# THE CHRISTMAS STOCKING MURDERS

### DENZIL MEYRICK

bantam

TRANSWORLD PUBLISHERS
Penguin Random House, One Embassy Gardens,
8 Viaduct Gardens, London sw11 7bw
www.penguin.co.uk

Transworld is part of the Penguin Random House group of companies
whose addresses can be found at global.penguinrandomhouse.com

Penguin
Random House
UK

First published in Great Britain in 2024 by Bantam
an imprint of Transworld Publishers

A CIP catalogue record for this book
is available from the British Library.

ISBN 9780857506399

Typeset in 12.75/16pt Minion Pro by Jouve (UK), Milton Keynes
Printed and bound in Great Britain by Clays Ltd, Elcograf S.p.A.

The authorized representative in the EEA is Penguin Random House Ireland,
Morrison Chambers, 32 Nassau Street, Dublin D02 YH68.

# THE CHRISTMAS
# STOCKING MURDERS

www.penguin.co.uk

*By Denzil Meyrick*

*The DCI Daley Thrillers*
Whisky From Small Glasses
The Last Witness
Dark Suits and Sad Songs
The Rat Stone Serenade
Well of the Winds
The Relentless Tide
A Breath on Dying Embers
Jeremiah's Bell
For Any Other Truth
The Death of Remembrance
No Sweet Sorrow

*Kinloch Novellas*
A Large Measure of Snow
A Toast to the Old Stones
Ghosts in the Gloaming

*Short-Story Collections*
One Last Dram Before Midnight
The Kinloch Tales

*Standalones*
Terms of Restitution
The Estate

*The Inspector Grasby Novels*
Murder at Holly House

For John and Mary Mason

# PROLOGUE

As was the case with Frank Grasby's previous remembrances, here follows an extraordinary tale that could only have happened when it did.

The early 1950s were a time when the country was trying to find itself after the Second World War, and all manner of odd trading deals and restrictions had been enabled to help UK goods and services re-establish themselves ahead of foreign imports.

Frank is bullish about this in his memoirs, and you'll see why when you read this book. He's in good form, his stock clearly on the rise following events in Elderby the previous Christmas.

As always, all I've done is try and fill in missing narrative, lost or misremembered by Grasby, as well as presenting documents pertaining to the case that have come to light during the intervening years.

I have taken the liberty of replacing some of the saltier language, lest it should offend the contemporary reader. But the rest is, and will remain, the very particular voice of its author, Inspector Frank Grasby.

Here are Frank's memories, beginning just before Christmas 1953.

# Original Note from the Author

*When I happened on my diary entries covering the period I'm about to inflict upon you, I was surprised how much detail I'd forgotten. You'd think the taste of blood in one's mouth, peering into the abyss, and witnessing the late Superintendent Arthur Juggers emerging from the North Sea as nature intended, might be indelibly inked onto one's mind. But I'd forgotten all of that. Odd, really.*

*I suppose, during such an eventful time, the grey matter tries to recall only the most salient details – there were plenty of them. But as my bonce has been thoroughly put through the ringer between then and now, it's perhaps no wonder these extraordinary days come back to me in vivid sparks and flashes, rather than a logical narrative.*

*Reading these yellowed, sometimes stained and torn pages of my old journal brings it all back.*

*'As real as a kick from an 'os,' as dear old Juggers would have said. But the least time spent on our equine friends, the better, eh? You well know my aversion to horses by now – and the reason for my distaste.*

*The whole tale was strange and unexpected. For me – as was usually the case – it began with a visit to Superintendent Juggers's office. I'm glad that I happened upon a piece from the local newspaper that underpins the whole bloody thing. I enclose it, and any other relevant* documents that have come my way since. They do fill in the blanks, you know.

My only advice? Jolly well hold on to your hats before you read this. You'll need to, as, yet again, I marvel at the fact I'm still here at all.

I hope you enjoy the meanderings of this old chap.

Frank Grasby
York, May 1976

# The Scarborough and Filey Argos

## 18 December 1953

Following a report from Scarborough woman Mrs Ethel Grimley (53), police attended the shoreline at the village of Uthley Bay on the morning of Wednesday, 15th.

The remains of a man, who has yet to be identified, were found on the sand, only a few yards away from the wreck of a small fishing boat.

The dead man appears to have perished at sea and been washed ashore. Though we have no confirmation from the North Yorks. Constabulary, it is rumoured that the deceased was a local fisherman.

We'll keep you up to date with developments in the following days.

# 1

*22nd December 1953, York Central Police Station*

I must confess to having secretly enjoyed the year following my adventure last Christmas. Now that I'm safe and sound, that is. One became something of an overnight sensation. Rather spoiled by the fact that due to the nature of the events, so vital to national security, the press were unable to report the full details of my heroics.

I suppose the mystique enables members of the public to insert their own story, likely much more alluring than the reality.

While visiting a school, imparting sound advice to the children, I was asked by one young tyke if I'd been to the moon. I told him not to be ridiculous, and that such a feat is something for the cinema, not real life. But the young do have such fertile imaginations, bless them. The day we go to the moon, I'll eat my trilby. And I'll want proof too – not just a piece of old rock.

On this morning, I was feeling rather fragile following the CID Christmas do. I say *do* but I rather think *don't* to be much more appropriate. The whole thing consisted of a few crates of beer and some shared fish suppers in the canteen.

But one must make the best of it, whatever the venue. So, yours truly took full advantage, being unable to remember much after around eight o'clock on the evening in question.

Still, that's what Christmas is for, isn't it? Goodwill to all.

Secretly, though, nothing can obscure the fact that I'm dreading Christmas this year. The lingering image of my father and me, sitting round the table with a withered capon – his festive fowl of choice – wearing cheap paper hats, drinking his elderflower wine, and feeling utterly miserable, is one I'd rather avoid. But for the life of me, I can't think what else to do.

Dear old pater has been behaving oddly for a while. He's taken to disappearing – sometimes for days on end – without an explanation to his only son. In fact, he's most guarded about it – furtive, almost. Not a negative trait I recognize in my sire. You may cast the Reverend Cyril Grasby as a petty pedant, sceptic, cynic and contrarian as much as you like, and you'd be right. But sneaking about in the shadows isn't his *modus operandi*.

A few days ago, I was on a re-rostered rest day, with nothing to do, when a bishop arrived to take me away from my precious Wodehouse. He'd arranged lunch with the Reverend Grasby, and waited until almost teatime, until he was convinced my father wasn't going to appear. It's quite a strain for me making conversation for almost four hours with a bishop, but he turned out to be quite a jolly chap – had known my father when they were young.

'Can't tell you what we got up to, Francis,' said he with a stage wink unbefitting his position.

*Don't worry, I know,* I wanted to say, remembering the dolorous Hetty Gaunt, and my father's youthful abandonment. But for me, loyalty is all, so I dutifully said nothing. It's stressful being so principled, you know.

One of my favourite pastimes when feeling a little under the weather is reviewing my past cases that have never been brought to a satisfactory conclusion. That is, it's a perfectly reasonable way to spend one's time, with no real prospect of any hard work. And as you know, I like a bit of nostalgia.

For example, there's Herbert Foss, who back in 1949 managed to remove the entire contents of a furniture shop in York, without anyone knowing how he did it. Not one piece of hard evidence against him could be found.

Then there's Dudley Price, a Welshman, who found his way north and terrorized just about everyone who owed money to certain criminal types in and around the city. Not a soul would come forward with anything we could use to bring about a conviction. In the end, he *retired* to Maidenhead, of all places, free as a bird.

Then there's Larry Hood. It was round about 1946 he came to my attention. He and his wife – whose name escapes me – were proper old lags, London crooks from way back. They had developed a sophisticated fraud technique, preying on the upper-middle classes who wanted to make more money but didn't fancy working for it. Larry had connections all over the place, even abroad, some said. I interviewed him once in connection with a bogus scheme to build a bridge across the Humber, an impossible task, I'm sure. He'd relieved a few very rich people across Yorkshire of their cash. Again, we could find nothing against him, and the Crown Office decided not to prosecute, rather bide their time and catch him hook, line and sinker. He was a charming old chap – gave me some marvellous racing tips, all of which came in at grand prices.

Larry and Mrs Hood soon disappeared. She was the grand-daughter of some earl or other. Some say the aristocracy helped them escape, that they went to America, others that they landed in Yorkshire. But I've always been sceptical of that.

I sigh at the thought of all these missed opportunities. Such is a policeman's lot, unfortunately. The chaps at D'Oyly Carte knew that, and they were right.

Sitting at my desk in York Central, with yet another cup of tea, I'm surprised to have Wilson lean into me in passing and say Juggers wants to see me, pronto. Quickly, I scan my feeble memories of the night before for any hint of a perceived misdemeanour, but can't think of anything. Mind you, that doesn't say much. I went out for a pint in York one evening a few years ago and woke ten hours later in Wetherby. I knew I was uncomfortably close to Hull but had absolutely no idea how I got there. So, you see, drink can render me uncomfortably vulnerable.

I knock on the stout oaken door of Juggers's office, still straining to remember anything that might have impugned my good standing.

The familiar 'come' from Superintendent Juggers bids me enter his hallowed office. As always, it reeks of stale beer and tobacco, which is good, considering that's how I smell today too.

'You wanted to see me, sir,' say I, as jauntily as possible.

He fixes me with his piggy eyes, and for quite an agonizing period of time says nothing. I note that his large desk is festooned with boxed items in various stages of adornment in festive wrapping paper.

'Put your finger there while I tie a knot in this ribbon, will you?' he commands.

'Of course,' say I, surprised the much-feted Inspector Frank Grasby has been summoned merely to help with the wrapping of presents for the Juggers family. But such is life.

'That'll do nicely,' remarks my superior, examining his handiwork. 'Trust Helen to be off sick today, of all days,' he says, referring to his secretary. 'Wraps a lovely parcel, she does.'

I feel a stirring in the midst of my hangover.

'Some bugger took her to Malton for a late-night drink at some bloody farm last night. Left her high and dry in the morning, the unprincipled swine.'

Oh dear, here we go. I did wake up at Bertie's opulent home in Malton this morning. It was early, mind. You know the hours farmers keep. I was up and at 'em quickly, anxious to escape the agricultural odour, and the awful racket made by the livestock. I had no idea I'd left Helen behind. In fact, no idea she was there at all, to be honest. I'd stirred from a drunken sleep on an old couch beside an extinct fire. I decide to remain silent on this damning revelation. My last memory is of trying to sing 'Underneath the Spreading Chestnut Tree', complete with choreography, to the merriment of all.

'I decided to give her the day off. She's a good lass, she is. Sounded tired and out of sorts. No wonder, being let down like that. Mind, if I find out who the lad was that abandoned her, he'll know all about it!' Rather alarmingly, Juggers bunches a fist and swings a punch into thin air, sufficient to knock any block off, I reckon. 'I know she doesn't drink.'

Now my memory is clearing, I remember the said Helen knocking back brandy and sodas as though they were about to become extinct. But enlightening Juggers will do nothing but bring his wrath down on me.

'What a damned bounder,' say I, with just the right emphasis and gravitas.

Juggers takes a seat and dons his reading spectacles. He

has a thin piece of white paper in one hand. Looks like a ripped-off telex message to me. He bites his lip, as though he wants to say something but can't quite find the words.

'Is there a problem?' say I, fearing the worst.

'In a way, there might be – in a manner of speaking, that is.'

I find this most alarming. Juggers is a man of action, who doesn't normally mince his words. If he's finding whatever it is he wishes to articulate to me difficult, how am I going to feel about it? I stare round the room at the wood panelling, the painting of Headingley cricket ground, group photographs of young police officers, and citations for bravery, anxious not to catch his eye. Hoping beyond hope that whatever he's finding hard to put across is intended for someone else.

'Now, lad.'

This is the cue for a horror, no doubt.

'You know the esteem in which I hold you – after all that happened last year, and the like.'

'Gosh, yes, sir. And I'm most appreciative of it.' Flattery will help in any situation, but it's not always enough.

'Don't go too far, Grasby. Any man who faced down what you did is to be applauded, but he can't be dismissed of his many flaws.'

How encouraging.

'We're all flawed creatures, to be sure. But these things leave a mark on one,' say I, further alarmed at his sudden change of tone.

'Truth is, I hate myself for saying this.' Juggers passes a handkerchief across his broad forehead, despite it being a very cold December day.

*Just get on with it*, I want to say. I'm expecting something in my past has been dredged up and is about to be used against me. In fact, I have a good idea what it is. I damn my youthful self once again.

'I know you had to spend Christmas away from your family last year, lad. Never easy, is it?'

My fear begins to dissipate. 'Go on, sir.'

'Well, I want you to do the same thing again this year. In fact, it's on the orders of the Chief Constable. He picked you out himself, no less. Needs someone who can be discreet.'

My goodness, what a difference a year makes. Last December, the Chief would have quite happily strung me up by my ears.

'I'm ready to do my duty as you and the Chief Constable see fit, sir.'

'You're a sound lad. When you're on form, that is.'

Another backhanded compliment. But heigh-ho.

'You may have seen a little piece in the papers today.'

'No, sorry, sir. I've been rather busy with reports and taking a look at some old cases we never solved.'

This is Grasby for, *I've been suffering a bloody awful hangover, and can't face doing any real work.*

'An old chap was found dead yesterday on the beach at Uthley Bay. Fisherman, I'm told.'

I shake my head. 'What a terrible place the sea can be, sir.'

'Aye, that's just the thing. The sea had nowt to do with it. He were strangled.'

I must look bemused as he summons me to his side of the desk.

'Take a look at this photograph. Tell me what that is.'

I squint at the monochrome image. It's a stained length of material. 'One half of a pair of stockings – I'm sure of it. There's the heel,' I say, pointing.

'Clever, Grasby. That's exactly what it is. And it's what was used to strangle our man.'

13

Gosh, I don't know what to think. Uthley Bay is a quiet fishing village. Not a place you'd expect such a horror to occur. But I feel I should venture some reasonable explanation.

'Pirates, sir?'

'What?'

'I mean, it could be the work of pirates, sir.'

'So, you think Long John Silver and his chums are hanging about Uthley Bay with half a pair of stockings? It'd make sense, mind you, if you've got one wooden leg.' He shakes his head. 'I knew you wouldn't be able to keep the facade of excellence going much longer, lad. Pirates, indeed.'

Again, I look on as Juggers's head shakes and his jowls follow on just slightly behind.

'The Chief wants you down there to find out what's afoot. The press know nothing yet, and that's the way we want to keep it. Locals are identifying him as Jack Wardle, but the press can't publish that until it's confirmed. You're the only man for the job. You're not a blabber, that's certain.' Juggers lowers his voice. 'You kept the fact we failed to find a rather large sum of money last year to yourself. Could have been tricky, that.'

I smile nobly, knowing all the time that the big bag of cash was given to me by the glorious Deedee, intended to help me improve my lot. Since then, it's been on top of my wardrobe, untouched. The whole thing has depressed me beyond reason. No point handing it in. That would get me into all kinds of strife. I've been planning to sink it in the Ouse with a couple of bricks in the bag, but finding the right moment is the problem, and somehow, I haven't been able to face it. Anyhow, just another complication in my life.

In the meantime – and I am a man of the moment – I give thanks in a silent prayer. I can leave Pops and his dry capon behind. I have a question, though.

'Double time for this, sir?'

I see Juggers's hands bunch once more into fists. 'Abso-bloody-lutely not! You'll get time and a half for Christmas Day and Boxing Day. Aye, and days in lieu. Try not to be a mercenary all your life, Grasby. It's unbecoming.'

'No, of course, sir. Greedy of me,' say I. But the extra money and days off are most welcome.

Juggers glances at the piece of paper now crushed in his right hand. 'I'll be coming along too.'

Initially, I'm shocked by this. But quickly, I come round to the idea. After all, Juggers likes his ale, and I've seen him quite merry at various functions that don't involve police work. Could be a jolly good wheeze, as my form tutor at Hymers used to say. As usual, I spend little time wondering why he's accompanying me. I should have done – you'll see why soon.

'Go home and get yourself packed and ready. I'll pick you up at one, sharp. Got it?'

As I make to leave, I see Superintendent Juggers read whatever is on the piece of paper and stroke his ample chins. His face forms an expression I've never seen there before.

He looks scared.

# 2

Following a series of unsatisfactory cars, I've been given a blue Morris Minor to aid me in my duties. Stubby Watts, our station mechanic and resident miracle-worker, handed the keys over to me in the summer as though it were a Bentley.

'You won't have any bother with her,' says he with no little pride. 'My little project, is that. I've tuned her to near perfection, lad. Stirling Moss could do a turn in her, and no mistake. I'm told they want to make another version of this model. But they'll have to come up with something special to improve her.' He stroked the engine in an almost sensual manner, which I found rather off-putting.

With this endorsement in mind, I set out confidently from the police garage, thankful that this vehicle could only be an improvement on last year's mode of transport, which refused to go uphill in any other manner but reverse, if it started at all. Unfortunately, I made it to the end of the road before, with a splutter and an unsettling jolting motion, my new Morris suddenly gave up the ghost.

When I returned *à pied* to report this inadequacy to Stubby, damning him for his failings, the bugger set about me with an oily rag, which he wielded like a cat-o-nine-tails.

'I don't care what they're saying about you these days, Grasby. Put you behind the wheel of a car, and it's bedlam!'

*Steady on.*

Eventually, he fixed her back up, with some excuse about below-par fuel blocking the carburettor. But I'm not convinced. I fear Stubby – despite his reputation – may be the most hapless mechanic in Yorkshire. Though, to be fair, the car has given me little trouble since.

In it, I pull up outside my father's two-bedroom cottage on the outskirts of York, a *consideration* from the Church for services rendered over nearly fifty years. He has to fill in for vacationing vicars now and again. But such is his fire and brimstone approach, these temporary stipends are – as time goes on – becoming fewer and further between. No incumbent clergyman wants to return from a relaxing sabbatical to discover my father has managed to ostracize half of the congregation. He does this on purpose, of course. Apparently, he had a whole troop of Girl Guides in tears following an exploration of the Book of Revelation. The Guides returned home expecting to see the Horsemen of the Apocalypse appear at the end of their streets at any moment. In all honesty, though he feels he's done his bit, and the cottage should be his by right alone, I'm always expecting the archbishop to send his henchmen round to evict us.

In the garden, his roses are nothing but knotted, thorned fingers, reaching up to the heavy, leaden sky in vain hope of a roborative sun. But they'll have to wait until April in this neck of the woods, I reckon. A distinct chill has enveloped the day, the harbinger of heavy snow.

I bound inside, still buoyed by the fact that Juggers has saved Christmas by sending me to Uthley Bay. As I rattle up the narrow staircase, I glean no evidence that the

Reverend Grasby is at all in residence. As I wonder where he's sloped off to this time, I get the fright of my life as his head peers round the door.

'I see.' He rubs his chin, a sarcastic smile playing on his lips. 'The conquering hero no more. Have they found you out at last and pointed to the door?'

'Do we really have to go through this every time I arrive home unexpectedly, Father? It's all getting a bit wearing, you know.'

'Matter of time, you'll see. You were lucky last Christmas. Probably the only spell of good fortune you'll enjoy in your life. But these things are sent to try us.' He manufactures an expression that speaks of resigned inevitability.

'Gosh,' say I. 'I was feeling quite low in spirits. How you've cheered me up.' I open the door of my tiny wardrobe and push aside the length of a couple of rain jackets and my cashmere overcoat, searching for my suitcase. It belonged to my late mother. I use it for sentimental reasons. It's not all about being a paean to law and order, after all.

'Where's my suitcase?' I enquire of my dear father.

He adopts the expression I've been telling you about, shifty, evasive. 'How should I know? I can't be expected to keep tabs on your goods and chattels. I'll not be here much longer, Frank. You'll have to get used to looking after your-self. Either that or walk about in your birthday suit when I'm gone.' He shuffles off, and I hear his hesitant tread on the stairs. Hesitant, only because he's fallen down them so often when under the influence of his extremely potent elderflower wine.

I'm inordinately upset by my mother's missing suitcase. I see no sign of it under the bed either. But there, unused for years, is the old cardboard job with which I trotted off to the army. On examination, it's cracked and stained. But it will have to do. Only an hour before Juggers arrives, and I don't want to keep him waiting.

I pack quickly. It pays to travel light, I've always thought. It's a habit I picked up in the war. All that's required is the suit of clothes on one's back and another of the same in a bag. And don't forget your toothbrush, soap, towel, under-pants and socks. I've seen chaps who can't go away for the weekend without just about every stitch they possess. I know Juggers will appreciate my frugal approach. I can't think of him as abundant in the luggage department.

I lug the suitcase back downstairs, desperately in need of something to eat and a cup of tea. The thirst from the pre-vious evening's boozing hasn't abated. Any confirmed drinker will attest to the feeling.

I hear my father humming quietly to himself in the lounge, as I draw some water to fill the kettle. As I set it to boil, I spot a rusting drying rack propped up against the far wall of the kitchen. It is festooned with a selection of grey socks, and three massive pairs of string pants. Once white, they too have faded to grey over the years. They can only belong to my father and are so large I cannot conceive of how he keeps them from falling to his ankles. Strange, he's usually much more guarded with his undergarments. But here they are, parading across the wall, punctuated by a random sock or two, like improvised Christmas decorations.

'What are you looking at?' he bellows once more. 'I would have thought you're past the age of giggling at some-one's intimate items. But I should've known better.'

'How on earth do you keep them up, Father? They're far too big,' say I.

'A man needs to keep the air circulating around his nether regions. I doubt you'd be here if I hadn't taken the precaution. What passes for underwear these days wouldn't look out of place on an acrobat.' He tuts magnificently. 'Sit down and I'll make you a sandwich for the road. Where are you off to?'

'Uthley Bay, if you must know, Father.' He has his back to me, chopping some cheese beside the old Belfast sink. He stops, motionless, like a broken clock. 'Are you quite all right?' say I, worried he may be the first person ever to have a stroke and remain standing.

He clears his throat loudly. 'I'm fine, Francis, thank you.'

Though he says no more on the matter, I'm left feeling uneasy. I don't know why. Surely, he hasn't been up to anything unsavoury in Uthley? We know he has form as far as this is concerned. If I find another little indiscretion, he's verging on becoming a menace to the rurals.

'I'll likely miss Christmas, you know,' say I. 'This is a very important case, and I can't swear I'll be back.'

He pivots on one foot to look at me, rather like a super-annuated ballet dancer in a dog collar. 'I see. I'm sure I'll make the best of it. Anyhow, Christmas hasn't been the same since – well, since your mother passed on.'

I feel the same. We proceed to drink our tea and eat our cheese sandwiches in relative silence.

As we're about to finish, the telephone thumps away in the hall. I say *thumps*, as the bell has seen better days, sounding more like someone slamming a wooden stick repeatedly into a double decker. Most unusually, my father is on his feet in a split second and fairly sprints out to answer it.

I cock an ear as he mutters a few indistinguishable words before ending the call perfunctorily. He then returns to the kitchen table with a deliberately neutral look on his face.

'I say, who was that?' I gauge his response carefully.

'It was an ecumenical matter,' he says without looking at me.

'Didn't take long, then.'

'Ecumenical matters rarely do, in my experience.'

This tells me two things. First, that the Church of England's view of *ecumenical* is more akin to *do as we do*. And second, my father is lying. He's the least ecumenical vicar you'll ever encounter. Why on earth would anyone seek his opinion on the matter?

I reflect what a fine criminal or poker player my father would have made. His expression is impassive – inscrutable. There's no way through such a stout backfoot defence.

I glance at my wartime-issue Omega and realize I have only ten minutes to present myself to Juggers at our front gate. He will be bang on time, for sure. Even if, in order to avoid heavy traffic, he must crash through fences and roll over gardens. He's obsessed with punctuality, is old Juggers.

I dash upstairs to the loo.

# 3

At the very stroke of one o'clock, his black Rover pulls up at the cottage. Juggers is seated squarely behind the wheel, like an ancient monolith. This, before partially disappearing to rummage in the glove compartment.

'Good afternoon, sir,' say I, all jaunt and enthusiasm.

'Is it? I've just had the most awful time explaining my absence to Mrs J. If we don't get this sorted out quick smart, I'll be for the chop. She's a formidable woman when riled, you know, lad.'

*She must be formidable indeed to subdue you*, I think. I've only had the pleasure of her company once, at the police ball. As much as Juggers is squat and seemingly immovable, she's a tall wisp of a woman with a hooked nose. Somewhat uncharitably, my father – who knows them through a Church committee – described the couple as Jack Sprat and his wife in reverse.

I'm rather unnerved, as Juggers is in a brown suit with a thick pinstripe, a homburg hat placed on his great bull head. I never think he looks quite right out of uniform. Instead of presenting the trusty face of law and order to the world, in a suit he always appears more like a retired boxer who's turned to violent crime.

When I make to place myself in the passenger seat, he

holds out his hand with a bellow. 'No! Stay where you are, Grasby. There's been a change of plan.'

For a ghastly split second, I picture myself like a Roman prisoner being hauled behind the car in chains, all the way to Uthley Bay. A fertile imagination is a positive curse, let me tell you.

'Mrs J needs use of the car when we're away. So, we'll have to travel in yours.' He grabs some documents from the glove compartment, slipping them into the inside pocket of his pinstripe suit. 'Here, give me a hand, will you?'

For a big man, he seems quite lithe. He's out of the car in one fluid motion, with none of the groans and grimaces I'm notorious for when alighting from a vehicle, chair or just about anything else. It's a well-known Grasby trait. None of us are particularly supple.

Juggers heads to the back door and pulls it open. 'Right, we'll pull this out and you take one end. Over here, Grasby,' he says like a weary choreographer.

I dash round to the other side of the Rover, only to observe him manhandling something from the back seat that looks like a short man's coffin. It's made from a rich, dark-brown polished wood – oak maybe – with leather carry handles, held fast by big, brass studs.

'Right, you catch that handle at that end, and we'll get it onto the backseat of your car,' he commands.

When we manage to manoeuvre the casket out of the car and I take my share of its heft, I feel as though my arms are going to be pulled from their sockets. On the other hand, Juggers looks as though he's just picked up a cricket ball, neither red in the face nor grunting, like me.

'Come on, lad. Put your back into it,' he says impatiently.

When we get to my car, only a few feet away, I feel as though I may very well pass out from exertion.

'Open the door, then,' says Juggers.

I'm hanging on to the leather handle of the casket with both hands. Opening the back door of my car will involve removing one hand and finding the keys. To make matters worse, I'm not sure in which pocket I've put the damn things. 'I'll have to lower my end while I find the keys, sir,' say I, somewhat meekly.

'Dearie me.' Juggers shakes his head, jowls wobbling above his tight shirt collar. 'How you survived the army, I'll never know.'

'I sometimes wonder myself,' say I. I'm about to lower this awful thing to the floor when my father appears from nowhere.

'Arthur, how are you? I've just brought my son's over-coat. He'd forget his head if it weren't attached,' he says kindly. My dear father throws my cashmere overcoat in the back of the car as though it were an old rag. I hadn't forgotten it – honest.

'I'm well, Cyril. You look in fine fettle. Wish I could stay as trim as you, I must say.'

'Can't fatten a thoroughbred, Arthur.'

As this happy little exchange is taking place, I'm becoming ever more desperate.

'Father, could you grab my car keys, please? They're in one trouser pocket or the other. I can't quite remember.' This was spoken through gritted teeth. The leather handle seems to be separating my fingers from the rest of my hands.

'Just like you to be utterly disorganized,' says dear old Dad. 'I don't know if he'll make it as a police officer, Arthur.'

*I'm a bloody inspector! What on earth are you on about?* I trust Juggers will put the Reverend Grasby in his place.

'Must say, I've often wondered that myself,' he replies.

*Gosh, thanks, sir.*

If the pain of carrying this jockey's coffin isn't enough, the uncomfortable feeling of my father rummaging through my pockets adds to the unpleasantness of it all. After what can only be described as an interminable length of time, he manages to find my keys and opens the back door of the car.

More agony follows as I twist and turn, desperately trying to cajole this damned awful thing onto the back seat. Eventually, it's done, and Juggers pushes his end into the Morris. I'm alarmed to note the lowering of the suspension, though. I hope the road to Uthley Bay is free of potholes.

'I say, what's it for? The casket, I mean, sir?'

'*What's it for?*' Juggers looks incredulous, and my father has an amused smile playing on his lips. 'It's a bloody trunk! What do you think it is?'

'For your clothes?' say I innocently.

'No, it's for my pet dwarf. You see, I can't let him out of the box or he'll run off. Buggers for that, are dwarves.'

My father lets out a howl of mirth, the like of which I last heard at a cinema in Scarborough where he took me to watch Charlie Chaplin when I was a boy.

'You'll be prepared for every eventuality,' say I, hoping to alleviate the embarrassment.

'Where's your luggage?' asks Juggers.

Helpfully, my father lifts my old army suitcase from the pavement. 'This is the extent of my son's accoutrement, Arthur.' The suitcase looks even worse in the light of day than it did in my cramped, dingy bedroom. A flap of dark vinyl veneer is hanging off like slipped skin.

'One good shower and that'll disintegrate,' says Juggers, now joining in with my father's mirth.

I don't know what it is about the older generation, but it's hard not to find them pig ignorant at times. I mean, who, apart from an elephant, cuts about with a trunk these days? I would love to say something about the outsize nature of Juggers's clothes but that would be a mistake. He'd likely punch me to the road and look on while my father gets in a few kicks on the fly.

'I do have another one. Unfortunately, it's disappeared.' I search my father's face from under my brows.

'It looks like snow, Arthur,' he says, absolutely ignoring me.

'Aye, it does that, Cyril. We'd better get a shift on. Don't want to be caught on the moors in a blizzard. Come on, Grasby.'

*I don't know, we could live in your trunk for a few weeks – there's plenty room*, thinks I. Sometimes, I wonder if this kind of humour would amuse my superintendent but I'm not sure. Apparently, as a younger man, he threw a colleague over a hedge for mentioning a gain in his weight. Best not to push my luck, methinks.

As I jump behind the wheel, I hear my father wish my superior farewell.

'Safe journey, Arthur. Please pass on my best to your good lady.' He conveniently neglects to wish me a fond goodbye. But that's my father for you.

With that, I coax the engine into life, just as the first fat flakes of snow fall from the pearlescent sky over the city of York.

# 4

The Filey road is a lovely drive in the summer. But with Father Christmas about to force his great girth down the chimney, everything points to blizzards. It's something about the quality of the flakes that are gently spotting the window. There's more than one type of snow, and that's a fact. I think of Stamford Bridge across the fields as we set off. I picture brave King Harold fighting off hordes of Vikings, only to be told to get down to the south coast quick smart because the Normans are at it too. I always think of Harold as one of our unluckiest kings. He wins a dreadful battle with the vicious Norse then has to do the same all over again with their cousins, a forced march in between. His chaps must have been done in. If there had been a railway service back then, England would be a very different place now. Though the dining car may have been a bit rowdy.

It's strange how I've always been sympathetic to the good old Anglo Saxons. Being a Grasby from Yorkshire, the greater part of the old Danelaw, my ancestors were much likelier to have been in a horned helmet, bobbing along in a longship. That's national identity for you. All the confused myths and dodgy tales of our heritage. I smile, picturing my father belting up a beach with axe in hand. We all become one in the end, and just as well, I reckon.

'What are you grinning about?' says Juggers.

'I was thinking about the Battle of Stamford Bridge, sir.'

'Bloody Chelsea! You should be supporting Leeds United, never mind that soppy southern mob. Good grief.'

And there you have it. Juggers adequately illustrates the divide between the north and south of England. Here's me, all high-minded, while Juggers is well and truly stuck in the Danelaw. Mark you, I wouldn't fancy him charging up a beach at me.

Through the Morris Minor's grubby windows, the skies begin to look even more threatening. By the time we arrive at Garrowby there is a steady fall of snow. By Fridaythorpe, it's heavy.

'Put the foot down, Grasby,' says Juggers. I've been day-dreaming about nothing in particular. My mind does drift when I'm at the wheel.

'Bit faster than that,' Juggers insists. 'We won't be at Uthley Bay until Christmas, at this rate.'

I've never been a very fast driver, as you might imagine. I was used to being ferried about in my grandfather the bishop's Bentley. The car passed down to my father. He always drove at a stately medium pace. But it appears Juggers wants me to go full-on Freddie Trueman. When I put my foot down, I'm dismayed to experience the car revving loudly then jolting alarmingly, just as it did when I first drove it.

'Bloody Stubby Watts!' say I, almost forgetting Juggers is in the car.

'I'll not have you blaming our mechanic for the standard of your driving, Grasby. He's a miracle-worker, is Stubby. Pull in here. I'll drive.'

I manage to slow down enough to park at the head of a farm road. Now, I'm in a bit of a quandary. I'm not a very good passenger. And I know – from most bitter experience – that Juggers drives like Fangio.

'Are you sure, sir?'

'Aye, I'm bloody sure. Look over at that field. You'll be able to ski on it in ten minutes. Come on, get moving!'

Sure enough, the snow is lying now. It paints a felted white picture across fields, the odd tree and fence posts. I love snow. But not with Juggers about to drive. I sigh as I force my long legs back into action. Cars are generally a nightmare for the tall, you know. I end up feeling squashed in, like a sardine.

Juggers, however, is up and behind the wheel in a flash. I have the seat set well back to accommodate my legs – as far as it will go, in fact. I note his girth is touching the steering wheel, nonetheless.

'Are you ready, Grasby?'

Before I can reply, he's off! The tyres screech as he slides on the tarmac. The engine hits a note hitherto unattained during my time driving the Morris, and I manage to close the passenger door in the nick of time. Within a minute, we're fairly bombing along, Juggers's face positioned just above the wheel, his piggy eyes squinting intently through the snow, ample bottom on the very edge of the seat.

I've survived a war, goodness knows how many scrapes as a police officer, and I'm about to die in a Morris Minor driven by a mad superintendent.

Now places like Sledmere, Cowlam and Foxholes whizz past. I suppose the poetic rendering would be *as though in a dream*. But it's more like a tumbling nightmare for the chap in the passenger seat. You know the one where you think you're falling then wake up with a start as though you've landed in your bed? But there's no bed here.

Just as we pass some snowy fields and a signpost for

Filey, Juggers wrenches the wheel and turns full pelt onto a side road, the car sliding beneath us.

'Don't worry, lad. I know this place like the back of my hand,' says he.

Well, clearly, he should be paying much closer attention to his hands. Because, within a few minutes, we end up at a well-proportioned farmhouse, where the road abruptly ends.

'I'll be damned,' says Juggers. 'They change the bloody signpost more often than thee and me change our scants.'

*Speak for yourself*, thinks I. But I begin to worry when the man of the house appears in bib and braces, then bangs on the roof of the car, evidently wondering what the devil is going on.

Juggers winds down the window with the stiff and squeaky handle. Another triumph for Stubby, you'll note. He's muttering oaths under his breath as he does so.

'I'm on important police business. Bugger off and attend to yours!' With this, Juggers slams the car into reverse, and we retrace our steps, only backwards this time. I see the astonished farmer gazing after us, his mouth agape, as our speed increases. I can't drive *forwards* this quickly. I'm beginning to wish I'd not had that last cup of tea.

Soon – too soon – we hit the main single-track road towards Uthley Bay and Scarborough. As we skirt the coast, the sea is a cold, metallic grey, a fishing boat just visible on the horizon. But at least the snow isn't lying as deeply here. I reflect that Juggers was probably right to put his foot down. Goodness knows how long it would have taken us with yours truly at the wheel.

I'm studying a herd of sheep walking in a circle over a small patch of field. They're clever beasts, are sheep. And despite my aversion to the animals after being pinned atop

30

a wall by a savage sheep on a school trip, you have to admire their endeavour in clearing a bit of ground to sit down and weather the snow. I mean, it's not as though they have the forecast on the wireless, is it now?

Mercifully, Juggers slows the car in order to turn the next corner.

'Not far now,' says he.

We head down a sloping lane that points straight as a die for the sea. And, just when I think he's taken another wrong turn and we're about to land in the waves, I spy tell-tale wisps of smoke that can only come from a row of chimney pots.

Sure enough, the village of Uthley Bay begins to reveal itself. It's nothing more than some houses and a few shops strung out above a strand of sand, as far as I can tell in this blizzard. There's a little harbour, only big enough to shelter a couple of dozen or so of the wooden fishing boats that are popular hereabouts. It's much the same right up the coast of North Yorkshire, with the possible exception of Whitby, where there are some ocean-going vessels. It's down in the East Riding, in Hull – my bête noire – where the really big trawlers lurk, packed with men as hard as the ice that covers their vessels on their trips to the Baltic Sea. Hopefully, Uthley Bay, despite its community of fisher-men, is a rather gentler place.

Juggers decides his shift as driver is over. He pulls up against a cracked pavement at the front of the village and announces his desire to have a walk down the harbour.

I think it's only good form to join him on this meander, so off we go.

# 5

When I leave the car, the cold air hits me like a brick. It's bracing, though, what with the gentle lap of the sea against the harbour walls and the snow falling lightly on the sleeve of my tweed jacket. The place smells gloriously of Christmas. Coal fires and cooking; spices and that briskness that clears the old nose. Somebody is making something delicious, and I'm suddenly ravenous.

'Come on, lad. Don't dawdle,' insists Juggers. 'Let's take a look down at these boats, eh?'

Suddenly, it crosses my mind that Superintendent Arthur Juggers may not have secured any accommodation for us, and we're about to rough it on a fishing boat. I think of ways to protest this, as his solid, rather rotund figure paces ahead of me onto the cobbled pier.

As it turns out, a stout breakwater has masked the fact that there are only two vessels huddling in the little harbour. Both are fishing boats, though that's where the similarity ends. The first has sleek lines, painted in a shade of green, with a gold stripe traversing a perfectly wrought white gunwale. It has short masts, probably for catching of fish rather than for cloth sails. The rigging, ropes and other nautical essentials (don't ask me what they are, for I haven't a clue) are neatly stacked on deck or hanging from the tidy, newly varnished wheelhouse.

The second vessel is tied to the first, looking as though it's hanging on for dear life, and about to sink. It's the colour of a badly maintained sparrow. There are botched wooden patches on the hull, while aboard, everything is a shambles, with ropes and fish boxes scattered everywhere. An old yellow oilskin has been pushed through a hole in the wheelhouse window in the crudest of temporary repairs.

An old seadog is sitting on a silver bollard busily working with a huge bodkin on a straggling grey net. He's wrapped up well against the cold, with chamois gloves, and an off-white jumper peeking out above a thick pea jacket. The greasy cap on his head has been adorned with a little cone of snow. So, he's clearly oblivious to the cold. A stout pair of moleskin trousers are tucked into what could be the oldest pair of wellington boots I've ever seen. They're rolled down at the top, revealing grubby canvas. The boots look as though they've often been repaired with a bicycle puncture repair kit. There are so many little circles of black rubber dotted about, it's hard to know when the boots stop, and the patches begin.

'Afternoon,' says Juggers as breezily as I've heard him. 'Not much of the day left now, eh?'

The fisherman regards him levelly then glances at me.

'Always the same at this time of year. But I can't stand being cooped up in the house. I'm out here in all weathers unless I'm at sea. Houses are for womenfolk, thou knows. And this way, there are fewer arguments.'

Rather sweeping statement over, he sniffs loudly and passes a glove across his nose, leaving a snail-trail of snot as a marker. He's one of those chaps who looks as though his face has been used as a pincushion for a decade or two. His features are pitted and mottled, grey beard sparse, with traces of yellow nicotine at each corner of his mouth on once-white whiskers. A red, bulbous nose marks him out as someone who would be equally happy playing either Father Christmas or Rudolph in the village play. And though he's out in the cold, I reckon it also indicates an unhealthy fondness for alcohol.

Nothing of the hypocrite about me, eh?

'I must say, she must be a pleasure to sail,' say I, pointing to the sleek boat at his side.

'Oh aye, a fine vessel, is that. Like a dream, even in the roughest seas.' He sniffs again.

'I bet you're glad you're not sailing in that old tub. Looks like her next sail will be her last.' I laugh at my own observation – always a mistake.

The fisherman makes a face, a cross between a grimace and someone sucking on a sherbet dip. 'I don't know. I think she looks quite sweet. After all, I've been sailing her for the last fifty years.' He sends me a malevolent glance.

You see, that's my problem. I open my mouth when I should just shut up. I'd assumed that, as he was sitting on the pier beside the well-maintained craft, he was involved with it in some way. Wrong again.

'Don't pay any heed to Grasby. More sense in a gull,' says Juggers. Looking as though he may rush me at any moment and dash me over the seawall and into the waves. 'Can I ask your name, sir? I'm Arthur, by the way. And this is Frank.' Juggers holds out a gloved hand. Wise decision to keep them on, methinks. You don't want this old duffer's snot all over your paw.

'I'm Ogden,' says old Sam Salt. 'Ogden Barclay. Been fishing here for nigh-on sixty year. Since I were a lad.'

He and Juggers engage in a manly handshake, each trying to squeeze the other's hand to smithereens. I've always found this a damnable waste of time – painful too. An old pal of mine – Turvey Colinston, a fine pianist I met in the army in Italy – came across this giant German prisoner of war. Turned out this bear of a man, who could have easily ripped your arm off and beaten you to death with the soggy end, was a full-on musician. He'd played double bass in a Berlin ensemble. They chatted away for a while, then on parting the German grabbed Turvey's hand and pumped it for all it was worth. He ended up with two fractured fingers on his right hand, unable to play for over a year.

Take my advice. Avoid handshaking at all costs. After the war, poor old Turvey fell off a tram in Blackpool and bought it under an approaching horse. I'm not sure this had anything to do with our musical German. But one never knows.

When old Ogden, man of the sea and captain of a dilapidated fishing boat, holds out his hand to me, I pretend to be preoccupied by a seagull.

'You pair will be here to find out what happened to old Jack Wardle?' He nods his head sadly. 'Don't often see the constabulary hereabouts.'

For once, Juggers is lost for words. 'Well spotted,' he says eventually, clearly put out that despite our arrival in civvy clobber, this old son of the sea has marked us out for coppers in a jiffy. 'Bad business, is that. Did you know Mr Wardle?'

'All me life. We were just about the same age, in the village school at the same time.' Ogden sets his chin against the sadness of it all. 'Aye, sailed on a few grand waves together. I hope you catch the bugger what did it. Wouldn't mind a kick at him. Once you have him subdued, that is.'

'Despicable behaviour,' says Juggers. 'We just bring wrongdoers to justice without fear or favour. There's no kicking folk about, not these days.'

I have to look away at this calumny.

Ogden regards Juggers with a grave expression that quickly turns into a smile then a full-throated laugh. 'Aye, and I come home to a song from Vera Lynn while she's making me tea.' He laughs heartily again. 'I live in Uthley Bay but I'm not ignorant of what goes on in the world.' An odd look passes across his face. 'Well aware of all that's rotten, me.'

I watch as Juggers takes one step towards the old man. And for a minute, I must confess, I think he's going to punch the old boy halfway back down the pier for his less than endearing comments about the constabulary. In the end, he smiles in a way I can only describe as menacing. Bit like a pantomime bad guy in some of the American gangster movies. George Raft, after sixty years of fish suppers and gallons of stout.

'That's me in my place, eh?' Juggers turns to me briefly, his eyes boring into mine. He turns his attention again to Ogden. 'Hope our paths don't cross in a professional capacity and I have to disappoint you,' he says to the fisherman. But I saw the bunched fist, the jaw working as though he was chewing a particularly recalcitrant steak.

'Oh,' say I. 'Quite a small fleet in Uthley Bay, no?'

Ogden narrows his eyes. 'What makes you say that?'

*Oh, I don't know. Maybe the fact there're only two boats here, you decrepit oaf.*

'There are other boats?'

'Aye, a few more.'

'Good-oh. Where are they?'

Slowly, our new nautical acquaintance removes his left

glove and raises a finger towards the grey sea and points, a grim expression on his face. I spot a gold wedding ring.

He can point out to sea as much as he likes. Ogden must surely realize that I didn't expect them to be traversing the North York moors. I've seen this before with nautical types. All sullen and mysterious about what they do, as though they're navigating Cape Horn every day of the week. That, and the odd names they have for just about everything – it gets my goat. He'll be spouting forth about davits and binnacles next, I shouldn't wonder.

'Is fishing good this time of year?' says Juggers, good temper barely regained.

'Bloody awful. Not bad deeper out, but they won't go there. Not now.'

'Why?' say I, all innocence.

'That's for you to find out, I reckon.' He taps his nose knowingly.

*Ha! Case solved, if you ask me.* We'll just pump this old soak for information and be back in York in a trice. I await a rejoinder from Juggers.

'Right, then. We better be off. Good day to you, Mr Barclay,' he says instead.

'You two staying in the Trout?' says Ogden as we turn to go.

'Yes, as a matter of fact we are,' says Juggers.

News to me. But there you are. Accommodation is obviously on a need-to-know basis.

'Good luck to you, then. You'll need plenty,' says he, somewhat enigmatically. Conversation over, Ogden Barclay attends his net again, pulling a long strand through the weft with the gigantic bodkin.

*Oh dear.* Doesn't say too much for our hotel – inn – whatever it is. At least we won't be kipping on a fishing boat.

# 6

I take in Uthley Bay as we're walking back up the pier. It's a pretty little place. Steep-gabled houses made of stout red brick face boldly out to sea. All small windows and salt-blasted walls. A long row of these cottages and a couple of tiny shops march the length of the village, abutted by two larger domiciles. One is rendered in sandstone, with a turret – likely an affectation – and window frames painted red. It's a jolly-looking place – somewhere one wouldn't mind going home to. At the other end of the village, to the left of the hotel, right as we look at it, is an austere place made of dressed stone, set back from the road with a driveway leading up to it. It's flat-faced and featureless, more like a small fort than a home or even offices. Reminds me of a police station I once attended in Oxfordshire. And it looks much more suited to the turret its companion at the other end of the village boasts. Somehow, that utilitarian appearance gives me the shivers.

Then to the very midst of Uthley Bay. There's a three-storey building with large bay windows, built in what I believe they now call the *Art Deco* style. It looks as though it would be more at home in a cove in Cornwall or Devon, with a flat roof, white rendered walls stained by wind, waves and weather, replete with a rather jaunty appearance. It's designed with the tourist in mind, I'm sure. Our hotel is on the main road of the village but not part of it, if you get my drift.

For some reason, I shiver at the sight of the Trout Hotel.

'Right, bring the car up and we'll grab a couple of porters to shift this bloody trunk.' Juggers points down the street to where my car is parked. Why he didn't just stop outside our hotel in the first place, I don't know. Maybe he was finding his bearings. But my irascible superintendent seemed too keen on getting down the pier.

As I stride off to the Morris, I thank the dear Lord for hotel porters. I don't fancy hefting Juggers's trunk up three flights of stairs. I glance at it as I insert myself into the car; it's solid as a boulder. How an inanimate object can exude a feeling of malevolence, I'm not sure. I'm so glad my father's not here. He hates all this otherworldly stuff, you know. Strange, for a vicar. I get this supernatural prescience from my late mother. The Scots are like that, you know. Forever having one strange experience or another. Apparently, my great-uncle had a long conversation with the ghost of a Highland soldier in an old hotel in Killiecrankie. What they talked about, I don't know. But it appeared that nobody on my mother's side of the family thought this in the slightest bit odd.

The car now neatly parked outside the Trout, I make my way through the front door, only to discover Juggers banging his fist on a bell in a tiny room off the lobby. The space is the size of a small front parlour, made even smaller by the presence of an outsized Christmas tree. Fully decorated in gaudy baubles and tinsel. Juggers's persistent din with the bell reminds me of the typing pool at York Central. How these young women manage to type at such a pace, I don't know. I'm sure most of them would make passable concert pianists, such is their manual dexterity.

'Bloody pain, is this,' says Juggers, clearly out of sorts. He gives up on the bell and starts shouting for assistance. 'Hello! Is there anybody there?' He's like an impatient clairvoyant.

'Shall I have a go, sir?' say I, desperate for quiet. I'm getting that prickly face I used to experience during the war when the firing started. He mutters something and steps away from the reception desk.

I give the little brass bell two sharp taps. 'I say, can we check in, please?' Though my voice is raised, I refrain from my superintendent's full-bodied roar. In a jiffy, the tiniest woman I've ever seen appears, it seems, from under the counter. She has a very strange appearance – big dark eyes and blonde hair cut in a fashion that would make a bowl tut.

'Hello,' say I, all smiles and approachability. 'We have a booking. It's—'

Before I can finish this sentence, Juggers pushes me aside and addresses the tiny receptionist.

'I'm Juggers and this is Grasby. We've a room booked. We're ornithologists, you know. Can't get enough of the birds – neither of us.'

I see why Juggers is so keen to butt in. Clearly, we're supposed to be undercover. I wish he'd told me. Though the very fact that Yorkshire's oldest fisherman marked us out for policemen not five minutes ago rather makes a nonsense of the whole thing, I reckon.

The receptionist blinks at Juggers a couple of times then produces a massive visitors' book from under the counter. I swear, it's all she can do to heft it up. Purposefully, she turns to a blank page and asks for our full names, addresses and next of kin. Though I've been asked this before in hotels and guest houses, it always sets my nerves on edge. It's as though the sudden deaths of guests are a routine business, and it's unlikely we'll last the night.

Once Juggers signs and fills in the relevant information, he tries to turn back through the pages, to see who the other guests have been, I suppose.

The receptionist grabs one end of the massive tome and bangs it down on Juggers's left hand.

'Hey, steady on!' he shouts, face instantly the colour of a mid-season Cox's Pippin. 'What on earth did you do that for?'

'To protect the privacy of our guests,' says Tom Thumb's little sister, her shoulders barely visible behind the reception desk. 'It's nobody's business but theirs that they've stayed here.' She gives Juggers the most magnificent glare, her brow furrowed and big eyes flashing. 'My, you are very inquisitive for an ornithologist. Looking for like-minded folk, I daresay.' This, with a lopsided grin.

'Well, I'm sure I'm not bothered,' says Juggers. It's obvious, for the sake of the investigation, that he's being as circumspect as he can. I'm sure it's a supreme effort. Well done him!

He stands aside to give me my go at signing the register. I smile winningly at our host and wait for her to open at the correct page. It's polite, after all, and I have quite delicate hands, you know. My father says it's because I've never done a proper day's work in my life. I always think this quite rich, considering his former employment. Hypocrite is his middle name, of course.

The receptionist smiles insipidly back at me as I fill in my details. She stands on her toes and flips the register round, to make sure we've filled it in correctly.

'Your name is Grasby?' She fixes me with a frown.

'Yes,' say I. 'What of it?'

'Oh, nothing at all,' she says. But I can see the shifty look. I wonder why? Maybe she's heard something of my exploits. Gosh, I hope it's the good ones.

'My name is Dot,' says our diminutive host, almost making me laugh out loud. 'Here's two sets of keys to your room and the front door. Though we'd be grateful if you were in your rooms before midnight.'

'Not going to happen,' says Juggers, unused to being told what to do. 'We've birds to spot. And they don't keep regular hours.'

Dot thinks about this for a moment or two. 'Don't they roost in the dark?'

This direct question has clearly troubled my superior, as he shifts his not inconsiderable weight from one foot to another.

'Good question,' says he, obviously playing for time while he thinks up a serviceable excuse.

'We await their calls at night, don't you know,' say I. Yes, it's quick-witted Grasby to the rescue. 'We rather specialize in birds of the night. And there are many examples.'

I instantly regret this. If she asks me to identify these nocturnal birds, I'm up the creek without a paddle.

'Well, you learn something new every day,' says Dot. 'But you'll need good luck round here. In this weather, any sensible bird has its head under its wing by teatime.' She nods over to the large window, where the snow is falling much more heavily now.

Juggers has had enough of this tittle-tattle. 'We'll be requiring the services of a porter – two of them, in fact.'

Dot looks at him as though he's speaking Swahili. 'What?' She cocks her head. You know, the way spaniels do.

'Porters. Men what carries luggage.' Juggers is really struggling now. His grammar is breaking down dreadfully. He's biting his lip to stem a tide of fury.

'We only have a porter in the summer. It's nearly Christmas. Any porterage you require will have to be done by yourselves.'

My heart sinks. I picture the massive trunk lying on the back seat of my car. 'You have a lift, of course?' say I hopefully.

'Of course,' says Dot. She's rather put out again, by the look on her face.

'Good-oh,' say I. Though it'll be a pain getting the damned thing from the car and into the lift, it's preferable to carting it up three flights of stairs.

'We're waiting for the maintenance folk arriving from Leeds. Broke down on Saturday. They were supposed to be here today.' Dot glances again at the window. 'Doubt they'll make it in this.'

The inevitable happens. 'Buggeration!' shouts Juggers. 'This must be the worst hotel I've ever been in. And let me tell you, young lady, I've been in some bloody awful hotels in my time.'

'We have a rather large trunk as part of our luggage,' say I, by way of scant mitigation. 'It contains our ornithological kit.'

'Why didn't you say?' says Dot. 'I'll give Tom and Wilf a shout. They'll have it up in your room in a jiffy.' She smiles, her head going up and down behind the counter. 'It'll cost you a bob or two, mind.'

'Don't worry about that. Just get them on the phone, and be quick about it,' says Juggers.

Dot gives him a nasty look then takes a deep breath.

I'm sure she's about to give the superintendent a piece of

her mind. But instead she puts one hand to her mouth, and gives a piercing yell quite out of proportion to her size.

'Tom, Wilf! Get down here!'

It's odd being a policeman. You get suspicious of just about everyone. Goodness knows how many times I've suspected my dear father of some wrongdoing or other. Of course, in his case, my suspicions have been entirely justified. But when the aforementioned Tom and Wilf appear behind Dot, they instantly raise my hackles. One of them is just about the biggest man I've ever seen. I'm pretty tall, but he dwarfs me. And it's not just his height that's impressive. He's broad into the bargain. A bit like Juggers through a telescope at close quarters. This man and Dot look like a different species, almost.

The other man is small, rat-like, with a shifty expression. He wrinkles his sharp nose, and rolls up one sleeve, revealing a badly rendered tattoo of a crown on his left forearm. It's an old lag's thing. It tells other criminals he's spent one term in prison. Pays to know these things.

'Good day, gents,' he says in a distinctly Cockney twang. 'A guinea and the job's done. What do you think, Tommaso?'

The huge man smiles broadly. 'Si, Wilf,' he says.

I met a lot of Italians during the war. I know one when I see one, and Tommaso's about the biggest I've ever seen.

My Grasby instinct is piqued. Suddenly, I have a bad feeling about Uthley Bay.

# 7

We accompany the odd couple of improvised porters out to the car. The snow is really heavy now, a true blizzard. Had we departed York any later, we'd never have made it.

'Right, lads,' says Juggers as I open the back door of the Morris. 'I'll leave it up to you. She's heavy, mind. Don't drop her.' He places a few coins in Wilf's scrawny hand.

I've seen some feats of strength in my time, both before and after my sojourn to Uthley Bay. But I tell you, what I witness now beggars belief. Tommaso leans his huge frame into the car, pulls out one end of the trunk, and before you can say *buongiorno* or whatever it is, it's off the back seat and in his huge paws. With no signs of difficulty, he strolls off in the direction of the hotel, Wilf rushing at his side to open the door.

'What room are you in?' shouts Wilf.

'Thirty-three,' says Juggers and throws him his keys.

'Is there anything else? Not that you'll need it with the size of this bugger.' Wilf sniffs loudly.

'Just my hand luggage,' say I. 'I'll manage that myself, thank you.'

'Ain't you the clever boy.' With that, Wilf disappears through the door behind his colossal friend.

'He's a big 'un,' says Juggers as we follow on into the hotel the up the stairs.

Tommaso is placing the chest in our room by the time we arrive. My goodness, the stairs were hard enough without a two-ton weight. The sweat is fairly pouring down Juggers's face. I fear he may have a coronary.

'Anything further we can do for you, just shout,' says Wilf. 'We're in the kitchen from early doors until all hours.'

'Are you the chef?' says Juggers.

'No, he is.' Wilf flicks a thumb at Tommaso, who is smiling benignly behind him like an affable giant. 'And I tell you this, gents. You're in for a treat – oh yes.' He fairly tugs his forelock and nods to his companion. 'Hope you 'ave a *good* time.' Wilf manages an impressive stage wink. 'By the way, you don't have to lock your door here. Safe as houses, it is. I hate a locked door, me. Makes me feel – you know.'

'Claustrophobic?' say I.

'That's the one!' With that, he's off.

'What's up with him?' says Juggers.

'I reckon he misunderstands our relationship, sir.' I give Juggers a knowing look.

'What do you mean?'

'You know, young man and older man sharing a hotel room.'

'Don't be daft, lad. Mind you, I can understand why he might think you're playing for Lancashire, but not me. And anyhow, if I were that way inclined, I wouldn't be tipping my hat at a long streak of haplessness like you.'

Only slightly abashed, I look round our room. It's tidy enough, in a cheap, chintzy kind of way. There's a decorative dressing table, an oak wardrobe and matching chest of drawers. At the far end of the room is a wash-hand basin with a shaving mirror above, complete with glass to rinse one's mouth after brushing. But there's a glaring problem in the furniture department. The bed is big and looks most comfortable. But it is *bed*, singular.

'This won't do,' I say to Juggers.

'It's a bed, lad. What were you expecting – a chaise longue?'

'I'll be honest, sir. I was rather expecting a twin room.'

'You were in the army. You must have had to share a bed with another chap before now.'

I do Juggers the courtesy of having a quick think about this. It's true to say that I bedded down in some strange places while fighting the war with Hitler, including a barn in Piedmont, stables just outside Athens and a fairground ride in Austria. But I never did so in the same bed as another bloke. 'No, sir,' say I. 'And I'd rather not begin now.'

'Don't be a jessie. It's big enough for both of us. We can sleep top and tail, if it would make you happier.'

'I'd be happier in a different bed. Or come to that, a room of my own, sir!'

'They only have four twin rooms and they're booked out. Lucky to get a room at this time of year. So, thee and me will have to cosy up together. Come on, Grasby, I know what goes on in these public schools. It should be me making a fuss, having to hit the hay with you.'

'Sir?'

'You know well what I mean. You're on the effete side, you have to admit.'

'Me? Don't be ridiculous – sir,' I nearly forget to say.

Juggers bites his lips. This is a sure sign that he has something awkward to impart.

'This has been praying on my mind for a while. I have a confession to make, Grasby.' He looks suddenly uneasy.

*Damn!* If he declares his undying love for me, it's out the window, three storeys or not.

'This trip might be a lot more dangerous than you think, lad. All I'm saying is, be on your guard, Grasby.'

I remember the piece of paper in Juggers's big hand back at York Central. The scared look on his face.

'Don't worry about me, sir. Always ready.'

'Good! Because there's trouble afoot hereabouts, let me tell you.'

I look out the window. All I can see through the snow is the North Sea and the harbour, barely visible. Now, you can call me feckless and as scatty as you like, but I'm sharper of mind than most of my colleagues. This isn't a boast. Your average peeler isn't usually the brightest chap.

'The fact we're in this room – this *particular* room – is no coincidence, is it, sir?'

'Aye, you're not slow, Grasby. Great mind, just not so good on the practical side, eh?'

I want to say *steady on, old boy*. But that will just create ill-feeling. And it looks as though I'm about to be at close quarters with Juggers for a while. *Very* close quarters, as I've just discovered.

'We each have our own little talents, I find,' say I, by way of mitigation.

'And some are well hidden, and all.' The retort is typical of your average senior officer.

'Well, what's afoot then, sir? I mean *really*.'

'We're here to investigate this strangled man on the beach. Plain and simple, Grasby.'

'But we must keep our eyes and ears open, yes?'

'Never any harm in that, lad.'

Yet again, I feel like a pawn being moved about the board to suit the aims and intentions of others. Don't get me wrong, a policeman's lot is to do his or her duty and not reason why. But it would be handy to know what's actually going on – just once or twice would be nice.

'What are we really about, then, sir?'

'Never you mind. You'll find out more when it's time.'

See what I mean?

'We're a bit out on a limb here, sir. I mean, there's not even a police station, is there?'

'The local bobby retired last year. They've never got round to replacing him. That's the rurals for you, Grasby.'

With a great deal of effort, he kneels in front of his trunk. A vein on his forehead is pulsing like a ticking clock. I hope he doesn't expect me to drag him back to his feet. We'll need Tommaso and maybe some of his brothers for that little task.

Juggers pulls something from the inside pocket of his jacket. He inserts a brass key into the formidable lock on the trunk. It all has the air of Long John Silver and missing treasure about it. Though rather than Spanish doubloons, I fear I am to witness the removal of Arthur Juggers's smalls. Not a happy prospect. It's not often one encounters the intimate garments of one's father and boss on the same day. He rummages around at the bottom of the trunk, cursing here and there as he goes.

'Ah, here we are,' says he, producing a police-issue side-arm from the chest. 'You have this. I've my own in here somewhere. I'll give you some rounds too.'

My heart sinks. There's nothing worse than having a gun thrust upon one. Their very heft and the accompanying stench of gun oil make me recoil. Guns kill people, and I've seen more than my fair share of that, thank you.

'Gosh, this is unexpected. I thought we were just here on a murder investigation, not taking up arms.'

49

'If something turns up, all the better. We'll be prepared.'

I spy rifles and round upon round of ammunition at the bottom of the trunk. It's as though we're about to start a revolution. No wonder it was so heavy!

I do wish people would stop talking in riddles to me, like Juggers is doing now. It reminds me of discussing transubstantiation with my father. As mystifying as it is frustrating.

'Hard to be prepared when one doesn't know what to be prepared for,' say I.

'Well, that's just tough cheddar. *One* will have to wait,' says Juggers rather sarcastically. 'Grab this, it's a shoulder holster, and here's a box of rounds. Carry that weapon at all times, do you hear? Aye, and don't make a song and dance about it neither.'

There follows the pantomime I had predicted when Juggers first lowered himself down on one knee. He leans a meaty paw on the trunk in order to push himself up but fails miserably. He gives it another go to no avail.

'Bloody hell! These trousers are too tight. Come on, don't just stand there. Give me a hand up.' He reaches out to me, his face the colour of beetroot. I place my pale, slender paw in his. It feels like assisting a bear. He's a dead weight. I hope I don't strain something.

'Lean forward,' say I. I want to say his great weight will propel him forward as I pull him up but settle for the rather cowardly, 'It's all a matter of mechanics, you know.'

With one last heave, we're there! Juggers stands before me, gasping for breath.

'Trust me, lad, old age is a curse. Enjoy your youth while it's there. Aye, and not in some sleazy bookie shop or tired old pub. I'm sad to see you've still not managed to find a wife.' He takes a seat on the bed and mops his brow of the beads of sweat that have formed there during his exertions.

While he mops, I mope. I'm sad too, about this talk of wives. It's been a year since I first met Deedee, and I can't get her out of my head. It's a long story. But she's the woman of my dreams.

Heigh-ho, another cross to bear, as my father would say. But she made a big impression on me in a very short time. Saved my life, into the bargain. That's bound to mark anyone out, isn't it?

# 8

By the time we're unpacked and suitably equipped with holstered sidearms, it's as black as pitch outside. Juggers looks at his watch and declares it time for a couple of pints then *tea*, as he calls it. It appears I'm to eat at an uncommonly early hour and spend the rest of the evening ravenous. But *when in Rome,* and all that. Or in this case, *when with Juggers.*

The tiny bar is next to a larger restaurant. We take a look inside at the set tables as we pass by en route for a drink. It all seems fine – neatly folded napkins on crisp white tablecloths, under a sea of mainly improvised Christmas decorations, sugar paper streamers, and the like. The war still casting its shadow. However, it looks nice enough. There's even a tree, the decoration of which has clearly benefitted from an artistic touch, with little candles and red ribbons placed hither and yon. Lovely; I like a proper Christmas tree, you know.

The bar is small, more suited to aperitifs than a good session with the lads from York Central. But I suppose my notion of drinking is rather at odds with those who normally come here to visit.

'What's your poison?' says Juggers, standing at the little corner bar while I sit at one of six small tables.

Now, I'm not keen on drinking too much before a meal. Drinking beer fills you up, meaning once you get to the food, you're too full to enjoy it properly. As I have an aversion to any wine, apart from my father's elderflower brew – which he will never turn into the blood of the Saviour, trust me – it's not an option either. I try to think of something less heavy.

'A Pimm's for me, sir. That would be just the ticket.'

Juggers fixes me with one of his formidable glares. 'What?' he says incredulously.

'Pimm's, sir – you know.' I think of describing the drink but merely shrug instead.

'My goodness. I've been drinking for damn near half a century, and I've never ordered a *Pimm's* in my life.'

'You know what they say, sir.'

'No, what do *they* say?'

'Every day is the dawn of a new opportunity.'

Juggers slings me the dirtiest look possible, before turning his attention to the bar. There's nobody about, so he begins to batter away again at one of the little counter bells, ubiquitous here, evidently. 'Shop!' he yells at the top of his voice.

A door swings open, seemingly of its own accord. And not until I see the top of her head do I realize that Dot has arrived behind the bar.

'Do you do everything in this place?' asks Juggers, with all the charm of a rampaging rhinoceros.

'At this time of year, yes. We all have to do our bit. We've extra staff coming in for Christmas, mind.'

'And what if there's somebody at reception, lass?'

'If there is, they must have flown here. The moor road's blocked, coast road, too. There won't be anyone coming here until the ploughs get through in the morning.'

*So, we're cut off from civilization,* I ponder, *with little chance of rousing any help. Good-oh.*

53

'I'd like a pint of bitter and a *Pimm's*, please.' He spits out the name of my drink as though expelling something unpleasant from his mouth.

There's a loud *tut* from our host. 'Are you sure you don't want some wine, or perhaps a nice drop of sherry?' says she.

'Bloody Pimm's isn't for me! I'm a proper ale man. It's for him.' He sounds as though he's been accused of being from Lancashire.

I take the opportunity to give Dot a little wave. Pays to be nice to the person serving the drinks, I always think.

'I would like one, if you have it,' say I. 'I always think it's a good aperitif, don't you?' I smile weakly.

'Fine,' says Dot. 'The customer's always right. Hand me over a chair, would you?'

'What for?' says Juggers.

'For me to stand on while I get the Pimm's, what else?'

'I see,' says Juggers. 'You should have one of them little step ladders. I have a set in the garage for reaching my bits and bobs. They have them in the bars in York too, you know.' He turns to me. 'Hand me that chair, Grasby.'

I do as I'm bid and look on as Juggers passes the chair across the bar. All I can see are Dot's arms, head and shoulders as she grabs the legs. Fair play, she's up on the chair in a jiffy, and with a further stretch, grabs a bottle of Pimm's from the gantry. She jumps from the chair and is soon pouring the drinks.

'There you go. One pint of bitter and a Pimm's,' says she, her eyes flashing at me from just above an ashtray on the bar. 'Sorry, it's not up to the high standards of York's establishments.'

'Much obliged, I'm sure. Can you put it on the bill, please?' says Juggers.

'Aye, I can that. But please note, all outstanding bar and meal bills must be cleared the next morning, no later.'

Juggers makes a face. 'I'm not going to run off without paying, lass.'

'You're telling me that now. But I don't know you from Adam. House rules, it is. Sign here,' she demands, producing a receipt for the drinks.

Having reluctantly appended his name to the drinks bill, Juggers brings them over to the table. The pint tumbler looks tiny in his big, meaty hands.

'Not much of a welcome by the seaside here, I must say,' says Juggers. He holds his pint of bitter up to the light. 'Aye, and this is cloudier than I'd like, and all.'

I sip my Pimm's. 'Ah, that hits the spot.' I smack my lips.

'I'm pleased for you. I always thought it was a drink for lasses and geriatrics. Shows you how much I know.' Juggers gulps down half a pint then burps magnificently. 'Don't taste much better than it looks, lad. But as my father used to say, it's better than a kick in the head from a goat.'

Clearly, Juggers senior was something of a philosopher.

As if by magic, Dot appears again. This time, as she has a little notebook and pencil in her hand, I reckon she's doing waitress duties. Gosh, one has to admire her stamina.

'Can I take your orders, please?'

'How can I do that when I don't know what's on the menu?' says Juggers.

Dot nods her head towards the centre of our table. There stands a toast rack with a little card propped up inside. 'That's the menu,' she says wearily.

I grab the card and read, hoping beyond hope that we might enjoy better fare than was available in the Hanging

Beggar last Christmas. The menu is neatly penned in that rounded hand I've noticed youngsters prefer these days. A few of the clerical staff back in York write in a similar way.

## The Trout Hotel

*Menu*

*

*Soup*

*

*Uthley Bay Fried Cod, served with Boiled Potatoes or Chips and Mixed Vegetables*

*

*As above with Fried Haddock*

*

*Uthley Bay Fish Pie with Chips and Peas*

*

*Steak and Kidney Pie with Mash and Boiled Carrots*

*

*Desserts*
*Steam Pudding and Custard*
*Fruit Trifle*
*Biscuits and Cheese*

*

*Tea and Coffee*

You know, that doesn't look half bad. I am, as usual, famished, and could eat just about anything. But Juggers has a complaint.

'Hang on. Where's the goose, mince pies, Christmas pudding, eh? Not very festive, this.'

'The festive menu isn't served until tomorrow, when the guests arrive.' Dot sniffs. 'If they can get here through all the snow, that is.'

'Way behind York,' says Juggers.

'Makes me wonder why you didn't just stay there,' says Dot with a sigh. 'Oh, and while we're at it. Steak and kidney pie is off. It's because of rationing.'

*Oh dear*, thinks I. Another place in jolly old England made less so by saving the world from tyranny. I think back to happier days when one could gorge on just about anything. Hopefully they'll return soon.

'And there's only Stilton, if it's cheese you're after.'

'Does the fish pie just have fish in it?' says Juggers, sarcastically.

'No, don't be ridiculous.' She raises her eyes heavenward. 'It's mainly whitebait and winkles in a sauce. But we never have any complaints about the food. Tommaso knows what he's doing.'

'I hope he does. Looks a bit heavy-handed to me,' says Juggers dismissively.

I always try to be careful when it comes to restaurant staff. A friend of mine used to work in a posh eatery in Harrogate before the war. If they encountered any snotty customers who handed food back, they used to do all manner of unspeakable things to it before returning it to the table. Trust me, never irritate a chef – you'll be eating their bodily fluids in no time.

To this end, I flash my most winning smile and order the

haddock with boiled potatoes, followed by the trifle and some biscuits and cheese.

'Steady the Buffs,' says Juggers, before turning to Dot. 'Give us a minute longer, lass.'

She sighs once more and retreats behind the bar.

'The constabulary isn't made of money, Grasby,' Juggers resumes in a low tone. 'Aye, and what there is should be spent on catching criminals. You can't have two desserts!'

'Two desserts?' say I. 'Surely, one ends a civilized meal on biscuits and cheese – after dessert, I mean. And you'll note, I'm not having soup.'

I don't mind soup. But in my experience, when you're hungry and order soup first, they'll leave you waiting an age for the main course.

'When I was a nipper, we were lucky to have a main meal, never mind three courses. No, you can have the trifle or the cheese, simple as that.' Juggers folds his arms to emphasise the point, before beckoning Dot with a cursory bob of his head.

'Just the Stilton, please, no trifle,' say I, sipping my Pimm's in as indignant a fashion as I can muster.

'What's the soup?' says Juggers.

'Minestrone,' replies Dot.

'Mini-what?' says Juggers.

'It's Italian. Tommaso makes fabulous soup.'

'That's as maybe. But I like good old English fare. No, I'll have the fish pie. Aye, and it better not be an 'alf empty job, neither.'

'We're not in the habit of serving half-empty pies in this establishment, sir.' Dot thrusts out her chin defiantly.

You have to give this general factotum her due, she's not afraid to lock horns with Juggers. You don't see that too often.

My superior confirms his order, and Dot disappears to the kitchen. I'll keep an eye out, but I'm sure Tommaso is busy urinating in the pie as we speak.

I feel sorry for restaurants these days. What with rationing still firmly in place, it must be hard to make ends meet and manage to concoct something that isn't easily knocked up at home. The war ended years ago, but it sometimes feels as though we'll never be out from under its shadow. I'm becoming more reflective in my old age. I'm not sure whether that's good or bad. They say they'll lift food restrictions next year, but that's a likely story, which I've heard many times before.

As I'm busy pondering the state of the nation, movement in the bar catches my attention. The oddest-looking man I've ever seen wanders in. He's dressed in a suit Disraeli would have likely drooled over, and his white hair is astonishingly unkempt. It looks as though a mattress is in the process of divesting itself of its straw.

He gazes about dolefully, his eyes inevitably landing on us.

'Good evening, gentlemen,' he says in an accent that makes me sound like a rugby league player. 'You haven't seen Dot, have you?'

'She's taking our meal order to the kitchen. And no doubt she'll have to paint a bedroom or two then rewire the place before she gets back here,' says Juggers sarcastically.

You can always tell when he's rattled, you know. And though I'm not immune to it, I'm a gentler soul than Arthur Juggers.

'She's a fine young lady,' says the man with the hair. 'Gets through a power of work in this place. I don't know what we'd do without her.' He nods his head vigorously to underline this. 'I'm Professor Blunt, by the way. Pleased to meet you both.' He nods again, this time by way of a greeting.

'Aye, likewise,' says Juggers. 'I'm Arthur and this is Frank.'

'Good-oh.' With that he disappears through the door momentarily, then reappears behind the bar, where he grabs a bottle of Scotch and pours himself a very generous gentleman's measure. He raises his glass to us. 'Have a lovely evening, gents.' With that, he's off.

'Right lot we have here,' says Juggers, puffing his pipe into life. 'Plain case of theft there, for a start.'

'Maybe he's a long-term resident,' say I.

I'm damned if I'll adopt the tendency my colleagues harbour of seeing the very worst in people. It's depressing and – more often than not – wrong.

Dot's little head appears just above the bar.

'You've been robbed!' shouts Juggers at the top of his voice. 'A man who pays very little attention to his hair just wandered off with about a gallon of whisky.'

Dot looks puzzled.

'Old boy, rather eccentric hairstyle, if you know what I mean,' say I for clarification.

'Oh, the prof,' says Dot. 'He owns the hotel.'

Juggers looks surprised. 'I hope he takes care of business better than he does his barnet, or you'll be in right bother.'

'He's a genius. His family has owned this place and the hotel that was here before it for generations. He spent most of his life down in Oxford. He taught chemistry, has all kinds of letters after his name. I can never remember them.' Dot's expression is suddenly filled with pride.

'Good for him,' says Juggers dismissively.

He really can be a bit of a boor at times.

Our meals arrive quickly and are delicious. Even Juggers comments that his pie is one of the best he's tasted. And my fish is beautifully cooked and succulent. I can taste just a hint of tarragon, which sets things off nicely. I've fallen on my feet again in the dinner department, it seems.

I'm dabbing my mouth with a proper linen napkin, while Juggers is wiping his hands on what he calls a *serviette*, lodged permanently under his chin as he eats, when there's a commotion at the restaurant door. A man in bright yellow oilskins is standing there, gazing at us as though we're sitting in our birthday suits.

'Can I help you? Or are you the Uthley Bay staring champion?' says Juggers.

'Aye, you can help me, if you're the bobbies,' says he.

Juggers empties his pipe into the ashtray by banging the bowl on the glass with a clink. I really believe he might be a frustrated drummer, always rattling something.

'Never mind that. What's to do?'

Our new visitor pulls his sou'wester from his head and sways from foot to foot. 'It's down in Danby Cove, thou knows. They've found something.'

Juggers knits his brows. 'And who told you to come to us?'

'Old Ogden said you'd want to know. Mr Barclay – he's a fisherman, like me. I'm his first mate.'

'I've already had the pleasure,' says Juggers.

The fisherman looks confused. 'Pleasure of what?'

'Pleasure of meeting Mr Barclay!'

At this point, I know Juggers is about to call this son of the sea a name he won't like. So, I intervene.

'Can I ask your name, sir?'

'Don.' He hesitates. 'Don Haddy.'

'Right, Don,' says Juggers. 'How do we get to this cove? It's knee deep in snow out there.'

'I've a vehicle with me. We can put you in the back.

They've cleared a good bit of the road with shovels and sand, as usual.'

'Where?' says Juggers.

'Between here and the cove. They always try to keep it clear.'

'Why's that?' I ask.

Don Haddy makes an odd face, his mouth downturned at the corners. 'I'm not sure, 'cos there's nowt there but an old pier. Seen better days, it has.' This reply seems as guileless as the man himself. But I sense a sudden wariness on his part.

'Right, Grasby. Get a shift on. We better get down there.' Juggers pats his oxter with a wink. I realize this isn't merely some odd gesture, but a reminder we're both armed.

And so, with great reluctance, I leave the cosiness of the Trout Hotel, its Pimm's and my *tea*, and head out into the freezing cold, snowy night with Superintendent Juggers. Maybe it's the bitter weather, but the hair is standing up on the back of my neck.

# 9

Don Haddy is a bigger lad than I thought. He's as tall as me but much broader. I gauge this as we head out into the night. The Bedford van looks ancient, like the first of its kind ever built, with great holes in between the rust, which seems to be all that's holding the whole thing together. Haddy beckons us forward, shining a storm lantern on the canvas-covered rear of the vehicle.

'I'm sorry I can't have one of you in the front. It's packed with creels.' He shrugs.

This makes little difference to me. I know full well that if the passenger seat were free, Juggers would park himself in it. The joys of being a superintendent. As it is, I jump into the van and am almost overcome by the stench of fish. So much so, I rush a hankie from my pocket to protect my mouth and nose.

'Don't dawdle, Grasby. Give me a hand up, will you? When you're my age you'll not be as supple as you are now.' Juggers holds out one of his great shovel hands for me to grab.

Despite pulling with all my might, Juggers remains firmly on the snowy road.

'Can you put a foot on that fender, sir? It'll help us get you aboard,' say I, still choking at the smell.

With a glare and a murmured oath, Juggers tries to raise his foot onto the vehicle's bumper. He fails twice at this, before catching his suit trouser leg with one hand and pulling his foot onto the battered metal that way.

'If I tear this suit, there'll be hell to pay, lad,' says he querulously.

I pull at his hand again. And for a moment, he's up! But this levitation doesn't last long, as he falls back, almost pulling me from the van while he's at it. My superior is only saved by the bulky Don Haddy, who in one swift movement catches Juggers and propels him into the back beside me. I manage to catch him just before he stumbles onto the floor.

'What a bloody performance that was,' says Juggers, brushing down his jacket. 'Why you couldn't have just pulled me in, I don't know. Didn't take Haddy here a second to do the job.'

There are two bench seats on either side of the van's rear. I sit on one, Juggers the other.

It's odd, but even though Juggers has struggled to get in here, he's still as strong as an ox. I, on the other hand, am thin and tall but not very strong. I may have no problem levering myself into the back of a van, but when it comes to fisticuffs with some ne'er-do-well in the course of my duties, well, Juggers would be a much better choice than I. Takes all sorts, I suppose.

The stinking Bedford makes slow progress along the road to Danby Cove. Conveniently, neither of us saw fit to go to back to our room and bring overcoats. And while Juggers is puffing contentedly on his pipe as though it's a spring day, I'm chilled to the bone, shivering like a tramp asleep in a puddle.

'I hadn't realized until now what a daisy you are, Grasby,'

says my kindly boss. 'Shivering like a bloody jelly. Buck up, man!' says Juggers.

I'm quickly tiring of Juggers's barbs. There's a full moon, and I can see well enough to root about in the back of this travelling pelagic dustbin to attempt to find something warm. After a brief trawl, caught amongst some net and white buoys I discover a yellow oilskin jacket. It's certainly big enough, so I shrug it on over my suit.

'You can't wear that! We're police officers – there are standards!' Juggers shouts over the din of the engine.

I don't care what standards there are. I'm sure Napoleon's chaps were warmer than this fleeing Moscow.

'Needs must, sir,' say I. 'And we'll have to decide whether we're police officers or not, don't you think? I know you're keen to keep a low profile, but most of the village seem to know what we're about.'

You can tell I'm on edge. Normally, I wouldn't dream of speaking to Juggers like this. But in extremis, one can be pushed to the very limit.

Juggers puffs his pipe more rapidly, his teeth clenching the stem. I can't say I'm too unhappy about this, as his tobacco smoke is preferable to the stink back here in Davy Jones's locker.

'Aye, I reckon our cover is blown, if I'm honest. I'd hoped we'd be able to blend in, like,' he says.

I think about this as I pull the oilskin tighter about me. With me so tall and thin, and Juggers looking like an all-in wrestler about to tear your head off, the chances of us *blending in* were remote in the extreme. In any case, I'm confused why he thinks we need to. After all, we're here to find out what happened to the poor strangled fisherman. A job for the constabulary, I'd say.

This thought further unsettles me, until we're being

buffeted about as though we're driving across rocks. I peer through the canvas flaps of the Bedford, and in the moonlight all I can see is the white line of the snowy road marching behind us like a ship's wake in the moonlight.

Just then, the vehicle pulls up to a stop. I hear a door slam, and before we know it, there's Haddy with a storm lantern, staring at us again.

'Are we here – at the cove, I mean?' says Juggers.

'Aye, we are.'

But Don Haddy is taking me in open-mouthed.

'You weren't wearing that when we left,' says he.

'No, just trying to keep warm,' I offer. He still looks unsettled. It's as though I've sprouted wings and a beak.

'Right, let's get on with it, shall we!' shouts Juggers. Then in an aside to me, 'This lad's not the full shilling, Grasby. Let me tell you that for nowt.'

*Well spotted, sir*, thinks I. Gosh, he must think I'm a bit short on grey cells too.

Thankfully, with a hand from Haddy, Juggers makes a much better fist of exiting the vehicle than he did entering. I clamber out behind him to look out upon a monochrome landscape, leached of all colour under a dark, starry sky. It's even colder outside, of course. I long for my cashmere overcoat. Come to that, I'd be much happier sitting by the fire with a decent brandy. But it's the life of a policeman. One minute, you're living the good life, the next you're out in the elements facing goodness knows what with a pistol strapped under your armpit. It's damnably unpredictable.

We reach the edge of a cliff, and looking down, the sea is lapping at a beach, which is in the main covered with the white stuff. We have to clamber down some treacherous steps, following Haddy's lead, to reach the strand. The moon seems brighter now, as though someone's switched on the ceiling light in a dark room. In the distance, I see a figure tramping towards us in silhouette.

'How do, gents?' says Ogden Barclay as he gets nearer. He glances at me in my oilskin. 'When in Rome, eh, Mr Grasby?'

Before I can reply, Juggers pipes up.

'Right then, Mr Barclay. What's to do? Why have you pulled us away from our tea?'

'Follow me,' says he, tramping along the beach, his ancient wellington boots crumping on the snow and sand.

I'm at the tail of this little band of brothers. As we turn a corner, another tiny bay opens out in front of us. In the moonlight, I can see a broken-down jetty at the far end. I say far, but the beach can't be more than a couple of hundred yards in length. At this short distance, it's clear there are little spots all along its snowy surface, like polka dots on a white dress.

We tramp on further. Then Juggers stoops to pick up an item.

'It's a pair of stockings,' says he. 'Still in the packet.' But it's the way he says it that piques my interest. It's almost as though anyone taking a walk across a snowbound beach, just before Christmas in Yorkshire, might expect to find a pair of nylons wrapped in cellophane. 'This were where they found poor old Wardle, thou knows.'

Juggers nods his head and surveys the scene. Somehow, it's an even bleaker prospect now we know a murdered man was found here. Aye, and not long ago, either. But as the local police report strongly suggests, Wardle was dead long before he washed up on this strand. Then there's the stockings, of course.

And there's plenty of them, too. As we walk on, I count at least five dozen little packets, all exactly the same. I pick one up, and in the light of Haddy's lantern discover they're forty denier, which is quite thick for a stocking. Intended for a more senior lady, I reckon. Oh yes, I know a thing or two about stockings, it has to be said.

Juggers turns to me, Haddy holding the lantern close to his face, making him look even more formidable than he already is. Bit like an evil genie from a lamp. 'Right, Grasby. We'll need this lot picking up. We'll all pitch in. Shouldn't take too long.' His breath billows over him in the lamplight, as though he's on fire.

And so, we go about it. Haddy is sent to the van and arrives back with two old sacks that smell just as bad as the vehicle itself. He hands me a pair of rough gloves that I'd normally have steered a hundred miles from, but such is the cold, I pull them on as though they were Dents' very best.

Juggers, whom I note isn't doing much bending to retrieve stockings, turns to Barclay. 'How come you found these, then?'

'I've a smaller boat the other side of that pier, Mr Juggers. A crab boat, you know. I'm not using it at the moment, this not being the season. But I didn't want her filling up with snow and sinking. So, me and Don here were going to pull her further up on the shore. These were just scattered about, as you see them now. It was either get a message to you or go into business selling them. I'm an honest chap, you'll note.'

Now, most people probably wouldn't have spotted this, but I do. When he finishes his explanation, he fairly nods at Juggers. It's hard to put across, but I find it conspiratorial in some way I can't explain. It's as though they share a secret, one to which I'm not party. Come to think of it, I had a similar notion earlier in the day when we first met the craggy old fisherman. There was something unsaid between the two. Though what, I've no idea.

It doesn't take too long to pack away the hosiery in our sacks, Haddy and I doing most of the work. The four of us head back to the Bedford with the stockings. As we draw near the vehicle, Juggers hangs back a bit, summoning me with a tilt of his head.

'There's a lot I don't like about this, lad,' says he.

I think for a moment. 'Because that poor old bugger was strangled by a stocking, sir? Bit of a coincidence, don't you think?'

He turns and sniffs the air, looking at the dark sea under the moonlight. The great orb is huge in the winter sky, casting a path of shimmering light across the waves.

'Aye, it is a bit, Grasby.'

He shrugs and we join Barclay and Haddy at the van.

But the Grasby instinct is hard at work. And what it's saying to me isn't good. Not good at all.

# 10

When we arrive back at the hotel, Juggers and I grab a sack each and sling them over our respective shoulders.

'I thank you, Mr Barclay. We'll hang on to these in the meantime. Until we can find out where they came from, that is,' says Juggers in a pleasant manner.

I divest myself of the oilskin jacket, though Haddy is still staring at me as though I'm from another planet – or maybe Scotland. It's hard to tell what he finds so fascinating. Though he is a few fish short of a good catch, I'm sure.

When we enter the hotel, Dot is passing with tea and sandwiches on a tray.

'Oh, it's Santa and his not so little helper,' she says with a giggle, referring to the sacks over our shoulders. 'You're a couple of nights early. Where's Rudolph?'

Juggers casts her a beady eye. 'With the rest of the little elves. Friends of yours, are they?'

That's one thing I'll say for him – Juggers rarely misses the chance to put someone in their place, especially if they're trying to be smart. I suppose he's had plenty young constables to practise on over the years. I remember being terrified of him when I joined up. And he was only an inspector back then.

'What's that smell?' says Dot. 'It's disgusting!'

'It's the sacks,' say I. 'We borrowed them from a fisherman.'

Juggers is heading for the lift – it's out of order sign having been removed – when she calls out again.

'Don't you dare! I'm not having that stench in our newly fixed lift. Wilf managed to get it going. You can empty whatever you've got stashed away in them when you get to your room. Then bring them back down here and I'll have Wilf set them on fire. Most of our Christmas guests arrive tomorrow. You're not going to have the place smelling like a fish market!'

'I'll have you know this is police business,' says Juggers.

'Gosh, policemen *and* bird watchers. What a combination!'

Juggers knows when he's beaten. Unless he decides to arrest her for impeding an officer in the course of his duty. He did that once with an air raid warden, I'm told. Got into a bit of bother over it, too. Thankfully, he doesn't try to repeat the calumny.

So, cold, still hungry and miserable, and without as much as a dram to cheer me, I mount the stairs with Juggers, heading for our third-floor room, and the prospect of decanting sixty-odd pairs of stockings from the fish sacks.

When we turn the lock and get in, I'm absolutely exhausted. But at least it's warm. Though Juggers looks as though he's fit to drop.

'Bugger this,' says he, sitting down on the bed heavily. 'Sometimes I think I'm getting too old for this caper. Thirty years ago, I'd have run up those stairs, carrying you and the sacks. Not now.'

I'm not sure if it's because I'm so tired too – only just recovering from our chilly night-time excursion to the

beach – but his words make me feel a bit on the melancholy side. I'm not far from my fortieth birthday. And
according to my dear father, life just shoots right out from
under one at that age. No sooner have you blown out the
candles on the cake marking four decades on the planet,
than you're stiffly bending over one to mark your sixtieth.
No doubt, to the accompaniment of aching knees and a
wheeze into the bargain.

When I feel like this, I remember the chaps I knew
that didn't make it through the war. They don't have the
privilege of getting old. With this in mind, I tell Juggers
I'll empty the sacks in a flash and take them back down
to Dot.

'Good lad,' says he, slipping off his shoes and loosening
the button at his waistband. He levers himself up on the
bed and folds the fingers of both hands over his ample
belly. Before I've started on the second sack of stockings,
he's snoring fit to wake the village.

I finish my task quickly. I've counted sixty-two pairs of
cellophane-wrapped stockings, now piled neatly against
one wall.

On tiptoes, I leave the room with the offensive-smelling
sacks. I'm about to take the stairs when the old Grasby disregard for authority grips me. I press the white porcelain
'down' button beside the lift and wait while it clangs and
cranks its way up to the third floor.

If my father can fall out with a king over the meaning of
religious belief, then I can bally well take the hotel lift.
After all, I'm a guest.

Mind you, when the lift doors open in the vestibule, I'm
delighted to note that nobody is about to witness my strike
against authority. Still, I must find the ubiquitous Dot,
which shouldn't be too hard given the number of jobs she

performs. I wouldn't be surprised to find her delivering the milk first thing in the morning, or perhaps shovelling some coal into the cellar.

There are voices coming from behind the internal door to the tiny reception office. It's lying slightly ajar, so I approach, ready to push it open and find Dot busy with some chore or other. But something makes me stop in my tracks. Don't ask me why. Could be instinct or the fact the conversation is muted – whispered, almost.

'Foundered just off Withey Shingle,' says a man I've yet to identify, though he does sound a bit like Ogden Barclay, with perhaps a trace of somewhere other than Yorkshire in his voice.

'Not the first boat to do that, is it?' This is definitely Dot, I'd recognize her voice anywhere, though I've only known her for a few hours.

'They'll need to be told.' This, I assume, is Wilf – certainly sounds like his Cockney twang. And voices aside, who are *they*, and why do *they* have to be told?

It's at this moment I let myself down badly. I'm not sure whether it's the trip to find the stockings or just the seasonal temperature, but without warning, I sneeze magnificently. One of those sudden jobs, with absolutely no chance of holding it in.

The reception door swings open. It's Professor Blunt in round specs and an evening suit. He's calmed down his hair with pomade or something similar. Makes him look very different.

'What on earth happened to you?' he exclaims, noting my person and the filthy fish sacks through his tiny specs.

'Bit of beachcombing,' say I.

None of his damn business what I'm up to.

When he retreats back into the office, I try to peer round

the door to see if I can spot anyone else. But quickly Dot slips through the gap and closes the door behind her.

Now, it might be my imagination, but I can feel the tension. When you're a police officer for a while, you begin to notice things much quicker than your average member of the public.

'The sacks, of course,' says Dot, clearly flustered, though doing her best to hide it. 'Give them to me and I'll get rid of the damned things.' She holds her nose. 'I don't know how you can bear them, Mr Grasby.'

As she's grabbing the sacks, I take my opportunity. 'Who's in there?'

She falters for a second but soon finds her feet. 'Oh, just guests. Friends of the professor. He's resident here over Christmas. Wants to know what time the morning service is at the church on Christmas Day.'

This is, of course, a complete lie and she knows it. My job is to make sure she doesn't think I know it.

'Good-oh!' say I with a grin. 'My father's a vicar, you know.'

'The Reverend Grasby?' she retorts instantly.

It's a fair enough guess, given she knows my surname, and the nomenclature used to denote a man of the cloth. But I don't like it.

'Yes, that's him,' say I, maintaining my happy visage. 'Once seen, never forgotten, let me tell you. You'll definitely remember him if you've heard one of his sermons.'

'I'm sure.' She bites her lip disconcertingly. 'Where's Mr Juggers, if you don't mind me asking?'

'He's in the land of nod. Dropped off as soon as we got back upstairs.' I smile winningly. 'What with one thing and another, it's been a long day.'

'If you hang on until I remove these awful things from the premises, I'll pour you a Pimm's. You still look cold.'

'That would be very nice,' say I. 'Though a good brandy might warm me up a bit quicker than a Pimm's.'

'No problem. Make yourself comfortable in the bar. I'll be with you in a tick.'

And she's as good as her word. Dot, for all her diminutive size, fairly ushers me into the bar. And I've just enough time to find my cigarettes and light one before she's back, rather flushed and out of breath, as though she's been rushing.

'Now, that brandy.' She bustles behind the counter, locates the bottle, which is thankfully low down enough for her not to require the services of a chair to reach it. She pours me a large one, then places it on the bar. 'That'll put hairs on your chest,' she says with an uncertain smile.

As I sip my brandy – not especially good but more than welcome – I'm aware she's forcing the conversation. It's question after question in rapid succession, leaving me giddy. Worse than my police job interview, carried out by a panel of senior officers, none of whom were in the least interested in my replies. And I get that same feeling from Dot, too.

Only when I hear a door slam distantly, do I see her relax. It's as though the world's been lifted from her shoulders. But with this relaxation go the pleasantries. She's no longer interested in Francis Grasby, Esq., asking me to drink up, as she has to rise early for breakfasts in the morning. Such a swift change!

Of course, she must be daft to think that I fell for any of it. She wanted me out the way to let her anonymous guest slip out – the voice in the office I didn't quite recognize. I bid her a goodnight and take the lift back to the third floor.

I turn my key gently in the lock, so as not to wake Juggers. But I needn't have bothered. The noise coming from him in his sleep is truly monumental. I've never heard snoring like it. I swear, the whole room is vibrating!

I quickly review my options and decide on a course of action. My overcoat is hanging from a hook behind the door – I remove it and grab my trilby from the dressing table. Before you know it, I've turned a little paper napkin I stuffed into my pocket at dinner into two improvised earplugs. I end up sitting in the basket chair with my overcoat draped over me like a blanket, my trilby angled over my eyes, feet up on a little pouffe. I look like a thin Yorkshire cowboy.

The darkness of the room is leavened by a chink in the heavy curtains, allowing light from the street lamp below to shine through. But I'm too tired to get up and close them. The room is warm enough, and with my cashmere overcoat I'm cosy. That large brandy has helped too.

With Juggers's snoring a dull roar behind my make-and-mend earplugs, I drift off into what turns out to be a restless sleep, filled with dreams of snow, holstered pistols, stockings, and shifty-looking guests.

# 11

I'm woken by a badly whistled tune, and the curtains being flung open. This, even though it's still black as pitch outside.

'Right, lad. It's time to get up and at 'em,' says a rejuvenated Juggers, resplendent in a bulging vest, white underpants and a pair of socks held up by suspenders.

'Gosh, sir. What's the time?' I enquire, my eyes still squinting in the electric light to see my watch.

'Just before six. We've plenty to be about, so get moving. The bathroom's down the end of the hall. Water's nice and hot too, if you want a bath.'

At this point I spot a white fleck of shaving soap on his chin.

'I'll have a quick bath, if you don't mind, sir. An army one will suffice.'

Juggers evidently knows what I mean. An 'army bath' is about two inches of water and lasts two or three minutes. We were lucky to find hot water when I was a soldier, and if we happened upon a bath, the queues made Oxford Street on Christmas Eve look relatively deserted. It also means that you're up and about in quick time. Wouldn't do if Jerry set about us and we were all luxuriating in the bath.

All my life, I've been able to move from asleep to awake

rather sharpish. So, as Juggers is struggling into his trousers – not a pretty sight – I'm off to the bathroom at the end of the corridor with my towel under my arm.

It's a standard hotel bathroom. You know – old bath, toilet with a skew-whiff seat, and a wash-hand basin with a mirror above, the latter just as we have in our room. Here, though, there's a nasty brown stain under the taps where they've been left to drip, which is something I dislike in the extreme. In fact, I also have an odd phobia of tiles. It's something to do with the grouting. This is down to our old chemistry master at school, who saw fit to inform us that, while it is pretty easy to keep the tiles themselves clean, all manner of germs lurk in the grouting between them. He went on to list all sorts of dreadful maladies, including botulism. And like every bad thing I've ever been told, it sticks in my mind to this day.

The grouting in this bathroom isn't the worst I've seen, but it's not the best either. I rapidly draw just enough water while I'm shaving, and in a jiffy I'm bathed and drying myself off with the towel.

When I report back to HQ in our bedroom, I find Juggers fully clothed, in his overcoat. Rather surprisingly, he has a towel under his arm.

'Good-oh, sir. Have you decided on a bath after all?'

He pointedly looks under his arm. 'Aye, I'm well known for going to have a bath in my overcoat.' He tuts and shakes his head. 'We're off for a wander and I'm going to have a dip. That's what the towel's for.'

'A dip, sir?' I enquire.

'A swim, lad. I love being beside the sea, and you can't beat a quick dip in the morning to set you up for the day. The wife reckons I should go to the swimming baths in York of a morning. But it's not the same.'

I'm aware that I'm gaping, so force my mouth closed. 'It's freezing, sir. Snow on the ground.'

'Won't bother me. I got into the habit in the Great War. We spent some time off in Normandy. Nothing better than a dip in the morning. Our colonel swore by it. Most of us were lousy, you see.' He shakes his head at the thought. 'For us straight out of the trenches, it were the best thing ever.'

Now, I'm no expert on the water temperature in the English Channel, but I'm willing to wager it's rather warmer than the North Sea in December. But Juggers seems to be determined.

'If you're sure, sir,' I offer, quietly giving thanks that even though I had to participate in a war, it was the second calamity. I've never been able to imagine trench warfare. The very thought of it makes me shiver.

'Will we have breakfast first?' say I hopefully.

'Not a chance. It's dangerous to go into the water after a meal. Don't you know anything? It won't take long. I'm not swimming to Holland. We'll have breakfast when we get back.'

With this little mission in mind, we head into the lift and exit the hotel.

We tramp through the snow past various little dwellings. There's no sign of dawn fringing the skies to the east at this hour in December, and the stars are still out. Mercifully, it's not snowing, but it's bitterly, bitterly cold. Our breath tumbles under the street lamps like thunderclouds.

'Here we are,' says Juggers. He dashes across the road to a short length of promenade. 'I spotted this yesterday. Steps down onto the shore. What more could you want?'

For my sins, I hadn't noticed the steps at all. I am, you may have gleaned, not the most observant of chaps. It's not a handy thing for a police officer, you know. But there's no point lamenting the fact.

And I do possess other attributes that make up for this. I work on instinct, and I've found it rarely lets me down. I remember being sent to a château in Normandy, just before the end of the war. Of course, the brass had set up an HQ there. It's the kind of thing senior army officers do. I was tasked with delivering a communication to Major General Blithering Horse, or whatever his name was. I can't remember now. He read the note from my then captain, stroked his chin and hummed a tune. Something by Bach, if memory serves. Before dismissing me, he was good enough to offer me a meal. No doubt noting my emaciated frame.

'Get yourself down to the kitchens and grab some lunch, old boy,' says he. 'If you can, try a drop of the *Medoc cru classe*. A bloody good gargle, you'll see.' He'd clearly marked me out as a bon viveur on very short acquaintance.

A private – no doubt his batman, and old retainer in civvy street – showed me below stairs to the kitchen. My goodness, the place was magnificent, intricate cornicing, gilt furniture and lavish paintings. I was about to sit down to a meal when a dreadful feeling of doom enveloped me. My heart began to pound, and I felt as though I was coming down with some malady or other. I made my excuses and left damn sharp, revving my dear old Triumph motorcycle away from the château as quickly as it would travel over the rutted drive.

Having managed to get a couple of miles under my belt, the whole road in front of me shook as a massive explosion rent the air. It was resonant enough to knock me off my motorcycle and I ran for cover, fearing an artillery barrage or even those bloody Tiger tanks.

I was wrong on both counts.

Seeing billowing black smoke coming from roughly where I'd just been, once I was sure the coast was clear, I ventured back to see what on earth had happened. The château, where I should have been enjoying some pheasant and a good drop of the old vino, had taken a direct hit from a bomber, and was almost flattened. I ventured forth to see what I could do, of course. But I shan't describe to you the harrowing sights that are still imprinted on my mind. I never found out whether anyone managed to survive, though I can't see how it would have been possible. Soon the place was swarming with soldiers from a nearby unit, pulling at debris and calling for hush in case some poor blighter buried under the rubble was crying for help. All in all, it was a bloody tragedy – one of so many I happened upon.

I returned to my own unit, but I never forgot the feeling I'd had in that kitchen, which undoubtedly saved my life.

As Arthur Juggers surveys the unwelcoming tide, I have exactly the same feeling wash over me again. Not perhaps about my superintendent's morning swim, rather something about the whole place. Though my inclination is to bolt, I stay put. Not sure why.

'Aye, ripe for a dip,' says he, pulling his overcoat from his shoulders.

'I say, sir. Don't you think it'll be a bit on the chilly side?'

He tuts and shakes his bull head. 'Cold water is a well-known restorative, Grasby. Gets the circulation going, stimulates the brain. If anyone needs their brain stimulating, it's you. Join me! You'll never look back.'

I mutter something about feeling a cold coming on, and look on as Juggers removes his last stitch of clothes – an enormous pair of white pants. His body turns an unhealthy

81

blue, and he wobbles into the surf. Though I think him rather foolish, I have to admire his spirit. I mean, my teeth are chattering again, and I'm fully clothed, and huddled into a cashmere overcoat.

He takes a few steps into the waves, to just about mid-thigh depth. It's at this point I spot clear hesitation from my dear superintendent. However, knowing I'm watching, and his pride is at stake, he slaps himself on the back with crossed arms, takes a deep breath, bellows like an ox, then submerges himself under the waves.

Two things cross my mind at this point. One, that if he doesn't re-emerge soon, I'll have to swim to the rescue. And two, I might be the one to die in three feet of water. It would be typical of my luck, you know.

But just as I'm watching the waves for signs of life, getting into a bigger and bigger funk as I do, there shoots from the sea a pale-blue rotund shape, with all the grace of a leaping elephant. Juggers pirouettes in mid-air, and when he lands back in the sea, makes a noise I can only describe as a spine-chilling yell.

This is closely followed by a high-pitched scream, which appears to emanate not from Arthur Juggers but from just above my head. I look back up to the promenade, and under the street lamp which bleeds its light over our little stretch of sand and tide, I see a young woman frozen in shock, her hands tightly gripping the handle of a pram. Her mouth is actually forming a perfect 'O' shape as she regards Juggers's maritime antics.

Fair dos, I'd say. Juggers must be aware of her as he's now submerged just under the waves, with only his head above the waterline. At the moment, considering his thinning hair, he looks like a blue buoy placed there to mark something hazardous to shipping.

'Off you go!' comes the shivering call from the North Sea. 'Nothing to see here!' Juggers bellows, his voice wavering in the extreme cold.

*Nothing to see?* I have to beg his pardon. For this poor young mother has just been treated to an image of the flailing, naked Juggers, picked out in perfect clarity by the street lamp. And let me tell you, it wasn't a pretty sight.

'I do apologize,' say I, desperately trying to form an excuse for what this poor woman has just been forced to witness.

'It's the baby,' she replies, now looking out to sea blankly, as though still trying to process what she's seen. 'He's a bad sleeper. Must have an early morning walk or he won't settle for the rest of the day.' At this point, she appears to pull herself together and glares at yours truly. 'I don't know what you pair are up to, but I've a good mind to call the constabulary and have you both arrested! Decent folk shouldn't be exposed to such depravity. Wait until I tell my husband!'

I'm about to announce that we *are* the constabulary to whom she refers, before thinking better of it. As I'm about to say something else inane, she clips off, her heels echoing on the promenade like the beating of the retreat.

'Quick, Grasby! Grab me towel,' shouts Juggers as he emerges from the sea like the dread sea monsters of old myth and legend.

For a horrid moment, I think he's going to ask me to help dry him off, but he soon gets on with the job himself, shivering more and more as he does.

'Well,' say I, irritated by this unseemly performance. 'I don't know if your brain has been stimulated, sir, but I'm sure that young lady's is quite befuddled!' All he can say by means of a retort are a few garbled words through chattering teeth, roughly resembling expletives.

As I wait for him to dress, I ruminate upon the fact that not only are we sharing a double bed, but a member of the community has also just witnessed one of us leap naked from the sea, at what is – for most folk – the dead of night, while the other looks on from the shore.

So much for the *don't tell anyone you're a copper* approach. Now we look like members of a sexually liberated maritime exhibitionist cult.

I give Juggers a hand with his overcoat and help my trembling superior back to the warmth of the Trout.

As we stumble back along the seafront, Juggers coughing and shivering, I hear voices. I look up to see the harbour as busy as Shaftesbury Avenue, with chaps fairly milling about under the harbour lights. I also note there are many more fishing boats in evidence than when we arrived yesterday. I count eight vessels, though I'm unable to distinguish one from another at this distance in the dark.

I'm sure Ogden Barclay told us that this time of year was poor for fishing unless skippers were willing to brave the winter storms in the North Sea and beyond. Now, I'm no mariner, as you know. But these vessels don't look robust enough to travel too far out to sea. They're small, wooden affairs, not like the great steel trawlers I've seen leave the docks at Hull.

'Get a move on, lad. I'm bursting for the loo,' says Juggers as we stumble a few yards from the hotel.

He tumbles inside and heads immediately for the lift. I watch him shiver like billy-o as he waits for it to clank its way down.

'Just going to have a quick bath and change of clothes,' he stutters through chattering teeth. 'You g-go and have some breakfast. I'll join you as soon as I m-may.'

As he steps into the lift, I'm pleased to see a little

pinkness return to that bald, round head. A bath will do him the world of good, methinks. I hope this is the end of our early morning escapades. But one never knows with Juggers.

I'm already enticed by the glorious smell of frying bacon and eggs. It must be one of the most alluring olfactory experiences known to man. It certainly is for yours truly. Quickly, I make for the dining room.

# 12

I almost stop in my tracks when I see a young waitress that's not Dot. Doesn't seem right they have someone else front of house. Then I remember it's the day the Christmas guests arrive, if they manage to clear the snow.

Outside, it's getting brighter, and already it looks like being one of those magnificently clear winter mornings when the cold hits the back of your throat as you walk. A day for hats, gloves and long johns. I've loved winter weather like this all my life. Well, I remember long winter walks with my late mother, me with my bobble hat and mittens. My mother would wear what she termed a *toorie*. It's a Scottish name – one of many I remember with great fondness. How I miss her. It's the time of year for missing people, isn't it?

I sit myself down and order bacon, eggs and fried bread. When it arrives, it's not quite what I was expecting. Last night's meal was lovely, even though the menu was limited. My plate consists of one rasher of bacon, a greasy, shrivelled egg and a half slice of bread. It all looks as though it's been under the grill to keep it warm. Nonetheless, after my early morning antics with Juggers, anything is welcome, and I tuck in for a minute or so until it's finished. Still famished, I spread the sliver of butter that's been left on the table, and marmalade from the tiniest jar I've ever seen, onto a piece of toast. At least the tea's good and strong, taken in the manner of the county.

I look on as an ancient lady totters in on a stick. She smiles at me, and I return the compliment. She must like the cut of my jib, as she seats herself at the table next to mine. And once she's arranged her accoutrement to her satisfaction, she leans over to converse with me.

'Howdy,' she says with a big grin.

Now, I must confess that it's an unusual greeting here in England. And the only Americans I've heard use it are on screen. But I smile, assuming she's from across the pond. I reply in kind. Well, at least in the way I've seen done in Westerns.

'Howdy, ma'am. I'm delighted to make your acquaintance.' I'd have tipped my trilby if it hadn't been on the chair at my side. I'm quite the mimic, as you'll have gathered. I pride myself in being able to get many accents reasonably close. She grins from ear to ear, no doubt delighted to hear a familiar voice, bless her.

'I'll be needing five dozen more when you have them,' she whispers. But this time she doesn't sound in the least American, though it's hard to tell at this low level.

I decide to abandon the charade. 'I do beg your pardon,' say I. 'You have me at a disadvantage. Another five dozen of what?'

The old dear suddenly looks quite startled. 'You're English!' says she, as though I've just jumped out of a box in a clown suit.

'And damned proud of it too,' say I, chin jutting nobly.

'I didn't know they had any Englishmen. How nice.'

At this point, the conversation has become quite bizarre. And whoever *they* are isn't at all apparent. Deciding that this elderly specimen has entirely lost her marbles, I play along, for her sake. It doesn't do to mock the afflicted. One never knows when it'll be your own turn to babble a lot of nonsense. If Juggers was here, he'd say I've been doing it for years.

'Five dozen of what?' I enquire kindly.

Lady Methuselah regards me as though I'm speaking Cantonese. 'What do you think? My goodness, if you're the new man, I don't think you're quite on the ball, my dear. But I'm sure you'll catch on.'

*What on earth are you blithering about, you mad old bat?* I want to say. But that's unkind.

Just at this, the waitress arrives at her side.

'Hello, Mrs Smith-Wantley, the usual, is it?'

If *the usual* is bacon and eggs, it's no wonder there's not a pick on this poor old biddy, considering my breakfast proportions.

'Yes, just a slice of toast and jam,' says she. 'And a pot of tea, of course, dear.'

'I say, could I have another round of toast? For some reason, even after the bounteousness of breakfast, I'm still famished.' Sarcasm is the lowest form of wit.

'I'll have to ask the manager. I mean, you've already had bacon and eggs, and your toast. And I see you've eaten the butter and marmalade.' She regards me as though I'm a veritable Billy Bunter in the making.

'Yes, I'm aware of that. Unfortunately, I'm still hungry. Can't think for the life of me why. I must say, it's a pretty piece when the manager has to be consulted every time a guest wants another slice of toast at breakfast.'

This is, of course, wrong of me. After all, my state of hunger isn't this young lass's fault. But I go on to say, 'I know we're not up to mid-season pace as far as the availability of food is concerned here in dear old England, but it's hardly back to nineteen forty-two now, is it?'

Mrs Smith-Wantley glares at me in disgust, as though I've tried to snatch a kiss.

'You need to learn some manners, young man,' she chides with a gnarled, wagging finger. 'You're not in New York now, you know!'

'But I'm sure you think you might be, or perhaps New Year,' I mutter under my breath. 'I do apologize,' say I, not meaning it. 'I'm just a thoroughgoing glutton. Can't help myself.'

At this point the door swings open, and a renewed Arthur Juggers enters the room, all pink and normal-looking. He spies me quickly and makes his way to my table.

'Good morning,' he says affably to my new friend. You wouldn't think it's just over an hour since he was leaping out of the sea as nature intended in front of a traumatized young mother. 'Looks like it might be a nice day.' Juggers smiles benignly at the elderly simpleton. 'How many times have I told you to leave the young ladies alone, Grasby?' He fairly chuckles at his own joke.

At least I'm not an aquatic flasher.

'My,' says Juggers, patting his belly, 'I could eat an old horse.'

'You might have to,' say I. But he ignores me.

Our waitress appears with Mrs Smith-Wantley's toast, jam, and pot of tea.

'Can I help you?' she says to Juggers.

Now, I know how things are going to go here. He's going to be presented with a plate of food Oliver Twist would have turned his nose up at, and there's going to be one almighty fuss.

'A pot of tea, please. And a round of toast and jam, just like my friend here.'

Gosh, I'm almost lost for words.

'I thought you were hungry, sir?' say I.

'I am, lad. But once you've appraised yourself in the full-length mirror in that bathroom – well, let's say it's time to cut down. Aye, and then some.'

'Good for you!' opines the old dear, in between mashing the toast to death with her gums. 'Now, you look like a man with whom I can do business,' she declares after a sip of tea.

'I beg your pardon?' says Juggers, his expression turning from friendly to confused.

'I'd like five dozen pairs, please. The shop's still busy, and the New Year parties will be upon us in no time. Plus, it's always good to have some put by, don't you know.'

Now Juggers does something that surprises me. I suppose I should have thought of it, but I didn't.

'Do you mean five dozen pairs of stockings, by any chance, madam?'

'Yes, what else?' Mrs Smith-Wantley looks bewildered. But then, she has for the entirety of our acquaintance.

Before Juggers can reply, the door swings open once more, and the rat-faced Wilf appears from nowhere. He dashes across to where we're all seated.

'Now, Mrs Smith-Wantley, me and Tommaso have a little surprise for you in the kitchen. It's something special, I promise.'

'It isn't two rashers of bacon, is it?' I enquire.

'I haven't quite finished my toast, dear.'

But before you can say jack-got-the-girl, Wilf hauls the poor old duffer out of her seat and fairly frogmarches her out of the dining room.

'Now you've seen all you need to see. Eh, Grasby?' Juggers's piggy eyes are screwed up in distaste.

I must admit to being puzzled.

'She thought I was American,' say I to Juggers. And I swear, the pinkness absolutely leaves his cheeks.

'My friend were right,' he mutters.

'Friend, sir?' I enquire.

'Yes, I do have some, you know.'

'No, I mean what friend, sir?'

'Oh, never mind.' He rubs his hands together, no doubt still stunned following immersion in the North Sea. 'Don't listen to me. I'm still getting back to my normal temperature. Pity it's so early or I'd have a large Scotch.'

Now, this is more like it. I must assure you, I'm not a regular morning drinker. Only on high days and holidays. But I do find it helps the day positively whizz by. This is more of what I expected from Juggers. Spending Christmas in a happy fug, while solving the murder of old Sam Salt, sounded ideal.

I light up a cigarette and ponder whether that will be the case. On reflection, I fear not.

Soon, Juggers's breakfast arrives, and he sets to it in the manner of a hyena going at its prey.

The waitress dashes back through, and heads for our table.

'Sir, it's the phone for you,' she says to Juggers.

'Who is it?' he replies.

'I'm Caroline from Willowtough Farm, sir.'

'No, not you! Who's on the *phone*?'

Poor Caroline merely shrugs her shoulders. No doubt wishing she was still knee-deep in cow dung or whatever else it is farmers get up to.

'Don't worry, his bark is worse than his bite,' I tell her as

Juggers rushes off for the phone. It's a lie, of course. His bark is nothing compared to his bite. I've seen him in action.

Just as I'm lighting another smoke, he returns, his face a picture of misery.

'What's going on, sir?' say I.

'You don't want to know, Grasby. I hope you've got that little friend with you.'

For a moment, I'm nonplussed, suspecting that his 'swim' this morning may have robbed him of all reason. Then I remember the pistol in its holster. It's amazing how quickly one can get used to having a weapon, but, very sadly, it's second nature for yours truly. Another thing for which I blame the war.

Juggers dashes down his tea with a gulp.

'Come on, lad. Get a wiggle on and put out that bloody fag! We've business to be about.'

'Sir?'

'It was the station at Filey. A call's come in to them – the local publican here has been found dead!'

# 13

I'd misjudged the topography of Uthley Bay, which I believe is understandable given we arrived here in a blizzard and have since only been outside in the dark. Just behind the buildings on the seafront, there's another road. It consists of some shops, houses and a pub. It straggles more than its neighbour; fewer buildings, bigger spaces between them. Yes, and they look much older, too. I quickly form the theory that this was once the seafront, until someone decided it wasn't quite up to the job and built another.

The pub is called the Skipper and is an odd-looking place. Firstly, it appears as though it's been here since Old Henry. A bit like the Tower of Pisa, it leans into its neighbour to the left. Some heavy wooden joists are clamped to one side of the building to shore up its two storeys. But otherwise, it looks charming. Freshly whitewashed, all mullion-windowed and dainty, if you know what I mean. It's the sort of place that if Falstaff came bundling out of the low front door, one wouldn't be surprised. I can already picture myself seeking shelter here during a storm, with a nice drop of rum or something similar.

It's odd how people's tastes change depending on their location, don't you think? Every time I'm back in Scotland visiting my mother's family, I'm fairly gasping for a dram. Forget the Pimm's before *tea*. It's rum from now on!

But back to business.

Juggers has been uncharacteristically quiet on the short walk here. And I must admit, his haunted look isn't cheering me on.

'Knock that door, will you?' he commands.

It's one of these stout oaken jobs, complete with iron bracing and studs. Thicker than your average wall nowadays. I can promise you that doors made in the 1950s won't be standing sixty years from now, never mind the time this thing's been in situ. With my gloved fist, I knock briskly. Nothing worse than having to chap a door – as my mother would have said – on a cold day. It's like punching granite. Anyhow, there's no movement from inside, so I make to knock again.

'Give way!' Juggers demands, pushing past me. 'It's a wonder anyone ever answers a door to you. It's like you're caressing it with a powder puff. You need to put some effort into it!'

From his overcoat pocket, he produces what I can only describe as a small cosh. It's shell-shaped, tight black leather covering a hefty core, I'm sure. It pivots on a large brass ring at the bottom. With it, he goes at the door like a set of bongos. The racket is fit to wake the dead – an unfortunate analogy under the circumstances.

'Police, open up!' Juggers calls in his most commanding tone.

For a while, there's no response. In a few moments, though, I can hear faint footsteps. The iron letterbox opens, and a frail-sounding woman's voice calls through it.

'Hello, who is it?' she says, voice trembling every bit as much as Juggers's when he emerged from the sea earlier.

'It's the police, madam. We'd like to come in,' says he, with a little more understanding.

'Are you really the police?' the voice comes again.

'We most certainly are. Superintendent Juggers and Inspector Grasby. We're from York Central, madam.'

'My, that were quick,' says the voice behind the door. 'I only called Filey half an hour ago.'

'Could we please come in, madam?' Juggers's voice is strained now. And despite the sensitivity of the situation, I can tell that if this continues, he's likely to rush the door like a bull at a gate.

'Give me a few moments, please. I'll have to find the key. I didn't expect you so quickly.' I hear the footsteps retreating.

'Do you know,' says Juggers with a misanthropic look on his face, 'I'm sure half the folk round here aren't bowling a full over.'

'I like your little – truncheon,' say I, using the word for want of a better description.

He handles the cosh with great reverence, almost like a noble artefact.

'An old copper in Leeds gave me this when I was a young bobby,' says he with a smile. 'He was given it back when they were fighting street gangs and the like when Queen Vicky were on the throne. Told me to always keep it with me, he did. And I've been glad of it too many times to mention.'

'Not only for knocking doors, I presume?'

'Indeed not! I've walloped a good few wrong 'uns on the head with this over the years. Never leave the house without it. And when I'm in bed, it sits by my pipe on the nightstand.'

Gosh, must be a delight for Mrs J. I picture her as

Juggers unloads his arsenal of weapons onto the bedside table before lights out. Isn't very romantic, is it?

I hear the sound of a heavy key being turned in the big mortice lock on the door. It swings open and a thin, dark-haired woman of middle age is framed in the doorway.

'I'm so sorry to keep you waiting. It's not been a very good day.'

This must surely be an understatement, thinks I.

Juggers grabs her hand between his great meaty paws. 'I'm so sorry. You must be devastated to find your husband this way.' His face is a picture of empathy. And if I didn't know better, I'd swear there's the glint of a tear in his eye.

'No, I'm not!' says she indignantly.

*Uh-oh*, thinks I. *Instant suspect here.* Wife who doesn't give a fig for her dead husband. She's put her foot right in it.

'I'm sorry,' says Juggers, no doubt thinking the same. 'Were you not getting on?'

'We got on fine. I've been with him for nearly thirty years.' She looks most puzzled.

As does Juggers. 'Right, well, we better come in and take a look at your late husband.'

'I wish you'd stop saying that! He's not – he *wasn't* – my husband. I'm Mrs Jinks. My husband is a fisherman. I'm the cleaner!'

'Oh, right. I see,' says Juggers, with a cough of embarrassment.

'I came in the back way, not an hour ago. The back door was lying open. Most unusual. I always come in that way, you see. I have a key.' She shakes her head sadly. I can see her hands tremble as she wrings them before her apron. 'You better follow me.'

We walk into a dark space. It's hard to see anything, as the curtains are still closed over the mullioned windows.

'Wait now, and I'll get the lights,' says Mrs Jinks.

Soon the place is enveloped in a warm glow. And it's exactly as I expected. A few tables and chairs, scattered hither and thon, storm lanterns and a buoy on the wall, stout beams on the ceiling, and a bar, complete with pewter pint pots hanging from a little false canopy above. Apart from the fireplace being dark as the grave, this looks like the perfect place to spend a few hours on a cold winter's night, with some convivial company, of course.

'Where is the proprietor?' says Juggers, all business.

'This way,' says Mrs Jinks, before bursting into tears.

'There, there. You've had a terrible shock. Once we have a good look at the deceased, Grasby here will make you a nice cup of sweet tea.'

*Yes, roll up! Tea and scones at Grasby's.* I mean to say, I am an inspector, not the tea lady. But it's nice to be nice, I suppose.

We're led through to the back of the pub, via a small room filled with bits and pieces: old ledgers, beer barrels and empty bottles neatly stacked in wooden crates. The smell alone is making me thirsty. That's how inured to death I've become. We're about to see a murdered man, and I'm thinking a nice pint of mild would go down a treat.

Once through this little cellar room, it's into a short hall-way. A *lobby*, my mother would have called it. And there he is, the landlord, lying on his back. He's a spare man, but I can't see his face properly because his head is covered by a stocking. He looks like a dead bank robber. His nose is pugilistic, pulled into a snout by the hosiery. His eyes are tight shut. His big hands are almost black, so he's been dead for a while.

With no little effort, Juggers bends over the body. 'I'm going to get this stocking off, Mrs Jinks. You should turn away, I recommend.' She does as she's bid. Slowly, Juggers pulls the hosiery from the head of the deceased, and damn me, I get the shock of my life. So much so, I take a step back. For, despite the blackened features of death, I can see our dead man is Ogden Barclay!

# 14

Even Juggers is silent for a few moments, as he takes in what's before us. Mrs Jinks cranes her neck round and begins to sob at the sight of her murdered boss.

'Look, Grasby,' Juggers says to me in an undertone. 'He's been strangled with a stocking, lad. Just like the other old bloke.'

Sure enough, I can see that the garment has cut into Mr Barclay's neck in exactly the same way it did his murdered friend Mr Wardle. I'm rather on the back foot here. It's odd that he never mentioned he owned the local pub when we talked to him yesterday. On the other hand, maybe that's why he was so dismissive about the hotel. They were his competition, in a way.

'Poor Mr Barclay,' says Juggers. 'He were a solid old bloke. May I ask, where's his wife, Mrs Jinks?'

'Sorry?' she says, still sobbing. 'What do you mean?'

'We spoke to him yesterday, and he mentioned his wife,' say I. 'We'll have to wait for the doctor, then the mortuary van. But it's only right we inform Mrs Barclay first, if only to come down and identify him officially.'

'I think he's past needing a doctor, don't you?' she cries, fit to burst.

'We need a doctor to declare life extinct, Mrs Jinks. I

know it sounds odd. But that's just part of our procedures.' Juggers shrugs apologetically.

'I don't know why you keep going on about a wife. Mr Barclay weren't the marrying kind.'

'What do you mean?' says Juggers.

'Oh, I don't like to say.'

'It would be helpful to know,' say I.

'He were . . .'

'What?' says Juggers.

'He were – oh, you know.'

'No, I don't,' replies Juggers.

'It's others that say it, not me, thou knows.' Mrs Jinks looks at a loss.

'It's fine to tell us, madam. It'll go no further.' I intervene quickly as I can see Juggers getting impatient beside the murder victim.

'They say he were . . .'

'Go on,' say I. 'Nothing we've not come across before. We're men of the world – and all its little *ways*.' I feel as though I should give her a nudge and a wink at this point, but I know it won't help.

'All right, then. But I'm just repeating what I heard, 'cos he never told me himself.'

At last!

'They say he were jilted a long time ago. The lass married someone else. Oh, I don't know if it's true. But he never looked at another woman. Not in all the years I've known him. And I started cleaning here long since.'

'Why on earth did he tell us about his wife?' say I, puzzled.

'Were you talking to him in here?'

'No,' says Juggers. 'He were down on the pier mending his nets yesterday. Hale and hearty he was too, poor man.

We saw him last night, as well.' I note Juggers decides to say no more on that subject.

Mrs Jinks shakes her head. 'How silly of me, I am sorry. Just with the shock, I should have told you.'

'Told us what?' I ask.

'You'll have met Ogden, Mr Barclay's twin brother. This is Perkin – Perkin Barclay.'

Gosh, the resemblance is astonishing – the dog-rough features exactly the same. But I'm glad we've established his true identity.

'He's bloody identical,' says Juggers.

'Everyone in the village says that. But they're never seen together – not on the best of terms, you see – so it's hard to make a comparison,' says Mrs Jinks, just about to weep again. 'But he's had those clothes for years. Wasn't one for spending when it weren't necessary, wasn't Perkin.'

Going through my habitual mental processes, my eye drifts to the late Perkin Barclay's boots. They're black leather, covered with mud. Drying in the pub has left white tidemarks, as though they've been very wet recently. Likely the snow.

'Do you think Mr Barclay came here late last night? Maybe forgot something after he shut up shop, and had to come back?' say I.

'He lives upstairs, sir,' says Mrs Jinks. 'Though I must say, he does like a turn about the village after closing time. He always said it blew away the cobwebs of the pub. You know, smoke, stuffiness and the like. Walked in all weathers, he did.'

Juggers gives me a meaningful look. 'I'll need to use the telephone, if I may, Mrs Jinks.'

'It's through in the bar. Come with me, please.' She steps over the remains of her dead boss gingerly and heads back up the hallway, while I give Juggers my arm to help him off the floor.

He hangs back and whispers in my ear. 'What odds would you give me on mistaken identity, eh?'

And do you know, I think he might be right. We've stumbled into something criminal in Uthley Bay, that's clear. And the bounders are ruthless into the bargain.

While Juggers is gone, I kneel over the remains of Perkin Barclay, mulling over the phenomenon of twins. A long time ago, I stepped out with a young lady called Eva Bellings. I was newly in uniform – just before the war – and fancied that, with a job already sorted out, I should find a wife quick smart. Eva was such a lovely girl, a librarian, a couple of years older than me. She looked Italian, almost, with lustrous dark hair and huge brown eyes. I was quite smitten.

Anyhow, one night we attended the cinema. I can't remember the film. But I'm sure Humphrey Bogart was in it. It was a regular little thing we did once a week. The pictures were so cheap in those days. It had opened up a new world to us all. During the intermission, I gallantly offered to go and grab some sweetmeats from the stall in the foyer. I asked if she would like some chocolate, and perhaps one of these new sodas from America. They were popular at the time, and everyone was knocking them back. I've never seen the attraction. Give me a decent pint of mild or bitter any day. But I knew Eva enjoyed them and loved milk chocolate.

'Oh, no!' said she to my offer. 'I can't abide those fizzy drinks, and I'd prefer a nice bar of Bournville and a cherry cordial, if they have it, please,' says she.

It was then I began to smell a rat. I too like Bournville – any dark chocolate, come to that. But I remembered offering Eva a square once, and she'd positively screwed up her face in disgust. And as far as the fizzy drinks were concerned, she absolutely gulped them down like a chap who's been hanging about the Sahara for too long. Something was wrong. Was this some kind of test? I had no idea.

One thing I did worry about was a *shock*, as my dear mother called it. Most people would term it a nasty turn or a stroke. But 'shock' appeared to be a Scottish term. It appeared that my mother regularly scanned the congregations during my father's church services just to see if anyone was behaving out of character – sure sign of a shock, if ever there was one. Apparently, she had an Uncle Tommy, who was quite an irascible chap. Sadly, I don't remember him, as he died when I was a nipper. Strangely, after his shock, he became a different man, with a smile and a good word for everyone. His personality changed absolutely.

This in mind, I returned to my cinema seat and the lovely Eva, determined to ascertain if she'd suffered any kind of brain malady, which had altered her taste.

A few gently probing questions later, she did something I didn't expect; Eva burst into tears.

Now, as you know, I'm a sensitive chap. So, this sudden emotion left me at silly point without a stout cap and a pair of short pads. Such was her distress, she fairly sprinted from the picture house, blubbing all the way.

Now convinced she was a victim of shock, I raced after her, only to find her sitting on a bench in Dean's Park, near the Minster. It was a glorious summer evening, and I was devastated that I'd upset her – worse still, maybe brought on another shock.

After a few moments, she regained her poise. When I enquired about her health and told her I suspected she'd had some seizure of the noggin, she confessed. For this wasn't my lovely Eva. No, it was her twin sister Enid. Apparently, the pair, being almost identical, loved to play jolly japes on their respective boyfriends by swapping places now and then. Particularly – and this is the real blow – if they were finding them a bore. I recall walking away with a heavy heart and a melting bar of Bournville in my pocket. Soon after, Eva and her family moved away – I never saw her again.

Although a pal of mine who knew them both said the twins were quite easy to tell apart when they were together, one can be forgiven for not spotting a subtle change in appearance when ignorant of the twin's existence.

Hardly surprising, then, that Juggers and I had both assumed the body in the pub was Ogden.

In the fullness of time, Juggers appears back from the phone.

'I called Filey. They're going to send over three constables. There's a doc to find, too. The local GP is away, so it's nearest one around, apparently.'

'Gosh, that's bad luck if you're in the middle of a shock,' say I.

'A what?' Juggers looks indignant.

'Oh, nothing, sir. Passing thoughts. Just ignore me.'

'No need to worry on that score, lad. I do, as a matter of course. Instead of daydreaming, you can make yourself useful.'

'In what way, sir?' say I.

'We should tell Ogden Barclay about his brother. Apparently, he lives along the road. Turn left out of here, and it's the last house. You can't miss it. He has his gate painted bright red, Mrs Jinks says. I'll stay here with her.'

'Just don't get up to any *high jinks*, sir.' I wink at him companionably.

'I don't know how many times I've told you, Grasby, but there is a time and place for levity. And standing over the body of a murdered man isn't it. Off you go!'

Duly chastised, I make my way back through the pub. Mrs Jinks smiles at me as I pass.

'You'll find Ogden no bother,' says she. 'Mind you, I don't know how keen he'll be to come here.'

'Not a drinker, Mr Barclay?'

'Ogden? Why, he'd drink furniture polish strained through a soiled bairn's nappy, he would. No, it's as I said – Perkin and his brother aren't on good terms, haven't spoken in years. Something to do with money when their father died. Don't ask me the details, for I've no idea. And anyhow, it were none of my business.'

She lets me out the big oak door and I turn left and head up the snowy street. The sun's out now, and it's a glorious day, but it's bitterly cold. No sign of a thaw, that's for certain.

Sure enough, at the end of the road sits one rather run-down-looking cottage. The red on the gate is the only paint about that isn't peeling or gone altogether. The small windows are curtained, and the roof is missing a few tiles and adorned with moss. Funny, I took Ogden for quite a fastidious man when I watched him mending his nets yesterday. Mind you, his boat wasn't up to much, so perhaps I shouldn't be surprised.

Remembering Juggers's admonishment earlier, I make sure to knock on the door as loudly as possible. In a few moments it creaks open, and Ogden Barclay peers through a crack. Seeing me, he opens the door an inch further but it's no warm welcome.

'How do?' He lowers his voice. 'Is it something to do with them stockings?'

'As a matter of fact, no, it isn't. Could I trouble you to let me in, Mr Barclay? I'm afraid I have some bad news.' I whip off my trilby as a mark of respect.

Barclay clears his throat and looks to the side furtively.

'Sorry, Inspector. My wife's not been well. Not well at all. Give me a moment, and I'll join you outside.'

This is surprising in a way. But I imagine the cottage as a cluttered place; unwashed dishes and dust piled high on old, done-for furniture. Much like my first flat, if this is indeed the case.

Soon, Ogden Barclay joins me on the cracked path outside his home. It's been cleared of snow, which is something. Had it not been for Mrs Jinks telling me about his drinking, I may not have noticed, but there's the whiff of stale alcohol on Barclay's breath.

'What kind of bad news, Inspector?' says he, his pitted face so like his dead brother's.

'I'm afraid your brother Perkin is dead, Mr Barclay. In fact, we suspect foul play.' Getting straight to the point is the only way, you know. No room for prevarication when it comes to the dreaded death message.

Ogden Barclay doesn't say anything for a while. He squints into the distance, shading his eyes against the sun with one gnarled paw, as though he's spied the Spanish Armada out at sea.

'I'm so sorry,' say I, hoping for a reaction.

'Aye, as like as not,' says he, still staring into space. 'You best know something, Inspector. Me and our Perkin haven't spoken in many a year.' He swallows hard. 'Don't get me wrong, I've never wished him any harm – certainly not this. But he had his life and I had mine. It's as simple as that. I'm sorry he's gone. Our mam would be heartbroken if she were still around.'

'Well, families are funny things,' say I, thinking of my father. 'We thought you should know.'

'Aye, right kind of you, I'm sure.' Barclay rummages in his pocket. 'It may explain this.' He hands me a piece of screwed-up paper. 'Came through the door some time during the night, in an envelope addressed to my wife, it were. That's why she's not herself this morning.'

I unravel the paper and examine it in the bright sunlight. It's one of those anonymous jobs. The letters have been cut from a newspaper and pasted into place to form the message.

**MRS BARCLAY. YOUR HUSBAND IS DEAD. HE WONT BE FISHING NO MORE. AND HE WONT BE A TRAYTOR NO MORE, NEITHER.**
**BE WARNED! THE SAME COULD HAPPEN TO YOU IF YOU OPEN YOUR BLUDDY MOUTH TO THE POLICE.**

Of course, the first thing I notice is the misspellings of 'traitor' and 'bloody', as well as the poor punctuation; in fact, the short note is distinctively local in tone and feel. Whoever wrote this is no great literary shakes, by the look of things. Still, it's a menacing missive, if ever I saw one.

'You've no idea who put this through your door? You didn't hear or see anyone, Mr Barclay?'

'No. Whoever done this were quiet as a mouse. I'm a light sleeper. I wake at a drop of rain on the window, but this didn't rouse me.'

Suddenly, his mouth gapes open. Shock is a funny thing. It rarely moves at the same pace as language. I think the truth has just dawned on him.

'They were after me, weren't they? I should be the one lying dead, not our Perkin.'

'It rather looks that way, Mr Barclay. I think this letter may go some way to proving it. I'd like the envelope if you still have it, please.'

I feel sorry for him. Death befuddles the mind, you know. People do all sorts of strange things when they hear about the demise of a friend or family member. I remember how dislocated I was when my father told me my mother had passed away. My instant reaction was to lay into him verbally as regards his many shortcomings as a husband and father. It was wrong, and I've been ashamed about it ever since. I see that same confusion on Ogden Barclay's face.

Then he does something I don't expect. He gives me a great bear hug and starts sobbing on my shoulder like a distressed infant.

I have to admit, this isn't my strongest suit. Emotion, I mean. I have always been advised that tears are best shed in private, and public moping is a sign of extreme weakness. I'm sure this English trait isn't good for one. I've had my fair share of contact with the Continentals, you know. Both during the war and since. They're always bursting into tears in France, Italy and Spain. The Welsh don't need any encouragement either. If something good happens, the floodgates swing open – the same if it's something of a darker nature. There's no stopping the blighters. Though the Germans are a bit more like us: stoic and understated in grief; a ripple of the jaw and a paling of complexion is about as far as it goes. The Scots are a different matter, however. Mention death to them and the whisky bottle is whipped out, and before you know it there are tales and sad songs. Everyone seems to thoroughly enjoy a funeral. And perhaps that's the right way to be.

Clearly, old Ogden has a bit of the Continental about

him, as he's weeping like a sore eye. Goodness, I hope he doesn't stain my cashmere overcoat.

'Right,' say I, desperate to bring this effusive outpouring to a speedy conclusion. 'I better get going and find out who did this awful thing. Grab me that envelope, please, and I'll be off. You do have my sympathies.'

'Aye.' He sniffs prodigiously and wipes his nose along the arm of his fisherman's cable-knit jumper. He disappears into his hovel for a few moments, returning with the envelope. It bears the same newspaper print on the front:

**MRS BARCLAY.**

I wrap it in a hankie. Well, they can do all sorts of things these days with fingerprints and the like. Who knows? Our killer may well have revealed himself on this envelope or the missive within.

Yet somehow, I doubt it.

I turn to go, expressing my condolences yet again to Ogden Barclay.

'Hold your ho'ses,' says he. 'They'll soon realize they missed me and got my poor brother. Then what, eh? It'll only be a matter of time until they try again.'

'Good point,' I reply.

'I want police protection, Inspector. I did my civic duty telling you about them stockings, and look where it's got me! Not to mention where it put our Perkin. You and Mr Jacobs owe it to me, thou knows!'

I'm confused. 'Jacobs?'

'Aye, Jacobs, your superior.'

'Juggers, you mean,' I correct him.

'Aye, aye. It's all the shock, lad. The fat bloke with the bald head.'

*Well,* think I. *Better not say that to his face or you won't have to worry about marauding murderers.* But something about the way he trots out this description reminds me of someone repeating something they've been told, rather than experienced. I put it down to the unpleasant news. It can affect us all in different ways.

'We're getting some reinforcements from Filey. I'm afraid it's only me and my superior at the moment. And we've a murder to investigate. You can come along, if you want?' I shrug my shoulders.

'Aye, good thinking. I'm coming with you, in that case.'

'I'm heading back to the Skipper, Mr Barclay. It's not a pretty sight.'

'Aye, and it won't be a pretty sight when they knock me on the head, neither.'

Gosh, here's a thing.

'What about Mrs Barclay? I mean, she's already been threatened,' say I.

Ogden Barclay rubs his chin for a moment, deep in thought. Without another word, he heads for the front door of the cottage.

He opens the door a crack and leans in.

'Elizabeth! I'm helping the bobbies with their investigations. Shut the door and bolt it until I come back. Aye, and lock the windows too. Don't answer the door if anyone knocks. And grab the carving knife and that old belaying pin from the windowsill. I'll be back with help as soon as I can.'

I'm quite concerned by this. After all, your average murderer won't think twice about kicking in a door to get to a potential victim. And it's fair to say Barclay's front door doesn't look the most robust I've ever seen. This, and the fact that Mrs Barclay must now be utterly scared witless. I picture her in the curtained darkness, belaying pin in one hand, carving knife in the other.

'I wonder if your wife should like to join us too?' say I.

'Don't fret, lad. She'll be fine. She's got a kick like a mule. Goodness knows what she'll manage now she's armed.'

I make a mental note to send someone to the house as soon as the Filey boys arrive, and to forewarn them, too. Despite Mrs Barclay sounding like Attila the Hun's little sister, she should still be protected by a bobby.

'Aren't you going to tell her about your brother?' I ask in a whisper,

'Best not.' Barclay puts a finger to his mouth in a hushing gesture. 'She's of a nervous disposition. I'll break it to her gently later.'

It's hardly the ideal solution. But what can I do?

Ogden Barclay disappears inside again and grabs his shabby pea coat.

As we head back down the street towards the Skipper, I can't help but feel a certain unease. It's an odd sensation, and I've had it before. You know by now my belief in instinct, and I'm now sure we're being watched. I turn sharply a couple of times on our passage down the street, but there's nobody to be seen.

# 15

When we arrive back at the Skipper, I knock the door vigorously, knowing that Juggers is bound to critique my percussive performance. Though it's Mrs Jinks who lets us in. She stares at Ogden Barclay as though she's witnessed the resurrection, which I suppose she has, in a way. He and his late brother are so alike as to be unsettling. They even appear to dress alike.

'Mrs Jinks, how do?' says Barclay sheepishly.

'A bit shocked, if I'm honest. Who wouldn't be? Mind, I never thought I'd see you cross this threshold, I must say.'

'One of those things. You get in the habit of something. Once I'd passed my brother in the street a couple of times – well, it became easier. Same goes for him, I reckon. Pity neither of us had the sense to call a halt to it all. But it's too late now.'

'Aye,' says she with a tear in her eye. 'A lesson in this for us all. I were fond of him, as you know.'

Gosh, lucky she doesn't know it's all a case of mistaken identity, and the man who should be lying dead in the lobby is Ogden here. I try to keep my expression as neutral as possible.

Barclay looks at me, then speaks hesitantly. 'I'd like to have one last look at him, if that's in order, Inspector?'

'Yes, I should say so. I'll go and have a quick word with my superintendent first. Keep him up to date, eh?' I tap my pocket, illustrating to Barclay that I'm going to show Juggers the anonymous missive.

'Yes. Thank you.' His head is bowed. 'I'm obliged to you.'

I leave Ogden and Mrs Jinks in an awkward silence. It must be bad enough losing one's sibling without knowing you're the one who should be heading for the mortuary.

You know, I never wanted a little brother or sister. My mother insisted I clapped and jumped up and down when she asked me the question, as a child. It became clear in later years that she was obviously trying to persuade my father to have more children, and I'd been schooled what to do when asked. But let's be honest, it's a miracle I'm here at all, such is my father's complete indifference to children. Clearly, his answer was in the negative, as I firmly remained an only child. And I can't say that troubles me. Any of my friends with siblings appear to despise them. I don't have time in my life for that. It must be so wearing and unproductive. Why can't people just get on with their own lives, and leave others to it, flesh and blood or not?!

When I reach the hallway, the victim is still where I left him, which is good, under the circumstances. Meanwhile, Juggers is smoking his pipe like there's a tobacco display on. The place is thick with smoke.

'Is Mr Barclay here, Grasby? I heard voices.'

I want to point down at the corpse, but that would be facetious, and Juggers would likely pulverize me. So, I merely nod instead.

'What's he saying, lad?'

'Ogden? He's not saying much. But this says plenty.' I fish into my pocket and hand Juggers the letter.

'So, as we expected. This poor bugger copped it for his brother. Who likely was going to get walloped because he helped us.' He takes a deep puff. 'It just shows you how one thing affects the other.'

'He'd like to see the remains, sir.'

'Aye, of course. Blood's thicker than water, lad.' Another puff. 'I have a brother, you know.'

'You do?' say I.

'Aye, I do. Haven't spoken to him in three or four years. After this little lot, I'm tempted to try and mend bridges.'

'I would, sir. You don't want to be too late – like this pair. What does your brother do, if you don't mind me asking, sir?'

Juggers coughs. 'He has a good job. Not to everyone's taste. But it has to be done.'

I imagine everything from tax collector to royal executioner.

'He's in charge of every drop of sewage in Leeds, you know. And let me tell you, lad, that's no picnic.'

'I can imagine,' says I, a mental picture developing in my head as I do. 'Busy, I'd say. How on earth does he manage?'

Juggers narrows his beady eyes. 'When I say *in charge of every drop*, I don't mean he's waiting by the toilet for everyone to do their business!'

'No, of course not, sir. He's overseeing the – the sewage.'

'Yes, Inspector of Human Waste is his official title.'

'Goodness me, your mother must be so proud.' I could kick myself for saying this but it's out too soon. With Juggers hitting sixty, the likelihood his mother is still knocking about is pretty slim. And so it proves.

'Sadly, no longer with us, lad. My, but she were a fine woman. Died of overwork when we were both in our twenties. Even though we were in lowly jobs, she saw what we'd become.'

'Really?'

'Alfred – my brother – was shovelling shit instead of inspecting it back then. And I was in charge of packing giblets for the Co-op Fleshings in Bradford.'

My goodness. Poor old Mrs Juggers must have spent a fair amount of her time at the wash board before her sons found wives. No wonder she was worked to death. The whole thing sounds ghastly. One can only shudder at the thought of the water she washed their work garments in. And imagine the conversation during *tea* when the question, 'What did you do today, boys?' came up. Dear me.

'She told us to do our best, and the best would happen to us. Aye, and she were right, too.'

'Gosh, yes,' say I. But it's hard to think how they could have been doing any worse. Therefore, the prophecy of better times ahead was surely a reasonably certain one. 'What did your father think of it all?'

Juggers's face turns red. 'He ran off to London with my Aunt Hilda, the bugger.' My superintendent is clearly still angry about this. 'Told our ma he were helping her with a troublesome ballcock on her cistern. He were round there night after night. Called it a *tricky job*. I'll say. He were the tricky blighter! He'd have been dealing with troublesome ballcocks if I'd got a hold of him, and no mistake.'

Now, this is the problem with being a policeman. You can't stop asking questions. And sometimes these enquiries take one to places it would have been better never to venture. I'll struggle to see my superior now without picturing the scene round that dinner table, him stinking of chicken giblets, his brother reeking like a blocked toilet.

Then there's the manhandling of his father's genitals. I do hope Aunt Hilda was worth it.

'Enough of reminiscing, Grasby! I have a job for you. Get down to the hotel and see if they can find space for three constables from Filey. They're sending the mortuary van from Scarborough. Until then, I'll keep a watching brief here. Make some notes for my report.'

'I'll try to find accommodation, sir. But you'll remember that the festive guests are arriving today. Might be no room at the inn.'

'The place will soon empty when they find out they've a more than even chance of getting strangled with a pair of stockings. At any rate, these coppers aren't fussy. They'll bunk up together and won't be a bit of bother. Not many hotels can turn away trade at this time of year. I trust your innate charm, lad.'

Just at this, I hear something at the back of the pub.

Juggers and I rush out. And there is Ogden Barclay poking about in the messy yard.

'Get out!' shouts Juggers. 'You might be disturbing evidence, Mr Barclay.'

Barclay jumps like a scalded cat.

'Sorry, I didn't think of that, Mr Juggers,' says Barclay, scuttling off.

I shake my head. 'Honestly, people never think, do they?'

'No worse than half of your colleagues back at York Central. Been trying to teach them best practice for years and it still hasn't rubbed off.'

And he's right, you know. Some of the chaps I work with are damned careless. But I'm not immune to this malady. I've made the odd gaffe in my time, as you're aware. The trick is trying not to repeat the exercise.

So, wrapping my scarf tightly round my neck, and

pushing my trilby down on my head against the strong breeze now coming off the North Sea, I make my way back down the mean, snowy streets of Uthley Bay, heading to the hotel. It's bitterly cold. A cup of nice, hot tea will go down a treat. I resolve to find one.

# 16

When I arrive at the Trout, it's all go. There's an omnibus sitting by the pavement, disgorging its band of happy holidaymakers. The passengers are mostly of the elderly variety, some looking quite bewildered. The bus itself is stained down the sides by the grey residue of rock salt they've had to put down to help keep the roads passable.

Welcome to Uthley Bay! Spend your Christmas freezing to death. If you're lucky, you might spy a York superintendent leaping from the sea naked as the day he was born, or perhaps be strangled with a pair of stockings. Have a lovely time.

I smile and excuse myself as I push through the throng of people waiting for their luggage to be offloaded from the bus. One old dear taps me on the shoulder and asks when they start serving lunch, and can she place her order with me now? She looks rather put-out when I tell her I'm a police officer, not a member of staff. I mean, how on earth could she mistake me for a waiter? I'm wearing a cashmere overcoat!

The little reception room is already crowded when I glance in. So, I wait in the adjoining lobby, just glad to be out of the biting cold.

It's then I spot something that makes me catch my breath. There, sitting against the wall, is my mother's suitcase. At first I close my eyes, putting this apparition down to the early start and an over-eventful morning. But it's still there when I open them again. Surely there can't be two identical suitcases knocking about? I'd recognize this one anywhere.

Then I hear a very familiar voice.

'Thank goodness there wasn't a queue for the facilities, dear. I was as overcome as you.' Stepping into the lobby from another door are my father and the distinctive figure of Hetty Gaunt. I met her last year on another of my policing adventures. She looks almost exactly as I remember, apart from a thick, black fur coat, and blood-red, lace-up boots – you know, the kind your granny would have worn. Not only does she dress oddly, Mrs Gaunt, a widow, has a penchant for the occult – she sees things in the future, would you believe. It turned out that she and my father had a rather lurid shared past, and it seems they have chosen to rekindle the flames of their old romance. Dash it all!

My father is standing beside her, drab and painfully thin as always. Both he and Hetty look at me impassively.

'I knew I'd find you idle, hanging about the hotel. Since you joined the police, I must admit I've reconsidered my choice of career. I swear, I've never seen you do any work in all these years. It's the life of Riley, and no mistake.'

Now I know why my father hesitated at the sink when I told him I was coming here. He's clearly had this little assignation planned for some time.

Hetty takes me in with narrow eyes. 'I can smell death off you, young man,' she says with a glare. Quite alarming, really, given where I've just been.

'Well, you are standing beside my father,' say I.

'Huh! When I heard you were coming here, I can't say I was happy about it. However, we'd paid a sizeable deposit, so I was determined not to throw it away,' opines my dear father. 'You're all the man you're going to be now, Frank. You'll have to get used to the fact that men and women must have companionship. Well, most of them, apart from you.'

'Aye, and we have our needs, too,' says Hetty. 'You'll be mindful of that, young man.'

I recall being introduced to Mrs Gaunt as my landlady last Christmas. At the time, she warned me against any shenanigans under her roof.

'Ah yes,' say I. 'I seem to recall you prefer lovemaking to be conducted outdoors, *as nature intended*. I wish you both luck here.' I turn to my father. 'I'd keep my long johns on if I were you, Pa.'

He shoots me a dark look. 'Just the kind of base comment I'd expect from you, Francis.'

The little corridor is getting crowded now, as people pour in and very few come out of the reception room. In fact, despite the chill outside, it's becoming rather claustrophobic. I look behind me to a sea of grey heads jostling for position, all waiting patiently to sign the hotel register. Gosh, the cumulative age in this small space must be approaching two thousand.

It's too much for my father, anyway. I look on as he blows out his cheeks and removes the woollen scarf from about his neck. And to my surprise, the dog collar I've rarely seen him abandon in almost forty years is missing. Instead, my father is sporting a neat shirt and tie, which gives him the air of a retired civil servant, which I suppose is what he is, in a funny kind of way.

120

'Going incognito, Father?' say I, fingering my tie by way of explanation.

'May I remind you, I'm retired. And furthermore, the festive season is the very worst time for the clergy. Why, you can't turn a corner without someone wanting you to talk to them about Christmas this, or prayer that. This is the first time I've not been ministering to a festive flock for nigh-on sixty years. I'm due a break.' My father shakes his head and looks at his most sour.

At this point, an elderly gentleman pokes his head over my shoulder.

'Why, it'll be lovely to have the services of a man of the cloth on Christmas Day. How splendid!'

He's clearly been listening to our conversation.

My father narrows his eyes. I know what's coming, but Hetty Gaunt beats him to it.

'Only the devil loves eavesdroppers. I fear this could well be your last Christmas, sir,' she says chillingly.

I hear the gentleman behind me laugh this off. But if he knew my former landlady the way I do, he'd be rushing to the nearest solicitor to make good his affairs. She might be as mad as a horse, but Hetty Gaunt knows a thing or two, and that's a fact.

Mercifully, the door to the reception room swings open, and a couple leave, having signed the register.

'They want the next pair in,' shouts one of these new guests as they push their way back through the crowded corridor.

My father takes a long stride forward, Hetty trailing in his wake.

'Not so fast,' say I. 'Police business of a most urgent nature. I'm going in now.'

There follows a most unseemly struggle, akin to two

beanpoles in a wrestling match. My father isn't the least interested in my duty. In fact, he still sees me as an annoying little boy who prefers cricket to Bible class. He grabs my scarf to pull me back from the doorway, while at the same time trying to step round me. With my left arm, I force him backwards. This works, though it also serves to tighten the scarf at my neck, making me squawk like some of these characters from a Walt Disney cartoon – you know, the duck chap. My arms are flailing in mid-air trying to find purchase on the door jamb to pull myself forward.

'What on earth is going on here?' shouts a disembodied voice.

My father looks round, as though he's finally been contacted by the deity. But I know better. I crane my neck down, and there is Dot, looking disapprovingly at the unseemly fracas.

'Constable Grasby, you should know better!' she chides, wagging an admonishing finger.

Quietly, my father lets go of my scarf, forcing me into two involuntary steps forward. Poor Dot thinks I'm taking an aggressive run at her and puts her hand to her mouth, letting out a little yelp of surprise. She backs away, looking at me with big, wide eyes.

'I must say, Constable, I've seen another side to you altogether.'

'Nasty piece of work, he is,' says my father.

'Aye, and watch him with the hot water, an' all,' Hetty adds. 'He'll never be out of the bath if you give him half a chance. I know from bitter experience.'

It's time for me to reassert my authority. 'For a start, Dot, I'm an inspector, not a constable. Secondly, I must discuss an urgent piece of police business with you. It can't wait, I'm afraid.'

Dot looks confused. 'Do you know these people?' she says, nodding to my father and Hetty.

'Yes, this is my father, the Reverend Cyril Grasby. And his *companion*, Mrs Hetty Gaunt.'

She addresses my father quizzically. 'Are you the Grasby who booked the honeymoon suite?'

'The what?!' say I.

My father draws himself to his full height, like a guardsman on parade. 'Yes, that is correct. And if you don't mind, Mrs Gaunt and I wish to avail ourselves of the facilities we've bought and paid for.' He looks down his nose at Dot, which, given her size, can't be a novel experience.

'I'll be with you as soon as I've dealt with the police, Reverend Grasby.'

'It's *Mr* Grasby, as far as you're concerned, young lady.'

Clearly put out, Dot dashes past me and closes the door in my father's face. 'Wait your turn, I'll be with you in a moment,' she chides. She bustles back behind the reception desk and faces me, her head poking just above the counter. 'Now, what can I do for you, Inspector?'

'We have three constables arriving from Filey,' say I. 'What with the snow, and other operational considerations, we'll need accommodation, please. I know how busy you are, so they're perfectly willing to share the one room. Two singles and camp bed, for example.'

'It's out of the question. We're fully booked. First Christmas in years, as it happens. I think it has something to do with the entertainment.'

'Entertainment?'

'We have Geraldo on for Christmas Day and Boxing Day.' Dot smiles wanly.

'Gosh, I can't abide magicians,' say I.

'He's a singer, damned good one. A celebrated tenor

from New York. Italian, originally, of course. He's a friend of Tommaso's. He gave us a good rate. It's all very exciting; reminds me a bit of Mario Lanza.'

'You don't have some little nook or cranny we can put our constables? They'll be no trouble, I promise.'

'No, I'm sorry. Unless you and Mr Juggers move out, there's no room at the inn.'

*How festive*, thinks I.

'Then I shall have to find a stable. Is there anywhere else in town that takes guests? A B&B, perhaps?'

'No. Everyone goes to Filey or Scarborough. Only room for one hotel in this village. I am sorry.' She stands on tiptoe and leans over the counter. 'I've heard a terrible tale about Mr Barclay at the Skipper. Is it true?'

Of course, it's no secret – or won't be one for long in a village this size.

'Yes, I'm rather sorry to say that it is. But I must rely on you not to breathe a word of it, please, Dot. There will be a public statement soon enough, I imagine.'

'How awful.' Dot looks genuinely sad. 'Perkin were a lovely man, and so soon after poor old Wardle. I'm beginning to worry. Folk in the village will, too.'

'Not to mention your guests,' say I.

Just as Dot is coming to terms with this news, there's a loud knock at the door.

'We can't wait out here all day, you know!' shouts my father.

Dot sucks her teeth. 'Maybe it's a shame Geraldo isn't a magician, Inspector. Perhaps he could make your father disappear. No harm, mind.' She winks at me, and we share a moment of mirth before dear old Dad appears through the door.

'I must demand access to our room. Mrs Gaunt and I

aren't in the first flush of youth. And hanging about in a crowded corridor isn't my idea of a holiday. So, if you don't mind, let's get on with it.' My father folds his arms, a gesture he's performed on many occasions since I was boy. It means he's unhappy – *most* unhappy.

I decide to leave them all to it and force my way out of the reception room and then the corridor. This place is badly designed, I decide, as I push my way past the last ancient holidaymaker.

I'll have to go back and tell Juggers there is literally no room at the inn. I decide to have a poke about, just in case a solution presents itself. I'm a born optimist, it must be said. I've had to be, really. Especially when my father's about.

# 17

It's back out into the snow for poor Frank. As I leave the hotel, I hear voices. Thin, cold air like today's always seems to amplify sound. Sure enough, when I turn my gaze towards the harbour, there's a small crowd gathered, with a lot of shouting and waving of hands.

I toy with the idea of taking a wander down to see what's afoot. But with two dead men, and Juggers not far away, I'd better stick to the task in hand.

I notice a lane, just beyond the hotel. Common sense tells me this is a shortcut back to the Skipper, our murder scene. And I'm right. The lane leads to Uthley Bay's second street. As I make my way along it, I'm surprised to find my way open up, and there, in a little cul-de-sac, is a squat building, for all the world like one of those bungalows that were so popular just before the war. Hull is full of them.

But this is no domestic residence. Just above the door is a blue lamp with the word 'Police' painted across it in bold, white letters.

I know an opportunity when I see one. I seem to remember hearing that Uthley Bay lost its only bobby when the last incumbent retired about a year ago. Now, unless the county council has opted to sell off the building, it must surely still be available for its original purpose – a police station.

I step through a rusting iron gate and take a poke about. Shading my hand at the window, I see a neat little bar office, with some old posters warning about the dangers of crossing the road, and other public information guff. This nonsense began in the war, you know. And since it ended, the government have taken it upon themselves to tell us all the bloody obvious. I, for one, don't need to be told how to get off a train, where to take a swim or how to avoid imminent death under the wheels of a lorry – it's common sense. But the nation's nanny must keep us right, for our own sakes.

I read a book by a chap called Orwell a couple of years ago. He painted a shocking picture of how things might be in 1984, when the authoritarianism all politicians crave runs riot. Well, I think these posters are the thin end of the wedge. I can envisage a time when you'll be told what to eat and drink. I'm not joking. One wag at York Central – I think it was Jocky Burroughs – told us that he could see a day when smoking will be banned. Of course, he's a dour Scot; how they love misery. I mean, even Orwell didn't go that far. Can you imagine? It's damned uncivilized. And if they manage to prise tobacco from the trembling hands of the committed smoker, how safe is booze?

The horrors of wars have led some to believe that we should expunge human frailty and live forever in peace and happiness. It won't happen. The human condition may be contorted this way and that. But basically, we'll never change. And to survive it all, I, for one, need fish and chips, a packet of ciggies and a pint or two. Where's the harm?

Anyhow, dragging my thoughts away from the horrors of dictatorship, I take a wander round the back. The garden could do with a bit of attention, all weeds and unruly grass sticking up in little green spikes in the snow. A quick look through the window reveals a neat bedroom, complete with wardrobe, chest of drawers and an old iron bed.

Just the ticket! Time to re-open Uthley Bay Police Station, say I. Not only will it afford us a base of operations, it'll provide temporary accommodation for our constables. Juggers will be chuffed. And that can only be a good thing.

I step from the curtilage of the police station, and back onto the lane. It gets broader as I head for the village's second street. I suppose that only makes sense. After all, how would they get police vehicles to and from the station, otherwise?

I'm reaching the end of the lane when two bulky chaps appear round the corner. By the look of their cable-knit sweaters and seaboots they are fishermen. Either that or aquatic cricketers. I discount the latter.

They stop in their tracks when they see me, then swagger in my direction on the snowy lane, grins on their unshaven faces.

'You're one of them perverts, aren't you?' says the larger of the two. He has a tuft of dark hair poking out from under his woolly hat.

'I beg your pardon?' say I, momentarily taken aback by the cheek of this oaf.

'You and your pal exposed yourselves to his wife this morning,' says the other. He's a broad-shouldered chap with bright red hair and a missing front tooth.

'I did no such thing!' I protest. I'd like to say *we* but – though he is no pervert – Juggers did, inadvertently, reveal too much to this chap's good lady.

'She said you were fat,' says woolly hat man.

'As you can see, I'm not. Now, move aside.'

'But there were two of them, George. He must look on for some fun, eh?' Red hair spits into the snow.

Woolly hat, whom I now know to be George, edges in my direction. 'You tell your boyfriend I'm looking for him. And when I find him, he's going to be right sorry.' He holds up a fist.

'Right, that's enough,' say I. 'I'll have you know I'm a—' The wind is driven out of my lungs by a sharp blow to the solar plexus. Instantly, I double up and fall onto my knees in the snow, as one is wont to do after a punch to the gut.

The pair leave me groaning on the lane, as they make their way down towards the harbour, giggling like a couple of schoolgirls.

It's pretty low, catching a chap unawares like that. If they had any idea what I've been through over the years, during the war and in my police career, they may have thought twice. As I get up on one knee, my wind returning, I feel utterly despoiled. It's typical, isn't it? Juggers decides to go for an early morning swim, and I end up getting a punch to the guts for it.

When I arrive back at the Skipper, a dark blue police car is sitting outside. So, the chaps from Filey have arrived. The road is clear, as I know from my father's omnibus. But yet again, the sky is beginning to thicken with snow-laden clouds. We'll be cut off again before it gets dark, I'll wager.

Just before I knock the pub's door, I hear the rattle of a diesel engine. A black Bedford van pulls into the pavement at my side, with two men and a woman on the bench seat. The men are dressed in white coats, and clearly from the mortuary. The woman, who steps out of the vehicle, is dressed in a tweed two-piece, and has a pair of glasses hanging round her neck on a chain. She's carrying one of those little doctors' bags, you know the kind, long, thin, in black leather.

'Are you Juggers?' she says to me in a guttural accent

that makes my heart soar. This lady of a certain age is a Scot. And every time I hear the Scots speak, I'm instantly reminded of my dear, late mother.

'No, I'm Inspector Grasby. Superintendent Juggers is inside.' I offer a hand, which she grips most firmly.

'I'm Dr McKay,' says she.

Gosh, a lady doctor. Here's a thing. The second lady doctor I've met in the space of a year.

We stand in silence for a heartbeat or two, while I digest this.

'Well, let's get a move on, young man,' says the doc. 'I'm not about to examine the patient standing out here, am I?'

'Well, not so much a patient as a corpse,' say I.

'I'll decide that. Until I declare life extinct, whatever poor soul you have in there is a patient, do you understand?'

She's as brusque as Juggers, and roughly the same age, I reckon. A small woman, with grey hair piled on top of her head in woven braids. This reminds me of some German girls I'd seen during the war, with their blonde tresses. On Dr McKay, however, the hairstyle looks more a steel helmet. At this short acquaintance, she exudes an air of bustling command. I'll bet you any money she's ex-army.

I knock the door and a tall constable opens up.

'I'm Inspector Grasby and this is the force doctor. Let us in, there's a good chap.'

The bobby looks at me blankly, and for a moment I think he's going to close the door in my face.

'I'll need to see your credentials, sir,' says he in a mono-tone voice.

As I'm poking about in my jacket, under my thick over-coat, I hear a familiar bellow.

'Let him in! What passes for brains in Filey, I don't know.

I reckon the closer to the sea folk get, the more their minds are addled. Get a move on, lad!'

The door swings open, allowing us entry into the Skipper. I'm surprised to find Juggers sitting at the bar with Ogden Barclay, Mrs Jinks busy washing glasses. It could be a scene from any drinking establishment in the country, were it not for the fact that the publican is lying dead in the back passage.

Juggers registers my surprise at his imbibing. 'It's been a right shock for Mr Barclay here, and I couldn't let him drink alone. Misery loves company, Grasby.' He places his pint jug on the bar and removes himself somewhat inelegantly from the stool upon which he's been perched.

'Now, then, who are you?' he enquires of Dr McKay.

'Oh, I'm here to paint the ceiling. Who the bloody hell do you think I am?'

I fear Juggers may erupt into a panoply of unflattering invective. But he registers the white-coated mortuary attendants who have entered the premises at our back and comes to a reasonable conclusion.

'My goodness, a female doctor, what next? You better come with me.'

'Aye, and you better get used to it,' says McKay. 'Though I had to join the army for my qualifications, the days of medicine being a cosy club for the male of the species are over, I'm pleased to say. It's amazing what the exigencies of war will do for prejudice, Superintendent. It's the National Health Service now. And that means everyone.'

'Like as not,' says Juggers, clearing his throat.

He can dish it out, you know, but my superior is no great shakes at taking it. Juggers looks quite subdued as we head to the back of the pub once more.

Two Filey constables are deep in conversation when we

arrive in the small passageway where lies Perkin Barclay. If Doctor McKay is at all put off by the fact the man lying on the floor bears an astonishing resemblance to the chap Juggers was just sharing a pint with, she doesn't say. Instead, she does the doctorly thing and fishes about in her black leather medical bag. However, instead of producing a stethoscope or some other instrument of her trade, she reveals a long cheroot, which she proceeds to ignite in a few puffs, using a Zippo gas lighter – the kind favoured by American GIs during the war, and yours truly.

Juggers and the Filey men look on open-mouthed as she stares at the man on the floor dispassionately through a cloud of smoke.

'Aye, he's dead, right enough,' says she with another puff.

'Aren't you going to examine him?' says Juggers.

'He's not breathing and is turning black, Superintendent. If I was able to save him, I should look for a career in the Kirk rather than as a doctor, don't you think?'

Ah, the *Kirk*. My mother always used the Scottish form of Church – or do we use the English form of it? I've never been too sure. Though I do know it used to infuriate my father, which in turn pleased me no end.

'I daresay you know your business, Doctor,' says Juggers rather stiffly.

'Of course, they'll have to perform a post-mortem. But that's no business o' mine.' McKay looks over her shoulder. 'Right, lads, bring in the stretcher and get this poor soul back to Scarborough.'

So, a few minutes later, Perkin Barclay leaves the Skipper for the very last time, carried by two men in white coats, covered in a green mortuary blanket. There's a dreadful inevitability about life, you know. Though his brother manages to restrain himself from blubbing again,

Mrs Jinks is as pale as a ghost, tears slipping silently down her cheeks.

'What will I do now?' she says, as the deceased landlord is finally removed. 'I mean, we can't open up, can we? I don't even know who owns the place after this.'

I see Ogden Barclay raise an interested eyebrow. No doubt, despite being estranged from his publican brother, he has a fair chance of inheriting the business. You'll be amazed how many people don't write wills. Especially when they live alone with no family. I ponder on the irony of it all. The twins haven't spoken for years, and Perkin was likely murdered in his brother's stead, but his public house could well end up in the hands of his sibling. I know this possibility isn't lost on Ogden Barclay, as he begins a quiet assessment of the place, squinting at fixtures and fittings rather too avariciously for a man who's just lost his brother. There's nowt as funny as folk, as the Yorkshire saying goes.

Juggers reaches out a meaty paw to Dr McKay. 'Sorry you came all the way from Scarborough for so little.'

McKay looks momentarily confused. 'We're at crossed purposes, Superintendent. I'm the local doctor here in Uthley Bay. I have a cottage a mile or so outside the village. I was in Scarborough doing some last-minute Christmas shopping. Tomorrow is Christmas Eve, after all. When I heard what had happened, I volunteered to come back with the mortuary van. Saves the bus fare, for a start.'

I'm not sure why Scots present this front of parsimony, you know. My mother was one of the most generous women you'll never meet. So are my Scottish relatives. My Auntie Moira told me that the whole thing dates back to before the Scottish currency was linked to sterling. It turned out that a Scottish pound was worth considerably less than its English counterpart. From a mythical twist in this fiscal imbalance over the years stemmed the notion that the Scots were miserable and mean. So unfair, if you ask me. My father is one of the most mean, miserable men you'll ever come across, and he doesn't have a drop of Scottish blood.

'I'd be obliged if one of your constables could take me home. I'm not keen on driving in the snow. That's why I took the bus to Scarborough,' says McKay.

'That won't be a problem, Doctor,' says Juggers, no doubt relieved that this formidable woman is about to leave our presence. 'Keithley, see that the doctor gets home, please.'

'You won't mind stopping at the grocer on the way, will you, Constable? The lads from the mortuary were kind enough to take my bags home before we came here, but I've nothing in the house to eat.'

Juggers nods to Keithley with a reluctant expression.

'You might be able to help me,' say I. Dr McKay must possess some local knowledge, I reckon. After all, she lives here. 'Who can I speak to in order to gain access to the old police station?'

'You mean the building on Kissing Lane?' says the doc.

My goodness, the irony. My first visit to Kissing Lane left me on my knees after a nasty blow from a swaggering local tough.

'I do believe that Constable Armley left the keys with Mrs Smith-Wantley in case of an emergency. She owns the haberdashery, and is chairwoman of the parish council.'

'You mean the mad old bat?'

'Aye, she can be on the scatty side, right enough. But she's not as daft as she's painted, and that's more than can be said for many hereabouts.'

'I don't know what's going on,' says Juggers.

'No room at the Trout, sir. But I came across the police

station. Perfectly sound, by the look of things, with accommodation. I thought we could use it for the chaps to rest their heads, and as a base of operations. Well, now that we know things aren't *straightforward*, if you know what I mean.'

Juggers regards me with a leery eye. 'You thought of all this by yourself, did you, Grasby?'

'Yes, as a matter of fact, I did. Hardly a great leap of intellect, I'm sure you'll agree.'

I know Juggers is still smarting from the way McKay casually put him in his place. But I'm damned if I'll be his whipping boy in her stead.

'He was a nice man, Constable Armley,' says McKay. 'I wish I could afford to retire to France.'

'France, you say?' says Juggers, as though such a change of scene should be subject to trial for treason.

'Aye, France. His wife was left some money or something like that. Shame they never replaced him.' She smiles rather nervously.

I see a sudden look of regret on McKay's face. It's almost as though she thinks she's said too much. But I have no idea from where this notion comes. Instinct again?

Juggers announces that he'll come with me to see Mrs Smith-Wantley at the haberdashery, while the remaining constables poke about for any evidence we may have missed.

'What about me?' says Ogden Barclay, rather forlornly.

'You stay where you are, while we sort ourselves out.' Then to me, 'Right, get a move on.' He looks me up and down. 'What happened to the knees of your trousers, lad? They're sodden.'

'Long story,' say I.

But I haven't forgotten George.

# 18

As Juggers and I set off, flakes of snow begin to fall again over Uthley Bay. The superintendent looks into the sky and makes a face.

'If it's another snowfall like yesterday, they'll have a job clearing the road, lad. There's only so many times a plough can push the white stuff onto the verge before it takes over.'

It occurs to me that – even with the three coppers from Filey – we are woefully undermanned for a double murder inquiry. I wonder why Juggers hasn't thought of this.

'We're a bit thin on the ground, sir. Especially if the snow cuts us off,' say I, hoping for a reaction.

'Aye, like as not we are. But there's help at hand if we need it,' he says knowingly.

'There is?' I take a glance at his expression as we walk along, the snow crumping under our feet. Juggers looks as determined as I've seen him, face set like a bronze statue.

'Rest assured, we'll be fine. Nothing to worry about.'

Now, this instantly sends me into a funk. You see, I heard this type of thing so many times during the war from senior officers. Almost inevitably, there would follow an utter catastrophe, involving swooping Stukas, tanks appearing out of nowhere through a hedge in the bocage or a division of German paratroopers landing on one's head. However, I must remember that the war is over, though for me and so many others, we carry it with us like a millstone every day. One that becomes ever more cumbersome as the years go by and the memories crowd in on dark, lonely nights.

I pull myself out of this self-indulgent malaise and fix the images of two local men, killed by the dangerous misuse of stockings, firmly in my mind as we pass the local news-agent. The place is firmly shuttered, no doubt because of events at the Skipper. It's not unusual for tight-knit places like Uthley Bay to close down in the wake of some local tra-gedy or other. I wonder if our trip to reacquaint ourselves with the mad Mrs Smith-Wantley will be a wasted one.

I shouldn't have worried, as towards the end of the road we find two shops huddled together. The first is a grocer of sorts, with netting bags of parsnips and carrots laid out on the pavement on trestle tables. Christmas staples, if I ever saw them. I glance inside the dimly lit shop as we pass and am fleetingly greeted by the stern face of a bald man in a brown dustcoat staring right back. He shakes his head and walks into the back, clearly wanting nothing to do with us. I'm sure word has got around that we're police detectives. You'd be amazed how the attitude of some people changes almost instantly when you reveal yourself to be one of the *boys in blue*. And this isn't reserved for the criminal frater-nity, either. Hatred of the police runs in some families, though they be honest and upstanding in every way. Huh, they should try living under the Gestapo; or maybe that's what they fear. After all, liberty is only a breath away from collapse. As I well know – and not just because of my father.

Though, let me tell you, most people are glad of the con-stabulary in times of trouble. It's an odd paradox. Thankfully, I can't envisage a time in England when the bobby won't be walking the beat, a solid reminder of law and order on every street corner. It'll be a dark day indeed if that changes.

In contrast to the gloom of the grocery shop, Mrs Smith-Wantley's emporium is positively bathed in light. In the window are mannequins dressed in staid tweed skirts, party frocks that look as though they've sprung from the early forties, and dresses that look as though they've survived from the thirties. One headless creature displays a fine leg encased in a fishnet stocking.

We tarry for a moment at the window. Juggers looks at me, no words necessary.

When we enter the shop, a little bell tinkles. Inside, it's as though we've walked into heaven. The light is golden, and the magnificent aroma of perfume is almost heady. We could be on 5th Avenue.

'Like a bloody bordello in here,' says Juggers, his nose turned up at the smell. 'Did I ever tell you about the time me and the lads found ourselves in a little place near Dunkirk in the first war?'

Thankfully, before he has time to relate this no doubt bawdy tale, he's interrupted by the swish of a curtain, and in walks Mrs Smith-Wantley. She's in a black frock with three rows of pearls adorning her neck. She looks at me and smiles broadly.

'Now, you are a naughty boy,' she says. 'I thought you were from my supplier when I spoke to you at breakfast. But I find that you are both police officers, here to find justice for poor Mr Wardle. I do hope you arrest the dreadful people who ended his life.'

It's strange – Mrs S-W seems to be more on the ball now. Earlier, in the hotel dining room, she looked much frailer and certainly not as lucid. Maybe she just needed her toast and jam.

One thing is clear, however: the proprietor seems to have no idea of the calamity at the Skipper earlier. I look at Juggers and he shakes his head almost imperceptibly. Unless we're going to ask this elderly lady if she saw anything amiss late last night, we should leave her to find out about Perkin Barclay under her own steam. Somehow, she doesn't look the type to be parading about in the wee small hours.

'May I formally introduce ourselves, madam,' says Juggers. 'I'm Superintendent Juggers, and this is Inspector Grasby.'

Mrs Smith-Wantley performs the shadow of a curtsey. By which I mean, she sinks an inch or two then grabs the counter to pull herself back up again. She does this while maintaining a perfect smile of greeting. No small feat for a woman of her age, if you ask me. 'Pleased to meet you both, *properly*,' she replies.

'You're the chairwoman of the local council, I believe?' says Juggers.

'Yes, I am. But only by dint of the fact nobody else wanted the job.' She giggles like a much younger woman. 'I do my best to keep things in order, as it were. One can do no more.'

'I'd like the keys for the police station in Kissing Lane, if you don't mind. We'll have to recommission it for a short while, at least. I have the authority from the Chief Constable at Northallerton. I believe the keys were left with the local council as a courtesy, and so that the station could be kept wind- and watertight.' Juggers is doing his best to be pleasant. But he's not very good at it. Everything he says sounds like an accusation.

'You're absolutely right, Superintendent. Constable Armley was such a lovely man. He did so much for the village. How we miss him. You'll be glad to know I have them safe and sound in my little office through the back. I'll be with you in a jiffy.' With that, Mrs Smith-Wantley slips through the curtain like a superannuated magician.

While she's away, I take a poke about. There are all manner of things in the haberdashery, everything from hair clips to brassieres, tweed skirts to blouses. All in various fabrics, colours and styles. But one thing strikes me instantly.

'Sir, have you noticed something strange?' I whisper to Juggers.

'What? Like what's a place like this doing in a tiny fishing village? Aye, I have.'

'Well, yes. That is a good point. But apart from the lady with one leg in the window, I can't see any stockings at all.'

Juggers looks around, his eyes darting from shelf to display cabinet and back again. 'Why, I do believe you're right.' He strokes his chin. 'Let's probe a bit.'

Before I can worry just what he might do, Mrs Smith-Wantley reappears, waving a brass key ring upon which are attached two large mortice keys.

'Here we are. I knew I'd left them safely.' She hands the key ring to Juggers.

'I'm much obliged to you,' says Juggers, pocketing it. 'Now, maybe you can indulge me again, if that's in order?'

'Yes, of course. Anything I can do to help.'

As she says this, I'm sure I detect a brief flinch. It's momentary but there, nonetheless.

'It's my wife, you see,' Juggers continues. 'She does love a pair of nylons. I was hoping you might have such a thing – as a Christmas present, you understand.'

Mrs Smith-Wantley shakes her head sadly. 'I'm so sorry, Superintendent. I sold my last pair yesterday afternoon. You may not realize, being a gentleman, but it's almost impossible to find stockings of any decent quality these days. And I refuse to burden my customers with the liquid variety. I'm told it's because of some embargo or other. All I know is, my clientele is furious.' She turns to me. 'You'll remember that's what I was asking you for this morning at breakfast, Inspector. Imagine me thinking you were a hosiery salesman. I am sorry.'

'Perfectly understandable,' says Juggers. 'He dresses just like a salesman. I've told him many times.'

'And he was pretending to be an American. Young people are such fun these days, don't you think?'

Juggers looks at me from the corner of his eye. It's a bit like a lion trying not to let the antelope know he's about to devour it. 'Now, how many times, Inspector Grasby? You're from York, not New York.' He turns his attention back to the proprietor. 'He's such a card, you know. Born comedian. In fact, I'm surprised he didn't take it up professionally. Still time, mind you.'

'You don't need your stick in the shop, I see,' say I, trying to avoid a scene.

'Oh no, Inspector. How clever of you to realize. I only use it outside. My old legs aren't as strong as they once were. Age is damnable.'

'Your shop is so lovely. Not what you expect in a little Yorkshire fishing village.' I smile.

'My husband worked in Harrods, Inspector. There for thirty years, he was. When he retired, well, he couldn't give it up. So, we opened this little place.' Suddenly her expression becomes sorrowful. 'He's been dead for almost five years. This is my little monument to him, you see. Better than some stone in a graveyard. It carries on his life's work, and I shall tend to it as long as I'm able.'

Now, I don't want to seem glib or heartless, but one wonders just how long this poor old dear can carry on. Can't be long until she joins her dearly departed. I know this is cynical, but I'm always rather taken aback by people who refuse to bow to the inevitable.

'I know what you're thinking, Inspector.' Mrs Smith-Wantley fixes me with a surprisingly steely gaze.

*Gosh, I do hope she doesn't!*

'You're wondering how on earth I can keep a shop like this open in Uthley Bay, aren't you?'

'Must say, it did cross our minds, ma'am,' Juggers interjects, no doubt terrified of what I might say.

'You'd be amazed. Folk come from all parts to sample my wares. It's just as Charles – my husband – said: make something special and customers will come. And he was right. I have regulars from as far away as Leeds.'

'Most gratifying to hear,' says Juggers unctuously. His expression sits uneasily on his fleshy, bold face. 'Now, thank you so much. We must be about our business.'

'Good luck to you both,' says the old dear. But as she does, again, a flash of something I can't quite gauge passes over her face. I can't explain it, but it's there. Something left unsaid, perhaps. Or maybe it's just me becoming paranoid in this village of stocking-related premature death.

So, with the keys to Uthley Bay Police Station now lodged in Juggers's pocket, we bid Mrs Smith-Wantley good day. Once we're back on the street, I ask my superior what he thinks of her having no stockings.

'She's lying through her teeth, Grasby,' says he roughly.

So, not just me, then. Juggers has a much less nuanced approach to these subtleties. But maybe his way is the more effective. I spend too much time riddled with self-doubt and the fear of making a complete arse of myself. I must break out and have more confidence.

Juggers nods to the grocer shop. 'Let's take a trip in here before we have a look at the station.'

# 19

The word 'grocer' hardly covers what's on offer in this shop. There are pots and pans, cuts of meat, shelves of detergent, vegetables and all manner of domestic necessities dotted about. The odd thing is, they're not behind the counter but all round the shop, a bit like a flea market. I lean over and squeeze a loaf, just the way my mother taught me. You can always tell when bread is about to go stale. But surely this place must be the pilfering capital of Yorkshire. You'd need eyes like a hawk to stop people nicking stuff on the fly when the shopkeeper's attention is elsewhere.

'How do?' says the solid figure behind the counter. He's wearing a white apron over his dustcoat now. It's stained here and there and sets off his ruddy, dour-set face. He's as bald as a coot, his dome shining, even in this low light. His mien shouts, *Leave me alone.*

Juggers does the introductions then goes for the inevitable question. 'Can I ask your name, sir?'

'What for?'

'Just for our records, sir. You'll be aware that all is not well here in Uthley Bay.' I can see Juggers is about to bridle.

'My name is Jeremiah Payne, owner of this establishment. And you're damned right all isn't well. First, old

Wardle, now Perkin Barclay. It's a disgrace. And I want to know what you bobbies are going to do about it.'

Juggers shuffles from foot to foot, a clear sign of irritation. I intervene.

'We'll be happy to answer your questions, if we can. First, though, we'd like to ask you a few, if you don't mind?'

'Here we go. You're about to pick out the first man with a criminal record and blame him. I knew it as soon as I saw thee walking past. Well, let me tell you, I won't take the blame for something I haven't done. The past is the past, and I've paid for my mistakes!'

Gosh, an old lag, as they say in London. I must say, he's honest enough about his previous misdemeanours. While I find this refreshing, Juggers, I know, will be of another persuasion. To him, as I've learned from bitter experience, once a criminal, always a criminal. I don't have to wait long for his response.

'For starters, is that your real name? Tell us, and then we can discuss what you did to put you in gaol.'

Our man shakes his head. 'So much for honesty, eh?'

I don't blame him for feeling this way. But Juggers is a dog with a bone at the best of times.

'What did you do, Mr Payne?'

'If you must know, I stole two loaves of bread and a tin of sardines from a shop in Bradford.'

'I see,' says Juggers. 'Feeding the five thousand at Valley Parade, were you?'

'Funny, Superintendent. Very funny. If you must know, it were before the war. I'd been made redundant from a flour mill. No job, and three kids to feed. What would you do? I got precious little from the parish council, let me tell you. And what I did get they made me grovel for.'

144

'So, you just thought you'd go on the rob instead. Aye, that were a good idea.'

Jeremiah Payne slams both fists onto the counter. 'I did six months at Wakefield for my pains. During which time my wife ran off with a pal of mine, and I've never seen my children again. To add to that, I served all through the war for little thanks. I got bugger all when they didn't need me to stand in front of the bullets no more. A white fiver and cheap suit that didn't last the year.'

'I say, I'm sorry to hear all that, old boy. You've had a rough time.' And I mean it too. They were foolish enough to place me in charge of a platoon of men during the war. Good chaps, from Bradford, Leeds, Hull, Sheffield – all over. They were on the rough side and didn't give much for my toffee accent. But when the chips were down – really down, I mean – they were the bravest men I've ever seen. We looked out for each other and had a real bond. Mr Payne reminds me of my old sergeant, a career soldier from Beverley called Tommy Monkton. He'd been through scrape after scrape before he joined the army. But let me tell you, though I was nominally in charge, it was him who was really in command. You see, he knew about war, he knew about loyalty, and most of all, he understood men. I learned a lot from him. And just as well. He was shot dead at my feet outside Berlin. The bullet could have hit either of us, but fate chose poor Tommy.

I miss that honourable, capable man to this day. What a police officer he would have made. Mr Payne is of that stock, I'm sure. You see, it's not the ex-choirboys like me who sustain the army. It's the tough fighting men who know what struggle is all about, and who their true friends are. That's what wins wars. Funnily enough, the grocer reminds me more of a police officer than a former prison inmate. Something about his manner, I think.

'Well, a touching story, I must say,' says Juggers with no real conviction. 'I'll be more direct. You obviously know about Mr Barclay. I wonder, did you see anything odd last night – just after closing time?'

'Aye, as a matter of fact, I did. I saw two bobbies get packed into the back of an old Bedford van and spirited off into the snow.' Jeremiah Payne's expression turns from a frown to a sneer.

'I'm well aware what we did last night, sir. I want to know where you were, and what you saw.'

'I were minding me own business. Which, let me tell you, is getting too hard to do in this village. And though I didn't see Perkin, God rest him, I did wonder why the bobbies were off on some wild goose chase when there were more important things to be about.'

I look on as Juggers hesitates. It's not the response he's expecting.

'What do you mean?' say I. 'Really, Mr Payne, if you know something you must tell us. Two men are dead.'

Payne shrugs his shoulders. 'I'll sell you some carrots, a tin of beans – maybe a bottle of pop. That's my business, you see. I'm of the opinion every man and woman should attend to their own fate to the best of their ability. This shop, for instance. I got the idea of folk helping themselves from an American magazine. See, I can carry a much larger and varied stock, and therefore make more money. I'm good at this. So, I keep my hand on my ha'penny and get on with it. I suggest you do likewise, as far as I'm concerned.'

'What on earth has that got to do with the questions we've asked you?' says Juggers in a growl.

'It says, you should know your business better. Because

you're going to find bugger all chewing the fat up here with me. Go and find the people what are destroying this village, before some other decent sod is lying dead.' Payne rubs his hands on his apron. 'Now, if you don't mind, I've orders to attend to.' He turns his back, our exchange clearly at an end.

I'm deep in thought as we head back down Kissing Lane. Everyone appears a bit shifty, yet ready with an excuse. Still, two men have been found murdered in the village in a week. And even given the fact that one of them may have been killed out at sea, he was still a local man.

And what about all the stockings washed up last night? Could that really have been used to divert our attention? If that is the case, then Ogden Barclay has a few questions to answer. And while we're asking him, we should perhaps press him more on the murder of his brother. My, it's turning into a right can of worms.

Juggers has said very little since we left Jeremiah Payne. And though the walk from his shop to the village police station is by no means a long one, such an extended period of silence is rare for him.

'What did you make of Payne?' say I, to break the ice.

'A wrong 'un, aye, to his bootstraps. That's what I make of him. He's hiding something, you can trust me on that.'

'Really? I didn't get that at all, sir. Thought him quite honourable, to be honest.'

'In that case, you've chosen the wrong profession. Aye, and I've let you maintain that role. He wanted us out of there as quickly as our little legs would carry us. Mark my words, if he's not involved in what's going on, I'm a Dutchman.'

Instantly, I picture Juggers in a pair of clogs, getting stuck into a wheel of Gouda.

'What about the stockings, sir?'

'Who goes to all the trouble of scattering little cellophane packs of stockings on a beach in the dark? Be reasonable, Grasby. Aye, and a damn sight more sensible an' all.'

In a few minutes we're standing outside Uthley Bay Police Station.

Juggers admires it from the lane. 'Just the job, is this.'

And for a moment, I think of Juggers's brother, the effluent inspector in Leeds. After all, there's plenty of it about. And I'd bet we're being fed much of it. Uthley Bay is not as it appears. What on earth have I got myself into this time? I really should learn to take the festive break.

Just as we enter our new base of operations, it starts to snow again. Though now in big, feathery flakes. By the time Juggers has given the place the standard tour of inspection, and he's given it the thumbs up, it's a whiteout beyond the windows.

'That'll be it until after Christmas, Grasby. It's a bugger, is snow in Yorkshire.'

As I stare out at the blizzard, I tend to agree with him. We're on our own. I wonder who's next for the stocking treatment. Not yours truly, I hope.

# 20

It's time for lunch. Also, a good moment to hatch our plans to stop the killer, and whatever is behind it all. But by the time we trudge back to the Trout in the snow, it's like a visit to Wembley. The entire dining room is packed with elderly holidaymakers desperate enough to come to Uthley Bay for Christmas.

Juggers decides he must go to the loo, leaving me standing about like a lemon until Dot approaches, just level with my oxter, bearing a letter.

'Found this at reception. It's addressed to you, so here it is. Not a clue who it's from, mind.'

'Maybe says inside,' say I.

'Likely it will,' she replies, before bustling off to see to the multitudes.

I find a corner in which to stand and open the letter with my thumb. The handwriting on the envelope is carried on inside, neat and well formed. It's a short note:

*Dear Inspector Grasby,*
*You'll be seeing much that isn't to your taste in our little village, I'm sure.*
*Please remember, this is a divided place, and there is good and bad. Please don't confuse the two. I'm not*

*sure your superior has your broad outlook. But be ready*
*to see behind the obvious.*
   *Good luck,*
   *A friend*


Gosh, this is a turn-up for the books. I look up and spy Juggers striding back from the toilet. At first, I'm anxious to tell him about this funny little message. But something stops me. Don't ask me why.

With Juggers back at my side, I scan the room for anything resembling a spare table. As he's muttering oaths under his breath, I spot the upright figure of my father, sitting at a table set for four, with only Hetty Gaunt for company.

'Sir, something I neglected to tell you,' I say into Juggers's ear over the din of conversation, the chink of glasses and the plink of cutlery on plates.

'You haven't found another body, have you? I don't think I could take it, Grasby.'

'No, I forgot to tell you that my father is in residence. I met him earlier. He's here with his friend for Christmas.'

'That's a bit of a coincidence, isn't it? Was he missing you that much he thought he'd come here for the festivities? Don't sound much like the Cyril Grasby I know.'

'I think he'd already booked. When he heard it's where we were going to be too, he didn't want to rock the boat.'

This is, of course, a lie. But what else can I say? I'm just glad that my father and Juggers didn't cross each other's paths in Elderby last year. My superior knows nothing of his romance with Hetty Gaunt. But he's about to find out.

I manage to catch my father's eye. I smile in his direction, and he lowers his head into his hands in a display of utter misery. Happy Christmas! I don't think.

'There are a couple of spare chairs at his table, sir. Best I can do, I'm afraid.'

Juggers follows my gaze to Grasby senior's table. 'Aye, I see, right enough. Who's with him, the village witch?'

I knew Juggers would comment on Hetty Gaunt as soon as he set eyes on her. She's still wearing her odd little bowler hat with the red feather in the headband. Oh dear, I could happily strangle my father. Though, perhaps that's not the right kind of emotion to bear, under the circumstances. Uthley Bay has seen more than its fair share of strangling lately.

'Any port in a storm,' says Juggers, brushing a ledge of snow from the shoulder of his overcoat, which nearly lands in the middle of an old gentleman's lunch. He throws us a dirty look. I'm just glad he doesn't protest. The poor chap would likely have found himself the first prisoner of the newly reopened Uthley Bay Police Station. That's the kind of mood my superior is in.

We make our way through the throng to my dear pater's table.

'Hello, Arthur,' he says to Juggers, utterly ignoring his son, and as though his presence here is nothing out of the ordinary. 'This is Hetty Gaunt, my companion.'

Juggers offers a meaty paw. 'Pleased to make your acquaintance, I'm sure. I like your hat.'

While she glares at him, having known the man for so long, I can see Juggers's mind working. It's something in his expression. Obviously, he's heard the name before, but as there was no court case following events last year, the only reason he'll remember is that he directed me to her guest house before I drove to Elderby. But he will remember soon, I'm sure of it.

'Pleased to meet you,' says Hetty, with a face like a sharp hatchet.

'I hope you don't mind if myself and young Grasby here join you? Just about no room at the inn, as you see.'

We sit ourselves down, and for a moment or two there's an awkward silence. As always in these circumstances, I feel it's my job to bowl the first over.

'I say, that was a thoroughgoing blizzard for a while. Luckily, we missed the worst of it on the way down.'

I don't what it is about the English, but the weather is an obsession. I suppose it's because we have so much of it. I mean, you go to France on a sunny day, and it's a fair bet it'll stay that way until dark. Here, well, you could experience anything from snow, hail, rain, hurricanes, a plague of frogs or flying kippers before bedtime.

'I'm sure it's not possible,' says my father wearily. 'But I'm convinced you become duller by the year. It's no wonder I usually fall asleep listening to you over dinner.'

It's on the tip of my tongue to say that his sudden bouts of tiredness are down to being pissed on his homemade wine, but I refrain for the sake of a united Grasby front.

'Aye, you're right, Cyril. He can be a bit on the dull side,' says Juggers.

Hurrah for comradely togetherness!

'Though I must say, I find that all the time with the youth of today,' Juggers continues. 'I blame cinema. They spend that much time with their heads in the clouds, they don't have time to live the way we do. No appreciation of the finer things in life. Jess and I were at a wonderful amateur dramatic show at Tockwith village hall a few weeks ago. My, it were a riot. We even had some community singing. Not a young person in sight, Cyril.'

Damn! Wish I'd been there. It would have been a good excuse to end it all before I wound up here.

Juggers turns to Hetty. 'Now, then, how did you and Cyril meet?'

I'm dreading this, and I'm right so to do.

'We met a long time ago. At the dawn of day, when the sap was still rising, Arthur.' Hetty Gaunt delivers this like a failing poet.

'I see,' says Juggers.

He's looking rather mystified and trying to put a brave face on it. Serves him right, I think silently. But it's not over.

'We made love under the stars.' Hetty addresses my father. 'Do you remember, Cyril? Just down by the beck, behind the old village pump.'

There we are! Curtain closed, the show's over. I'm glad Juggers isn't currently in the process of masticating his lunch. By the horrified look on his face, it would have been bound to scatter everywhere.

'We all mourn our younger days with great sorrow,' says my father, quite unabashed.

But he and Hetty don't know that the young Arthur Juggers spent his tender years counting giblets, while his brother was shifting the excrement of an entire city from one place to another.

'Your name is familiar, Hetty. I can't quite place from where.' Juggers strokes his chin for inspiration.

'You lodged my son at her guest house last year, Arthur. Don't you remember?'

'Oh, aye! That's it.' Juggers snaps his fingers at the memory.

'He has some strange habits, does the lad,' says Hetty. 'Always wants to be in the bath, he does. It's a sign of some uncleanliness of the mind, is that. Mind you, the way he chased after that young American lass like a puppy dog,

I'm not surprised. Young enough to be his daughter, she were.'

Here we go again. She refers to Deedee, a young lady I met last year. She was just six years my junior – in her thirties!

'I distinctly remember warning you off affairs of the heart on duty, Grasby,' says Juggers. 'I can see I wasted my time.'

'Now, listen here, all of you. Miss Dean was acting as my intern. I was merely teaching her the ropes, in the process of investigating a very difficult case.'

'I don't know what perversion this *intern* business is,' says my father. 'But it sounds like the kind of thing I've come to expect of you, Frank. I'd rather hear no more on the subject, if you don't mind.'

'And his sheets were a disgrace,' says Hetty into the bargain. 'Worst I've seen.'

'I was covered in soot! You wouldn't let me have a proper bath.'

Juggers puts his hand on my forearm. 'Now, young Grasby. We've all done things we're ashamed of, I'm sure. Let's talk about this later, lad.'

It's the gentlest warning to change the subject that one is likely to get from Juggers, so I take his advice and shut up. Maybe he's ascertained that there's something not quite right about dear old Hetty. My father too, come to that.

'They tell me there's been trouble afoot in the village, Arthur,' says my father. 'More since you and Francis arrived, I hear. I pray for the poor souls lost, whoever they are.' My father's nose is bothering him.

Juggers bridles, recognizing his motive. 'Now, Cyril, you know I can't talk shop. It's not a policeman's way.'

'I just hope you catch the buggers before one of us is

hanging off the Christmas tree with a stocking round our necks,' says Hetty Gaunt. 'I could feel the evil in this place as soon as I arrived.'

Here we go.

'She has the sight,' says my father proudly.

'Really?' says Juggers. 'I didn't think a man of the cloth like you would approve of such things, Cyril.'

My father points to his button-down collar and tie. 'I'm off duty, Arthur. I'm sure you don't go chasing miscreants on your days off.'

I know what's coming here. It appears my father thinks that he's free to be about anything the moment he removes his dog collar. The mind boggles! But I know Juggers is of a very different caste.

'Not true, Cyril. As far as I'm concerned, a police officer is never off duty. If were to come across someone committing a crime during my leisure hours, I'd have them behind bars before you could say Jack-the-lad, and no mistake. My work is a calling, just as yours is.' He eyes my father's tie with distaste. 'Doesn't do to forget that, you know.'

Three cheers for Superintendent Arthur Juggers! That's put the damned old letch in his place. Thankfully, before my father can respond, a harassed waitress appears.

'Sorry, we've not had time to look at the menu,' say I. 'If you could give us a few moments, please.'

'No point looking at the menu. All that's left is haddock and chips. The chef's had to pop out until dinner.'

'That's not good,' say I, picturing the massive figure of Tommaso bowling off somewhere to lift up a bus or something like that. 'And you with so many guests.'

'It's not so bad. You're the last to be served, I reckon.' She stands poised with her notepad. 'Is it haddock and chips, then?'

'Yes, it is,' says Juggers sharply. 'Haddock and chips twice. And I hope you don't need to write it down, lass, or my fears for the youth of today are definitely not mis-placed. Quick as you like, now. We haven't got all day.'

I note a certain hardening of our waitress's expression. But she turns on her heel and dances back to the kitchen, through the close-set tables of jabbering geriatrics.

'Well,' says my father. 'That's us just about done here. Sorry to be rude. But you'll excuse us. We're going to take a turn along the seafront.'

'Take your huskies with you,' says Juggers. 'You'll need them.'

'And then we're going to go to the little pub up the way for a drink or two,' says Hetty.

'Pub's closed,' says Juggers.

'Bad time of year to shut the pub, Arthur,' says my father.

'Publican's indisposed, Cyril. Can't be helped.'

My father murmurs something to Hetty, and for the first time in my experience, she smiles from ear to ear. It's such a strange sight. Quite off-putting, actually.

'Don't worry, Cyril's thought of something much better than sitting in an old pub.' She nudges my father with her elbow.

Dash it all, the implication is obvious. I shan't want any lunch at this rate.

Thankfully, they get ready to leave. My father shakes Juggers's hand manfully, while ignoring me completely again. With that, they're off. I see Juggers watch them go.

'An odd couple, sir,' I venture.

'You can say that again, lad. Like a tiger courting a gir-affe. I've seen a few things in my time, but that's plain odd.'

'You don't need to tell me.'

'We won't say any more about you pestering the lasses.

But if hygiene is a problem, you must smarten up, lad. I dread to imagine these sheets of yours.'

I long to put the record straight. But what's the point?

'Lean in, Grasby. We have things to discuss.'

I do as I'm bid. I've heard of hiding in plain sight, but this takes the biscuit. It appears we're about to plan to put the ills of Uthley Bay to rights in front of half the elderly population of Yorkshire. Mind you, I'll be hard pushed to hear Juggers over this din, so any potential eavesdropper will struggle.

'The key to this is the stockings. Plain and simple,' says Juggers emphatically.

Gosh, it's clear that you need to develop keen insight to become a superintendent. It's a wonder there aren't more ten-year-olds in that exalted position. But I must play the game.

'Yes, sir. I think you've well and truly got to the nub of the matter there.'

It's not easy being a toad. However, needs must.

'So, my theory is that the fishing fleet are bringing in these stockings from abroad. We just have to follow them.'

'Abroad, sir? They seem to leave first thing then they're back for tea. I can't see them heading to the Continent and back in that time, can you?'

At first, I think Juggers may haul me up by the collar and administer his famous foghorn-in-the-face routine. But once he's digested what I've said, he seems more sanguine than I expect.

'Good thinking. I'm not right up with the ways of the sea. How quick the craft can travel, and that. I'm glad to note that you are. So, the question is, where are they coming from?'

'I should think a larger vessel. Offload them a few miles

out, then drop the smuggled items off at some covert spot, I shouldn't wonder.'

'I don't care how many young ladies you've pestered, Grasby. You're right up there when it comes to inspiration, and that's a fact.'

'Sir, I haven't—'

'Don't you worry. All forgotten, as far as I'm concerned. You may have the method right, but I think I know who the mastermind behind it all must be.' Juggers smiles in triumph.

'You do? I mean, who, sir?' I whisper. This has me taken aback slightly.

'Thought you'd have picked up on it, to be honest, lad.'

'No, not so far,' say I, meaning it.

'Plain as the nose on your face. It's that old Smyth-Windley.' Juggers leans back, happy he's solved these dreadful crimes.

'Do you mean Mrs Smith-Wantley, sir?'

'Aye, that's what I said.'

Now, there are a number of reasons why I can't think this to be true. Firstly, the lady in question is reasonably frail – though that doesn't mean she's an innocent abroad. But if she is the woman responsible for the mass smuggling of stockings, not to mention murder most foul, my instincts have failed me utterly.

'May I present the case against, sir? Merely as a discussion topic, you understand.'

'Go ahead, if you must,' says Juggers wearily.

'If this is the case, sir, why did she ask for five dozen pairs of stockings this very morning?'

'She were testing your resolve. Trying to find out who you were. You pretending to be an American must have put her off her stride, mind you. Did you do that on purpose?'

I begin to try and explain my discourse with Mrs Smith-Wantley over breakfast this morning. But you had to be there. So, in the end, I just nod my head and enjoy Juggers's praise.

'I agree that she must have accomplices. Otherwise, how could she keep order, eh? These fishermen are a rough bunch. There will be some muscle keeping them in tow. But she's the money, and that's where the power is.'

'Indeed, sir. I rather think that Wilf might be a guilty party. He seemed thick as thieves with the old dear this morning.'

'That weasel-faced lad that helped us with our luggage? No, I can't see him having the wit to be a master criminal.' It's a shake of the jowls from my superior.

I picture Wilf spiriting our main suspect away during breakfast, lest she say too much, for sure. And to be honest, I just don't fancy the cut of his jib. Instinct again. Rarely fails me. If Juggers is willing to write him off so quickly, I'm not. I shall quietly investigate. My superior need never know. After all, I am an inspector.

'What's our plan of attack, sir? As you know, we must prove that this stocking smuggling is indeed taking place before we rush off and start blaming people.'

'You've learned well from me, Grasby. Here's what's going to happen. I want one bobby in the police station at all times with Barclay. The other two will do some door-to-door enquiries about poor old Perkin. See if we can't dig up something.'

'What about us, sir?'

'We have a few things to be at for the rest of the day. You get the phone reconnected at the station. Calling from here is likely best. And then organize the lads. I'll go and find a boat. And make sure Mrs Jinks gets the pub dubbed up. Oh, and get the lads down to the station and square the place off. We'll have to find coal and bedding. I'll leave that to you, lad. Aye, and teamaking facilities. Can't leave the boys without a cup of tea. Inhumane, is that.'

Yes, stick them in an old police station that's needing aired, with no creature comforts, and that's fine. But for any sake, don't leave them without tea. Like the weather, it's another national obsession. Mind you, I'm as bad as everyone else. I love tea more than just about anything else in the world. But during Juggers's monologue, and list of things to do, I notice something out of the ordinary.

'Did you say boat, sir?'

'Oh, yes. We're off first thing tomorrow to find out what's happening out at sea.'

For some reason, I picture Juggers and me sailing into an endless ocean in a rowing boat, never to be seen again. A bit like the chaps that thought they'd fall off the edge of the world, back in the good old days. It's not a pleasant prospect.

# 21

Thanks to Dot, I'm permitted access to the little office behind reception to make my calls. From there, I organize the reinstatement of the phone at Uthley Bay Police Station. It's just a case of informing the exchange in Filey. They'll reconnect it as soon as possible.

Next, I telephone the Skipper. Mrs Jinks is glad to be getting away from the place. I don't doubt she's had enough of policemen poking about, not to mention the presence of her murdered boss's estranged twin brother.

I speak to Keithley, who appears to be the senior man amongst the bobbies from Filey. He seems a sound enough chap. He explains they've 'been about' but can't find anything that might help us find the murderer of poor Perkin Barclay. I tell him about the station and point out what's required. He accepts this with good grace and assures me he'll get going right away.

My telephone conversation with Ogden Barclay isn't as straightforward, however. He has no intention of being placed under guard at the rejuvenated Uthley Bay Police Station and tells me he now intends going home to be with his wife. They want to be alone in their grief. There's something assertive about him I didn't spot on the pier at our first meeting. The murder of one's brother will do that, I suppose.

The best I can do for now is have one of our constables escort him there and await Juggers's instructions. I'm surprised by this casual approach towards his own safety, especially considering his brother was likely murdered in his stead. It makes me all the more suspicious of our rugged-faced fisherman.

All this done, I thank Dot. But before I depart, I note the wringing of her hands and take it to mean she's uneasy about something.

'Problem?' I ask in a friendly, conversational way.

'It's nothing, really,' says Dot, looking up at me. 'I suppose I'm a bit unsettled. I mean, we've never had so much as a theft here in the village. It's all a bit of a shock, Inspector. I'm so glad you and the superintendent are here to keep us safe.'

Then she does something I don't expect. She rushes me like a prop forward going at a winger, clinging to me like a limpet. There follows an awkward moment when she stands on tiptoes to kiss me on the cheek. She's still short by a few inches, so I have to lean down in order to receive said kiss.

Of course, as you'll know by now, my luck doesn't extend much past my nose. And in the midst of this awkward embrace, Juggers, who has apparently been trying to attract someone's attention at reception, pokes his head round the door.

'Put that young lady down this minute!' he yells, making us both jump, and Dot's head collide with my bottom lip.

'I can explain, sir,' say I, as Dot rubs her head.

'It's quite plain you're insatiable, Grasby. Though now certain facts about your father have come to light, it's likely inherited. Leave the lass alone while I ask her a question.'

Almost without thinking, I shove Dot away, subconsciously wanting Juggers to believe I am not some rampant womanizer. She stumbles a bit but manages to right herself in the nick of time. Mind you, not much distance between her and the floor. So, I daresay there wouldn't have been much damage if she had toppled over.

Juggers takes the whole thing in with a look of disgust.

'Now, I know that you're very busy,' says he. 'Busier than I thought, to be honest.' He casts me a dirty look. 'But I have three constables who have to be fed and watered. I've found them accommodation. But if you'd supply their meals, you'll be handsomely rewarded by the constabulary.'

'I suppose so,' says Dot. 'It'll be a push. But the more the merrier.' She looks up at me. 'And I can explain what you saw pass between myself and Inspector Grasby. I was merely thanking him for being here to keep us safe, nothing more.'

Juggers frowns. 'Like as not you were. Inspector Grasby has a great deal to do. I'd be grateful if you *thank* him when he's off duty. Though his personal hygiene is in question. Best you're forewarned.'

Dot looks slightly bemused by this comment, though I know Juggers now thinks me a thoroughgoing sexual deviant and sees it as his duty to keep the female populace of Uthley Bay safe. No surprise. I'm the most misunderstood man I know.

'Come with me, Grasby.' The order is palpable.

'Have you found a boat?' say I as we cross the lobby.

'I have. Though I'm surprised you didn't come up with the idea. I can't be expected to do all the planning, you know.'

'Sir, I was doing other things.'

163

'Oh, I know what you were at, don't worry. I fully expect to find you in the arms of Mrs Smythe-Winsey before we're finished here. Get yourself a wife, lad. All very well sowing your wild oats, but you must have acres of crops by now, eh?'

'Smith-Wantley,' say I, glad to have some retort to hand. 'The boat, sir. Where did you find it?' As you can tell, I'm anxious to change the subject.

'Why, Ogden Barclay's fishing vessel is the very thing! He can damn well sail us there, too.'

I want to say that I have my suspicions about Ogden Barclay. However, with no real evidence, I can't put my case to Juggers until I have something more solid.

'Come on. I'll need your help.' He heads for the lift. I follow on meekly behind.

Not only do I suspect that our soon-to-be skipper may be involved in all this horror, but one look at his fishing boat is enough to send the surest of mariners off the edge. Dash it all, it's a veritable death trap. No two parts of it are hanging together the right way. I mean to say, a hole in the wheelhouse window has been patched with an old oilskin! I can just picture us huddling in there as a storm whips up out on the North Sea, completely at its mercy.

I fret on this as we ascend to the third floor in the lift. I'm unable to describe my fears to Juggers or he'll think me a coward. As you know, dear reader, I am anything but. Just a bit on the cautious side. Who isn't when it concerns the continuation of their life?

We alight from the lift and make for our shared room. About three doors away, a woman is moaning loudly.

'What's all that about?' says Juggers in a low voice.

Suddenly, I feel a shiver down my spine. It's because there's already been so much death around Uthley Bay, no

164

doubt. Then, some other fear takes over. My father and Hetty Gaunt are in one of the hotel rooms, this we know for a fact. I'm a betting man, as you know, but I wouldn't take any odds against this being their room.

As the moaning gets louder, Juggers's sense of duty kicks in.

'Right, lad, we better see what's going on. It's our job.'

'Sir, but what if it's a private matter?' say I desperately.

'A private matter? What on earth do you think's going on, the Inquisition?'

At this point, I feel Juggers may well have led a rather sheltered life. But, undaunted, he chaps the door loudly with his ball of a fist.

'York Police! What's going on in there? Open up!'

Now, quite why he has to identify us as *York Police*, I'm not sure. It will be a big enough shock for those potentially in the throes of passion to discover the police are banging on their door at all, never mind the fact they've come all the way from York for the privilege.

I hear footsteps thudding in the room. As predicted, there is my father, standing in a pair of candy-striped flannelette pyjamas, buttoned up to the neck.

'Cyril! What on earth . . .?'

As Juggers speaks, the moaning continues behind my father's tall, thin frame.

'Thank goodness you're here, Arthur. I've been trying my best, but to no avail, I fear.'

Juggers bursts past him into the room. I follow in his wake. Dressed in a dark blue silk dressing gown is Hetty Gaunt, her face contorted in pain, standing in a bowl of water.

'It was an early start,' says my father haltingly. 'We were tired, so we thought to have an hour or two's nap. I filled a

165

hot-water bottle to take the chill off. The damned thing burst all over Hetty's foot. She's been scalded.'

In a flash, Juggers grabs the tiny figure of Hetty Gaunt in his arms and, despite her protestations, carries her out of the room, down the corridor, and into the bathroom. Both my father and I rush after him.

I look on as Juggers lifts Hetty into a bath, orders her to stand still, inserts the bath plug, and turns the cold tap on full.

'Get down there and fetch a bucket of ice, Grasby,' he shouts to me. But, clearly flapping, my father runs towards the lift at my side.

'He meant me, Father,' say I. 'Get back and help Juggers.'

My father looks as though I've ordered him to kill his congregation. Nonetheless, he turns on his heel as I step into the lift.

You've got to give credit where credit is due. When it comes to quick, on-the-spot action, always find a police officer. Though I wonder, perhaps unfairly, just what my father and Hetty were really up to when the bottle burst. Mind you, how much fun can one have in a pair of buttoned-up candy-stripe pyjamas?

By the time I get back with the ice, my father is holding Hetty's hand as she shivers, standing in the bath.

'Give that here,' orders Juggers. He grabs the full ice bucket from me and pours its contents into the bath. Hetty gives a little yelp but I daresay realizes that it's in her best interest.

'You'll need to stand there for a while, Mrs Gaunt. The scald doesn't look too bad. But a trip to the doctor might be wise. That'll come up as some blister, I reckon.' He turns to my father. 'You were lucky there, Cyril. Nasty shock, when you're lying in bed minding your own business. Aye, nasty indeed.'

And, somewhat uncharitably, I wish it were my father standing in a bath of freezing cold water with a scalded foot. He deserves it!

Leaving them to their own devices, we head for our own room. Juggers goes straight to the great trunk we hauled here with us.

'We'll need to arm the bobbies,' says Juggers.

'What if they don't have a permit, sir?'

'You know, Grasby, you're a strange mix. A man that thinks nothing of clandestine dalliances with all and sundry, when he should be working, worries about other rules and regulations. I made sure the Filey boys were all ex-army. Face it, lad, how many chaps your age do you know who've never carried a gun?'

He's right, and it's a salutary thought. This sceptred little isle of farmers, fisherfolk and shopkeepers has been turned into a place where most men have been in a fight to the death, whether in the First or Second World Wars.

'Bring me your suitcase, Grasby.' When I hand it to him, Juggers packs three pistols and a box of rounds into my old army luggage.

'I can see you suspect there'll be trouble, sir.'

'Not just suspect, lad. I know. I had the word earlier.'

This puzzles me. *Had the word* from whom? I must trust that Juggers has his ways. But I must confess, they're a mystery to me.

Packed up, it's time to head back to Uthley Bay Police Station through the snow. But just after we turn into Kissing Lane, I hear a shout behind us. It echoes in this snowy place.

'You pair! It's time to put you both right this time!'

I turn to see George and his red-haired pal. That they're spoiling for a fight is obvious.

'Sir,' I say. 'The man who's doing the shouting is married to the lass from this morning. You know, with the pram.'

'Oh aye,' says Juggers. His face is impassive.

George and his pal catch up with us.

'Out for a little stroll, are you, ladies?' says he, to much hilarity from his red-haired friend.

Juggers just stares at him, his eyes as blank as I've seen them. Like those of a shark or bird of prey, they seem almost black, focused and intent. I fear the worst.

'Like younger lads, do you?' says George. He's half a head taller than Juggers, and thirty years younger at least.

'I'll give thee one chance,' says Juggers. 'Get yourself home quietly, and we can forget about this. Off you go.' His voice is calm, even.

'Oh aye. Just go home and wait to hear who you've displayed yourself to next. Not likely, old man.'

Without warning, George flashes a bunched fist directly at Juggers's head. I wince, waiting for the blow to connect and that sickening sound of fist on flesh and bone, like the cross between a slap and someone kicking a football. But I'm wrong.

In a trice Juggers ducks under the blow, and before I can blink sets about George with a three-punch combination to the stomach, doubling the fisherman in two. For good measure, Juggers shifts his weight, carrying himself behind his would-be attacker, and twists one of the fisherman's arms round his back, making him squeal. It's all very balletic, you know. As George is gasping for breath, Juggers forces him face down into the snow.

'I'll tell thee something for nothing. I've come across people like you all me life. People that never know when to shut up and walk away. This is why you should listen.' He leans his head into George's.

I want to cheer – to clap, even. But that would be unseemly for a man in my position. So, instead, I turn my attention to George's pal. He's looking on, mouth agape, as though he's just witnessed the impossible. He catches my eye for a split second before he's off, pelting back down Kissing Lane, slipping and sliding as he goes, billows of frozen breath reaching into the air.

'Right, time you learn some manners behind bars, lad.' Juggers hauls a pair of handcuffs from his back pocket, and in a flash, born out of forty years' experience, has them on our local miscreant. 'Grab the bag, Grasby,' says he, nodding to my shabby suitcase, which he dropped, ready to lay into George.

As Juggers pushes him along in the direction of the station, I have a quiet word with the young fisherman. 'Don't go about assaulting police officers. You've not faced me in a fair go yet, you know.'

Of course, I'm safe as houses here. No chance of yours truly being inconvenienced in any way. I rather like seeing wrongdoers face their comeuppance. It's probably at the heart of why I joined up in the first place.

It's with no little pleasure that I look on bright lights spilling from the newly resurrected police station. It's beginning to get dark now, and it all looks quite impressive. One of the young constables greets us at the door. He's staring at our newly arrested prisoner.

'George Beckwith, what a surprise. I've not seen you since I sorted you out at school in Filey. You haven't learned nowt, by the look of things. Shall I take over, sir?' he says to Juggers.

'Aye, do that, lad. What's your name again?'

169

'Wood, sir.'

'That's it, Constable Wood. Get him in the book and charge him with police assault.'

Wood looks at Juggers doubtfully. 'Pardon me, sir. But there isn't a book, if you know what I mean. At least not that we've found as yet.'

'Just note the arrest down in your notebook, lad, until we get things up and running.'

'Custody, sir?'

'Bloody right, it is!' says Juggers.

As Constable Wood takes George Beckwith away, Juggers smiles. 'You know, I've not enjoyed myself as much for years. That's the trouble with the job, Grasby. You're taken from where you're most effective – aye, and happy – and stuck behind a desk. Damn shame, it is. I'd go back on the beat in a moment.'

*With a superintendent's pay, no doubt.* And that leads us to another foible of human nature. Who is really ever happy and content? I'm sure, no matter what one achieves in one's lifetime, few are ever really happy. I always wanted to be a policeman, but there are many days I'd happily chuck it in and do something else. It's not being able to identify that *something else* that's kept me in this job.

We head into what must be the only private office in Uthley Bay Police Station and, yet again, I'm impressed by the Filey contingent's industry – they've managed to light a fire, though it's still in its early stages. From much experience lighting fires at home when I was a child, one of the many chores my father imposed upon me, the construction of the coals looks spot-on. It's a rough pyramidal shape, with plentiful gaps to allow the flames to breathe, little sticks of kindling poking out here and there.

There are two chairs; an old wooden affair, and a rather

grander captain's chair, with a small palisade of wooden batons bearing the weight of a semi-circular armrest. These sit on either side of a plain desk that has been much infested by woodworm. Automatically, I take the plain chair. Juggers, however, objects.

'I can't settle on one of these. Last time I sat in one, when I got up, I took the bloody thing with me.'

But he hasn't lost his sense of superiority. He grabs my plain chair and places it behind the desk. In turn, I put mine down on the other side. Everything is in its place.

'Time for a poke about,' says Juggers, rifling through drawer after drawer on the desk. He's about halfway through this when he stops. He pulls a leatherbound desk diary from it, and sniffs at the binding like a dog. 'Good quality, is this.' Juggers opens the daybook, the like of which you'll see in police stations up and down the country. It literally does what it says, bearing witness to everything that happened in that station on any particular day of the year.

But I see something flutter to the ground when Juggers opens it.

'Boring, is this. Nothing in it but the comings and goings of the days, as you'd expect.'

'Something fell from the pages,' say I.

Juggers cranes his neck and searches the floor.

It's an odd thing, one's health. Juggers took to the altercation in the lane with George like a duck to water. He was utterly calm and unflustered. No sense that he was struggling with the burden of his weight or age. Just the calculated moves of a well-practised street fighter. However, when he appears from behind the desk, having retrieved whatever fell, his face is like a Cox's Pippin, and there are beads of sweat on his forehead.

'That weren't easy,' says he.

'No, I can see,' I reply. 'What is it, sir?'

'Just greed and old age, Grasby.'

'No, what do have in your hand?'

Juggers examines the paper. 'Damn me, it's a bookie's slip. He's written out the ho'ses' names and the odds. Maybe that's how he could afford to go and retire to France, eh?' He hands me the slip, a scribbled-on sheet from a book-maker's notepad, in the full knowledge I am much more au fait with all things equine than he.

I cast my eyes over the horses and must say I haven't heard of any of them, which is most odd, I assure you. And though it doesn't come to me straight away, in a few moments, I have it.

'Sir,' I venture, with no little trepidation, 'I think I may have stumbled upon something. Something bloody import-ant, too.'

'What do you mean? It's a list of the ponies he fancies. Can't see the importance of that.'

'These horses don't exist.'

'How do you know? You're not claiming to know every racehorse in the country, are you?'

'Just about, sir.'

Juggers shakes his head. 'You do waste so much of your time.'

'Maybe not in this case, sir.' I hold up the list between us. For all the world, it looks like someone jotting down his naps for the day. But it's really a warning:

*Blue Stockings – Evens*

*High Tide 14/2*

*Yesterday's Man 2/1 On*

*Run Away – Evens favourite*

*Dirty Business 2/1*

*The American 30/1*

*Dorothy's Dad 30/1*

'I can't see what you're getting at, Grasby,' says Juggers. 'I note the mention of stockings, obviously. But that's a bit tenuous, isn't it?'

'Look more carefully, sir. I mean, *Blue Stockings* and *High Tide*, for a start. The goods are coming on the high tide – the stockings.'

Juggers looks unsure.

'*Yesterday's Man, Run Away*. If this is Constable Armley, he's off, had enough. He's literally yesterday's man.'

Juggers raises an eyebrow.

'It's *Dirty Business*. And I'll lay a wager it's something to do with *The American* and *Dorothy's Dad*, sir. But I can't work out why their odds are so poor.'

It's as though the scales have fallen from Juggers's eyes. 'By heck, Grasby. I think you might be onto something. You're right about the odds, though.'

'Yes, that's a puzzle. May just be for effect. But you'll note that *Yesterday's Man* and *Run Away* are absolute certainties, if you go by those odds. So, he's definitely had all he can take, and he's off. That's for sure.'

'And the poor bugger has tried to pass the information on in the subtlest way he can. Obviously in the hope some bright spark will work it out.'

'Well, he has,' say I, less than modestly.

'Took a bloody year, though. Whoever cleared this place wants sacking.'

'We just need to work out who these people are, sir.'

'Well done. Well done indeed! Haven't I always said you can be an inspired detective, when you're not chasing the fairer sex or gambling?'

Dash it all, even my praise is tainted these days. But this is a find. Good for me!

# 22

A quiet evening in the Trout is to follow. We've to be up at four, ready to hit the waves. So, Juggers decides that it's time we have an early night.

Now, normally, as you might have guessed, I'd be less than happy about being told when to go to bed. But it's been a bloody tiring day that seems to have gone on for a week.

Before we leave the police station, I ask Keithley to find out where we can contact Constable Armley in France. It may take a while to find him. But as recent events dictate, what he knows may well be priceless. It can't have been easy being the only policeman around for miles, considering what's been going on in Uthley Bay. Thankfully, he was lucky enough to miss out on the murders. Or perhaps it was his presence that stopped them. Time will tell.

Meanwhile, Juggers issues our three men with sidearms and ammunition. To be fair to them, they make little fuss. Two of the bobbies are ex-army, while the third, Herbert Watson, is of farming stock, so well used to handling firearms. One of them is to accompany Ogden Barclay home, and stay with him, while the other two take turns to kip and keep an eye on George Beckwith. They've to sort a roster between themselves. I must say, Juggers has always been good at this, allowing people to use their own initiative, and not treating grown men like infants.

We leave for the hotel to the braying of George Beckwith demanding to see a doctor, as he thinks his arm is broken. Tough! As I used to hear the GIs I fought with during the war say. Wood made him some sandwiches with the back-enders of a loaf and some meat paste he acquired from somewhere.

Back at the Trout, Juggers and I discuss the case and what we know so far as we eat some soup and sandwiches sent up to our room. Then, as we're getting ready to sleep, Juggers produces a bottle of malt whisky, along with two small glasses.

'Nightcap, lad,' he says.

And it's most welcome. As the spirit warms my gullet, I relax almost instantly. It's then I remember tomorrow is Christmas Eve. Instead of shopping for last-minute presents or decorating the tree, we'll be on the North Sea in a vessel that has most certainly seen better days.

After a couple of drams, and Juggers's pungent pipe, it's time for bed. I'm on the chair with my feet up on the pouffe again. It's comfy enough, and with my earplugs as defence against Juggers's snoring, I soon slip off to sleep.

My rest, though, is fitful. I dream of the great galleons of old, filled to bursting with illicit hosiery. Juggers, complete with eye patch, is making me walk the plank. And the shock when I plunge off the end and land not in the sea but in snow is jarring.

It's with this start I awake to the ringing of Juggers's alarm clock – yes, he's brought one. It's four in the morning.

Soon, I'm padding along to the bathroom. My mind wanders as I'm shaving. I wonder what my poor mother would have made of my father's dalliance with Gaunt. But she was a kind soul, so would probably have nodded and flashed that smile I'll never forget. She'd have put it down to life's rich tapestry. The world would be a better place if there were more people like my mother.

'Everyone is in their own canoe, whether they share the same house or the same bed,' she used to say. 'You must give people room to breathe in a relationship, Francis.'

This advice came hot on the heels of one of my youthful broken hearts, of which I had plenty. Not sure which canoe I'm in. Probably one with a great hole in the bottom. Hope this doesn't extend to Ogden Barclay's fishing boat.

'The right lassie will come along. You'll see,' she would always say.

Well, mother of mine, whoever she is, she better make it quick, or I'll be an old man. I'm only a kick in the backside away from forty, sadly.

Just then, as I'm dabbing shaving soap from my chin with a towel, the most melancholy thought crosses my mind. What if the *right girl* has already come and gone?

I remember Deedee's beautiful cornflower-blue eyes, and her bright, welcoming smile. She was working for the American government when I met her last year, and I can't seem to forget her. She wasn't the person I thought, but then, which one of us is? We all have our own carapace, which we deploy to face the world. I hope our paths will cross again one day.

'Are you in there for the duration?' Juggers is tapping gently on the door, with that half-whisper, half-shout thing people do early in the morning when there are others sleeping.

On the way back to the room, I stare at the door to my father and Hetty's little love nest. The honeymoon suite, indeed!

As I dress, I'm glad I brought a jumper, a bloody warm old cricket sweater, minus the badge. I stare out of the window over the dark sea, a shiver threading its way down my spine, and it doesn't want to stop. I have no particular fear of the sea. Always quite liked it, in fact. We always spent Easter at Scarborough when I was a child. This would invariably involve a fishing trip on a boat, from which we'd usually return cold and fishless. Still, I found the whole thing bracing, with the hint of danger.

Mind you, these jaunts took place with spring in the air, on calm waters. December's North Sea is a rather different prospect.

Juggers manages to fit two jumpers on under his overcoat. This serves to make him look even more rotund than normal.

Our trudge down to the harbour isn't a long one. But my goodness, it's cold. When I mention this to Juggers, he cheers me up.

'It'll be a lot chillier out at sea. Aye, bitter, likely.'

Good-oh, just the thing for a chap whose only sustenance has been a couple of cups of tea, and some dubious hotel biscuits left in our room.

It's as black as the Earl of Haig's waistcoat as we plod through the accumulated snow. When we get to the harbour, it's plain the rest of the fleet has sailed, leaving behind Barclay's old tub and the sleek green fishing vessel we spotted on first arriving in Uthley Bay.

Ogden Barclay is waiting for us, cowering with Constable Wood in the lee of a wooden building on the quay, the faint glow of the harbour lights picking out the two figures.

'There's to be a sea haar,' says Barclay with a frown. 'It'll be all right until we get a mile or so out. If it's too bad, we'll have to turn back. Won't see nowt in conditions like that.

Aye, and you run the risk of collision into the bargain. We'll see how she goes.'

'Do you want me aboard, sir?' says Wood to Juggers.

'No, lad. You get back to the station and get some kip. You three know what you've to be about.'

'Just as well, because they won't get any reinforcements today. There's no way the snowploughs are getting through drifts at Wally's Hill or Dugden's Fell. The road's blocked both ends. When it's this bad here, you can guarantee it'll be worse back on the moor roads,' says our cheery captain.

This news isn't unexpected. Though at the same time, it's unwelcome.

'Follow me, gents,' says Barclay, coughing fit to wake the dead as he steps onto the fine vessel between the pier and his boat.

Dutifully, we do as we're asked, parading across the snowbound deck to the other side of the green fishing boat. Barclay's boat is considerably smaller, and notwithstanding the gap between them, the deck we're on is a good yard higher than the one we need to get to.

'How does one go about this caper?' says Juggers.

'That's right, I'm forgetting you lads aren't sailors. Just watch me, and you won't go wrong. It's what we do every day. All the boats aren't the same height.'

With this, Ogden Barclay takes a couple of steps back – a bit like a leg spinner – and flings himself off one fishing boat onto the other. I'm rather surprised when he tumbles forward and lands flat on his face in the snow on the deck of his own dilapidated vessel. I mean, how many times has the man done this? It doesn't bode well for us.

He looks up at us with a smile. 'Right, who's next? Just aim for the bit where I landed, and you'll be fine. There's enough snow about to cushion a fall if you make a misstep.'

It's typical of seafarers in my experience. If he was showing us the *right* way to go about things, goodness, we'll likely break our necks!

'You next, Grasby,' says Juggers. 'I'd like to study that jump again.'

I must say, though some things send me into an instant funk, I'm not too worried by heights. That said, I'm not usually throwing myself off them. And I find that dark gap between the boats very off-putting. It's pitch black down there, and there's a lapping, sucking noise that makes one feel like a giant is licking his lips, waiting to swallow me whole.

'I say, Mr Barclay. What would happen if one lands down there?' I point to the gap.

Barclay removes his greasy cap and scratches his head. 'Well, if you don't knock yourself out and drown, at this time of year the cold will kill you long before we can fish you out.' He shrugs. 'My advice would be to jump over the few inches the way I did. But each to their own.'

He's a bluff cove, I'll give him that. Especially when he made a backside of it himself. But I feel the nerves in the pit of my stomach that always indicate I'm about something dangerous. I remind myself that I've jumped out of a plane over occupied France, so how much more dangerous is this? Mark you, I don't have a parachute. Bad luck.

I catch my courage, take my spinner's steps backwards and fling myself into the freezing Yorkshire morning air. Before I know it, I see the deck of Barclay's boat rise up to meet me. I bend my legs, ready to cushion my landing. But when I do, I slip forward on the slick snow. My heart races for a second, until the wiry figure of Barclay halts my progress by grabbing my shoulders.

'There, that weren't too bad. Need to work on planting your feet better. All told though, a bloody good effort.'

*Huh, I did better than you, methinks.* As is the case when one has overcome trepidation, there follows a brief period of euphoria. I feel as though I could jump round the harbour. And for the first time since I arrived in Uthley Bay, I'm as warm as toast. I even consider removing my overcoat; though I realize this feeling is a passing one, and just stand there with a broad grin.

When I look up at Juggers, he's most definitely not smiling. In fact, he's as pale as a ghost.

'It's not as bad as it looks, sir,' say I by way of encouragement.

'It is with my knees, lad. If I land like that, I'll spend the rest of my life parading about with bent legs. Oh no, I'll have to take a different approach. You be ready to grab my legs, Grasby.'

With this, he lowers himself down onto his backside, and shoots his stubby pins over the gunwale of the larger vessel.

'I'll slide forward. You grab me shins and guide me aboard, got it?'

'Sort of, sir. Are you sure this is going to work? I mean, you'll have to propel yourself over this damned gap.'

'What a performance,' says Barclay. 'I'll stand by to clean up the mess.'

I'm beginning to bear an unreasonable dislike for old Ogden.

'You're getting well paid by the constabulary. You'll damn well help out, Barclay.'

I should have known Juggers would brook no nonsense.

'If you say so, Superintendent.' He turns to me. 'I'll grab

one leg and you get the other. I hope he knows what he's about.'

'Never mind the chit-chat. I'll count to three. Be ready, you pair.'

There's a moment of hesitation that's almost palpable.

'Right,' says Juggers. 'One, two, three!'

Juggers shuffles forward a bit on his backside, then pushes himself off the other boat like we used to do when sledging as children. Unfortunately, his is not the same frictionless passage, for though his legs are heading towards us, they're not close enough to grab.

Juggers is now teetering on the edge of the gunwale, the merest part of his ample backside the only thing between him and the freezing sea.

'Lever yourself further down!' shouts Barclay.

With one more effort – likely all that's in him – Juggers forces himself off the gunwale and hurtles towards us. I make to grab his right knee but end up with his ankle. Barclay, on the other hand, has grabbed Juggers's left thigh with both hands, and is holding on for dear life. It's a bit like trying to move an extended ladder. Under Juggers's not inconsiderable weight, we're tottering about on the deck, trying not to drop him.

Suddenly, I feel a dreadful pain in my head, and wonder if I'm having one of those *shocks* I described earlier. I realize that Juggers has grabbed a huge handful of my hair and is using it to try and right himself.

I yelp in pain. But it's done the trick for my boss. With Barclay straining with the solo effort of keeping Juggers upright, I try to grab his right leg again. And though he's loosened his grip on my hair, it's like trying to balance an elephant on a plank of wood. I look on in horror, when, as if the world has suddenly decided to move much more slowly, Barclay slips on the snowy deck, dragging us with him.

We land in a collective heap, Juggers snorting like a bull heading for a herd of cows.

'Aye, that weren't as bad as I thought it might be,' says he, holding his hand out for me to pull him off the deck.

'Not too bad?' shouts Barclay. 'I think I've broken my ankle.'

By the time I get Juggers to his feet, judging by the beet-root colour of his face, he's absolutely done in.

Barclay is walking rather gingerly up and down on the deck, clearly favouring his right ankle.

'When we get back, remind me to break out the rope ladder from down below,' says he.

'The what?' says Juggers.

'A rope ladder. Are you deaf?'

'No, but you must be stupid. Why didn't you fetch it in the first place?' says Juggers.

'I didn't think, sorry.'

During this exchange, I'm trying to get my hair back into some sort of shape.

'You don't have a comb, do you, sir?'

He takes me in with a chilling stare for a few moments.

'Bugger off, Grasby!' says he. Quite unkindly, in my opinion.

Anxious now I'm aboard, I watch Ogden Barclay at work in the wheelhouse, likely trying to get us underway. He's scratching his head again. What should surely be second nature after all these years afloat is taking an age. After what seems like an eternity, I hear the engine putter weakly into life, and wonder how it will stand up against the great North Sea.

With me still fretting, we leave port, heading out into

the cold, dark sea. Juggers is complaining that he may well have jarred his knee too, and his backside is wet from hunkering down on the snowy deck of the other boat. Meanwhile, Ogden Barclay is exaggerating a limp as he heads out of the wheelhouse. And I plant my trilby firmly down over my ruined hair.

I always find that unhappy hair does nothing for one's confidence. I'm lucky to have a thick thatch of auburn hair, of which I'm inordinately proud. My mother used to compliment me on it. Of course, the colour comes from my Scottish roots. Something my father has never been slow to point out.

'Too much Scotch in you, Francis. That's why you're so restless,' he often says. Though quite what restlessness has to do with the Scots and one's hair colour has yet to be discussed. During a very brief period, when I was between sixteen and seventeen, I seriously considered following my father into the Church. However, he thought it unlikely that the *C of E* would see fit to employ anyone who wasn't of pure English stock, making the Church sound more like a fascist organization than the institution we like to think of as being so benign. There's always been a touch of Oliver Cromwell about my father, you know.

Thankfully, I quickly lost my ecclesiastical notions when I considered how miserable everyone seemed to be. Vicars fitted nicely into three categories, as far as I could tell. The first, those like my father who wanted to take the Church back to the seventeenth century; then nervous chaps who finger their dog collars, waiting for a knock on the vicarage door from the bishop to tell them they are surplus to requirements; and lastly the breed who, despite being employed by the Church, aren't religious at all, and don't really believe anything they preach. My father reserves his

184

greatest opprobrium for this group, and I'm sure would happily see them burning at the stake, should such an action still be tolerated. He reckons they'll pull it all down brick by brick, eventually.

Therefore, all things considered, I opted for the police, and of course a rather unwelcome sojourn into the army. That reminds me how easily kept my hair was back then. There's nothing like a short back and sides to keep things tidy, you know.

As I feel a ghastly gust of freezing wind pulling at my trilby, I discover that Ogden Barclay's boat is called the *Empty Heart*, which is indeed a gloomy name for any vessel. However, as I hear it putter, creak and groan as it ploughs an uncertain path through the waves, I feel the name may well be appropriate.

'How long until we get to where we think all this skulduggery is afoot, Barclay?' shouts Juggers into the wheelhouse. Ogden had been informed of our broad theory, as he would be the one navigating to a likely spot for exchanging the cargo.

'A good two hours,' our skipper replies. 'And then there's no guarantees. Just a best guess based on what you've told me, that's all.'

It's now a thought springs to my mind. If we do come across a group of tiny fishing boats surrounding a larger vessel filling their holds with illicit hosiery, what are we to do? I mean, they're bound to spot us out here at sea. They even know Barclay's boat. Not a hard spot, mind you. Does Juggers intend to make a sprint back for port to rouse the authorities, or are we to open fire on the smugglers with our pistols, in an echo of sea battles of old?

Oh gosh, I do feel bloody uncomfortable.

# 23

I intend to question Juggers on his intentions. But as I'm about to, he grabs my arm and tells me that Barclay thinks we should go below and have some tea. I must admit, as this sounds infinitely preferable to standing on deck, quietly shedding the family jewels, I agree instanter.

Juggers shuffles off to a hatch, which he pulls open, no doubt as instructed by Barclay. Below, in near-complete darkness, one can discern a steep set of steps heading down into the abyss. Of course, utterly undaunted, Juggers takes to them as though he were jumping out of a car on a sunny day in York.

Before I can comment, the place is illuminated by the torch that Juggers has produced from his coat pocket. I swear, he's like a veritable ironmonger.

'Stick on your torch too. Barclay says there's a lantern down here.'

'Sorry, sir. I don't carry one,' say I, rather sheepishly.

'You what?'

'I had a torch when I was in uniform, obviously. For checking locks on the nightshift, and suchlike. But I've never seen the point of having one in plain clothes, sir.'

Juggers shakes his head in the sepia light of the torch. 'I don't know. That's the whole art of being prepared, is that.

Carry stuff you don't need day to day but might be essential at some point in the future – like now! You'll be telling me you don't have your truncheon next.' He laughs at the thought.

Luckily, Juggers thinks this such an unlikely occurrence that he doesn't question me any further on the matter. In actual fact, I stopped carrying a truncheon not long after I became a detective. In the absence of the special baton pockets sewn into police uniform trousers, one can hang a truncheon from a belt by use of a leather thong. But it's so unsightly as to be utterly impractical, certainly for yours truly. Though if Juggers had asked, I'd have been happy to remind him that I'm carrying a Colt pistol under my armpit.

Soon enough, resourceful man that he is, Juggers locates the big storm lantern and sets it into life with one of his long pipe matches. It produces a cosy, flickering glow that would be quite welcoming, were it not for the shambles below deck of the *Empty Heart*. There are two unmade bunks bearing filthy sheets, a tiny table about which are two chairs, and, worst of all, a bucket with a toilet seat affixed to its rim. It's hanging in a rough metal frame, no doubt fabricated by our captain himself.

'Goodness, how primitive,' I say to Juggers. 'One will just have to cross one's legs until we get back to port.'

'I'll never understand how you managed in the army. Places I had to bunk down in in the first war make this look like a palace.'

Mind you, with a brother who shovels shit for a living, the great giblet-packer's idea of what constitutes a palace is no doubt far removed from mine.

'Be a good lad and get the tea on. Oh, and don't forget to make a cup for Barclay. He's gasping, apparently.'

187

I might have known. You know, I must make more tea than any inspector in the country. Some will say that's because I move in exalted circles. True or not, when I locate the teamaking facilities, my love of the beverage is almost utterly banished. There, beside four stained tin mugs, is a tiny metal sink that looks for all the world as though an elephant has just defecated in it. Behind this disgusting artefact is a half-finished bottle of milk, wedged onto a little shelf, no doubt stopping it from tumbling over in a heavy sea.

I sniff at the milk tentatively and discover to my amazement that it is still fresh. At the side of the sink is a gas burner, atop which sits what looks like the oldest kettle in the world. Holding my head as far from the process as possible, I fill this kettle from the single tap above the sink. It sputters in some fetid-looking water, then I proceed to light the stove with the help of my cigarette lighter. It blooms into life like an internal combustion engine, but soon settles to a steady enough blue flame, upon which I place the kettle.

The space is tiny. So, when I turn round, I'm standing almost cheek by jowl with Juggers.

'I think I'll give tea a miss, sir.'

'Why, in case you need to pee in that bucket?'

'Not really. I daresay I could force myself if necessary. I just don't like the look of the mugs.'

'You're drinking boiling water, man! Get into it. Look at Barclay, he's lasted long enough on it.'

I'd like to draw attention to his haggard, pock-marked face. But I know Juggers would dismiss this immediately. Therefore, it's for the sake of peace that I locate a little tin caddy that holds sugar at one side of a divide, with tea on the other. Though for the life of me, I can't find a tea strainer.

'No strainer, sir. I suppose that knocks tea on the head.'

'The leaves will fall to the bottom! This isn't Betty's tea-room in Harrogate! Do you know, I've never seen so much fuss over a cup of tea in me life. Now serve the brew up. I need to tell you something.'

I must say, this statement makes tea from filthy mugs seem like a minor inconvenience. For in my experience, when Juggers has something to relate – especially in a private setting – it's rarely good.

I choose the best-looking mug, rinse it under the tap and pour my tea into it, then select another mug for Juggers. I hand it over before clambering back on deck with a mug for Barclay, only scalding myself twice in the process. Soon, Juggers and I are sitting round the tiny table as the floor moves beneath our feet at the pleasure of the waves.

'Right.' Juggers takes a sip of tea and winces at the result. He carries on regardless. 'We both have our doubts about you-know-who.' He points his right index finger skywards.

I frown at this. 'Not me, sir. I'm a confirmed believer. I'm surprised to find you're not.'

For a fleeting moment, Juggers looks confused. Then it dawns on him. 'No, not *the man upstairs*. I mean Barclay,' he says in that whispered shout he's becoming so good at.

'Ah, yes, I have you now, sir.' I'm feeling like a bit of a twit, to be honest.

'Our captain told me he had a good idea where the exchange might be taking place. If he has anything to do with this stocking smuggling, he won't take us there, but make some excuse. Any funny business when we get there, and I've taken steps.' Juggers taps the side of his nose.

Right, so we don't know if we can trust Barclay. But if it turns out we can't, Juggers has it all in hand. Good-oh! I must say, I find all this on-the-hoof stuff rather alarming. If I was in charge, I'd have called up the Royal Navy, and they could have jolly well blown the smugglers to smithereens. I know this sounds rather brutal, but better them than me. Under the current circumstances, by Juggers's devising, we're out at sea in a terrible craft, with a skipper we can't trust. I don't like the odds, I tell you. And the very thought of our skipper reminds me of poor old Perkin. I don't want to be next! There's something else I can't put my finger on, but it won't settle in my mind.

Back on deck, we're not much longer into our voyage when the darkness becomes thicker, somehow. There's a taint to the air, too. Nothing unpleasant. But all of a sudden the sea smells much more like the sea, if you know what I mean. And Juggers and Barclay's chatter starts to sound as though they're in a very small room, not out under the elements.

'That's the haar setting in. Just like I said,' says Barclay.

'You never mind the haar,' says Juggers. 'Just concentrate on that heading.'

My goodness, Juggers has suddenly become all nautical. There are clearly things I don't know about this trip. But it seems to me as though sailing headlong into nothingness isn't a good idea. I'm even more alarmed when I look back down the length of the vessel and can barely see the light above the wheelhouse, nor the one inside it.

'I say,' I shout in the padded darkness. 'Don't you think we should turn back?'

'Shut up, Grasby!' the disembodied voice of Juggers returns. 'I know what I'm about.'

'You better had,' says Barclay, also unseen. 'Either that or you'll have to pay me for a new vessel. Aye, and they don't come cheap, neither. That's if we survive!'

I probably have enough cash in my pocket to replace the *Empty Heart*, but I won't give a fig for that if I'm drowning. Dash it all! How on earth do I find myself in such situations? It's a question that regularly springs to mind.

As if things weren't bad enough, I hear the mournful tone of a foghorn in the near distance.

'That's the foghorn at Dunnet Head,' says Barclay. 'I'm turning back.'

What follows sounds like a wrestling match on the wireless. There are various grunts and thuds, followed by a strangled yelp. I feel as though I should make my way aft to find out what's afoot. But as this will entail walking into a black nothingness, towards the shrouded gloom of a misted light, I decide that I must deploy the only Grasby tactic and nail my colours to the mast. Well, in this case, the bow, to which I'm clinging for dear life.

You won't be surprised to discover that I spent much of my childhood reading adventure novels by the likes of H. Rider Haggard, John Buchan and Robert Louis Stevenson. It's *Treasure Island* that crosses my mind now, and I worry that we have perhaps been boarded by ruthless smugglers, who have subdued Juggers and Barclay in the murk, and are now stealthily making their way towards me, cutlasses firmly grasped between clenched teeth, or whatever the modern equivalent is.

I crouch at the bow and await some dread shape to emerge from the murk.

I can hear my heart beating in my chest, as everything else is silence, save for the lapping of water at the sides of the boat, and the throaty putter of the engine. Even it seems muffled.

They tell me that the human instinct when faced with danger is to flee or stand and fight. Since the former – my

191

default inclination – isn't an option, I must gird my loins and be prepared to fight for my life, or to feel a collared stocking slipped over my neck, and tightened until my eyes pop out.

Sure enough, out of the misty darkness emerges a huddled figure. You'd need to have good eyesight to spot it, but luckily my late mother was a strong believer in the power of carrots, feeding them to me by the dozen when I was a nipper. I can see a dark shadow in the fog. I scream at the top of my voice, sending an unseen seagull squawking off into the gloom.

'What the bloody hell has come over you, Grasby?' says Juggers.

'Sorry, sir,' I mutter in embarrassment. 'I had it in my head that you and Barclay had been attacked by boarders. Quite lost my reason.'

'Do you know, you have the strangest notions of anyone I've ever worked with,' says Juggers. 'I'm not sure you're facing a ball with everything you should be, lad. Half a bat, at best.'

'But I heard a scuffle,' say I, doing my best to straighten up.

'That were me and Barclay. He were trying to make way for me to get out that damned tiny wheelhouse. He's an irascible bugger.'

Pot calling the kettle black, as far as I'm concerned. Maybe he should have stayed in the Co-op Fleshings or wherever it was.

We make our way carefully back to said wheelhouse, Juggers leading the way. Well, better he falls in than me.

There's Ogden Barclay, standing quite the thing by the binnacle, a big smile on his face.

'Mr Juggers said you'd be up there hiding. He fell over that capstan – he's harder to move than a full net of cod, and that's a fact. That's the racket thee heard.' He laughs uproariously.

Juggers appears behind me. 'Sorry, lad. But I might have known you'd have some odd idea. You have a healthy imagination, that's for sure. Doesn't make you a bad man, mind.'

*Au contraire.* My imagination has been responsible for the solving of many a crime that stumped my less inspired colleagues.

'What about this fog?' say I. 'How on earth will we find anything in this?'

'We've decided to go along at a steady pace,' says Juggers. 'It's do or die, young man.'

I always think there's steel in the older generation that I have somehow missed out on. Maybe it's living through two world wars that's done it. But they seem to be much more sanguine as to their personal fate than us younger chaps. Well, this one at any rate.

I glance at Barclay as he grips the ship's wheel, or whatever it's called. There's no sign of the big, gold wedding ring I spotted on our first acquaintance. Perhaps he doesn't wear it out at sea in case it gets lost.

Now all there is to do is wait, as we make our way through the darkness to goodness knows where. I study Juggers's face in the gloom. It's set like granite.

# 24

Some things in life can be relied upon. And it is with a certain weariness I read the time on the luminous display of my wartime Omega, only to find we've been on the waves for almost three hours. I have been huddled under a tarpaulin next to a hawser roll, and despite the cold and growing fear, I must have dropped off.

It's another Grasby trait, you know. Legend has it that my grandfather – the bishop – once fell asleep during an audience with the Archbishop of Canterbury. It's said that the senior bishop of the Church took this in his stride, making sure my grandfather was covered by a blanket, and buggered off to do something else. Quite what went through my grandfather's mind on waking up in the archbishop's palace, covered by a blanket, is open to interpretation. Though my father tells the tale that he folded said blanket neatly, got up, and left the place, quite unconcerned.

I only remember my grandfather fleetingly, from when I was a very small child. My mother told me that he was the only person she'd ever seen my father defer to. And that she was convinced he was scared of him until my grandfather's dying day.

Well done, Gramps! That's what I say. I wish you were still around to witness your only son kicking about without his dog collar, in the company of a superannuated seer.

On the subject of seeing, as more time rolls by, I'm sure I can see limpid sunshine through the dolorous gloom. It's like the headlight of a car in a London fog, so diffused it's hard to discern a shape or purpose.

I spend a few minutes watching this until something else attracts my attention. I swear I can hear voices on the roke-muffled air.

Juggers and Barclay are chatting away companionably enough in the wheelhouse. I stand and hold my index finger to silently warn them to shut up. Juggers makes his way over.

'Can't you hear it, sir?' say I.

He listens, one ear cocked. 'Damned if I can hear anything.'

But though the sound is modulating on the air, I catch another burst of chatter. It's the voices of young men, laughing, joking. It's either real or I'm back to some point in the war, my mind finally packed up and wandered off; I wouldn't blame it. This, of course, isn't impossible. I worked with a young sergeant during the war who was normal in every way, apart from the fact he was convinced that his dead mother was whispering advice into his ear every hour of the day. He used to stop in mid-flow of conversation to reply to her. Otherwise, he was a bloody good soldier.

'I can hear it!' says Juggers, and turns to Barclay. 'Cut the engine,' he relates, aided by improvised sign language, a flat hand to the throat.

The steady putter of the *Empty Heart*'s engine stops, and we're floating on an ominously silent sea.

I hear the noises again. And without saying anything,

Juggers waves me back to the wheelhouse, where we join Barclay.

'Where are we?' asks Juggers.

Barclay attends a tattered map under the dim light of the little wheelhouse binnacle with his brass magnifying glass. 'Where you wanted to be, Superintendent. It took a bit longer because of the haar. But by my calculations, we're just off Wicker's Bank.'

'Good! Well done, Barclay.' Juggers has a broad smile spread across his face. 'This fog is a blessing in disguise.'

'How so?' say I, hearing voices at much closer range now.

'Because we can stay put here, undercover, awaiting events.'

Just as he says this, it's as though some celestial body flicks a switch. In seconds the fog lifts, and we find ourselves a few hundred yards away from a large vessel with a sweeping metal prow. Around it are dotted four fishing boats by my count, too far away to identify. They're busy filling large nets with wooden crates. All are being transferred from the large ship to the small boats by way of two big cranes, or whatever it is you call such things at sea.

But just as we can see them, they can see us. We are both frozen on a little patch of sea, amidst a clearing in the fog, eyeing each other like baying stags.

I hear a few words that sound for all the world like German but aren't. However, their meaning is clear enough.

'Quick, Mr Barclay, get the engine back on. They intend to come after us!'

As Ogden Barclay goes about his business, I see Juggers stand with his legs apart, a huge smile on his chubby face.

From the vessels in front of us, the last thing I hear is 'Go and get them!' before Barclay engages the putter of our engine once more and describes a neat circle on the waves with the *Empty Heart*. Soon, we're dashing off towards a bank of fog. I say *dashing*, but I really mean something resembling a robust meander, the limit of which the vessel is capable.

As I glance behind, I note the fishing boats are in pursuit. The larger vessel slowly receding into the murk.

Less speedily than I'd have liked, we breach the haar and are once more enveloped in our own little world. However, I have no delusions as to the nature of the chasing pack. These are vicious criminals, who have certainly killed people. I can still hear their calls, and the syncopated thud from their diesel engines.

I peer at Juggers through the gloom. He's still smiling. But he's doing something else, fondling an object between both hands. It's his police-issue pistol.

Juggers raises the pistol above his head with a straight arm and delivers a three-shot volley into the air. Gosh, he's deliberately giving away our position. It's stupid, like a cocksure cowboy yelling and halloing as the Apache creep up from behind. Yes, I know I read too many potboilers. Sorry, it's the way I'm made.

'You damned fool!' shouts Barclay from the door of the wheelhouse. 'You're going to bring them down on us!'

It's now that everything seems to happen at once. A massive shadow appears from the direction of the diffused sun, and a split-second later the *Empty Heart* shifts under my feet like jelly. It's one snooker ball hitting another. We're being deflected out of the way by something much larger than ourselves.

Needless to say, I end up on my backside, almost battering my head off the gunwale. I see Juggers tumble too, his pistol flying through the air like a deadly boomerang, butt over barrel.

A shot rings out. Now I'm beginning to understand what's happening, despite my shock and confusion. The ship delivering crates onto the fishing boats has been following us all the time, merely by an alternative route. It's rammed us, and now we're helpless. Judging by its list to port, the *Empty Heart* is sinking. My days are going to end in the freezing North Sea, as my ever-slowing breaststroke gradually fails, before I'm consigned to Davy Jones's locker. That or a bullet through the head from a stocking smuggler. Either way, this isn't how I want to go. Damn, I don't even have a lifejacket!

I've survived a world war, only to die in the Battle of the Stocking.

# 25

O ur boat is now listing at an angle of almost forty-five
degrees. I'm holding on to various ropes, fish boxes
or anything that will prevent me from tipping into the sea.
As I glance across the slanting deck, I see Juggers desperately holding on to the side of the boat, a look of extreme
irritation on his face. For a fleeting second, it crosses my
mind that it's an unusual way to express his inner feelings
when he's clearly about to die. I expect he'll shake his fist at
the heavens, cursing his luck.

*Wait, I hear a voice.* Yet again, a dark shadow appears
over my head, just about where Juggers is clinging to the
gunwale.

'I'm throwing rope ladders down. Grab them! We'll turn
the light on you.'

The accent is odd-sounding and familiar all at once.

Suddenly, my grey world is illuminated in a blindingly
bright light, just as the *Empty Heart* lets out a splintering
groan and lists over even further.

I thank my mother for all those carrots when I see what
looks like an unfurling flag. However, it's grey-brown and
colourless, and much too long and thin to be a standard of
any kind. It dawns on me; this is one of the rope ladders.

I take a deep breath, as though I'm climbing Mont Blanc,

and grab various nautical detritus hand-over-hand, making my way up the slanting deck to where I can see the ladder flapping freely under the illuminated mist.

'Grasby, lad. Give me a hand up!'

I manage to grab the bottom of the rope ladder, leaning across to Juggers, my other hand outstretched. But just as our fingers touch, the roll of the sea pulls me up, away from my superior.

'Come on, get up the ladder!' shouts a voice from above.

With strength I never thought I possessed, I drag myself up the slimy rungs. Eventually, I feel a strong grip on my wrist, and thank all that is holy as I'm pulled aboard this larger vessel, landing in a heap on the deck.

You'll be aware – as always when my life's at stake – I'm in a damned funk. Now that I've been saved from a demise in the watery depths, all I have to worry about is being shot by furious smugglers. Even though I'm flat out, I raise my hands above my head in meek surrender.

'Don't hurt me, please. I'll tell you all I know. Don't shoot!' I can hear my teeth chatter with a cold I don't think I've ever felt before.

The reply to my plea is rather confusing.

'Poor chap, must have banged his head. Thinks he's back in the war. Away below with him and break out the rum, Chief.'

Whoever this smuggler is, he must be of the kind, generous variety. And though I'm by no means mentally incapacitated, a good glug of rum will do wonders for my nerves, which are at breaking point, I must admit.

I'm aware that I'm being half-carried down a gangway. The cold air disappears, to be replaced by the warmth of a large cabin.

'You stay there, mate. I'll fetch you a blanket and a tot of that rum.'

This angel, whoever he is, has a distinct Cockney twang. I instantly think of the porter at the Trout.

'Thanks, Wilf, that's very kind of you.'

My rescuer chuckles as he leaves the cabin. 'You're thinking of someone else, me old china. I'm Harry, not Wilf.'

I sit in silence for a minute or two. This peace is broken when I hear a familiar voice call my name.

'Grasby! Where the devil are you?'

It's Juggers, and he's not happy – not happy at all, by the sound of it.

'Father, is that you?' say I, lying back on the chair, making sure it looks as though a bang to the head was responsible for me not managing to grab his hand and pull him to safety. He and Barclay must have climbed another rope ladder.

At this moment, I hear another set of feet.

'Excuse me, sir. The old man says this gentleman is to have a large tot of rum.'

'Don't be daft,' says Juggers brusquely. 'He's away with the fairies. He thinks I'm his father – or mother – I'm not sure which. He's likely been walloped on the head by flying debris. The worst thing you can give in that case is alcohol. Give it here.'

I open one eye just enough to see Juggers grab a tiny brass mug and knock back the contents in one glug.

'Aye, that's better,' says he, licking his lips. 'I'll have another, if you don't mind, lad.'

'I can only distribute rum on orders from the captain, sir. I can ask him, if you'd like?'

'Don't be daft. I'm a captain of police. It's the same

bloody thing. You cut along and get that rum. That's an order!'

'Are you fetching my cocoa, Mummy?' say I, playing along with the ga-ga routine. Yes, I'm bloody fed up that Juggers has dispatched my rum. But it's better than facing his wrath.

'My goodness, you must have taken a right bang on the head,' he replies.

'Father,' say I. 'Pray for me. I don't want to go to hell.'

It's tricky being devious. Best not take it too far, is my motto. However, in this case, I still feel I haven't played out the string as far as I can. I sit up, looking intentionally startled – which isn't a lie, when you think about it.

'Who the bloody hell are you?' I enquire of Juggers less than politely.

'It's me, Arthur Juggers. Your superintendent, lad.'

Just as he says this, the second tot arrives.

'Good, you're up,' says Harry. He hands the little brass mug to Juggers. 'How's he doing?' Harry points to his head.

Juggers takes another monumental slug of rum. 'It's plain he isn't in his right mind. He's one of the bravest we have, is our Frank, you know. He'll need a medic sharpish.'

Gosh, I'm so touched by this, I feel tears welling up in my eyes. Who'd have thought Juggers held me in such esteem? Especially since I nearly let him drown not ten minutes ago.

I stare at him as he stands in a puddle created by his dripping clothes.

'Best get you pair something to wear,' says Harry. 'You'll catch your death in that clobber, lads.' With that, he's off again to find us dry figs.

'You're very wet,' say I, keeping it all going for a bit longer. 'Been for a swim, old chap?'

202

'Aye, something like that,' says Juggers. 'But you're as wet as me.'

I adopt an intentionally confused expression. 'You know, I was sure I saw a man who looked just like you jumping from the sea like a seal.' I lean forward. 'You were in your birthday suit.' I place my hand before my mouth to stifle a giggle.

Juggers makes an unhappy face. 'Seems as though you're beginning to remember things again. Try to rest.'

Another person arrives in our cabin. He's in a sailor's uniform. He whispers something in Juggers's ear.

'Are you sure?' says he, a note of incredulity in his voice.

The sailor nods gravely, turns on his heel and removes himself from the cabin.

'Damn and blast!' says Juggers, banging his fist on the superstructure of the boat, sending a spray of drips all over the place. 'Damn and blast!'

High time I grasped reality, methinks.

'Sir, what on earth's the matter?' I look around the cabin as though I've never seen it before.

'You're back in the land of the sane, then. I thought you'd finally lost it.' Juggers rubs his hand across his face and sighs. 'I've some bad news, if you're up for it, Frank?'

Without giving the game away, I wiggle my fingers and toes one at a time. It would just be like me not to have noticed I'm missing a foot, such has been my determination to convince Juggers I'm temporarily bonkers. Thankfully, I reckon I'm intact from head to toe.

'What on earth's happened?' I blink at him. 'This isn't the *Empty Heart*, sir.'

'No, it damn well isn't. It appears she's heading for the bottom of the North Sea, as we speak.' Juggers pauses, fingering the folds of his chin. 'That's what I have to tell you, lad. Looks like we've lost Ogden Barclay.' He shakes his head miserably.

Good grief! I was that busy saving my own skin, the fate of our skipper never crossed my mind.

'I'm so sorry, sir,' is all I can muster to say.

I feel like a bit of a heel now, to be honest. Poor old Ogden. He and his twin brother die one day after the other.

'Those separated in life, now together in death,' I mutter.

'Still not quite on the ball yet. You sound like your father.'

And in that moment of sadness, I know he's right. I've survived yet again, leaving some poor bugger behind, dead as a dodo. And that's the uncertainty of life, you know. You can be quite happily going about your business, and the next minute you're dead – forever. I can never understand why everyone appears so calm about this, when we should all be dashing about bemoaning our lot. Eternity is catching up with us – bloody quickly, too. I feel so sorry for Odgen Barclay. He died helping us, poor sod.

# 26

Turns out we're in a Royal Navy minesweeper, tasked by the Revenue with catching the smugglers. The vessel is carrying a dozen Royal Marines, armed to the teeth, plus it has a gun at its prow. No doubt the crew of hardened matelots are up for the fight too. There's still something of the marauder about Royal Navy men, you know. It comes from having chaps like Nelson and Cochrane to look up to. Pity they don't always swash their buckle in the right direction – certainly for poor Ogden.

Mind you, this job was considered too big for the Customs cutter that patrols the coast, which gives me further cause for concern. It's clear the people behind this are not to be messed with.

Dressed in overalls – Juggers's barely big enough – we are shown to the captain's cabin, a small but cosy affair behind the bridge. He makes apologetic noises while handing us each a large glass of whisky. His name's Commander Madden, and it's his voice that sounded familiar to me when we were being rescued. He's a Scot, and sounds uncannily like my Uncle James.

'Sorry things have gone the way they have, Superintendent. Not what we planned when we spoke of this last night. Dear me, no. Was always going to be risky in the fog. We have to head back to port following the collision, but rest assured we have two vessels, plus the lifeboats from Filey and Scarborough, out looking for Mr Barclay.'

The hopeless expression on his face says it all, though. Remember, Juggers spent exactly two seconds in the sea before removing his naked self by jumping ten feet in the air. I'm no maritime expert, but I don't reckon you have more than a few minutes in the freezing North Sea at this time of year before it's goodnight forever.

Madden may be from north of the border, but he's picked up the English talent of understatement. Not only have we let a gang of murderous smugglers escape, we've killed one of our only allies. I'm not sure, 'dear me' covers it.

'Worse things happen at sea,' says Juggers, clearly too full of rum and whisky to remember we are, actually, at sea.

'Jolly bad luck for poor Barclay,' say I. 'Won't do much for our standing in Uthley Bay, eh? So far, the score is three to the smugglers, and we're lagging well behind.'

'Not the time for levity,' chides Juggers. 'We've missed out on breaking a seriously dangerous smuggling ring here, Grasby. There could be millions of pounds at stake. Aye, a huge loss to Her Majesty's Revenue, I can tell you.'

'I'm sure Mrs Barclay will feel the loss terribly,' I mutter.

Juggers clears his throat, choosing to ignore me. 'It were a risk from the outset. But the only chance of catching them at sea was under cover of that fog. We took the risk and failed. Now, we must hunt them down by land.'

'Yes, we've tried and tried to catch them in the act. But they must have a good warning system. And they never rendezvous in the same place. Perhaps they're signalled from the coast, or maybe fishing boats with radios are ready to warn the smugglers ahead of our arrival. It's got me right scunnered.'

Hurrah! At last, a Scottish expression of frustration from Commander Madden.

'All the same, Superintendent, once the vessel has been checked over, we'll sit off the point if you need any assistance. It's just a matter of procedure, after all. That old wreck of a boat won't have caused us much in the way of damage. Although our Marines aren't permitted to be part of the operation on land, they can be asked to intervene in a case of mutual assistance, if lives are in danger, you understand. We're under orders from the Admiralty, don't you know.'

'It's a kind offer, is that, Commander. But I'm not sure how I'd raise you under such circumstances. Not as though I can lift the phone, is it?'

And there you have it. Everything this country lays its hands upon is stymied by red tape. Can't do this, must do that. It happened in the war over and over again. As the Germans were surging towards us on land, sea and air, we were busy discussing what colour the teacups should be in the NAAFI. Good old Winnie tried to clear a lot of that nonsense away. But like a persistent weed, it just grows back again, worse than ever. It means that while we police can't apprehend anyone at sea, the RN and Marines are in the same boat on land. It's like going into a boxing match with a right bruiser and deciding to punch oneself repeatedly in the eye before the first-round bell sounds.

'I may be able to mitigate that, to some extent,' says Madden. He reaches into a drawer and removes an item bearing a strange resemblance to a brass gun, with a short barrel. It reminds me of some of the starting pistols they used to have at Hymers for the school sports. He produces a fat, red cartridge, and proceeds to lodge it down the barrel.

'Quite easy, really. Push this chap down until you hear a click, then fire at will. It's a flare. I'll have lookouts with their eyes on Uthley Bay and the coast nearby, just in case. Not much comfort, I know. But the Royal Marines are a force to be reckoned with in times of trouble, I can assure you.'

And they are too. In the war, one always knew things were going to be rough when the green berets of the Royal Marine Commandos or the red headgear of their airborne counterparts, the Parachute Regiment, hove into view. These chaps can fight, by golly. And drink, as it happens.

'I say, couldn't we just call your base – or the Admiralty, come to that?' I say breezily.

'In an ideal world, yes, Inspector. But as we all know, this is anything but an ideal world.' Madden shrugs. 'Not if you want prompt action, that is. It'll be passed between three ratings, four lieutenants, a commander and a vice-admiral before they think of me.'

There you are. Nothing changes. People kept in jobs by the ludicrous rigmarole that governs our lives in this country. Much of it in place simply to keep the otherwise unemployable in a job. 'Bloody scandal,' I reflect.

Juggers gives me a withering stare. 'I'm right obliged to you, Commander. Very grateful, indeed.'

To my mind, this fallback position relies on too many intangibles. Will our flare be spotted? Will we even have the time to set it off? And what if there's fog like today – or snow? Too chancy for yours truly.

It turns out that the minesweeper's draught is shallow enough to land us at the pier at Uthley Bay. So it is to there we sail, prior to our minesweeper going in for the once-over following a collision at sea. More red tape.

And we're expected! There to greet us are two lines of sneering fishermen, straggling along the quayside like a welcoming party. Or in this case, an unwelcoming party.

By this time, we're on the bridge with Commander Madden. Our journey back to Uthley Bay has been so much quicker than our passage out on the *Empty Heart*.

'Look at the damned cheek of these devils!' says Madden. 'Surely you can arrest them on some charge or other, Superintendent?'

'If I could, I would,' says Juggers. 'But we've nothing on them, unless they have a go at Grasby and me. We certainly couldn't identify the boats earlier. And none of them have been caught in possession of smuggled materials. We'll just have to sit this out, and hope somebody makes a mistake. But I intend to put some pressure on them, just the same.'

Madden rubs his chin. 'I may not be able to station the Marines for your assistance, but I can have them escort you from the vessel. Chief, have Lieutenant Chusker come to the bridge.'

Chusker, it turns out, is in charge of the Royal Marine contingent. He's a jolly-looking fellow, with rosy cheeks and a ready smile. No doubt he's been splicing the mainbrace too often. There's nothing our Royal Navy and its various attachments enjoy more than getting absolutely plastered and toasting the monarch, you know. Worse than the Bradford Salvage Division. And let me tell you, a more inebriated band of men and women is hard to find. All dressed very well, too; though that's another tale.

I must admit, marching up the quay with seven rifle-toting Royal Marines makes one feel much better. When a fisherman calls Juggers and me something unspeakable, the Marine sergeant thumps the butt of his rifle into the chap's midriff with great gusto, while his colleagues point their weapons at the rest of the crowd. They're a bold bunch, but not foolish enough to carry on against this show of force. The fishermen drift away – for now.

Juggers and I are still clad in our naval overalls, our soaking civvy kit stored in a nautical kitbag slung over my shoulder. It's like an oversized duffel bag, and the damned thing is chafing me something rotten.

It's been snowing again at Uthley Bay, and while the streets are therefore quiet as we walk the short distance from the pier to the Trout, I notice a curtain twitch here or a suspicious glance there. As we bid our escort farewell at the hotel door, I can't help feeling isolated and alone, despite Juggers's formidable presence.

Now someone must tell Ogden Barclay's widow that he died bravely, trying to impound hundreds of pairs of stockings. How proud she'll be. You can guess who'll have to perform that unpleasant task, I'm sure.

And it's Christmas Day tomorrow, too.

# 27

We make for our rooms on arrival at the hotel. It's mid-afternoon, and I'm done in. It's a combination of the early start, all the sadness surrounding Barclay's death, and the fact I'm beginning to feel as though this might be my last Christmas, too. Just a feeling, but I'm sure you know what I mean.

As expected, Juggers takes advantage of his rank.

'Now, Grasby. I want you to get a bath and put on some dry clothes, lad. Don't want you getting ill.'

He hesitates for a moment, and I know what's coming.

'Then I'll need you to get up to see Barclay's widow. I'd do it myself, but it's never been something I've been very good at, to be honest.'

Surely not! I can barely believe it.

'Of course, sir,' I say dutifully. 'What shall I tell Mrs Barclay?' He's not getting off that easily. Good gracious, a couple of days ago Barclay was a contented old fisherman, happily mending his nets on the quayside. We arrive, and his brother is brutally murdered, then we manage to kill him on a mission which – let's face it – was hare-brained to begin with.

'Tell her he's missing, nothing more, lad.'

'Missing, sir?' He's been in the North Sea for the last few

hours, and it's December! I'd say missing, presumed dead, is the most we'll get away with.

Really, what a pantomime.

'Missing, that's what I want you to tell her, is that clear?' He stares at me with barely disguised irritation springing from those piggy eyes. 'I know you've had a difficult few days, lad.'

I'll say! I've had to cope with a naked boss, my truculent father and his odd paramour, a blow to the guts, nearly drowning, dead twins and the heartbreak of telling somebody that their husband of many years is 'missing'. This woman is – or was – a fisherman's wife. She'll know well that *missing* while at sea is merely a trite euphemism, deployed to save our blushes.

When I return from my bath, warmed but not altogether restored, Juggers is sitting in the armchair.

'Have a stiffener before you go. I have whisky here, as you know,' he says.

To be honest, I'd love a drink. But I don't want him thinking I'm some weedy individual who goes weak at the knees when telling someone a close relative has died. It's part and parcel of a policeman's lot, and I've been doing it for years. Though it never gets easier.

It's better than writing an impersonal letter to a family, like I had to with my little platoon in the army. That felt plain cowardly. Especially when the dead chap was someone you'd laughed, drank, fought and been generally chummy with besides. I can still picture myself at my dimly lit desk at the barracks or some hell hole that only war can throw up, poised with my pen and a blank sheet of paper. I mean, how does one pass on the fact that the person you've loved and cherished is gone and you'll never see them again?

'It'll be bloody cold out, sir. My overcoat is still wet; likely ruined. It's cashmere, you know, sir.'

'Cashmere comes from goats, don't it?' says Juggers.

'Yes, sir, I believe so.'

'Do these goats only come out when it's dry? Stick it on that radiator, it'll be right.'

He walks over to the wardrobe and removes something black and bulky. 'Here, wear this. It'll be on the big side, but it'll keep you warm. It's my spare.'

He hands me a black pea jacket that smells strongly of pipe tobacco. I shrug it on over my fresh shirt and tie and have a look at the mirror on the wardrobe. It reminds me of trying on my father's surplices when I was child. They used to trail along the floor like a bride's train. This – to be perfectly frank, and I always am – looks much worse. For a start, it looks like the jacket a matador might wear, high at the waist. Juggers is much shorter than I, and besides, my arms are protruding from the sleeves like razor clams from their shells at high tide. The main body of the jacket is way too large. One could fit two or three of me in here. But it's all I have. I must be grateful.

'I'll be off, sir,' say I, less than enthusiastically.

'Aye, no time like the present. I'll wait until you come back then we'll have a drink before dinner, eh?'

How nice of him. Poor old Barclay won't be having dinner this evening. I trudge out into the corridor, and soon I'm sharing the lift with two old ladies whose combined age must be at least three hundred.

'My, what a smart boy you are,' says one old biddy. 'And still growing too, the way your arms are sprouting out of those sleeves.' She smiles benignly.

'Could do with a good feed,' says the dourer of the pair. 'The thing's hanging off him like a snake's skin.' She shakes her head and sucks at her teeth. 'I hope he has nothing to do with what's happening in this place. Local folk are frightened. They're saying murder. But I don't believe that, not in Yorkshire.'

I want to tell her that I'm nearly forty years old, and an inspector of police here to protect them. I want to tell her to mind her own damned business, and that the murders are all too real. But I smile instead.

'My mummy said I'm not to talk to strange people,' I say.

The old ladies cast each other a glance. 'I think you mean *strangers*,' says Dourface.

'Oh, I don't know,' say I, as the lift doors open, and I'm mercifully liberated from their company.

I mean, why must old people be so pass-remarkable? My father's just the same – worse, in fact. It seems as though once you get past a certain age, being rude is the done thing. How would they enjoy me mentioning that they have dreadful teeth and smell like mothballs?

To make matters worse, I meet my father in the hotel lobby. Hetty is nowhere to be seen. Likely, she still has her feet in a bucket of ice.

I'm waiting for him to mention the pea jacket. But instead, he grabs me by the arm and pulls me into a corner.

'Something's going on in this hotel, Francis,' he says most earnestly. 'People are scared. The locals, at any rate.'

'I'll say,' I mutter glibly.

'There were noises – all night, you know.'

'Yes, I heard them. I assumed it was you and Hetty.' Easy to see my dear pater is getting jumpy. Not like him. All Hetty's mumbo-jumbo, no doubt. The only noise I heard last night was Juggers and his endless snoring.

'Don't be disgusting! I'm your father, and don't forget it!'

'And she's not my mother, or have you forgotten that,

214

*Daddy?*' Low blow, I know. But I'll be damned if I'm going to be treated like a ten-year-old by the third person in as many minutes. I thought he might storm off at this. But no, he doesn't.

'We overheard two of the young waitresses talking. They said they would be off if it weren't for the snow.' He stares at me. 'What's going on?'

'I can't tell you, Pa. You know how things are.'

'Hetty's consulted the tarot, and the spirit of a murdered man spoke to her. Said he wasn't who everyone thought he was. What's to be made of that?'

'Firstly, Father, please do me a favour and don't tell anyone in the Church that you're consulting the tarot.'

'I did nothing of the sort.' He folds his arms. 'I was on the bed and Hetty was at the table.'

It's now that something catches my eye. No more the checked shirt with the button-down collar and tie. No, his dog collar is proudly displayed round his neck.

'Have you decided you're a vicar again?' I say.

'Never mind that, Francis. Hetty has been having visions. I tell you, it's uncanny.'

What's been happening at Uthley Bay has clearly spooked my dear pater. He sees me eye his dog collar.

'I'm wearing my appointments by way of protection, if you must know. You should be careful, too. Mark my words!'

My father, as you may know, is a pretty blunt, no-nonsense character. Despite having spent a whole career in the Church, there's never been anything otherworldly about him. But now he's beginning to sound like Hetty Gaunt. I recall that he had an aunt who went mad. It's said this happened after she drank too much mescal sometime in the 1890s, or so my mother reckoned. She'd apparently morphed from a confident socialite into someone who couldn't go out and was frightened by her own shadow. As was the way back then, her husband – a businessman of considerable means – sent her to an asylum in Wales, and nothing more was ever heard of her. The good old days, my backside.

For a kick-off, sending someone with an uncertain disposition to Wales is asking for trouble. I remember being horrified that nobody from the family bothered about her. When I asked my mother when she died, the question foxed her.

'I'm not too sure, to be honest, Francis. She might still be there, for all I know. Your father doesn't like to speak about it.'

That felt so inhumane when I was a child that I burst into tears. But now, as I stare into my father's haunted features, I reckon if he gets any worse it'll be the first available train to Caerphilly for him. Yes, by golly, and he can take Hetty with him too.

Nonetheless, I feel a twinge of guilt when I walk away, leaving him looking distressed behind a pot plant adorned with tinsel. However, the feeling doesn't last long. Good-oh.

As I make my way up Kissing Lane, I spot some lights on in the newly recommissioned police station. I toy with the idea of popping in for a cup of tea, but decide I'll maybe leave it for the way back. I must say, it's been rather challenging working with Juggers, especially when I know he's keeping things from me. Like this morning's failed mission to bring the smugglers to justice, for instance. As an inspector, I'm pretty used to trundling along under my own steam, as it were. If Juggers ever thought to ask my advice, I'd have counselled that we sat back, enjoyed the fruits of Christmas in snowbound Uthley Bay, then sent for reinforcements as soon as the snow cleared. Like the full complement of the Coldstream Guards, for example. But he'd have ignored me, so there was no point. Juggers is one of these men of action who has been stuck behind a desk for too long. The minute he smells a fight, it's *tally-ho* and damn the consequences.

Darkness is falling upon Uthley Bay now. I can just see the stars and planets forming as the black velvet sky banishes the day. Another dusting of snow is settling on the little lanes and pathways cleared through the heavy falls by the locals. They'll have to do it all over again if this gets heavier. The village is, of course, still cut off. Even if they could, you try persuading the council to clear the roads on Christmas Eve.

The nearer I get to Ogden Barclay's domicile, the worse I feel. It's pure guilt. I should have checked the deck for his presence after we were inadvertently rammed by the navy. After all, I was the youngest, fittest man aboard. It was a moral duty to rescue my fellow crew.

Ultimately, though, who am I kidding? I was in *save myself* form.

As I approach Barclay's shabby home, I'm surprised not to see a constable about the place. I don't remember lifting the guard before we left earlier in the day. Perhaps the chap is inside warming his toes. I can't blame him. It really is bloody cold.

I knock twice on the tumbledown door. It's too cold to be using a fist, and my skills as far as door knocking is concerned have been well and truly dismissed by Juggers.

Thankfully, I hear the pad of feet along the corridor, and the door swings open. Revealed is one of the most handsome women I've ever seen. I was picturing some hunched-over fisher wife, decked out in an old shawl and wearing her hair in a bun. But Mrs Barclay is tall – statuesque, even. Her hair is down to her shoulders, a golden colour. She's wearing a tweed skirt and matching jumper, which exaggerates her superb figure.

And do you know, even as a policeman, if you asked me to put an age on her, I'd struggle. She could be anything from forty to sixty. Though I suspect she must be towards the older end of those parameters.

'I'm sorry to bother you,' say I, rather taken aback. 'Are you Mrs Barclay?'

'Yes, I am. And you must be Inspector Grasby. My husband has spoken of you. Well, you and your superior, I think.'

Her voice is a treat, smooth, honeyed. No trace of a Yorkshire accent, as far as I can hear. It only takes a split second for me to work something out. Ogden and Perkin Barclay fell out so badly that they never spoke again. Mrs Jinks told me that it was over money, but also that Perkin never married because the woman he loved chose someone else. Two brothers fighting over money is common enough, but the same could be said of fighting over a beautiful woman. How often in history has that happened, I wonder? Looking at Mrs B, it's easy to see why it might be the case here.

'Can I come in, please?' say I. For now, I face the dread moment. The death message must be delivered.

'Of course, please do.' She invites me in, closes the door and leads me into the lounge. Like her, it's a surprise – well decorated, with decent furniture and even a couple of paintings on the walls.

She must see my surprise, as she smiles and says, 'My husband is responsible for the exterior of our house,

Inspector. The interior is my preserve. You can tell just who places an emphasis on what, I daresay.'

It's been my job for many years to create swift impressions of people. Mrs Barclay is well educated, and not from some northern grammar school, either. She exudes the confidence of someone brought up with wealth and privilege, and I'd bet my last penny she's either been to a good university or one of those posh finishing schools one reads about. The next logical thought is to wonder what on earth she's doing in Uthley Bay. But I'm mesmerized by something else. She reminds me of somebody, and I just can't place who.

'Would you like some tea, Inspector?' she enquires of me. 'I baked some scones this morning. Ogden does love them so.'

It's a punch to the gut. No matter how strangely I feel the pair are – or *were* – matched. Hearing such regard for her husband makes my job all the more difficult.

'Please, don't trouble yourself, Mrs Barclay. Can we sit down and have a chat?'

I see a shadow of concern pass across her face.

'This business with poor Perkin. I do hope it's nothing to do with that. Are you any further forward with your enquiries? He and I – well, he and I were friends, once upon a time.' She wrings her hands as she speaks. I know my theory about the Barclay brothers is correct.

'No, nothing about that. Though, as you'll be aware, we're investigating the matter thoroughly.' I'm side-tracked for a moment, suddenly realizing there's no sign of a constable. 'I say, where's the officer we assigned for your protection?'

'Oh, he had to leave. One of his colleagues sent a message to say that he must attend the station immediately.'

She delves into a neat, patent leather handbag. 'Here it is. I picked it up from the floor in the hall. Your constable was in such a hurry to leave, he must have dropped it.'

She hands me a crumpled piece of paper.

*Come back to the station imeediately. Wood.*

Now, I'm not going to try and persuade you that all our chaps rival Shakespeare when it comes to the written word. But I would have hoped they might spell 'immediately' correctly. I curse myself for not popping in on my way here. Certainly, nothing looked out of place when I passed the station. I wonder what on earth could have happened.

'I see,' say I, pocketing the note. 'No doubt there will have been some crisis or other. Happens all the time in police stations, don't you know. Usually a storm in a teacup.'

It's usually just that, a teacup. When you see a police car racing through the streets of any town or city, it pays to remember they're more than likely heading for a tea break. My goodness, those leaves have us well and truly addicted.

But I must remember why I'm here. 'I'm sad to say I have bad news, Mrs Barclay.' She opens her mouth to speak, but I calm her words with a touch of her hand. Best to get to it. 'As you are aware, Mr Barclay took us out to sea earlier today. I'm afraid things didn't go quite as planned. I'm so sad to tell you that your husband is missing at sea.'

This is the unpredictable part. I've had all manner of responses from the suddenly bereaved, you know. Everything from complete denial, hugs and tears, complete indifference, or a physical attack on one's person. But Mrs Barclay just stares at me with her beautiful blue eyes, her face expressionless.

'A search for him commenced almost immediately. I'm told the lifeboats from Scarborough and Filey as well as Royal Navy vessels are involved. I'm so sorry. We can only pray for his safe return.'

'Dear me,' says she. 'I'm sure I don't know what to say. What a shock – a terrible shock.' She has the upper-class ability to hide grief, too. But I know utter devastation when I see it. Her bottom lip is trembling, and she's fighting to keep her composure.

I take Her hands in mine. 'I'm so sorry to be the bearer of such bad news. Is there anyone I can contact to come and sit with you, perhaps?'

'No.' Her face is still blank, disbelieving. 'The only person I can think of is dead, too.' She looks up at me quickly, as though she feels that she regrets what she's just said.

Instantly, I know who she means. It can only be Perkin Barclay.

'You must ignore me, Inspector. I must say, I'm rather in shock, I think.'

'In that case, we won't leave you alone. I'm not sure quite what's happening at the station, but I'll make sure that there's an officer here shortly.'

'There's really no need, Inspector. When our men go to sea, we know the risks. I shall go in to my neighbour. They're a kindly enough family. And being fisherfolk, they'll understand.' A fat tear trickles down her face. She wipes it away with a trembling hand.

Though there is no scene, I can tell what a blow this has been to Mrs Barclay. I hate leaving her, but I must see what's afoot down at the station.

'Do you have a telephone, ma'am?' I say perfunctorily. People having telephones is becoming reasonably normal. Though I'm not sure why. The damned things are always blasting off when they're least wanted. There's no doubting they have their uses, mind you.

'No – no, we don't have a telephone. Ogden always thought they were dangerous.'

'Dangerous?'

'I don't know. Something to do with them emitting damaging rays or the like. He has – had – some strange ideas, Inspector. I do believe he read about it in one of these awful penny dreadfuls he was so fond of.' She smiles weakly. 'And please, call me Elizabeth, Inspector. I know how difficult it must be for you to have to pass on such information.'

'It's my job, Elizabeth. Though never an easy part of it. I'm Frank, by the way. Of course, we'll let you know if there are any developments with the search. And you'll have a police officer with you at all times. I must apologize that he was called away. I'll go straight there now.'

I stand to leave, though seeing her in such pain makes me feel like a rotter. I'm sure the dam will break when I leave. Gosh, she's as pale as a ghost, poor woman.

I'm really angry, all of a sudden. What on earth did Juggers think he was going to achieve in such weather? Come to that, why did Barclay agree to the stupid plan in the first place? He must have known the potential pitfalls. My mind winds back to Ogden Barclay's awkward boarding of the *Empty Heart* and his missing wedding ring. God rest him, for he is surely as dead as his brother. I hope they parted on good terms earlier, he and the brave Elizabeth.

'You've been very kind, Inspector. Please tell him that if I'm not here, I'll be next door.'

'Of course,' say I. Then something occurs to me. 'The note, who delivered it?'

'One of the parsonage children. Becky, I think her name

is. They live down on Front Row.' Elizabeth Barclay shrugs. 'No doubt they gave her a penny for her trouble.'

I express my sympathy to Elizabeth once more and take my leave. If there's any chance of finding Barclay, I hope we do. But as I step out into the cold night air on this Christmas Eve, I fear that Ogden Barclay has long since been consigned to a watery grave.

# 28

During the brief time I was with Mrs Barclay, a rather brisk wind has blown up from the east. Flakes of snow are swirling under the streetlights. It's heavier now, no doubt about to settle in for a nocturnal blizzard. It's the last thing we need. Mind you, weather like this should bring crooks to a halt as well as police officers, surely. Though one thing has to be said for the criminal fraternity – they tend to stick to their task much better than those trying to catch them. I daresay this is because some looming overlord might just pan in their heads unless they carry everything through properly. And let's face it, the wage of your average policeman is pitiful. Not to mention, I have some naturally *relaxed* colleagues, who find it hard to shift themselves from the cosy office or whatever dive they use to hide away for a bit, no matter what crimes are being committed.

As I plod on, head down – one hand holding the collar of Juggers's pea coat together at my neck while the other is keeping my trilby in place – I ponder on it all. Who is the dread figure keeping the smugglers in line, and meting out punishment to those that say too much? Wilf? I don't think so. Mrs Smith-Wantley? Hardly. The bespectacled hotel owner? Well, you never know. Though he doesn't look the type. Tommaso has the right physicality – nobody's going to mess with him. But I detect something gentle about the man. Often the way with bigger chaps, in my experience.

When I turn down Kissing Lane, the wind and snow hit me square in the face and I squint ahead, trying not to trip or walk into a wall. Soon, I'm at the station. My goodness, I'm ready for a heat at the fire and a nice cup of tea. It's also good to have a break from Juggers. As I've said, I'm not used to having a senior officer so close at hand.

As a rule, and as good security practice, most police stations in the 'rurals' lock their doors at night. There's normally a sign advising one to ring a bell or knock to gain admittance. But I have no need for such a sign tonight, as the door to Uthley Bay Police Station is ajar. It's only the recessed nature of the place, lying off the lane, that's keeping the door from being blown off its hinges in the wind. I shall have to *have a word*, as they say.

I see they've set the place up well enough. There's a fire blazing in the little office in which Juggers and I sat, and the front bar is neat and tidy. A half-drunk mug of tea is on the counter, a couple of pens beside it.

I put my hand on the mug and discover that it's stone cold.

'Wood! Keithley!' I call. But nobody replies.

As I walk further into the body of the station, there's still no sign of life. I call again, but it's pretty clear that the police station is empty. Our prisoner, George Beckwith, is nowhere to be seen, his cell door lying open.

Now, though there are a number of things that could be happening here, the thumping in my chest says otherwise. I mean, our three constables could be out apprehending someone, having made progress in their investigations, but they would surely have left one of their number to man

225

the station. It's protocol, you know. Apart, that is, from in the direst of circumstance.

In the living quarters, just behind the operational portion of the station, things are even more concerning. In the little sitting room-cum-kitchen, there's no sign of life. On a counter under some cupboards, there's a sandwich under construction. The cheese intended to fill it is chopped on a plate, and beside it there's a small pat of butter with a knife protruding from it, half-wrapped in greaseproof paper. When I check the kettle, it's full, with the merest hint of warmth, and there's an empty, cracked mug at its side.

I remember my mother telling me the story of the lighthouse keepers on the Flannan Isles, living on nothing but a wild rock in the Outer Hebrides. In that case, I seem to recall, there was a meal on the table and overturned chairs. For all the world, it looked as though the three keepers of the light had been disturbed by something while enjoying a repast. Despite exhaustive searches and investigations, they were never seen again, and no definitive explanation as to why they disappeared has ever been arrived upon.

My mother, being Scottish, told the tale expertly, with a tremor of foreshadowing doom in her voice. And maybe because of that, or perhaps the unknown fate of the men, the story always chilled me to the bone.

But here I am, standing in a village police station on the east coast of Yorkshire, on Christmas Eve, living it again in real life.

In front of a broken-down settee is a small table. Bang in the middle is an envelope. It's been placed there deliberately, in the knowledge that even the most inept detective will find it.

I can feel my knees tremble as I make my way towards it. My hands shake as I pick the envelope up and roughly tear it open. Inside is a little note on a lined page that looks as though it's been torn from a notebook – a police notebook.

*When you read this be sure to know the lifes of your*
*bobbies are at steak. Go back to the hotel and stay*
*there. If you downt do what we say they'll die. They*
*will be safe if you obay this message*

I fumble in the pocket of the jacket and find the little crumpled note given to me by Mrs Barclay. Not only is the handwriting identical, the disregard for spelling and punctuation is also the same.

Our colleagues have been kidnapped. Now we're right in it!

I hurry to the door. When I pull it shut, I remember that I don't have the key. But what does it matter? There's nothing worth stealing inside, and those who should be manning the place have gone.

Despite the snow, wind, and difficult conditions underfoot, I positively sprint down what remains of Kissing Lane. The flakes are stinging my face like mad. They're hard little balls, more akin to tiny hailstones. In my haste, I slip a couple of times but manage to stay upright. When I turn onto the front row of Uthley Bay, I'm almost blown off my feet. The wind is gusting now, and it's getting stronger.

I'm at the Trout's threshold when a horrible thought crosses my mind. What if I go in and find that Juggers too is nowhere to be seen?

Desperately, I try to catch my breath. It's hard, not only because of my exertions, but because plain fear is coursing through my veins.

I look round, terrified to go in. Through the snow, I spot

something that wasn't there earlier. Under the harbour lights, I can see the outline of a vessel. And though its detail is impossible to make out in the tumult, it has long, sleek lines, which means that it belongs to someone very rich or the government. Hopefully, it's the latter.

I shake my head as I take off my trilby and bound into the hotel. In the bar, there's no sign of Juggers amongst the parade of early drinkers enjoying a libation before dinner. It crosses my mind how early it is, being not quite six in the evening. Still, it is Christmas Eve.

When I step into the dining room, there are two men at the far end of the room moving a set of drums into position. Of course, though the Italian singer's name escapes me, I remember he's performing for the guests this evening. One of the men looks at me, and instead of a nod to acknowledge my presence or a smile of hello, he's scowling.

'You're too early! The show starts later. Vamoose!' Though I have no idea what that last word means, I can hear his American accent.

I run to the lift to find Juggers, cursing when I find it in use. So, I dash to the stairwell, taking the steps to the third floor three at a time.

I race along the corridor towards our room and note that there's a wheelchair sitting outside the door to my father and Hetty's suite. Her foot must be too sore to walk on. How sad.

I get to our door, fumbling in my pocket for the key, and remember with no little irritation that I've left it in my cashmere overcoat. I have no choice but to bunch a fist and batter at the door instead.

'Arthur – sir! Are you in there? Open up!'

As I batter again, I look to my right and see little grey heads popping from doorways, my father's included.

'Are you drunk, Francis?' he berates me from down the hall. 'My goodness, you have no sense of propriety. There's a time and place, young man. And Christmas Eve or not, you have too much on your plate to be getting sozzled!'

He opens his mouth again, no doubt to offer some other pearls of wisdom. But I have neither the time nor inclination to listen. 'Get inside and mind your own business!' I call. It's strangely pleasing watching each head withdraw into the safety of their own rooms. A bit like superannuated turtles, I reckon.

Of course, my father stands his ground.

'You should be ashamed. Lord knows, I am. How could you make a fool of me this way? How dare you!'

It's wrong, but recent events have me in a right funk. 'Of course,' I say, with a large hint of irony in my voice. 'I'd forgotten that everything is about you. I do beg your pardon.'

'I should think so too!'

'But in the meantime, Father, get back in your damned room before I arrest you.'

The Reverend Grasby makes to object, but I reckon he's spotted the gleam of anger in my eye. I get it from my mother. She was the mildest-mannered of women, but when roused it was as though a switch flicked in her head, illuminating her blue eyes. Even my father beat the retreat on these rare occasions. I'm pleased to see him do it now.

As he disappears, I lift my fist to bang on the door once more, when it swings open. This all happens so quickly, I almost punch Juggers on the nose.

'What the bloody hell is going on?' he shouts. 'I were having a nap before dinner.'

I regain my wits. 'Quickly, sir. Back inside, I need to speak to you.'

He ushers me in and closes the door. 'Pull yourself

together. I know it's sad about Mr Barclay. Aye, and it can't have been easy having to tell his wife. But you can't go around behaving like this, and you a police officer. Won't do, won't do at all, lad.'

I'm about to sit down when I notice Juggers's bottle of whisky and two glasses sitting beside it.

I begin to pour two large measures. 'Here, sir, take this. You'll need it, trust me.' I hand him a good dram of whisky.

When he makes to speak, I silence him by beginning my story. I hand him the notes and explain the circumstances behind them and how they came into my possession. Though I rush through it, my tale of woe is still coherent.

Juggers sits down heavily on the bed and finishes his whisky in one long gulp. He wipes his lips clean with the back of his hand and opens his mouth to speak. But before he can, the lights go out, and we are plunged into darkness.

# 29

'Damn it!' shouts Juggers. 'This is all we bloody need. Three men missing, presumed kidnapped, and now no lights! I'm beginning to think we're in a bit of a pickle, lad.'

I pull my Zippo lighter from my pocket and flick it into life. 'I'll go and get some candles downstairs.'

'And I'll come with you. Wait until I put on me jacket.'

I'm glad to say my own overcoat is drier now, having been on the radiator. I swap it for Juggers's pea coat, which I hand him.

There follow a few moments of cursing while Juggers grabs said jacket, eventually heaves it on, and is already out of breath before we set out.

'I'm glad I'm not paying good brass to be here,' says he. 'Place is a disaster. Folk getting murdered all over, tragedy at every turn – not to mention the smuggling. I'm not sure there's a decent, honest person in the whole village.'

I consider this as we make our way out of our room. Thankfully, a member of staff is coming up the stairs with a tray of candles and holders. A single candle flame is dancing in the dark as we approach him.

'Are you guests?' he says guilelessly.

'No, we're just out for a stroll and we ended up on your

third floor,' says Juggers sarcastically. 'Give me a bloody candle.'

The lad puts one finger to his lip, deep in thought. 'I'm not sure that's in order, if you're not guests, you know.' He regards us both with great suspicion.

We don't have time for this.

'Of course we're guests. My friend is just pulling your leg,' say I.

'Aye, and I'll pull the bloody thing off and beat you to death with it, if you don't give me one right now!' Juggers snatches a candle from the tray, stuffs it, rather unceremoniously, into a little holder and asks me for a light.

I hope that sometime in the far future, police officers will discover the knack of being polite to the public. This new world of law and order, I daresay, will not include senior officers threatening to pull off your leg and kill you with it. It's just an idea, but it might work.

'I am sorry,' I say to the lad, as Juggers makes his way down the stairs with his flickering candle, for all the world like an overfed Wee Willie Winkie. I follow him, wondering about the absence of electricity. This is rural North Yorkshire in the depths of winter, during a blizzard. A power cut isn't exactly novel. And it's clear that the staff are used to such events, given how quickly the candles have arrived.

And in all honesty, what will darkness do to stop us? After all, we've been told to sit tight, otherwise our three colleagues will be harmed. And it's not as though we can put this down to an idle threat, either. These smugglers, or whatever they are, have proven themselves to be as ruthless as any criminals I can remember. It's all the worse when you consider that the folk here in the village all know each other and have likely shared this place for generations. People expect crime in our cities, but, in light of recent events, take a stroll in the countryside and you'll likely never come back. Even if you do, it'll be minus any belongings.

At this point, my father would undoubtedly bang on about the evils of Mammon. He wouldn't be all wrong, for once.

Juggers is puffing as we reach the hotel lobby. An old lady is standing there holding her candle. She wishes us the compliments of the season as we hurry past, heading for Dot's little reception room and its back office.

'Same to you, Mother,' says Juggers, leaving the elderly lady rather bemused.

Gosh, he's the giddy limit.

Juggers bounds into the little reception area like Attila the Hun on cream cakes. There's nobody about by the look of things.

'Bugger it!' says Juggers. 'We need to use the telephone. We need reinforcements, rapid, like, even if they arrive by sea. Get in there and call the nightshift superintendent in York. Should be Harry Darrow. He'll work out something.'

'I'll take the candle, sir.'

'Aye, that makes sense. Just leave me here in the dark.' Then he remembers. 'I've me torch here. All these goings-on have set my nerves on edge. Hurry up, lad!'

He hands me the candle, and I step inside the little office. Thankfully, someone has seen fit to place a fishing boat lantern in here. It shines with an odd hue of red and green.

'Can I help you?' The voice comes from the shadows and nearly shifts my heart. 'Ah, you're one of the police officers,' says the man before me, his odd appearance further exaggerated by the eerie light.

'Professor Blunt,' say I, glad that the office isn't full of desperate cut-throats. 'I wonder, can I use your phone? I have some urgent calls to make.'

He shows me the phone with a gesture. 'Please, be my guest.'

I fumble the phone into my trembling hands, still cold from my antics outside at the police station. 'Much appreciated, Professor.' I begin dialling the familiar number of York Central. But when nothing happens, I press the telephone closer to my ear and rattle the cradle. 'I say, the phone's dead, too.'

'Yes, not surprised, really. Did you know that the further you are from the exchange, the less likely it is for the telephone to work in a storm? It's called phantom power. And in this weather, well, the weight of the snow brings telephone and power lines down all the time.'

Smartarse. It's something about the teaching profession – and I include university professors in this. They spend so much time in front of impressionable young people that they come to believe they know better than anyone else. I tell you, go anywhere near a teacher of any stripe, and they'll start lecturing you on the bloody obvious.

For a dreadful moment, I ponder how setting Professor Blunt's odd hair on fire will affect his smug face. However, being the Grasby I am, I'll just remove myself from the situation before something beastly occurs. 'Back at York, we have a generator to use when there's a power cut at the station,' I say as smugly as possible.

'We have one too,' says the Prof, then goes back to what he's busy writing.

I know it's obvious, but the question as to why they're not using said generator immediately springs from my lips.

'Oh, it's a damnable old thing,' says Blunt. 'From my father's time in the twenties. Wilf and Tommaso are on the job now. It'll take them a good half an hour, if past experience is anything to by. I should have it replaced but it feels disloyal, somehow. My father tinkered with it so much that it's almost constructed by his own design.'

*Why don't you go down and patronize* them? I want to say. Though, you know the form by now. I mostly manage to keep these wicked thoughts to myself.

'I hope they hurry,' say I instead.

At this point, the prof looks at me from over the top of his half-moon spectacles.

'Are you quite all right, Inspector? You're as pale as a ghost. No wonder, with all that's happening.'

'We're not having a good day.' This is, of course, the understatement of the year.

'I'll go and hurry Wilf and Tommaso along once I've finished this. Why don't you have a drink in the bar in the meantime? We'll soon be back up and running.'

I'm about to follow his advice when my gaze lands on a Christmas card on the table before me. It's lying open, revealing a cloying message printed within. But someone has written inside it, too.

*To my dearest, dearest Dorothy. I wish you everything*
*you wish for yourself this Yuletide. From Daddy xx*

So, we now know that Dorothy has a dad close by the hotel. I remember Armley's curious bookie's odds – *Dorothy's Dad* – 30/1. And into the bargain, I've seen that hand before. Gosh!

I thank Professor Blunt and leave the little office a wiser man. I have to tell Juggers that the phones aren't working. Somewhat predictably, he's not happy about it.

'It's like the bloody Dark Ages,' says he dyspeptically.

'Mind you, I could do with another whisky. Helps me think, lad.'

Therefore, it is to the bar we head, where a dozen or so little grey-haired people are flitting about with their own candle sconces.

'Isn't this jolly good fun!' says one old duffer as he passes by, a huge smile spread across his wrinkled face.

'Halfwit,' replies Juggers. Though the old bloke must be deaf, as his big smile is unaffected.

'Good evening, gentlemen,' says Dot, popping up from behind the bar. 'I didn't know if you intended to be with us tonight for the show, but I've kept you a couple of seats, just in case, like.' Her face darkens. 'Not that most of us are feeling very jolly after – well, you know what.'

'How kind of you,' say I, hoping she won't try and question us on what's happening in Uthley Bay.

'I hope all this kerfuffle doesn't affect your pouring arm, lass? Two large whiskies, please,' says Juggers, with absolutely no finer feelings.

Dot raises her brows. 'Ornithologists, indeed. I knew you were police officers as soon as you walked through them doors.' She bustles off to the gantry.

No great feat of deduction, I reckon. Though Juggers murmurs something about me sticking out like a sore thumb. As if!

The Trout is most certainly no stranger to a power cut. Big sea lanterns are dotted round the room. In fact, with the tree and decorations, the effect is much more festive than it was before. There's still something magical about a flickering flame. It's elemental, I suppose. Going right back to our earliest times.

I note that Juggers's fists are fast frozen on our little table, like a boxer with nobody to hit. I've known him long enough to recognize that he desperately wants to belt someone in the mouth, such is his frustration. And I don't blame him, either. Losing one officer is bad enough. But having already killed a participating witness into the bargain, three is too many.

Whiskies delivered, we huddle round the table, a candle in the middle.

'Right, Grasby. It's time to put on our thinking caps, is this.'

I think back to the letter I found at the station. 'They clearly want us out of the way while they get up to something, sir.'

'Aye, I'd worked that much out for myself. And what better night to smuggle than Christmas Eve, eh? Hardly anyone about, and those that are will likely be three sheets to the wind.'

I can't fault his logic. Though something else troubles me.

'They've told us to stay put here in the hotel. But to make sure we do, they must have someone here watching our every move.'

Juggers takes a glug of his whisky. 'I was hoping you'd come to that conclusion, Grasby.'

Huh, a likely story. He hasn't thought of it.

Just as we're pondering what to do, there's a distinct buzz of excitement around the dining room. I turn in my chair to see a large gentleman in an evening suit glad-handing the guests. This can only be Geraldo, our Italian-American tenor. I watch as he ingratiates himself with his public. He's a big man, too, as rotund as Juggers, but being taller, carries the whole thing better. He reminds me a bit of some of the retired cricketers I know. Most of them run to fat when they leave the game. It's not really self-indulgence, just that they no longer run about for a living. It doesn't cross their collective minds that a surfeit of beer and pies will fatten you like a Christmas turkey when enjoying a more sedentary lifestyle.

Geraldo looks round the room, his gaze alighting on our table. I must say, for a big man, he's nimble enough. I look on as he weaves his way through the maze of tables and chairs towards us.

'Hey, guys. You ready for a song and dance tonight? I'll begin about ten.'

Geraldo winks at me with his dark eyes. His skin is sallow, his hair slicked back with some form of pomade. His breath reeks of garlic and red wine.

'I want you to know' – he talks in a New York drawl, complete with Italian inflection – 'guys like you are OK, as far as I'm concerned. Each man to his own, and all that malarky. I don't care what they're saying about you in the hotel.' He pats me on the shoulder companionably and makes off to find the next victim of his cheap charm.

'Didn't take him long to work out we're bobbies, either, eh?' says Juggers.

'I don't think that's what he means, sir.'

'You what?'

Without wanting to go through it all again, I simply shrug my shoulders. Geraldo, spotting an old chap with a much younger one, all set to enjoy a cosy Christmas in a double room at a nice seaside hotel, has drawn his own conclusions, spurred on by gossip from the staff and locals, no doubt. That's what happens when one of you decides to run about naked on the seafront at six in the morning. Suddenly, though, I feel a spark of anger. I don't know what it's like in New York, but generally, as a species, we're absolutely rotten to each other. How many of us live miserable, lonely lives, just to please convention and the likes and dislikes of others? Half the time, we make the world hard for ourselves. Live and let live, that's the ticket!

Dot – the top of her head poking up from behind the bar – is clinking a spoon against a crystal glass, to attract the attention of the room.

'Ladies and gentlemen, if I could ask you to place your order now, it'll make things a lot quicker and easier when it comes to serving our very special Christmas Eve dinner. And don't worry. We have a generator, so it'll be business as usual in no time!'

There's a murmur of contentment from the assembled guests, many of whom don't look likely to see another festive season. No wonder they're excited.

'Right, lad, I'm famished. We're going to get nowt done if we haven't eaten. See if the lass can organize something to keep us going. I start to feel quite faint if I don't eat properly.'

As I make my way to the bar, I consider that dear old Juggers has plentiful reserves to fall back on, should he miss a meal or two. Though I'm with him on this. We had no proper breakfast and no lunch. This may well be a long night, so, despite the plight of our brave constables, some kind of sustenance must be found. In any case, with the electricity off and no phones, I'm struggling to think what we can do.

At the bar, I ask Dot if she can knock something together for us to eat. 'I'm not too keen on tongue, and I know the superintendent doesn't like meat paste. Otherwise, you have a free rein. We'll likely be working tonight, so I'm afraid we're going to miss the festivities.'

'Oh dear,' says Dot. 'What a horrible way to spend Christmas Eve. It's up to us to take everyone's mind off what's been happening.'

'You've done wonders with the decorations. And once you get the power back on, I'm sure everyone will enjoy themselves.'

'I meant you two! The other guests are already having a wonderful time, thank you,' she says, quite put-out.

That's typical of me. Having too much on my mind makes me insensitive.

'Do you both like fish?' she asks, her smile restored. 'We have a little gas burner – for emergencies. I could cook you some fish, and bread and butter. Better than a sandwich, I reckon.'

'Gosh, how kind,' say I. 'That would be fabulous.'

'Well, you are guests, after all. And given all that's happened, I'm rather glad you're both here.'

Poor Dot – she thinks her safety is guaranteed by the pair of brave detectives billeted at her place of work. In actual fact, with our having already presided over the death of a fair percentage of Uthley Bay's small population, she'd likely be much safer throwing in her lot with the smugglers.

'What fish do you prefer? There'll be cod,' says Dot.

'Oh, what else do you have?' I reply. My love of cod came to an end when my father kindly told me that it was the filthiest fish in the sea. Not only that but, according to him, the fish mainly dines on dead bodies. I suddenly think of poor Ogden Barclay. Now, no doubt, resting beneath the waves being rapidly consumed by a large shoal of cod.

'I have a list somewhere,' says Dot, looking about the place while biting the corner of her lip. 'Ah, here it is,' says she, finding a small piece of paper under the bar. 'We get our pick of the local catch, you know. They leave us a note of the best fish every day, so that Tommaso can pick and choose. We pay them well. Now, let me see what I can offer you . . .'

Not that she knows it, but her voice is slipping away from me to the point where I can only hear a noise. I'm not being rude, neither am I ill. But what I've just spotted has frozen me stiff.

'Who wrote that note?' I ask urgently, without begging Dot's pardon.

'This? Oh, I have no idea. One of the fishermen, I suppose. As I say, the note is normally delivered to Tommaso or Wilf. They'll know who brought it.'

As she's talking, there's a flicker and suddenly we're bathed in electric light. It would appear that Wilf and Tommaso have managed to coax Blunt senior's generator back into life.

'Can you do me a favour, Dot?'

She shrugs. 'If I can.'

'Could you ask Wilf or Tommaso who handed that note in?' I lean over the bar to address her from on high. 'It's a surprise for the superintendent. He loves fresh fish. It would be nice to organize some for him when we leave. I can just see his little face light up.'

Sometimes I do go overboard. Damn, I wish I hadn't used those words.

'Gosh, is it a surprise?' she says.

'No, nothing like that, he hates surprises,' say I, rather pathetically. 'My boss fancies himself as something of a handwriting expert. I like to put him to the test now and again, don't you know.'

'And here's me thinking you'd be completely absorbed trying to find these murderers.'

You'll note 'these *murderers*', plural. It's unintentional, but Dot clearly believes that this isn't the work of one mariner-hating psychopath.

'Any form of planning helps us concentrate,' I say,

grabbing the note with trembling hands I hope Dot doesn't notice. 'Thank you, for this.' I turn away from the bar.

'What about tonight – what do you want?'

'Double cod, if you have it,' say I without thinking.

'And would you like some cocoa and marshmallows for afters? They're delicious. It's our little treat for the guests this year. We don't have enough for a range of desserts all round. Not with rationing. Thank goodness it's coming to an end.'

I turn to face her. 'Cocoa and marshmallows, you say?'

'Yes.'

'What a disgusting prospect. You won't catch me near that with a bargepole.'

Dot trots off with a shrug, and I return to the table, where Juggers is looking more irritated than when I left.

'You know, you can't help yourself, can you?'

'Sorry, sir?'

'With the lasses. I were watching you up there. My, she's only the height of tuppence.'

'You know what they say about small packages, sir.'

'I know what they say about poison too, Grasby.'

'Actually, I wasn't wasting my time up there, sir.' I hand Juggers the fish note.

'What's this, your list of suspects? Because if it is, some-body's pulling your leg, son.'

'Take a look at the handwriting.'

Juggers removes his reading glasses from the breast pocket of his jacket with a sigh.

'I'm not in the mood for funny business, Grasby. I must warn you. Nether the time nor the place.' Juggers puts his round spectacles over his pug nose and squints at the note. 'Good gracious!' says he. 'It's the same handwriting as the note you found at the station.'

I nod. 'It is, sir.'

I turn to see the large figure of Tommaso ambling to our table. He's rubbing his plate-sized hands on a stained white apron.

'What you wanna to know about the fishes?' says he in a thick Italian accent. Beads of sweat are breaking out across his forehead. Probably the remnant of stress at the prospect of having to cook a Christmas Eve dinner without electricity.

'Just our little bit of fun,' say I.

Tommaso shrugs in a particularly Latin fashion, and thinks for a moment. He rubs the dark stubble on his chin by way of an aide-mémoire. 'Mr Don – Don Haddy. It was this afternoon – about the time of lunch, I think.'

And there you have it. Now we know who is responsible for the kidnapping of our officers. And much more besides, I suspect. Be sure your sins will find you out, right enough.

But Don Haddy, really? I'm not surprised the note was misspelled. He didn't seem the sharpest tool in the box when we met him. The reverse, in fact – I recall his befuddlement at me popping on the coat I found in his van, as if I'd performed some magic trick. But I know enough about policing to realize that very little is as it seems. Clearly, beneath his bumbling, rather weak-minded veneer, there lies a ruthless criminal mastermind.

Who'd have thought it?

'Right,' says Juggers, as Tommaso ambles off the way he came. 'We'll have us fish and then we'll go upstairs. Tell folk we're having an early night, lots to do and the like.'

'Then we'll break out unseen and go in search of Haddy?' say I, with a frisson of excitement.

'That we will, lad. But we need to get something in our

bellies first. I don't want you coming over all weak at the knees with hunger, lad.'

I must say, I'm looking forward to having something to eat, but at this point I remember I've ordered cod. Sometimes one just has to shut one's eyes and get on with it. But still, I look for reassurance, sound in the knowledge only my father will have such a ridiculous idea about such a noble fish.

'We're having cod, sir.'

'Good, my favourite,' says Juggers.

There we are, cod back at the top of the list.

'Bloody scavenger, it is, mind. Do you know, there were a case in Hull just after the war. They dredged up the body of a man out at sea. An old detective sergeant pal of mine told me they had to prise the teeth of the cod from his flesh before they could go about the post-mortem. Makes you think, does that.'

Bugger.

# 30

In the end, I'm so hungry that the cod goes down a treat. Dot's done us proud, frying it in butter with a little lemon and thyme. She's also provided some fresh tartare sauce and an absolute mound of homemade bread. It's delicious.

Funny how the simplest meal can be elevated to fine dining in the memory of a hungry man. I recall eating snails in white wine and garlic butter in the bocage during the war. I'd never have considered putting the damned things in my mouth before. But after months of bully beef and stale bread, it was heavenly. The old woman who made it for us was so pleased to be free of the Germans, she'd have given us the last bite of food she had. War is indeed a terrible thing.

I'm wiping my plate clean with some bread when Juggers decides to become all business.

'Right, Grasby, I know you to be a brave lad or I wouldn't say this.'

Dash it all. What's he going to say? It crosses my mind he's realized the fish was poisoned and we are about to be convulsed by our death throes.

'If I'm not much mistaken, we're in for a difficult night.'

Happy Christmas!

'But we must keep in mind the bobbies, and the inno-cent folk of this village. We shan't spare ourselves, if it comes to the bit. Give us all for the betterment of mankind – or in this case, the good folk of Uthley Bay.'

I've heard this kind of awful guff before, all about noble sacrifice and the abandonment of fear in the face of the enemy. The old *Good luck, Grasby*; usually, a precursor to imminent death. Well, I'm here to tell you, though I have great regard for my fellow man, I'll be watching out for yours truly.

Suddenly, Juggers yawns massively, and flings his arms in the air as though he's just scored at Wembley. 'That's me beat. It's an early night in store for Arthur Juggers, thou knows.'

This attracts attention from around the dining room. No doubt there are a few of the assembled septuagenarians wishing they were still abed. But I see what Juggers is doing.

'Early start, sir.' I ape his yawn. 'Get the head down and all that.'

I note that, as yawns are for some reason catching, table after table of the Trout's patrons begin to do so magnifi-cently. With all eyes on us, we move from our table and make our way out of the room. One old wag attracts my attention as we pass.

'Here, he'd make a good Father Christmas!' says this wrinkled wit with a toothless grin.

I'm on the edge of saying that with his teeth, or the lack of them, he'll have to get his Christmas dinner mashed up and fed through a straw. But I merely cast him a weary smile, as his little table of pals bursts into giggles. They'll all be dead soon, so I don't let it annoy me. Mind you, if Juggers's little speech about self-sacrifice is anything to go by, I may well beat them to it.

When we step out of the lift on the third floor, all seems normal. There's a little sconce holding a flickering candle on a windowsill. That aside, you'd never know the power had been off.

But when we near our own room, the door is lying ajar, and there's the black imprint of the sole of a size-ten boot just under the lock.

'We've been broken into, Grasby. Quick!'

Inside, Juggers flicks on the ceiling light. Just about everything that could be cast asunder has been. The wardrobe is leaning on the bed, which has been stripped of blankets. Every drawer of the dressing table and chest of drawers is either hanging out or lying on the floor. Clothes are spread everywhere. A pair of Juggers's string underpants adorn a mirror like a pelmet. Not a pretty sight.

'Sir, they've taken the trunk!'

Sure enough, Juggers's heavy old chest is nowhere to be seen. And considering its contents, our smugglers are now armed to the teeth.

'This isn't good, sir,' say I, stating the obvious. Something I despise in others.

'You'd think not, lad,' says Juggers enigmatically. 'Come with me.'

Just as I think he's going to fly downstairs and give Dot and Professor Blunt what for, he walks past the stairs to the honeymoon suite, where my father and his singed-footed paramour are no doubt practising the occult.

Juggers knocks the door firmly. Something, as we know, I cannot do.

'Cyril, open up!'

For a horrible moment, I worry my father is part of all this. But when he arrives at the door in his shirt, no trousers, a pair of grey socks held up with little suspenders, and a bright red paper hat from a Christmas cracker, I know I was stupid to consider it.

'Francis,' he says, as though I'm taking my seat for evensong. 'Have you been eating cod? You fairly stink of it.'

Now, one would have thought that, following my father anxiously harassing me in the lobby earlier, he'd have more to worry about than what I've had for my dinner. Plainly not.

'C'mon, Cyril, let us in,' says Juggers.

My father looks back over his right shoulder. I can hear a wireless in the background – a big band playing something festive.

'Can you give me a moment, please?'

But in typical Juggers fashion, he pushes past my dear old daddy.

'Don't have time to stand on ceremony, Cyril. Lives are at stake, and duty calls.'

My father rushes in behind him, me taking up the rear. It's then something truly disturbing happens. There's a muffled noise from behind the bathroom door. I can tell it's Hetty Gaunt, but what she says sounds almost coquettish, not her normal doom-laden rasp. The door swings open, and teetering on a pair of stiletto heels, a heavy bandage showing on her ankle under a pair of black fishnet stockings, Hetty Gaunt is revealed. She's wearing a very low-cut, red silk nightdress, barely long enough to cover her modesty. And to top it off, through a red garter on her withered thigh is a spray of mistletoe. All-in-all, it's like discovering your granny has a nice little sideline in prostitution.

Hetty Gaunt raises a defiant chin and hobbles to the dressing table, where she takes a seat then lights a cigarette.

'It's Scarborough on August bank holiday in this place,' she opines, regarding me and Juggers witheringly as she takes another puff. 'Cyril, help me off with this damn shoe. It's playing havoc with my blistered foot.'

My father hurries to her aid, as Juggers surveys the room. 'Where's the trunk, Cyril?' he enquires impatiently.

'Behind the curtain. I didn't know where else to put it,' my father says as he slips off the shoe from Hetty's injured trotter. She yelps as he does so.

'Right, Grasby, help me with this.' He pulls one end of the trunk from behind the curtain.

I grab a leather handle and lift on Juggers's one-two-three. It's a relief to discover that the damned thing isn't as heavy as it was when we left my father's house. Mind you, that's pretty obvious, given so many clothes, weapons and rounds of ammunition have been removed from it. Dash it all, I didn't notice it wasn't in the room earlier. Good thinking on Juggers's part.

With my boss taking the lead, I note my father getting up stiffly from the floor.

'Aren't you going to give her a kiss under the mistletoe?' say I. 'It's good luck, you know.'

My father treats me to one of his baleful stares, like he used to when I was a child.

'Never whisper a word of this to anyone. Do you hear, Francis?'

'Not even the bishop? That's not fair, Pater.'

I'm well aware how disappointed some parents are in their children. For mysterious reasons, they believe that giving their child life entitles them governance and carte blanche to interfere with all aspects of their offspring's existence for evermore.

It's altogether different for the children themselves.

None of us asked to be born. I've known many who'd have happily cancelled the contract had they known what was in store. I, at least, feel under no particular obligation to point out that my father's behaviour is highly inappropriate for a man of his age, who's also a vicar. But he knows I think that. In a way, it's a liberating discovery. He'll never again be able to criticize my choice of lady friend or the amount of ale I consume. The picture I now have of them in my mind will cheer me through many a dark night of the soul – maybe this one.

As I leave love's young dream to it, all I can think of is what Cecil, Hetty Gaunt's overly protective and very vocal pet raven, would say at this point. But that's another story.

The door slams behind me as Juggers and I hurry the chest back into our room.

'Gosh, that was bloody awkward,' say I, as we lay the chest in the middle of the floor with just about everything else.

'None of my business,' says Juggers. 'Cyril was good enough to hide the chest for me. So, I can hardly comment on his conjugal arrangements, can I?'

'You're not his son.'

'Very true, lad. What can you say? I never walked in on my mother in such a circumstance. She weren't the type, I'm quite sure.'

Perhaps she was, and potential suitors were put off by the odour of her sons' dirty overalls from the Co-op Fleshings offal department and Leeds sewage works. It's hard to tell. I resolve to banish the whole incident from my mind.

'How on earth did you know they'd come for the guns?' say I.

'It were obvious. One thing I've never done in my entire career is underestimate the criminal. I've known old lags who are as smart as any chairman of the board. Who knows, given different circumstances I may have strayed from the righteous path. We should always remember that. I have my mother to thank for keeping me right.'

I can never say that for my father, can I now?

Our original sidearms were rendered unusable following the sinking of the *Empty Heart*. That in mind, Juggers decrees that we'll both need a rifle, pistol and relevant rounds for each weapon. I fancy myself like a Mexican bandit you see in the cowboy films, replete with a bandolier stretched across my chest, chewing a cigar. Though any flights of fancy are banished when I catch a look at Juggers's expression. It's as dark as the Earl of Haig's waistcoat, as my mother would have said. It's the same look he had on his face when I left his office in York Central, having agreed to accompany him on this ill-fated mission. I can see the hint of fear.

'Sir, can I ask you a question?'

'Aye, fire away,' says he, checking the sights of a Lee–Enfield rifle.

'I do apologize, but I've rather had the feeling that you've known much more about this case than you've been able to say.'

'You're a sharp lad, right enough. I'm sad to say, we've been let down. Aye, let down badly by folk I thought I could trust, and that's a fact.'

'Do you mind if I ask whom, sir?'

'It's complicated. And I shouldn't really say much more. But it's Special Branch.' He lowers his voice. 'They've known about this smuggling for some time – here in Uthley Bay. The black market is flooded with illegally imported stockings. It's a long tail of woe. But it starts out in America – New York, to be precise. The hosiery makes its way to Holland from there. We have trade restrictions, as you know. The Dutch smugglers have made arrangements with various mariners up and down the east coast. They started at Hull but they had trouble with the trawlermen.'

I'm not surprised about this. I had to deal with a Hull trawlerman's wife once. She was the toughest woman I've ever met. I dread to think what her husband was like.

'We knew they intended to move huge quantities over the festive period. Millions of pounds involved. A pair of illegal stockings on every woman in the country. Can you imagine?'

'I can indeed, sir.'

And I definitely can, you know. Hetty Gaunt's stockings flash before my mind's eye, and all joy is drained from me.

'Because the crime is an international one, it's too big for us bobbies alone.'

'Special Branch were supposed to liaise with us here, I presume?'

'That they were. They might have been held up by the snow, I suppose.' Juggers's expression says otherwise.

'Or we're the bait to flush them out, regardless of the consequences, eh? There's only so many times in a chap's life he gets away with things like this. And I've already had too many, sir.'

'It's speculation, Grasby. But not unwarranted, I'll give you that.'

The image of a worm wriggling on a fisherman's hook springs to mind. Appropriate, really, considering the fishermen here are clearly in league with the smugglers.

'Shouldn't we take a step back until we have reinforcements, sir? Or at least think carefully before we go getting ourselves killed?'

'Circumstances change, young man. But we must do our

duty as pre-ordained. Then, if we fail and the buggers get away, we can't be blamed. Not forgetting our duty to the lads.'

Clearly, Juggers and I differ greatly as far as the word *duty* is concerned. I mean, though I hated every minute of it, the war was noble in cause. More noble than we could ever have imagined, as it turns out. Hitler could not have been allowed to run roughshod over the whole of Europe – even the world.

But, despite myself, I can't become motivated about the prevention of an influx of stockings. Especially if that means me getting killed. It's hardly the same thing, is it? In two hundred years, they won't be studying how hosiery was to blame for the demise of democracy. If this is how I meet my end, it shall be a sadly wasted one.

Before I can raise my voice in reasoned debate, Juggers interrupts these melancholy thoughts.

'Right, lad. Here's what we're going to do . . .'

# 31

Juggers's plan is, to say the least, a flawed one. He believes that our only secure route from the hotel, without risking anyone seeing us, is via a drainpipe outside our third-floor window. I protest that in midwinter, with frozen hands and feet, it's tantamount to suicide. Not to mention the fact we'll be exposed to the whole village as we climb down the front of Uthley Bay's largest building, just as Father Christmas is due to make an appearance.

'My, you're a right cynic,' says Juggers with a frown. 'What's your bright idea, then?'

I have to think on my feet here, for if I don't come up with something workable, it'll be out of our bedroom window, and damn the consequences. This being the case, I decide to adopt Juggers's plan, tweaking it somewhat.

'Sir, as we know, it being Christmas Eve, the guests will be making their way down to the dining room.'

'Aye, so far what you're saying is sound enough. Though there's no guarantee it'll continue in that fashion.'

'Hear me out, sir.'

Honestly, it's like trying to persuade a bear not to bite your head off.

'I reckon we find a room on the first floor, with a window out onto the Kissing Lane side of the building. That way, it'll be easier to get down safely, and fewer people are likely to see us.'

Juggers thinks for a moment. But I can see by the ever-growing smile spreading across his face that he approves.

'Good, very good! Mind you, I can see a flaw in this.'

'What, sir?'

'How are we to gain access to the room? I don't want to go round damaging hotel doors, you know.'

'Don't let that worry you, sir. I take my skeleton keys everywhere.'

'You do?' says Juggers, looking less than sanguine. 'Where did you learn that? Was it on that temporary posting to Sheffield? Rum lot down there, and that's a fact.'

'It was during the war, sir. A chap called McNair taught me. He was a Glaswegian burglar.'

'The people you associate with, I don't know.'

'He was a corporal in my platoon, sir. Said I was as close to having a family as he'd ever had. Sad, really.'

'I'm beginning to think you should be the one with the dog collar on in your family, lad. Especially given recent events. I'm sure you know what I mean.' Juggers nods his head in the direction of my father's little love nest.

'Poor chap bought it, sir. Just two days before we were to be sent back to Blighty.'

'And he gave you the skeleton keys as a dying gift. Touching, is that.'

In actual fact, I found them amongst his effects. He showed me how to use the keys about a week before he died. It was the day heavy rain forced us to hide in a French cowshed. McNair bought it trying to save his friend by charging a large number of Germans. Such actions sound bizarre now peace has been restored. But they happened over and over again.

I reason that all of us have hidden strength. I just hope I can find mine as soon as possible.

Juggers reckons that our lads are being held in the big fishing sheds down on the quay. And while I'm not so sure – it is rather obvious – I don't have an alternative suggestion. At least we'll be out of this place, which is beginning to feel rather claustrophobic, with unknown eyes on us everywhere we go.

We decide to place the rifles in a blanket and carry them, rather than marching through the hotel like desperados with them slung over our shoulders. It looks odd, and I'll be the one to bear this burden, but such is life.

Juggers looks at his watch. 'I reckon we should leave it half an hour to make sure folk are down in the dining room,' says he.

It's a good idea, so we wait. It crosses my mind to have a quick game of 'I spy', a Grasby classic on long holiday drives. I'm not sure my superior is the I-spy type, mind you. So, in the end, we do something very English and make tea. There's no milk, and the sugar is in short supply. However, the soothing properties of the beverage make everything seem more palatable, somehow.

We chat away about cricket until Juggers decides that it's now or never. So, with my swag bag of rifles over one shoulder, we take the lift to the first floor. There's nobody about, it seems. Someone is playing mawkish tunes on an accordion downstairs. Likely, this is a prelude to Geraldo's great Christmas performance. Suddenly, I'm glad to be going out – sort of.

The problem is, which rooms are occupied, and which aren't? Juggers decides that listening at doors is the best way to determine this, so we walk until the corridor turns sharply right. Located here are the three rooms facing onto

Kissing Lane. Juggers clamps his ear to the first door we come to. He makes a face and shakes his head when he hears voices coming from inside. The same goes for the next room; he can hear a radio.

This could be a problem. Why aren't all the guests downstairs at the festivities?

We move to the third and last door. Juggers listens carefully then nods enthusiastically in my direction. It appears we have struck empty-hotel-room gold. I fetch the skeleton keys from my pocket and study the lock. It's the same as our door, and I know which of my specialist keys is likely to fit best. I wiggle it round in the lock, insert a small lever, and hey presto, it opens with a quiet click of the barrel.

'Well done,' whispers Juggers. 'Maybe a bit *too* well done, now I think on it.'

But I care not a jot. I've done the job, and the drop from a first-floor window is much easier than trying to climb down a drainpipe in this weather.

I push the door open, and we hold our collective breaths, just in case. In the shadows thrown by the light in the corridor, I can see the room is empty.

'OK, sir. Let's get this done as quickly as possible.'

'Aye,' says he.

Why we're on tiptoe, I'm not sure. Just the clandestine nature of our mission, I suppose. But we're soon by the wall. Juggers draws the curtains open and tries pushing up the big sash window. It doesn't budge.

'Hold on, I'll check the locks,' say I. However, on inspection, they're off the catch, so either the window is frozen shut or just stiff with lack of use.

'Right, Grasby. You do one end, and I'll do the other.'

Together, we push at the sash window, and sure enough

it moves up by half an inch or so, protesting with a sharp squeak.

'Same again. This time put more elbow grease into it,' says Juggers.

We repeat the exercise, and our joint efforts move the window up with a shriek like a banshee.

Just as we're congratulating ourselves, I hear a gasp from behind. I turn and see a head poking up from beside the bed.

'What on earth do you think you're doing?' says an old man now struggling to his feet from the floor.

'I could ask you the same thing,' says Juggers, forgetting that we're intruding on this chap's privacy.

Our man takes one look at the blanket of rifles on the floor and steps back. 'You've bloody robbed me.'

He makes to run off, but I grab his thin arm. It's time for a Grasby diversion, methinks.

'We're police officers. I'm afraid to say we think there are burglars about. We're just checking windows and the like are sound enough to thwart the rascals.'

'I'll need to see your credentials before I'll believe that tale,' says our old chap, clearly still in full possession of his senses.

'Switch on the light and show him, Grasby,' says Juggers wearily.

I walk to the door and flick the light switch, then delve into the inside pocket of my jacket to produce my warrant card. I've had to dry it after our rescue from the North Sea, but its details can still be made out.

The old man squints at it. 'That don't look right to me. It's all soggy,' he says. 'I don't trust the police, you know. One of them punched my Uncle Stanley in York in eighteen-ninety-nine. He had a squint nose until the day he died.'

'I don't believe it,' says Juggers, both unconvincingly and unhelpfully.

'It's bloody true!' Our man bunches his fists in front of his face like a prize fighter. 'I might be seventy-nine, but I can still pack a punch. Aye, good enough to knock you out, Fatty.'

'Now, just you listen here . . .' says Juggers, stepping towards him.

I manage to hold my superintendent back.

'I'm sorry, what's your name, sir?' I enquire with a smile.

'Toby, Toby Watson.'

'Mr Watson, my colleague and I are on a particularly difficult case. We'd appreciate it if you'd co-operate.'

'Co-operate? I'm no tell-tale!'

'Nothing like that,' say I. 'Just keep it to yourself that you've seen us.'

Toby Watson strokes his scrawny chin with his bony hand. 'What's it worth?'

'I beg your pardon?' says Juggers.

'How much money will you give me to shut me mouth? It's not a difficult concept to grasp, is that.'

Juggers is about to blow a fuse, when I decide to take action. Quickly, I open my wallet and produce a white fiver. 'Will this do, Toby?'

Toby Watson makes a face. 'I'd prefer a tenner, I must admit.'

'You'll get a punch on the nose like your Uncle Stanley, if you don't shut up,' says Juggers. Neatly confirming Watson's worst fears regarding the police.

'A'right, a'right. I know when it's time to shake hands,' says Toby. 'Aye, and I know how to shut up too. You won't have a problem with me.' He grabs the five-pound note from my hand. 'Though don't have me down as one of your snouts or the like. It's a one-off, as far as I'm concerned. I don't like the police.'

'You've said. Rest assured, the police aren't too fond of you, either,' says Juggers. He narrows his eyes at Watson. 'Where were you when we came in, under the bed?'

'No, nothing of the kind. My back's gone, you see. I was lying down on the hard floor to see if that helped. I must have dozed off. My wife's downstairs enjoying herself. To be honest, I didn't want to come. It's all a bit lame, if you ask me. I'd rather be in my local in Leeds with the lads.' He leans his head forward, almost whispering. 'Are you coppers here because of the murder of that old boy at the pub?'

'Can't say, sorry,' says Juggers.

'Well, you might like to know there's a vicar here with a witch, un all.' Toby Watson nods his head enthusiastically. 'Saw her staring at me like she were casting a spell or summat.'

'We know,' say I with a curl of the lip.

'It's a bloody odd place. That's all I'm saying,' he continues. 'Half the staff are frightened to death. Don't make for a happy Christmas, doesn't that.'

I can see what he means. This poor chap has been paid to keep his mouth shut by two police officers who are about to escape the establishment by way of his bedroom window. Hardly run of the mill.

'You go first, Grasby,' says Juggers.

Watson pokes his head out the open window. 'A bigger drop than you'd think, is that,' he says encouragingly.

And he's right. The rooms in the Trout have reasonably high ceilings. So, the distance between floors is greater than your average terraced house. The drainpipe is too far away to shin down. And in any case, it's likely frozen, which would make it more like an accelerated trip down a fireman's pole. On a happier note, the snow below will cushion our landing.

My plan is to manoeuvre myself out of the window, take a grip of the ledge – which is thankfully stout concrete – dangle by my outstretched arms, and drop the few feet onto the white stuff.

Of course, there's one thing thinking and another doing, as an old teacher of mine used to say. When I edge onto the window ledge, the drop below takes on what appear to be monumental proportions, reminding me of a holiday I had as a child to Cheddar Gorge. I tell myself that this is all in the mind, and with hands so numb I can barely feel the concrete ledge, I twist my legs and torso to get into the right position. Soon, I'm hanging like I used to from an oak tree in the old rectory garden at Malton, when my father was the vicar there.

Mind you, I managed to contain my tree-hanging to the summer months, back then. Now, I feel a bit like an icicle. It's strange what fears we have of heights, as a species. Though common sense tells me I haven't far to fall, I feel exposed and in peril. If I were an athlete, there'd be some hectoring coach ready to encourage me to let go. A bit like the games master at Hymers.

I needn't worry. Though my own resolve is failing me, my superior is there to lend a helping hand.

'Get a bloody move on, Grasby. We haven't all night, lad.'

I look up, and there he is, looming above me, his round face illuminated by the light of a single street lamp a few feet away.

I nail my courage the mast and let go. For a moment, I feel cold air rush past my face. But very quickly I make contact with the ground below. Bending my knees to cushion my landing, I take an involuntary step backwards, slip and land in a pile of snow. I hear Watson and Juggers cackling from above.

'About as elegant as a horse having a shot at ballet,' says Juggers.

It's helpful to be so encouraged. And though my pride is hurt a bit, and the backside of my trousers is damp and cold, I'm still in one piece. I console myself that Juggers is still to make his leap. Part of me hopes he breaks something. It's an uncharitable thought, I know. But I'm sure one can find a passage in the Bible that deals with these types of feelings. And though it would place us in even more dire peril, it would be good to see Juggers wrestling with the excruciating pain of a broken ankle or something similar. I sound even more like a vicar now. They're a vicious bunch.

All of you who are shocked by this, please look away now. Because, as these wicked thoughts are passing through my mind, I crane my neck and see a black brogue appear over the ledge. I can hear Arthur Juggers pant and strain as he tries to have his other leg follow suit. However, there's something wrong.

Though his stubby legs are now in mid-air above my head, Juggers appears to be unable to move any further.

'What's wrong, sir?' I call.

'His braces are caught on the handle of the window,' says Watson. 'Hang on, I'll try to slip them back over.' Meanwhile, Juggers's feet waggle with impatience.

'Hurry up, man! I can't spend the rest of Christmas Eve like this.'

Suddenly my heart is in my mouth, as I hear footsteps through the snow on Kissing Lane. I turn to see a woman holding the hand of a little boy, as they make their way through the snow towards us. She has a scarf wrapped over her head, while the lad is sporting a red, woollen bonnet.

They both stop in their tracks when they see what's going on. The little boy spots the rotund figure, half in, half out the hotel window, and points.

'Look, Ma, there's a fat man climbing out that window.' With his other hand, he rubs the sleeve of his coat across his dripping nose, leaving a silvery trail of snot that sparkles under the lamplight.

His mother casts me a dirty look. 'Oh, don't you know who that is?' she says to her son.

'Is it Grandpa? Me dad says he's having it away with Nessie Sidebottom. Is this what having it away means? His arse is the same size as Grandpa Pat's.'

'Don't be rude, Wattie. How many times have I told you? It's backside, not arse.' She shakes her head at me, by way of an apology. 'There's only one man who's climbing in and out of buildings at this time of year, silly.'

'Who?' says Wattie, sucking at his blocked nose in a most disgusting fashion.

'Why, it's Father Christmas!' His mother looks up at Juggers's little legs doubtfully. 'He's just practising for later on, getting in and out all these chimneys with presents for little boys and girls.'

I watch Wattie as he narrows his eyes and sticks one finger, temporarily, up his nose. 'Me dad says that's a load of bollocks, and anyone one who thinks Father Christmas is real is a right stupid bugger.'

For this, Wattie is in receipt of a quick slap round the ear. Quite right, too.

'What were that for?' he says innocently.

'You know fine well. Aye, and there's more of the same if

you keep speaking in that manner. I shall be having a word with your father when we get home.'

Wattie is dragged away from the entertainment, though he twists round to snatch a last glimpse of Juggers.

'The window's stuck. We're just freeing it!' I call after her. But I'm sure this woman isn't as stupid as her husband appears to be, and I worry that she'll tell half the village of what she's witnessed on Kissing Lane.

'I've nearly got it,' says Watson, the strain clear in his voice.

'Bloody hurry up!' says Juggers. 'My nether regions are taking a right battering here, thou knows.'

I've noticed this about my dear leader. The more stressful the situation, the more *Yorkshire* he becomes. Apparently, my bishop grandfather used to say 'He's as broad as James Stead', a saying my father still uses to this day. I believe that Mr Stead was a comedian from Hull in the old days. Amongst other things, he was famous for the song 'Pop Goes the Weasel'. Can you imagine such a thing? Not *the old days* or the song – I mean anyone from Hull being a comedian. The mind truly boggles.

There comes a great roar of effort from Watson, the sound of snapping elastic, and before I know it, Juggers is tumbling earthwards with a yelp.

For a split second I fear the worst, with memories of his arrival on poor Ogden Barclay's fishing boat still fresh in the mind. But I'm surprised. As he's about to land, Juggers curls himself into a ball and executes a perfect forward roll onto the snowy pavement.

'Don't just stand there, help me up!' he says most irascibly.

As I haul him to his feet, pulling on one arm, I congratulate him on this minor feat.

'If you're thinking about what happened on that fishing boat, don't bother. It's one thing landing on the ground, and quite another on a vessel. Only the biggest fool will tell you otherwise.' Now upright, he brushes himself down. 'You snapped me braces, you damned fool!' he calls up to Watson, now leaning out of the window, observing the scene below.

'You shouldn't have been daft enough to get them caught in the first place,' says the voice from above. 'You'll be wanting your washing,' says he, disappearing for a moment before coming back with our small arsenal, tied up in a hotel blanket. 'I have to say, your smalls are on the heavy side, eh?' He struggles to lift the bag onto the windowsill.

'Direct that down on that patch there, will you?' says Juggers.

Before he does, I dive behind some bins, images of a gun being coaxed into action by the fall. But the improvised bag of weapons lands safely enough on a mound of snow.

'Where on earth have you got to, Grasby?' Juggers turns to find me emerging from my cover. 'Some of the things you do bewilder me, lad,' says he.

And so, with my blanket of guns over my shoulder, we leave Mr Watson to his Christmas Eve, and make our way back down Kissing Lane. I wonder just how many times he'll dine out on the story of the two Yorkshire detectives breaking into his hotel room, only to jump out the window.

It's an odd world. Don't let anyone tell you otherwise.

# 32

'Hang on,' Juggers says, rubbing his chin for inspiration. 'If we march out here in front of the hotel, somebody's bound to see us. We'd be much better off going back up the lane and out onto the back row. We can use that little walkway between there and the quayside. Don't you agree, Grasby?'

I'm already freezing and adding time to our walk to the harbour is irritating. However, giving the proposition some thought, it does make sense, so I reluctantly agree.

Watson is still hanging from the window, smoking a cigarette. 'Lost, are you?' he says with a sneer.

'Bugger off,' says Juggers, and we plod on.

Shortly, we pass the police station, where a light shining from the window is casting its glow onto the lane, illuminating the snow. I remember the note, the feeling of sudden abandonment, and the chill it sent down my spine. It's strange how some things set one on edge. Down to life's experiences, I suppose.

We're walking as briskly as we can, firstly to get where we want to go as quickly as possible, and secondly to keep warm. It's absolutely bitter – the coldest night yet, here in Uthley Bay. We turn left at the top of Kissing Lane into Back Row. I feel somewhat nostalgic for Christmas as we walk past houses with lights shining from behind curtains and smoke billowing from chimneys. I picture families having a meal, looking forward to Christmas Day. The image of little children tucked up in bed, finding sleep hard to come by, just like me as a child, anticipating presents and nice things to eat. The smell of burning coal adds to this sensory experience. You know, if someone deposited me here, blindfolded, without a clue about the time of year, within seconds I'd be able to tell them it was Christmas Eve.

Though I still feel its magic, darker thoughts spoil my remembrances. My father in tearing bad humour because he can't find his sermon. Dashing about, wondering why he can't have the day off like everyone else. *You're a vicar, that's why!* I want to shout. It's your job. But still, he grumbles and grumps until we get to the church. In there, he's even worse, taking his ill temper out on the rosy-cheeked congregation. He must be the only man of the cloth in England who reads passages from Revelation on Christmas morning. I remember watching people's expressions change as they checked their watches, desperate to get home.

By tradition, the Christmas story was played out by the children of the parish in the middle of the service. There they were, with tea towels over their heads and toy sheep, marking the Saviour's birth with a little nativity play.

On one occasion, halfway through this re-enactment, with parents beaming at their putative thespian offspring, my father leaned over from the pulpit, stopping the play in its tracks with a scowl.

'Tommy Atkinson, have you messed yourself again? There's a right stench. Smells travel up the way, you know.'

The same Tommy Atkinson, now thoroughly ashamed,

burst into tears and instantly messed his pants. Bawling, he abandoned his frankincense – in reality a white stone from our rockery – and trailed up the aisle into the arms of his furious mother.

'You should be struck off, Reverend Grasby!' she shouted as the little family left the service. 'My lad can do as he pleases on Christmas Day.'

This merely enabled my father to bang on about *children rising up to smite their parents*, etc.

'My, you're quiet,' says Juggers as we pass the Skipper, so recently the scene of murder most foul.

'Just thinking of Christmases past, you know,' say I.

'I bet. None as bloody miserable – aye, or dangerous – as this one.'

'Dangerous, yes.' I leave it at that, remembering how my mother refused to take part in our own Christmas Day following my father's treatment of poor little Tommy Atkinson. It all left me most depressed. I ended up going to bed with a turkey sandwich, a glass of milk and a book. Thanks, Daddy.

We turn down the little worn path that leads to the seafront, likely a shortcut used by many seafarers over the years. The snow begins to fall again, and it's heavy, too.

'Dash it all,' say I, pulling the collar of my still-damp coat over my neck.

'It's good luck, is this,' opines Juggers. 'We're much less likely to be spotted in the snow.

And I suppose he's right. But as we're walking downhill, for no reason at all – apart from it being Christmas – Deedee's bright, pretty face crosses my mind. Happiness and memories are strange things. Events which at the time seemed like a buttock-clenching horror now seem warm and nostalgic. It's a year ago, but I still miss Miss Dean.

'Right, let's get crouched down,' says Juggers.

We're now at the very edge of Front Row, Uthley Bay. To get to the harbour, we must cross the road, and walk back on ourselves for a few yards.

The snow is so heavy, it will take somebody with exceptionally good eyesight to spot us. We're merely dark shadows in a blizzard, fleeting, and soon enveloped in the huge flakes of snow.

'Get a move on, Grasby!' Juggers is stepping out now, striding across the road and onto the seafront.

I catch him up, the bundle of rifles cold and heavy over my shoulder. Water laps at the sea wall. A bird is disturbed by our progress, and flaps into the night, its dark shadow passing between us and a street lamp. For a moment it appears frozen there, a black cross in a white sky. For me, this augurs very badly.

We're on the quay now. The fishing boats, packed tight in the little harbour, are already blanketed in snow, their outlines softened by the stuff. Against the dark sea, the world has suddenly taken on a monochrome aspect, stark, chilling.

Beneath the pool of light under a lamp post on the pier, Juggers darts behind one of the big sheds. They're stores for gear, and where catches are kept until they're sold and removed. The stench of fish is quite overwhelming.

For a moment, I lose Juggers in the blizzard.

'Over here,' he calls, quietly.

I find him standing beside large double doors, held fast by a huge rusting padlock.

'I hope you've still got them keys?'

Of course I have. And as impenetrable as the great iron padlock looks, I know I'll have it open in a jiffy. The only problem is my frozen hands. I grab the skeleton keys from my pocket and try to find the right tools for the job. Jug-gers is holding his torch over my numb fingers to help me along. Ordinarily, a flashlight would be too revelatory. But with the snow gusting all around us, it's quite safe.

'Can you do it, lad?' says Juggers, an edge of urgency in his voice.

'I can. Though the cold doesn't help.'

'Don't be a big jessie. Get us in there. I know you can do it, a man of your resourcefulness.'

He's trying his best to encourage me. But all my life, I've hated being watched over while I'm doing something fiddly. Trying to ignore him, I find the right little lever and a tiny key that may fit. I push them into the padlock, trying to get that click that tells you you've cracked it. I curse under my breath. It's the wrong size key. I search for the next one up.

'If all else fails, we could always shoot it off,' says Juggers.

'I don't think that's a good idea, sir. It'll attract folk from all over.'

'It won't matter a jot, as long as we find the lads. Time to crack a few heads and get some answers, I reckon.'

*Great.* As I'm struggling to open this damned padlock, my superior is coming over all Stalin. Trust me, this is how we descend into tyranny, ladies and gentlemen. It takes me three goes to find the right key. Mercifully, I hear the click, pull off the padlock, and we're in!

'Right, we'll need to go steady here, Grasby,' Juggers whispers. He's hiding the beam of his torch with his slab of a hand. 'This place isn't that big, we'll find them quickly, I reckon.'

I'm pleased he's come to this conclusion. Firstly, as I'm a firm believer in safety in numbers. Secondly – and I'm not going to tell Juggers this – because I still don't have a torch. Though, having been plunged into darkness so often in this case, it's definitely something in which I should invest.

Juggers shines his torch on our blanket of guns. 'Take a pistol for yourself and one for me,' he commands.

Untying the big knot is no easy matter with hands as cold as mine. But following a few clicks of Juggers's tongue on his teeth, I break through.

'Which one do you want, sir?' I hold the handguns up for my superior's examination.

'I'm not choosing a bloody suit, Grasby. Just give me one!'

I hand him the Webley, while I retain a Beretta. If I am to carry a gun, it might as well be one with a bit of style. The Webley weighs a ton, into the bargain.

'They're loaded, on the safety,' hisses Juggers, as I go through the time-honoured process of checking my weapon. Old habits die hard, you know. Of course, these are habits I'd rather never have acquired.

Now we're both armed, Juggers flicks the torchlight round the shed. There are fish boxes, nets, pieces of old rope, and buoys cast hither and thon, but essentially the building is empty. The smell of fish becomes overpowering, and suddenly I regret having cod for dinner. Well, my mother would have argued that, taken when it was, and the nature of the meal, it was high tea. But I must keep my mind on the task in hand. After all, we have three colleagues to find.

This shed, being set on the quay, is quite narrow. When Juggers casts the light of his torch to the far end, he picks out another wooden door. He nods at it, and we make our way through the maritime detritus on the floor in its direction.

In the dim light, I can just about make out a small gantry

above our heads. I reason that it might be used to hang nets out to dry in the winter months. That, or it's something for the fishermen to throw themselves off when they've had a bad day at sea. Though most of the jolly sailors of the Uthley Bay fleet are more concerned with stockings than they are with our pelagic friends, their catch.

When we reach the door, Juggers puts his ear to it. I don't really know what this will achieve. After all, the last time we tried this – about half an hour ago, or so – we ended up waking a man with a bad back, lying on the floor. I'm not sure listening at doors is a particularly reliable method of discovering what's behind them. But he's the boss.

'Can't hear anything,' he declares.

I'm not sure if Juggers expects our missing constables to be carrying on an endless lament at their plight. They're much likelier to be frozen stiff if they're being kept in here.

'Looks like we'll be needing your lock-opening skills again.' Juggers assesses the door without laying a finger on it. I decide to try the handle, and it creaks open onto another dark space.

'Well done, is that,' says Juggers. Great praise from a man not prone to dishing it out.

We enter the room, and Juggers flashes the torch about. This space proves much the same as its next-door neighbour, apart from a pile of boxes towering at the very end. Thinking about the length of the pier, we've come to the end of the sheds. It would appear that Juggers's theory is wrong, and wherever our constables are being held, it's not here.

'Looks like we've drawn a blank, sir,' say I, incurring a baleful stare from the superintendent.

'But ask yourself a question, lad. Why are these sheds so

empty, eh? I've been around the docks all over the place, and I've never seen the like. Usually, there's stuff spilling out of places like this.' He makes his way to the boxes at the end of the room. On closer examination, they're flimsy wooden crates. Juggers breaks into one and, unsurprisingly, stockings packed in Cellophane spill onto the rough floor.

'Well, that's all the evidence we need,' says Juggers. 'We've not been able to tie the local fishermen directly to the smuggling of hosiery. This is the proof!'

But something jars in my mind. Why on earth, given the fact the local fisherman know we're police officers, and know what we're about, would they leave the spoils of their crimes here on the quay, protected only by one padlock? Just as I'm processing this, I hear a noise in the darkness.

Juggers has heard it too, because he points the beam of his torch in its direction. There appear to be people pouring into the room. As soon as the light is turned on them, they start to shout and halloo in the darkness, the noise coming at us from every side. It's disorientating, especially when a powerful light is turned on us, so bright I have to hold my arm in front of my face to protect my eyes from the glare.

'Make for the door!' shouts Juggers. This is all very well, but I don't know where the door is. I can see he has dropped his torch and has something else in his hand – his pistol. A single shot rings through the shouts and yells coming from the darkness beyond the dazzling light. Juggers has fired into the air. Suddenly, the light flicks out, and all is silence.

'Just give yourselves up. I know you're still there!' shouts Juggers. 'We're armed, so you better think twice before doing anything stupid. I'm not very good at missing, you know. And I'm warning you, that was the last shot that goes in the air, and that's a promise!'

As he's busy with this, I search about his feet for his discarded torch.

'Don't bother with that. Get your own torch out, lad,' he hisses.

It's another case of being caught short just when it matters. But as I'm about to admit that I still don't have such a thing, my hand lands on Juggers's. I fumble the damned thing on, swinging it round the room like the big searchlights that used to search the wartime skies for German bombers. Somehow, though, the place is as deserted as when we first stepped into it.

'Get a move on, Grasby! They must have run when they discovered we had guns.' He's running off in the direction of the next room, the one we walked through to get here. I pelt after him. But there's something in the pit of my stomach telling me I'm doing the wrong thing. It's the Grasby intuition, you know. Though, for the life of me, I can't work out how we can be at a disadvantage. After all, as Juggers says, we're armed, and they aren't. It's then I remember that my Beretta is in the pocket of my overcoat. I reach for it but pause as Juggers comes to a standstill in front of me.

'Shine that light about!' he orders. And of course, I do.

There are the fish boxes, the old nets, buoys, and various other items. I see an old glove with two fingers missing, an empty pop bottle and a great spool, round which rope is wound, looking for all the world like an oversized counterpart of the one my mother used in her sewing. Our breath billows in great clouds of freezing air. But of those who have just assailed us with their shouts, there is no sign.

'Bugger this!' shouts Juggers. 'I'm warning you all. You may think you're going to get away with what you're doing.

But I tell you, we know where you all live, and we'll arrest you one by one. Better to come clean now!'

The thrill of the chase has, yet again, brought out the Yorkshire in my superior. But before he bursts into a chorus of 'On Ilkley Moor Baht 'at', I decide to shine the torch up onto the little gantry I spotted on the way in. Sure enough, there's movement. I see the figure of a man duck beyond the beam of the torch.

'Sir, up there, look!'

Juggers swings round. He points his Webley in the direction of the beam.

'You stay where you are!' he calls to the fleeing figure above. 'I promise you, I'll shoot!'

Finally, I manage to train the beam on the figure of a man. He stands stock still, his hands in the air. However, our sight of him doesn't last for long. Something heavy falls on our heads, and for a moment I fear the roof has caved in, but Juggers swears loudly as we seem to become entangled.

Having read the great adventure thrillers of H. Rider Haggard and John Buchan when I was young, the thought that we're being enveloped in the web of a giant spider comes to my mind and my heart nearly thuds itself out of my chest. It doesn't take me long to come to my senses, though. We're ensnared in a big net, the robust kind the Hull trawlers cast deep in the Baltic Sea. It's chunky and, above all, heavy.

Beside me, Juggers's thrashings are enough to knock him off his feet, and he joins me on the filthy floor. I notice his pistol has been dislodged from his grip, as has the torch from mine. It's shining on us but from somewhere under the net.

I needn't worry about light, though. There follows a loud

click then a ping like someone tapping a champagne glass with a spoon, and we're quickly bathed in bright light.

As I struggle to pull the Beretta from my pocket, a man appears before me. I can see him quite plainly through the tight squares of the net. He has a double-barrel shotgun pointed right in my face.

'That's enough, you two!' he shouts. 'Just stay still and you'll be fine. If you move, I'll have no choice, bobbies or not.' In my panic, I can't work out what's wrong with his face. I soon realize that he's wearing a stocking over his head, which is flattening his nose like that of a pugilist. But I recognize the voice – it's Don Haddy.

'What on earth have you got yourself caught up in, Don?' say I. 'Put down that gun and go home, man.'

'Easy for you to say, Mr Grasby. You don't know what I know. I must make amends.'

Goodness knows what the poor chap has been told. As I said before, he's not the brightest spark. And easily manip-ulated, I reckon. But by whom?

I toy with the idea of thrusting my hands in the air, by way of surrender. But I stop, quickly calculating that any movement under the great net could be considered as an attempt to get my gun.

'Please don't shoot, Don.'

'Jessie,' says Juggers. 'Shoot me all you bloody want. But you won't do that, will you, now?'

I fear the certainty in his voice may be misplaced, as Haddy points his shotgun in Juggers's direction.

'They tell me you're handy with your fists, Mr Juggers. We'll try that out later, if you want.' There's laughter at this, and I look past Haddy to see eight masked men waiting behind him.

Gosh, you can be so wrong about people.

'We'll see who's laughing at the end of this little lot,' says Juggers. His face is bright red, and I fear he's going to burst something.

Of course, I'm in my usual state of funk. To class these people as simple fishermen is a mistake. We know they've killed Jack Wardle and Perkin Barclay already – or someone has. And this someone had more than a hand in the death of Perkin's twin brother Ogden. Though we must take some responsibility for that, of course. In short, we're up the creek without a paddle. But Don seemed so gentle, so loyal to poor Ogden Barclay. Then another picture springs to mind. What if . . .? But this isn't the time for wild theories. We may be reaching the end of the road. I can picture cod-fish-gnawed bodies being washed up on a beach somewhere:

*Gosh, the old chap looks like he was at death's door already. But look at the noble features of the younger man. Such a waste of young life and potential.*

Yes, that's what they'll say.

Of course, though I am no stranger to life-threatening situations, the feeling of helpless despair never leaves me. And Juggers doesn't help matters.

'If you're going to do it, might as well be done now,' he says, nodding to Haddy. 'I've no time for this namby-pamby stuff. Shoot us! You know you're going to!'

Now, there's sang-froid, and there's plain foolishness. I'm almost dumbstruck by Juggers's attempts to call our captors' bluff. I desperately think of something to say that will appeal to these ruffians' better natures.

'Don't listen to him, he's having problems at home!' I wail.

Well, it's the first thing I can think of. What would you do under these circumstances?

'You what?' says Juggers to me through the net. 'What on earth are you blabbing on about?'

'It's his wife, you know. Very ill, very ill indeed.' I'm blethering now, as my mother used to say. 'She should have eaten more fish. Yes, definitely. Do you have some? I'm sure it might mean the difference between life and death.'

'Bloody hell,' says Juggers. 'You've lost your nerve, Grasby,' he whispers under his breath, just loud enough for me to hear.

'I knew you were a bloody jessie,' says one of the men. It's Beckwith – I recognize his voice now. 'Should have known that when I floored you on Kissing Lane.' He turns to his fellow ne'er-do-wells. 'Squealing like a pig, he were. Just one punch to the guts, an' all.' They all laugh heartily again.

'I've not been very well, either.' I rack my brains for a suitable illness. 'Dengue fever, you know. I caught it in Hull . . . just the other day. It's bloody infectious, let me tell you.'

I can see one of Juggers's eyes through the net. You may think it unlikely that one eye could convey such contempt. But it can.

'Bloody hell,' he says again, though once was most certainly enough.

'Let us go and we'll walk away and say nothing. You can smuggle as many stockings as you like. Trust me!'

Before Juggers can contradict this, one man leans over the net, pressing his face close to mine. I can smell stale beer on his breath. I reason that I'm not the only one frightened out of my wits. He is too. After all, it's one thing smuggling a few stockings, but quite another doing away with police officers.

'You listen to me. We're going on a short trip. Somewhere

nice and cosy.' Don Haddy chuckles. I can feel his spittle on my face.

That's it, then – we're going to be pushed to the edge of a cliff and shot. I can picture the scene in my mind's eye now. In no time at all, I'll be consumed by shoals of cod, thankful for a Christmas Day feed. My father will love it too.

*'I told him about cod, and he wouldn't listen. It reminds me of the parable of the blind monk, children.'*

It's amazing how men of the cloth can almost instantly refer to this action or that from the Bible to suit the circumstance. I'm sure they make half of them up.

'C'mon, lads.' Haddy pulls me from the clutches of the net. 'Let's get them packed and ready. Aye, and make sure they don't have the chance to get up to anything. Especially the fat one. This lad won't be up to much, I reckon.'

While two of our captors stand back, their shotguns pointed at us, the others move in and remove us from the net. I can hear Juggers struggling, so I make sure I'm as pliant as possible.

'He'll be thinking of his wife,' say I, as I'm pulled to my feet. The Beretta is removed from my pocket, an old sack is bundled over my head, and my hands are tied tightly behind my back. I hear a yelp and pray they haven't just strangled Juggers for the sake of it. I know I've thought about it a few times in the last few minutes.

'He bloody headbutted me!' I hear a man call out.

Juggers has left his mark. Though what good it will do us, I don't know.

We're forced along, one man at each arm. I stumble over something, and they hold me upright between them.

'Steady on!' I say, just as the cold air of the Christmas Eve night hits me squarely in the face. I hear a creak, metal on metal. One of the men pushes my back, and for a moment my bowels loosen, as I feel the sensation of flying through the air. Surely they're not going to do away with us in the harbour?

When my face hits a wooden floor, though, I know we're being loaded into a van. I hear Jugger's heavy bulk land beside me. He grunts in pain.

'You all right, sir?' I say dutifully.

'Don't talk to me. I can't believe I thought you were made of sterner stuff. It was embarrassing in there, listening to the drivel coming out of your mouth. And just so you know, Mrs Juggers has barely been ill a day in her life. What a lot of nonsense.'

The back door of the van we're being carried in slams shut with a hollow, metallic thud. This looks like being my final journey. Oh, the ignominy of being carted to one's death in a vehicle stinking of fish.

Such is life – or death, in this case.

# 33

The van thuds into life in a clatter of smoky, percussive syncopation. The driver – whoever he is – revs the engine, making the whole vehicle rattle. Wherever we're going, it'll be face down with our hands tied and the stinking sacks over our heads.

I listen as we move off, and picture the scene. I expect the van to head to the top of the pier then turn left. It's the only way in and out of Uthley Bay, as far as I know. But to my surprise, our driver pauses just as we hit Front Row, then turns right.

Though I can make out very little from inside the sack, just light and shade as we move along, my hearing is working perfectly well. We've only driven a few yards away from the harbour when I hear the tinkle of music on the air, over the puttering engine.

*Still the night, Holy the night . . .*

The carol is being sung in a deep American tenor. It's Geraldo serenading the Christmas Eve guests at the Trout. Suddenly I'm filled with a feeling of deep sadness at the injustice of it all. My father – the man who gave me life – is likely a few short feet away. If he only knew, I'm sure he'd burst out of the hotel and fling himself in front of the van.

Well, I'm not that sure, to be honest, but it's a comforting thought, under the circumstances.

As we trundle on, memories of past Christmas Eves flash before my mind's eye. I can see my mother dashing about, making sure everything was spick and span for the big day. Before I'd go to bed, I'd have some milk and mince pies, the same as was to be left out for Father Christmas. Only, he was also given a glass of the good whisky my mother kept for Christmas.

She'd kiss me goodnight, and I'd trot up the stairs, listening to my parents' voices from the lounge. My father's whining tenor, and my mother's quiet Scottish burr. The house – whatever vicarage we happened to be in at the time – would be warm and cosy, fires blazing in the hearths. The smells of the season were all round: cinnamon, clementines, Christmas pudding, mince pies, pine needles, giblets boiling on the stove. Gosh, what powerful memories.

Mind you, if I'd known then what I know now, it would have been a different matter. I'd likely have wrapped my meagre belongings in a checked cloth and tied them to a stick, like Dick Whittington, then headed off into the dark of night in the hope of a safer future.

It's just as well none of us know what's to come in our lives, I'm telling you. Enjoy the good times while you can. They don't last.

One thing I could not have predicted, happens now. No sooner have we passed the hotel than the van slows down, brakes protesting quietly. We turn onto a less even road. I'm trying to work out if we're now on Kissing Lane. But stones are popping under the tyres – a sure sign of loose gravel or stone chips. And in any case, we're too far beyond the hotel to have taken that route.

It's then it dawns on me. We're heading up the drive of

the austere, utilitarian-looking mansion I first spotted when we arrived in Uthley Bay. The van comes to a gentle halt, and I hear voices from the front cabin.

'Sir, I know where we are,' say I.

'In bloody disgrace, that's where you are, lad. Disgrace!' Juggers says again for further effect.

The back doors open, and in moments we're being hauled from the van.

'Just stay quiet, you pair,' says Haddy. 'This way.'

I'm pushed along the gravel then pulled to a stop. Through my sack blindfold, I can see a change in the light and hear the creak of a heavy door opening.

'It's three steps up. Come on!'

I'm dragged along, Juggers puffing behind me, muttering under his breath. My right foot lands on a step, and I take the next two, as advised.

At the top of the steps, it's warm and bright. Instead of rough chips under my feet, I'm walking on a deep-pile carpet. I can smell incense in the air. I try to recall what I remember of the big house, right at the end of the village; plain, with an institutional look. It reminded me of a police station, I remember – that big one in Oxfordshire.

'In here, the pair of you,' says the man with the deep voice. Juggers and I are pushed into a room, and the sacks pulled off our heads, though our hands remain tied behind our backs.

As I blink in the light, I see Juggers struggling against his bonds.

'I shouldn't bother, sir. If your hands are tied as tightly as mine, it's futile.'

'Only one futile thing in here, and that's you, Grasby. I can't believe what you were about. Have you taken leave of your senses or are you just frit, eh?'

'I was trying all I could to get us out of the predicament. Escaping alive isn't all about heroics, sir.'

I have to be emphatic now. If there's a slim chance we might survive this, I need to keep Juggers onside if my career is to continue. I know it's an odd thought in our current predicament, but right now, looking round this smart room, with its leather Chesterfield couch, winged armchairs, tasteful ornaments and fine paintings, I feel a whole lot more comfortable than I did only a few minutes ago.

'You listen to me, Grasby,' says Juggers. 'Don't be surprised if we're offered a bribe here. They've not brought us to a place like this just to knock us on the head.'

This is strangely reassuring, though I'm not convinced. As you can tell, I'm all over the place at the moment. Terror will do that to you.

'And I tell you summat else into the bargain. If you forget your duty and fall in with these bloody fishermen, I'll shoot you myself.'

It's clear that Juggers will never surrender. Therefore, they'd likely have to do away with him. Why on earth are people so stubborn in the face of such odds? After all, if I survive by acceding to the wishes of these smugglers, I've much more chance of bringing them to justice. If you're dead in the North Sea, there's very little one can do for the cause. My superintendent should think on this.

'I'll be damned,' says Juggers. 'That's a Moorcroft, if I'm not much mistaken.' He's staring at a squat, petrol-blue bowl, decorated with representations of pastel-coloured fruit. 'Mrs Juggers loves Moorcroft.'

Good. Note to self. If we survive this, I'll buy him some awful ornaments to get back in his good books.

I'm about to comment on one such chubby ornament

alongside the bowl, when, from behind, a heavy door opens over a thick carpet with a distinct swoosh. Momentarily, the big ceiling light goes out, and what can best be described as a dark lantern is carried into the room. When I say *dark lantern*, I mean the maritime type, with three sides shaded. The bright side of the lamp is pointing at us, semi-obscuring what's happening behind it. But it's clear that a small number of people are shuffling into the large lounge.

As you know, I have wonderful eyesight, thanks to my dear late mother feeding me endless carrots when I was a nipper. So, on the brightest day or the darkest night, I can be relied upon to see what's going on.

In this case, I make out five figures in the shadows. They shuffle in behind the light-bearer and stand in a row before us.

'What's this?' says Juggers. 'A game of postman's knock?'

'Please be quiet,' says the man who's just put the lamp on a little tea table between us and them. His voice is strange and familiar all at once. He's affecting a French accent, but only a fool would think him a native of that country. Sounds more like a friend of mine who made his way to London and became a waiter in some very posh establishments. When I met him in the restaurant in which he was working at the time, he greeted me in the most unusual way.

'Ah, mon-sir. Yew 'ave come here, efter all.'

Given he didn't speak this way when we were playing cricket for Malton Primary School Under-12s, I assumed that waiters gained added gravitas when they sounded French. But like the chap before us now, he wasn't making a very good job of it.

'Bloody Frenchman, that's all we need,' mutters Juggers, clearly missing the subtlety of it all.

285

'What part of France are you from?' say I. And instantly, I know I've foxed him.

'Thees is not omportant now,' says our faux Frenchman.

'I'm guessing somewhere near Putney, if I'm not much mistaken,' say I.

'There isn't no Putney in France, Grasby. Catch up, for any's sake.' Juggers is glaring at me again in the gloomy light.

Now that my eyes have adjusted, I can make out the figures before us more clearly. Our lantern man may be a most unconvincing Frenchman, but he's done a good job hiding the faces of his confederates. They're all silhouetted against one wall of the room, their features indistinguishable.

'We must talk to you,' says another chap. His attempted French accent is better than the other chap's, but it's still poor.

'Well, speak properly,' say I. 'What's all this bloody nonsense about, eh?'

Second from the right stands the dark shadow of a small woman – a very small woman. 'You must leesten carefully,' says she.

I throw my head back and laugh. 'I've seen some things in my time, but this takes the whole biscuit barrel, and then some. Professor, Dot, Wilf, why are you trying to treat us like idiots?'

There's a short silence while the party in the shade make various gasps of frustration, and Juggers glares at me again.

'I told you we shouldn't have brought the wee lassie with us,' says the instantly recognizable voice of Dr McKay.

There follows a fumbling at the wall, and soon we are illuminated once more by the ceiling light.

'By golly,' says Juggers. 'You're right, Grasby. I thought you'd gone daft with fear for a while there.'

Before us stand Professor Blunt, Dot, Dr McKay, Mrs Smith-Wantley and Wilf. The latter looking as though he's just chewed a wasp.

'It was your idea, Wilf,' says Smith-Wantley. 'I must say, I thought you made for a rather convincing Frenchman.' She smiles weakly. 'Gosh, we are all exposed now, aren't we?'

'Untie them, Wilf,' says the professor. 'Let's be civilized about this, at least.'

Reluctantly, Wilf goes about loosening my and Juggers's bonds. It's good to have the freedom of movement of one's arms for a change, and I stretch mine heavenwards by way of loosening off.

Unfortunately, my superior has other ideas. No sooner have his hands been untied than he jumps into action, grabbing Wilf and holding him round the neck in the crook of one arm, you know, in the fashion of a wrestler at a summer fair.

'Right, you lot. You're under arrest for the false imprisonment of police officers, assault, the illegal use of firearms, and anything else I can think of before it's Christmas Day. And let me tell you, that will be plenty!'

'Sir, if you don't loosen your grip, you're going to strangle him,' say I, watching Wilf's face turn red.

I hear the cocking of a gun, and when I look up, Dr McKay has a pistol pointed at us. A wartime job, by the look of it.

'Please let him go, Superintendent, and take a seat. We'll do this properly or not at all,' says she.

Juggers releases Wilf from the hold and pushes him away.

'So, as I suspected, you're all in this together, aren't you?' I say this looking between each one of them.

'Not just us,' says the professor. 'Most of our fellow villagers, in fact.'

'Smuggling stockings? Are you being serious?' Juggers is incredulous.

'Please don't be angry.' I swear Dot is on the verge of tears. 'You see, the village was dying on its feet. Our fishing fleet is made up of small boats. The big trawlers from Hull and Grimsby get the deep-sea fish, and the likes of Whitby, Scarborough and Filey leave us with precious little nearer the coast. Our lads were going further and further out. Aye, and it were dangerous, too.'

'The hotel had to close at the start of the war. We only managed to reopen three years ago.' The professor looks defiant. 'As a community, we'd no choice.'

'And apart from all that,' says Dr McKay, 'this marriage is a rather one-sided affair. It all started with them landing a few boxes. Before we knew it, they'd every boat from the village roped in. The rest of us became involved to try and persuade them to leave us alone.'

'But you failed,' I say.

'We did,' says the good doctor.

'When they threatened our village bobby, we knew there was nothing we could do to stop them.'

'Constable Armley was threatened?' asks Juggers.

'Aye, he bloody well was,' says Wilf in his waspy Cockney twang. 'Threatened to harm his dear old mother in Sheffield, they did.' Wilf shivers. 'He made some excuse to his bosses and went to France. He was paid to do it, mind you.'

Dot nods her head enthusiastically at this.

'You see, officers, it was carrot and stick all along,' says the professor. 'But soon, our fishermen – mostly young chaps – were making more money than they could possibly have earned by ploughing the seas. Until – well, until one of their number was killed for expressing doubts. I'm afraid things got rather out of hand.'

'Poor old Mr Wardle. What did he do?' asks Juggers.

'Like the late Ogden Barclay, he didn't agree with it all. At first, they weren't bothered about his refusal to cooperate, and the fisherman said he wouldn't be a problem. But then, as their shipments became larger and larger, they wanted his, the biggest vessel in the fleet.'

'The big green boat?' I ask. I remember wondering why it was in the harbour with Ogden's awful tub, while the rest of the fleet were out at sea.

'He refused. And as you know, was found near an old fishing boat. I read the report,' says Juggers.

'Correct, Superintendent,' says Dr McKay. 'But that was done on purpose, the way they'd arranged it. It was a warning to every fisherman – everyone in the village – what's yours is ours, and don't forget it.'

'We keep referring to *they*,' says Juggers. 'Who exactly do you mean?'

Uthley Bay's great and good, and Wilf, look between each other, clearly not wishing to put the finger on the people behind these crimes.

'They call it *the mob*.' Dot juts her chin determinedly when she says this.

'The mob?' I repeat, my intestines doing somersaults.

Dot nods, while the rest look both sheepish and scared, all at the same time.

Now, I'm a big cinema fan. In the process of finding another half, I've had many failed nights of romance at the pictures, don't you know. Amongst them the many films starring Edward G. Robinson, Jimmy Cagney and the like. And who can forget films like *Key Largo*, *High Sierra*, *White Heat* and *Dillinger*?

'*The mob*, that's all made up by Hollywood,' say I with a weak laugh. I search the faces of the Uthley Bay contingent and note that nobody's laughing.

'No, it isn't,' says Juggers with a dreadful finality. 'It's true enough. Our Customs and Excise, aye, and Special Branch, have had their eyes on this for a while. I'm not sure what happens in America, but I do know they're well organized and as ruthless as they come.'

'Why on earth aren't Customs or Special Branch dealing with this themselves, sir?'

Juggers sighs and shakes his head. 'Because the gang-sters get wind of it, and before you know, they're off to somewhere else. Nobody can pin them down or find enough evidence to get the buggers behind bars.'

'Hence our little trip here?'

'That's right, Grasby. They're not bothered about a couple of plods from York.'

'And you've known this all along?'

'Yes, I have, lad. Though, with the snow and that, things haven't quite worked out the way we'd hoped.'

'We thought this would be the case,' says the prof. 'You see, we had to come clean and tell you what's really been happening.'

'You didn't need to trap us under a net and bring us here trussed and at gunpoint.' Juggers fairly spits this out.

'That was my idea,' says Wilf with a leery grin.

'But if the snow keeps our cavalry from arriving, surely it's the same for this *mob*, sir?'

'But their men are already here, lad.'

This puzzles me for a moment. Then the scales fall from my eyes. 'Geraldo and his stage crew, sir?'

'The very same. And as I can't phone out to rustle anyone up by boat even, it's us and them, Grasby.'

Yet again, I see that frightened look on Juggers's face, while my mind drifts back to all the bloodthirsty gangster films I've ever seen.

'What about our constables?' I address the rather sheepish Uthley Bay party.

'Up at the lighthouse at Hadden Head,' says Wilf.

'On the cliffs,' adds the professor.

'And who is holding them, this *mob*?' I enquire.

'Well, of course,' says the prof. But there's something about his reply that doesn't convince.

'This is a right mess, and no mistake.' Juggers is shaking his round head irritably. 'We could never work out how these people were doing this under the noses of the villagers and getting away with it. Now we know, eh? You've all been in on it! You should be ashamed.'

'Yet, here we are,' says the professor. 'My advice to you both is to get back to the hotel and behave as normally as you can. That way, it won't arouse suspicion. Geraldo's chaps enjoy a lot to drink, you see.'

'They're relaxed – amongst friends, so they think – with nothing to worry about,' says the doctor. 'Once they're in their cups, we can sneak you both out, and try to get help.'

'Without my constables? Not a chance,' says Juggers.

There goes our shot at escape.

'Be under no illusion what you're facing.' Wilf's face looks even more rat-like than usual. 'For a start, Tommaso could pull you limb from limb and not get out of breath. And he's just one of them.'

I recall the huge Italian carrying Juggers's trunk up three flights of stairs as though it weighed nothing.

'Here's what we'll do,' says Juggers. 'We go back to the hotel and make our plans – not run away. Then, when they least expect it, we'll grab the lads, get them armed and do our best.' He looks at me. 'We might not all survive, Grasby. But we'll succeed, I'm sure of it.'

Super!

The locals give a little cheer – well, really a sigh of relief. I look on, unimpressed. It's us against the American mob.

Dash it all!

# 34

We're let through out the back of the house into a sizeable yard. To my dismay, the snow is coming down in great white sheets. I can barely see my hand in front of my face. Luckily, the distance between us and the hotel isn't too far, and there's a little lane, the type so common in Yorkshire, running along the back of the properties on the seafront. It's obviously been cleared after the previous snowfall, so isn't too difficult to navigate, with only three inches or so of new snow.

I love the white stuff, generally. By that, I mean under a bright blue sky, once the blizzard is over. Walking through a whiteout, however, is something I despise. It takes your very breath away. I plod on as fat flakes crowd into my mouth and nose. I try to cover my face with one hand but it's too cold, so I just have to endure it. My head is tilted down, and I'm hoping that whoever is leading the way – Wilf, I think – knows where he's going.

Behind me, I hear Juggers mumbling away. For a moment or two it sounds like a muttered prayer, the way monks go about things. However, on closer listening, he's producing an endless stream of invective, most of it unrepeatable. It's as though he's berating himself for being so stupid as to think whatever plan he concocted might have worked. And he's bloody right to be upset, too. Of course, compounding the felony by ensnaring me in it all.

I hope he falls in the snow, quite frankly.

And though I know it to be hopeless, part of me wonders how far I'd get if I shot off in this blizzard and made a run for it. The fact that I have little idea of the terrain, no equipment, and even less courage, leaves me tied to Juggers's cause. It's damnable.

After what seems like an hour but is in fact mere minutes, we stop behind the hotel. I hear a key rattling in a lock, and soon we're bathed in warmth and light in a part of the place unfamiliar to me. It's a small lobby, with some beer crates piled in a corner. I can hear muffled singing. So, the villainous Geraldo is still at it, warbling away like an outsized blackbird full of grappa.

'That's one of my favourites,' says Juggers. 'I've a record of Mario Lanza singing it, back at the house.'

*Gosh, you should throw a few shillings at him and ask for an encore*, I think to myself. I'm not sure I can carry on supressing my feelings about Juggers's determination to kill me much longer. If it's not leading me against the most dangerous men in America, he's inviting our erstwhile captors to just get on and blow our heads off. It's what I always say about the courageous. For every one of them, desperate to fill the grave in pursuit of some hopeless cause or other, there's a chap like me who ends up at their side, wondering how he got there, and how to survive the madness. Remember, if you ever meet a very brave person, stay as far away from them as you possibly can. You won't regret it.

'You pair go through that door,' says Dot. She looks at her wristwatch, having to brush snow from it to tell the time. 'They'll take a break at about nine, before starting up again just before midnight to bring in Christmas. That's when their guard will be down. There're some people who want to see you.'

Before I can ask who, she's off. So, Juggers and I troop in and through the door as directed. And, sure enough, we find ourselves in the small reception area, empty save us.

'I'm bloody soaked,' says Juggers, brushing accumulated snow from the shoulders of his jacket.

I fear I'm damp, too. I've probably wet myself in my current state of funk.

'We'll get in there, grab a drink or two and keep our eyes peeled,' says he.

I've noticed that Juggers's gait has been a bit off since we were trapped in the fish shed. He's definitely limping and seems overly inclined to fiddle around the zip of his trousers, an area that should most definitely be left alone in polite company. For all the world, he's like a chap who has delved into the drawer and donned his wife's undies by mistake.

'Are you quite all right?' I ask, casually, pretending my attention hasn't been drawn to the fact he's very obviously rearranging his family jewels. He then looks at me red-faced.

'I've got to get this out, Grasby.'

'I beg your pardon?' say I, looking on as he pulls down the zip of his trousers and starts tugging at something within.

'Good grief, sir. Have you entirely taken leave of your senses? This is neither the time nor the place!'

Of course, he's completely ignoring me, his face now crimson with the effort. There's a downturn to his mouth that would make one of these chaps who have gurning competitions up and down the county very proud indeed.

'Grab this!' says Juggers, gesturing to his crotch.

'Indeed I will not, sir! For my sake, if not the honour of

York Police, stop what you're doing. You must have taken a blow on the head earlier, because this type of behaviour is not on, I tell you.'

I recall arresting an old gent in a York restaurant when I was a young constable. He was well known to us, and well-to-do to boot. Sadly, something in his head went awry, and in this confused state he decided he could urinate anywhere he pleased. Juggers appears to be going the same way. My, he picks his moments.

Without warning, he lets out a yell that makes me jump.

'Managed to get the bugger out without having to unbutton my trousers. I'm glad of that, I'll tell you.' Juggers is now breathing heavily, while I avert my eyes.

'Good grief, this is an outrage, sir!' I protest as vociferously as I can muster – not hard, under the circumstances. No pun intended.

'Unbuttoning trousers won't be a problem for you, I daresay. But as you get a bit more ample round the middle, you'll see. Once you get your trousers fastened, you'll want to keep them that way as long as possible. The bloody thing was sticking into my leg all the way back here.'

'Please, contain yourself!'

If it weren't for our otherwise perilous circumstances, I'm sure I couldn't be more shocked. Facing death is bad enough without discovering one's superior is a rampant onanist into the bargain.

'Still in good working order, mark you. I was frightened it were going to go off back in that room when Mrs Smith-Wantley were talking. Now that would have left me in a right pickle, and no mistake. If it weren't for this snow, I'd go outside and let it off right now.'

'That's it!' say I.

Now, I've only ever assaulted two officers senior to me in

rank. The first was a captain in the Fourth Foot in Normandy, the second an inspector from Scragglethorpe at a Christmas party. But my golly, there's going to be a third. I turn round, my right fist bunched, ready to punch Juggers to the floor.

As I do, though, I see his eyes are cast downwards, examining something most carefully. Before I can protest, he shoves it in my face.

'These fishermen need to know more about searching a bloke for weapons. I stuffed this down my trousers when we were under that net.'

And there it is, the stubby little flare gun given to us by Madden, captain of the vessel that rescued us but failed to save poor Ogden Barclay.

'Well, that was clever, sir,' say I haltingly.

'Bloody uncomfortable, I'll tell you that.'

I picture the Royal Marines belting down Uthley Bay pier, ready to fire a few bullets into the American mobsters. Jolly good show – I feel quite elated! Then I remember it's unlikely to be clear enough outside for them to spot a flare, never mind navigate to the harbour in a blizzard.

It's damnable, you know. Two steps forward, three back. I look at Juggers with his little flare gun. I know we are to be returned of our sidearms and the rifles that accompany them. But the task before us is so enormous, a deep despair begins to settle on yours truly.

It's then I hear a familiar voice, and my world, already upside down, begins to spin so quickly it makes me dizzy.

'Hi, Frank. What have you been up to, buddy?'

I turn to face the voice, and there, with her blonde hair and cornflower-blue eyes, is Deedee – Daisy Dean – standing in this absurd little reception room of the Trout Hotel. And honestly, I can't believe it.

# 35

At first, I'm convinced my mind is playing tricks on me. I squeeze my eyes shut, ready to open them and for the world to be back to its rank misery. But no! Looking me straight in the eye is Deedee, as I've come to know her. Deedee works for the American government. And not only is she beautiful, she's a force to be reckoned with. Though I cannot work out why she's here.

I met her a year ago and, as you may have gathered, she's never been far from my thoughts.

With my heart thumping in my chest, my first instinct is to enfold her in my arms and tell her how I feel. That, though, would not be appropriate. In any event, standing behind her is the tall, broad-shouldered, suave chap I aspire to be. My goodness, you could positively hang your overcoat from his square jaw. And when he decides to smile, his teeth are so bright they give me a headache. Of course, this is just the type of guy I expect Deedee to be partnered with. My sudden elation is punctured like the flattest of tyres.

'Good evening, Miss Dean,' says Juggers, all sweetness and light. 'I'm so pleased to see you I can't put it into words, lass.'

'It wasn't easy, but we're here, Superintendent. Sorry we've had to lie low. But as you're aware, some of these guys know me by sight. It's a pity our plan is on the fritz.'

'And your colleague?' says Juggers, obviously looking for an introduction.

'Oh yes, how rude of me. This is Agent Terry O'Leary. It's his first time in England.'

'Pleased to make your acquaintance, sir,' says O'Leary, holding out a hand the size of a dinner plate. 'Gee, I thought it could snow in Boston, but you have us well beaten, sir.'

Of course! It just shows you how muddled my mind is. We're not bumping into Deedee by accident. She's here to bring her mobster countrymen to justice. And as for Flash Gordon, he's working with her. My mood takes another upward swing. Gosh, it's like being on a rollercoaster.

'Stop staring, Grasby. You look like a fish,' says Juggers.

'I do apologize. Just surprised to see you, Miss Dean. That's all.'

Face saved.

'Is there somewhere we can go? To be alone without interruption, I mean,' says Deedee. 'This is a bit public.'

'Rather!' say I, with a rush of blood to the head. I should, of course, have considered that she means all four of us, not just she and I.

'Come up to our room, we're on the top floor,' says Juggers. 'I must admit, I thought we were going to face this alone. Not a prospect I were looking forward to. Whereabouts are your men?' Juggers looks past her, as though whatever men Deedee has are standing behind her back in this small space.

'Not good news on that front. But hey, such is life, right? I'll let you know the lay of the land when we're sure nobody's listening.'

That's the confident Daisy Dean I know and love. She's as brave as a battalion of Commandos. Unfortunately, I'm not.

'Let's get upstairs,' says Juggers. 'You're right. This place has bigger ears than a bloody elephant.'

We decide to make our way to the third floor separately. Juggers and I walk through the main lobby, ensuring we're seen, while Deedee and O'Leary go by a back stair I've yet to discover. Trust her to know the place like the back of her hand.

We only have a few moments to wait before there's a knock at the door. Deedee and O'Leary enter. While she stands, O'Leary takes the chair by the dressing table – the only one in the room – meaning Juggers and I have to sit together on the bed.

The thing is, he weighs rather more than I, so the mattress is squashed to the springs where he's sitting. I have to resist tumbling into him, from where I'm perched. Something I'm sure our American friends would find odd. Just as well they didn't appear a little earlier, or they'd have been treated to the excruciating spectacle of Juggers removing a flare gun from his underpants. I often find life compensates here and there, when it can.

'Now,' says Deedee. 'I have good news and bad news.'

I love the way she pronounces *news* as though it rhymes with booze.

'If it weren't for bad news, we'd have none at all,' says Juggers bleakly.

Deedee reaches into her pocket and produces a single sheet of paper, which she hands to Juggers.

```
GPO TELEGRAM
Sender: Ethridge J Pughnam III
Recipient: RF 3
Date: 23-12-53
IN LIGHT OF WEATHER AND LOGISTICAL
PROBLEMS THE FURNITURE REMOVAL TEAM ARE
CANCELLED STOP STAND BY STOP MORE ANON
STOP
EJP
```

'I've heard the name,' says Juggers.

'He's my boss,' says Deedee.

*Good for him*, thinks I. And I note the telegram was sent yesterday. However, it's manna from heaven as far as I'm concerned. It means we won't have to fight the mob to the death. Hurrah and huzzah!

'Of course, we can't pay any attention to this now,' says Deedee.

It's amazing how one can go off a person, you know.

'Why on earth not?' say I. 'We're outnumbered, likely outgunned and trapped here in the snow. Even if we did round up the buggers, what on earth would we do with them?'

She smiles at me, a determined glint in her eye that I saw so often last Christmas. It's disconcerting. And I'm right to feel that way.

'Of course, things have changed since that communication was received.' Her polite New York accent is to the fore here, and she's sounding quite officious.

'I'll say,' say I. 'I've been punched, sunk, rescued, kidnapped, netted and I thought I was going to die at every point in between. We should shut ourselves in here, or better still, grab a fishing boat and escape as soon as we can!'

I don't know what it is, but seeing Deedee again has reminded me just how much I love life, and how I'm less than willing to give it up over a few smuggled stockings.

'And what about the folk here in Uthley Bay?' says Juggers. 'You just going to swan off and leave them to it, eh?'

'I rather think they've made their own beds, sir. In fact, they've been profiting from all this. If we're to do our jobs properly, then we should arrest every damned one of them.'

'Frank!' says Deedee, a look of disappointed surprise on her face. 'Your father's here, and Mrs Gaunt. You just going to abandon them?'

*Quite happily*, I muse.

'No way, Frank. This is the closest we'll ever come to bringing Geraldo Monza to justice. He's a senior member of an organized crime gang in New York. We're pretty sure he'll break under questioning, and we need to know more about these people before they run the world. We can cut a deal.'

More maniacs bent on world domination, I note with weary sadness. When will it end?

'Certainly, they're much more than just mobsters. It's our job to find out what that is,' says O'Leary casually.

'And stop them infiltrating Europe, too,' Deedee adds.

'They can do what they like in Europe, as far as I'm concerned,' say I. 'I've already nearly died saving Europe, thanks very much.'

'Frank, you're in Europe,' says Deedee flatly.

'Indeed, I am not!' I protest. 'Europe begins at Calais, and may I remind you, we're some distance from there.'

'You English,' says O'Leary. 'It's like me saying Manhattan isn't part of the USA, just because it's surrounded by water. I can never work you guys out.'

'You would know it instinctively if you were English,' I

say with a raise of my chin. The Americans don't like the high hand, you can be sure. I'm the very man for that, by golly.

'Shut up, Frank. You're making a show of yourself,' says Juggers. 'What do you suggest we do, Miss Dean, Mr O'Leary?'

I must admit to feeling a bit of a heel now, you know. But how many foxholes, ruined buildings, damp barracks or nights in the freezing cold has O'Leary spent defending Europe, eh? Not to mention being shot at, blown up, half-strangled, stabbed and near-starved to death. He doesn't know what he's talking about.

'I fought in France and Italy and I was aide to the Russians at the siege of Stalingrad,' says he, as though he's read my mind.

'Bloody hell,' says Juggers, clearly impressed. 'You've seen plenty, then.'

'I've seen my fair share.' O'Leary shrugs his shoulders disarmingly.

It doesn't matter what you achieve in life, you can always guarantee that an American has done it bigger and better.

'I did my bit, you know,' I pipe up, to little effect.

Deedee walks forward and places one hand on O'Leary's shoulder, making me madly jealous.

'Listen, you guys. They're going to have to take you out at one point this evening. They know you're cops, even though they don't think you'll be any trouble.'

'This might mean you being locked in a room or tied up,' says O'Leary, Deedee's hand still lingering on his shoulder. 'But more likely it'll mean – well, you know.'

'No, what will it mean?' I ask.

O'Leary drags one finger across his throat, leaving me in no doubt as to our likely fate.

'Here's what I propose,' says Deedee.

'Go ahead, lass,' says Juggers. Meanwhile, I'm calculating the chances of me ever seeing York again – or anywhere else, come to that.

'You guys go to the bar. Sit there like you're enjoying yourselves, but be alert.' She looks between Juggers and me as she says this. 'They have a delivery of cash – a lot of cash – coming over from Holland tonight. It's payment from the guys running the operation in Europe.'

Not this *Europe* again.

'How much money?' says Juggers.

'About two million dollars,' says O'Leary.

Gosh, I can't imagine so much money. What on earth would one do with it all? I mean, once you've bought a flashy car and a nice house?

'They won't want to make a fuss, so you'll probably be confronted by two of them only. Maybe at your table, maybe in the john, right? So, go there together,' says Deedee.

Dash it all.

'Could be guns, knives, we don't know.' O'Leary shrugs again. He seems most adept at that.

'What next?' I ask.

'They take you out of the room, quietly,' says O'Leary. 'And then, boom!' he shouts, making me jump. This has the unfortunate effect of propelling Juggers up with the force of the springy mattress. Before I know it, he's falling forward and ends up on his hands and knees on the floor, cursing like a fishwife.

'Hey, you guys are sure jumpy,' says O'Leary, helping Juggers to his feet. 'You don't have to worry, we'll be watching. Once we have two of them, we can take out the rest, one by one, if necessary. Shadows and confusion are our friends, right?'

Good, I've been confused all my life. And spent plenty time in the shadows, too. But it all sounds too easy. And in my experience, that's rarely the case once the talk stops and the action begins. I let out a deep sigh of despair.

Deedee looks at me with a little smile. But there's something else behind her blue, blue eyes I can't quite fathom.

# 36

Deedee and O'Leary disappear from our room. No doubt into the shadows the latter is so keen on. Mind you, I'd happily court the shadows with Deedee at my side. But no such luck, I've Juggers for company.

There's a quiet knock on the door. It's Dot. From a laundry bag, she produces our sidearms. My hand goes out immediately for the Beretta, leaving Juggers the bulky Webley again.

'There's an old sack lying behind the reception desk,' says Dot. 'Your rifles are in it. I'll make sure the door's left open at all times.' She smiles at us both. 'Good luck. You have the whole village behind you. Well, most of it.' With that, she's off.

I can't help wondering what she means by *Well, most of it.*

Juggers examines his weapon. I give mine a cursory glance. But my mind isn't on the job. I mean, I'm pretty sure I can trust Deedee. But O'Leary is an unknown quantity. And as you know, I find it hard to have faith in anyone. If you had a father like mine, you'd be the same.

'Right then, Francis,' says Juggers, ominously using my Christian name proper. 'No time like the present.'

And so, with Juggers's hands unconsciously bunched

into fists, and my heart consciously jumping through my chest, we leave our room and enter the lift.

Lifts make me pretty giddy at the best of times, especially the variety with the iron shutters, through which one can see floors rushing by. And though our journey is a very short one, I begin to feel queasy.

'It's do or die, lad,' says Juggers helpfully.

Oh, great. Just what I wanted to hear. Do, please!

We alight from the lift, and head straight into the bar. It's pretty busy, which I suppose it has every right to be on Christmas Eve. People are flitting between it and the dining room, where Geraldo has been performing. I spot two of his men in an enclave by a large aspidistra plant. It looks quite comical, actually. It's as though they're trying to be inconspicuous. It isn't working. They look horribly out of place with their sleek hair and pinkie rings.

Trying to ignore them, Juggers and I head for the bar.

'What would you like, Grasby?' says he.

Well, at least I'm not buying the drinks.

'A large Scotch, please. Very large,' I say under my breath.

Juggers orders a pint of stout and my whisky. And Dot, newly returned behind the bar and looking a tad pale about the gills, goes about her business. We grab the drinks and scan the room for a table. Deedee reckons this cosy little place is the perfect spot for them to make a move on us. Luckily, there are two tables right at the end, both unoccupied.

'That'll do us, lad,' says Juggers. We head to the seats closest to the wall.

Juggers takes a chair and moves the table near to his large gut. All of a sudden I feel trapped, as though I'm meat being prepared for the oven. Prime Grasby – just roast for a couple of hours in a hot oven until his skin is crisp. Oh, and you'll need stuffing; that was knocked out of him years ago.

I take a gulp of my whisky. It's a poor blend, likely the best they could manage during rationing. Gosh, here's a thought. Will I live to see the end of rationing? It's anyone's guess at the moment.

Then, the worst possible thing happens: a tall, very thin chap appears in the bar, followed by a woman dressed in black from head to toe, staggering on a walking stick. They look about the place, eventually see us, and make a beeline for our table.

'Now then, Arthur,' says my father, again wearing a shirt and tie rather than his dog collar.

'Cyril, Mrs Gaunt. How do you do this evening?'

I can see Juggers is rather put out. The last thing we need is my father getting in the middle of us and the mobsters. Goodness knows what might happen. The whole point of this exercise is for us to be quietly accosted by these villainous Americans, then let Deedee and O'Leary do their bit.

'Actually, we're waiting for someone, Father,' say I.

Well, it's not a lie.

'Ever the gentleman, my son,' says my dearest father. 'Surely you can see the effort Hetty made to come over here. Look at her.'

Sure enough, Hetty Gaunt is leaning on the back of a chair looking as though she might expire at any moment.

'Take a seat and get your breath back,' says Juggers. 'But your lad's right. We're here on business tonight, Cyril. Police business, you'll understand.'

'I see. Like that, is it?' The Reverend Grasby isn't best pleased. But while he'll happily have a go at me, he defers to Juggers.

Hetty sits down with a thump on the chair facing me.

'You look as though you've seen a ghost, young Frank. Eaten some old goose?'

*There's only one old goose in here*, thinks I. Though she's right about me being pale. It's a tendency in times of trouble and stress. An old flame of mine, Gertie Blenkinsop, sat beside me at my mother's funeral to keep me company. She was always a decent lass. Married to an accountant from Durham now, you know. In any case, she thought I was going to faint the longer the funeral went on. It's just the way I am. I looked like a ghost all the way through the war. Imminent death round every corner; that's how I feel now, and how I felt then.

Hetty Gaunt, having retrieved her puff, leans across the table.

'You have a dark aura, you know, Frank.'

She's wrong, of course. As you know, I drive a blue Morris Minor.

She holds out a gnarled hand, finger bent with rheumatism and old age. 'Take my hand, lad.'

I want to shout, *Go way, you stupid old crone!* Though, knowing the woman as I do, it's best to let her get on with what she's doing, so that it'll all come to a more rapid conclusion. I surrender my hand.

She turns it over and reads my left palm.

'Oh dear, oh dearie, dearie me.' Our family seer shakes her head repeatedly. 'Cyril, is it in order for a father to bury a son?' says she.

For once, I can count on Juggers. 'Right, as we said, we're expecting someone. So, I must ask you to find another table.'

'I'm not surprised the two of you are being so secretive. We've seen some odd things in this place, Arthur. I hope Francis told you.'

'He did that.' Juggers is lying now, and I'm proud of him. 'I hope you can get to the bottom of it.'

With that, the oddest couple in Yorkshire make off, one hobbling, the other stalking like a guardsman, making for a table across the room just vacated by an elderly couple. A plump woman has had the same idea, though, and sends her equally plump husband to claim the table. Fortunately, my father – being lithe as he is – beats him to it and sits down triumphantly, urging Hetty forward on her stick. Table claimed, my father goes to the bar, while Hetty stares at me, shaking her head and muttering under her breath.

Just what I need to cheer me up. I wonder if I could hit her with an ashtray from this distance. But that's an uncharitable thought. After all, if I survive this, she might be my new mummy. Gosh, I hope my father pops his clogs before he gets the chance to make an honest woman of her.

Juggers dunts my arm with his elbow, rousing me from mental pictures of my father and Hetty walking down the aisle.

I follow his eyeline, and spot what he's looking at so intently. Geraldo Monza is making a beeline for our table. And he looks a far from happy troubadour.

He arrives, all dark-eyed and unsmiling. There's none of the gushing of earlier on show now. He takes a seat and mops his brow with a handkerchief.

'Did you guys enjoy your walk earlier this evening?'

'Yes, we did, rather,' say I, suddenly determined not to be cowed by this great lump of pomade and lard.

He casts me a baleful glare. 'You're the feeble one. Half an idiot, so I hear.' He says it with flat authority, as though my status as *idiot* has been signed in triplicate by some government department.

'I beg your pardon?' say I.

'I know you guys are cops,' says Geraldo in his Jimmy Cagney drawl. He gives a shrug. 'And hey, I'm pleased.'

'You are?' says Juggers.

Geraldo leans in. There's sweat on his brow, his dark hair matching his black eyes, bright and sparkling, nothing behind them but a chilling void. I wait for the threat of the knife and the bullet, for the intimidation to begin. He seems to exude menace. Gosh, I feel myself shiver involuntarily, even though I know Deedee is close at hand.

If this master criminal is trying hard to put the wind up us, he needn't bother. He's already succeeded by his sheer presence. The gangster movies parade past my mind's eye once more. And to make matters worse, I know Juggers will want to fight on, no matter the odds. This isn't a good place to be, and I'm working myself up into a right funk.

'I have something to say. I want you to listen and listen good, got it?'

Here we go!

'We haven't got all night,' says Juggers. 'Father Christmas is on his way, you know.'

'He is for some.' Geraldo nods his head. 'But not for me.' The statement is again matter-of-fact.

I'm puzzled.

'I need your help. The pair of youse.' The Italian-American monster looks between us. 'Just smile, that's all you need to do. Because someone is going to die tonight. And I'm the favourite.'

Gosh, here's a turn-up for the books, if ever there was one.

'What do you mean?' says Juggers, looking more than a little bemused.

'Just what I say.' He rubs his forehead dry of sweat with

one great paw and looks round the room with a smile. 'Just keep those faces happy, as though we're talking about nothing in particular, just shooting the breeze.'

I look at Juggers with a smile. Well, it's best to do what one is told when dealing with cold-hearted killers, I always think.

'You're talking in bloody riddles,' says Juggers.

Geraldo lowers his voice. 'They have my wife.' He nods with a grin, as though conforming this happily. 'I brought her here to see England, and they took her.'

'Who took her?' I pipe up, feeling some of the fear drain away.

'These people. These damned *villagers*. Hey, I was told England was a quiet little place, with lords, earls and all that malarkey. It's worse than a visit to Harlem! And let me tell you, a man like me doesn't go to Harlem unless he has to.'

Hurrah for Harlem, that's all I can say. Dash it all, this is turning out to have more twists than a Raymond Chandler novel. I bought *The Little Sister* in Ken Spelman's bookshop in York in the summer. Gosh, it was exciting. Kept me up for nights on end.

Geraldo isn't quite what I expected. Not that I had any real preconceptions. I detect a vulnerability there, but maybe it's all an act.

'Who's that old guy?' says the American.

I follow his line of sight. 'That's my father,' I say with some regret.

'Really, that's your old man?' says Geraldo, as though he's happened upon two parts of the Holy Trinity. 'I love my father. Well, did love him. He passed some years ago thanks to the government. Your old man keeps calling me Geronimo.'

'You want to hear some of the things he calls me,' say I.

Not for the first time in my life, I silently rationalize the relationship I have with my father. It never adds up. Feel free to bury him in a concrete block.

'He's a character.' I feel my brows rise as I stare across at Grasby senior.

'Then you're a lucky guy! What I wouldn't give for just one night with my father for company.'

'You miss him?' I ask.

'Yeah, of course. But I'd also like to know where he hid the money from the Santino job.' He smiles. 'I'm breaking your balls.'

Gosh, I hope not.

'Hey, I've left you my calling card. Read it carefully, right?'

With that, Geraldo Monza takes to his feet and wanders back through the tables towards the stage.

'I'm at a loss with all this,' says Juggers. 'I mean, what was all that about the villagers?'

'It's a puzzle, sir.'

'And what's happened to your little American friend?'

He's right, there's absolutely no sign of Deedee.

I'm casting about, trying to work out what's happening. I picture Dot and the professor capturing Geraldo's wife and ruthlessly blackmailing her husband. It just doesn't make sense.

'Grab the card, Grasby,' says Juggers.

I pick it up and examine it.

'Here, sir. Something written on the back.'

Juggers snatches the business card from me and instantly turns it over.

*Be at the Skipper at 1 a.m. G*

The note is short and sweet. Of course, there's no way Juggers is going to fall for this old trick.

'Right, drink up. We better be up at the Skipper for one,' he says.

'Sir, this is madness. We can't trust him!'

'Maybe not. Though I'm not sure we can trust anyone, the way things are going. At least with Miss Dean and her boyfriend in the shadows, we can't go wrong. Anyhow, we've got to get to the bottom of this, Frank. What do you think?'

I ponder upon what he's said. 'I don't think he's her boyfriend, sir. Just colleagues, I'm sure.'

Juggers raises his eyes to the heavens.

Gosh, I hope Deedee appears quick smart. It's time to take the lift again. There's a while to go before one on Christmas morning. Let me tell you, I've been in many places in times past, early on Christmas Day. But freezing outside a dead man's pub isn't one of them. Though I suppose it's marginally better than being the dead man inside. There's plenty time for that, mark you.

We needn't have worried – Deedee and square-jawed O'Leary are already in our room when we arrive. She's propped up on the bed, while he's sitting on the chair by the dressing table.

'That was quick,' say I.

'Speed is the essence of our work, Mr Grasby,' says O'Leary. It's typical of a man like him. Good-looking, confident – full of himself. My goodness, the world's absolutely teeming with them – swines.

Juggers regales our American colleagues with what passed between us and Geraldo.

Deedee narrows her eyes as she listens. I'm convinced O'Leary takes her in with far too much enthusiasm. Leary by name, leery by nature, I suppose. Damn him!

'OK, you do as he says.' Deedee looks between Juggers and I.

'Surely that's asking for trouble,' say I.

'No, it isn't. Remember, we're one step ahead of them now. And we have your backs, Frank.'

'Is he being honest, do you think?' says Juggers. 'It sounds unlikely to me.'

I see another look pass between Deedee and her colleague. No wonder folk think they're involved. It's like that telepathy that everyone's going on about. I read about it in the *Picture Post* a while ago. Most unsettling.

'We take things as they come. We're pragmatic,' says leery O'Leary.

*I bet you're not as pragmatic as me.* Any more of this, and I'll be pragmatically heading for York on foot, blizzards or no blizzards. I'm sure I can rustle up an igloo. I must also thank the *Picture Post* for this idea. It's a fabulous publication.

Deedee walks over to me and takes my hand in hers. She looks up at me with such affection. Gosh, I'm weak at the knees.

'I know you can do this, Frank. I just do.' She stands on her tiptoes and plants a brief kiss on my lips.

And for a moment, she's absolutely right. I feel as though I could face down a Panzer division single-handed. But this sensation lasts mere moments. Before she walks back to the bed, I'm pondering the fine art of cutting blocks of compressed snow and fitting them together. It can't be that hard, surely?

Juggers lights his pipe and shakes his head. 'I don't know, you young folk. I'll just settle for a good shag any day,' he says, shaking a box of matches.

I know he means his odorous pipe tobacco. It brings

him comfort. The only thing that will comfort me now is the road home.

'We're going to disappear,' says O'Leary. 'Rest assured, though, we're there for you both.'

Deedee smiles at me. I can only return the gesture weakly. Even great admiration can't break through my feeling of utter hopelessness and fear.

# 37

When Deedee and O'Leary depart, we resort to Juggers's whisky bottle. I have a stiff drink and prepare myself for another adventure in the freezing cold – probably my last. With that in mind, I take a look at my remaining clean clothes. I have another shirt and sweater available. I put them on over my existing kit. It'll go some way towards keeping out the cold.

'What are you about, lad?' says Juggers. When I tell him, he announces that this seems a good idea and decides to copy me.

'Sir, are you quite able to move your arms?'

After all, he's going to need them, I'm certain.

'No problem. I'm as lithe as a gymnast, me.'

To prove this, he attempts a star jump, which ends up with him falling back on the bed and being consumed by a paroxysm of coughing.

'I'll be fine once we get going, lad.'

All this time, I'm planning my escape. If Juggers does survive, I can say I was disoriented in the snow. It's possible, after all. When I look out the window, it's coming down heavily enough, but not as much as I'd hoped. Still, it might get worse – or better, depending on one's opinion.

The noise downstairs subsides, and I hear people traipsing up the stairs for bed. Christmas Eve is over, and the big day is here.

'A good Christmas to you, lad,' says Juggers, holding out his big hand for me to shake.

'And you, sir,' say I, grabbing it.

'I wonder what's for Christmas dinner in this place?' says he.

I must say, this is an empty gesture. It's like General Custer and a lieutenant discussing their holiday plans at Little Big Horn. It's going to be another unhappy Christmas for me. I'm getting used to them.

Juggers, with no little difficulty, rolls his wrist to check his watch.

'Right, it's time. Best to be a little early to see how the land lies,' says Juggers.

Fabulous! More time freezing in the snow.

Before I know it, we're outside again. And for once, my mood lightens. The snow is much heavier again. The whole place – what you can see of it – resembles the Yukon. It foreshortens buildings, makes cars like round baps at the side of the pavement, and banishes understanding of where the road begins or ends. Even the twinkling light from the street lamps is diffused, making Uthley Bay look almost picture-perfectly beautiful.

My plan, though, is well advanced.

As we turn into Kissing Lane, I'm ready. I know there are little blind spots of darkness, street lamps more spaced out here than on Front Row and Back Row. As we approach one, I call out to Juggers.

'Sir, my lace is undone. I'll need to tie it!'

'You know where we're going, Grasby,' says he, head down, plodding into the heavy snow.

And it's as easy as that. I look on as his rotund frame disappears.

Of course, my lace is perfectly secure. But it's a damn good diversionary tactic. Once he turns round – if he does – he'll just assume I'm following on through the whiteout.

I've noticed a few things since I've been here. Most people seem to have little sheds in their back gardens. I shall break into one, huddle down out of the weather for a couple of hours, and return to life, as Dickens said, suitably dishevelled, desperate and frozen, anxious to find out what happened to my colleague.

I know this sounds cowardly. But it's not as though I'm leaving Juggers to it on his own. He has the Americans in tow, somewhere – the covert Deedee and O'Leary.

I give Juggers a couple of minutes before carrying on up Kissing Lane. Instead of turning right at its end, I turn left. The dirty deed has begun.

The snow is coming down like cheap confetti. From the north-east, wind is gusting into my face. Though progress is slow, I'm making my way from trouble rather than towards it.

Despite the hour, there are still one or two lights shining from houses on Back Row. I see a garden gate, lying ajar, with snow piled up in the gap between it and the fence-post. I'm about to navigate this when I hear something. Though the wind and snow fill my ears, as well as my nose, I hear a definite crunch, like the crump of a boot on soft snow.

'Who's there?' I shout. I'm really scared now. This place is full of demons, as far as I'm concerned.

Of course, there is no reply. So, putting it all down to the deleterious impact of blind funk, I place my hand on the gate, to steady me as I go in search of a shed in which to hide.

It's then I'm grabbed from behind, a strong arm round my neck. The shock knocks the very breath from me, and quickly I begin to panic.

'Hey! Have a care, I'm a police officer!' I squeal in protest.

'Oh, I know who you are,' says a voice in my ear. It's a woman, and for the life of me I can't work out who she is, and why her voice is familiar.

Someone else grabs my arms and pulls them behind my back. And so it is, for the second time in a few hours, my hands are tightly tied.

There are a few of them. I can see shadowy figures through the snow, under the street lights. I count five, though there may be more out of my line of sight. They're all wearing balaclavas that have little holes for their eyes and mouths. Instantly, I'm taken back to a similar garment knitted for my birthday by my mother's Aunt Mamie. Of course, at the first sign of cold weather, it was forced over my head and I was sent on my way to school. I was told to take it off when Martha Ackroyd almost collapsed in fear on seeing me in the playground.

I can honestly bet you any money she wasn't as terrified as I am at this very moment.

'How lucky,' says the woman. 'You'll come in very handy, I'm sure.'

Such is my panic, I still can't place the voice.

'What do you want from me?' I venture. 'You'll find yourself in a world of trouble, you know.'

I hear laughter and a few indistinct mutterings.

'We're really scared. But we're going to take the risk.' It's the woman again, mocking me. 'Let's get going. Push him along!' says she, as though I was a beast of burden.

320

I want to protest, to shout to anyone who'll listen, that I'm being abducted – again. It'll do no good, though. My escape plan has failed before it has begun. And now I'm in the hands of the very people I was running from. It would seem that Geraldo wasn't lying. Or maybe he was. Who knows? Everything is so confused.

Happy Christmas, I don't think!

We head up one side of Back Row, then down the other. We're definitely making for the Skipper.

Despite the snow, progress is good, and before we know it I can see the pub's sign, swinging on the wind, the painting of a bearded man with a Breton cap partially obscured on one side by snow, illuminated by a single lamp.

There is another group huddled around the front door, their collective breath pooling in a cloud. Instantly, I spot the rotund figure of Juggers, which in a way is comforting. Geraldo Monza is alongside him.

'Missing one, are we?' says the woman with a laugh.

'Grasby, what on earth . . .?' Juggers is confused. I don't blame him.

'I heard a noise, sir. Went to investigate, in case we were being followed.'

'I can see we were,' says Juggers.

'Enough of the chit-chat. We all know why we're here,' says the woman I still can't place.

'I'm here for my wife,' says Geraldo. 'Where is she?'

'You know what I really want. I do hope your lovely cruiser is in good working order.' There's a certain note of triumph in her voice.

'Wait, you never said nothing about going to sea. In this weather, are you crazy?' Geraldo gestures. 'You ever been lost at sea?'

*Yes, as it happens. And not long ago, either*, thinks I.

'We don't have far to go. And you know exactly where the meeting point is. Your men were going to sneak out there while the rest of us were making for the lighthouse. You're a good singer, Mr Monza. But you aren't that clever. Just goes to show, you can trust no one.'

Geraldo is suddenly animated. He looks round his men angrily; there are four of them. 'Which one of you guys is a rat? I will find out, and I'll kill you!'

There are various protests to the contrary from the other mobsters. Mind you, I didn't expect one of them to thrust an arm in the air and shout, 'It's me!'

'I have the keys to the pub here. Your men will be held in there. Search them, please,' says our bandit queen.

It's then I realize who she is.

'Mrs Barclay!' I stutter. I should have recognized her soft, upper-class accent earlier. I suppose it was the present context that put me off.

'You sure catch on quick, kid,' says Geraldo.

Elizabeth Barclay ignores me, as her men search the four American ruffians, guns pointed at their heads.

'They've nowt on them,' says a Yorkshire voice. Clearly one of these villainous villagers.

'Do you have any idea what trouble you're in?' I say, hoping to give this deluded fisherman second thoughts.

'Aye, I do, as it happens. And from where I'm standing, you're in no position to threaten nobody,' says he.

'Just get on with it,' says Elizabeth Barclay.

In moments, the door to the Skipper is opened, a light flickers on, and three of the balaclava-clad locals usher Geraldo's henchmen into the pub. I was right – there are more gun-toting villagers than I thought. I count another three at least, though the darkness and the snow makes it confusing.

'Now, gentlemen. You won't mind your hands being tied, like Sergeant Grasby's here.'

'Inspector, actually,' say I automatically. Juggers shakes his head at the comment.

The door of the Skipper is locked and bolted from the inside. Now we are fewer in number. I count Mrs Barclay, Geraldo, Juggers and myself. We're being guarded by four of the local men – assuming they are local. They certainly sound it.

'This is where crime gets you,' says Juggers, as though he's preaching to children about the dangers of crossing the road. It's something we have to do now in schools. I'm sure it makes not a jot of difference to the little tykes. One of them threw a half-chewed caramel at me the last time I attempted this unenviable task.

'Enough from you all!' shouts Mrs Barclay. 'The sooner we get this done, the sooner your wife will be free, Monza.'

'Let's get on with it, then,' says he in reply.

So it is, in the snowstorm, under the flickering street lamps of Uthley Bay, that we are force-marched at gun-point to the harbour. There's not a soul about now, so early on Christmas morning. Even the Trout is shuttered up, and not a light to be seen from the bedroom windows around the building. I think again of my father, no doubt snuggled up to Hetty, while his son is being forced towards a cold, watery grave. I wonder if he'll cry the way he did when my mother died. I doubt it. And that's sad.

This little fishing village has become so familiar over the last few days. Who'd have thought such evil lurked beneath its surface? Three dead men – that we know of – and a fortune from hosiery. American gangsters, ruthless locals, and us. Caught in the middle of this nightmare. It's damnable bad luck. And it just shows how money corrupts even the most ordinary folk.

We pass like shadows under the lights on the quay. A casual observer may reckon the fleet is taking to sea unexpectedly, instead of the horrible reality of it all. I glance at Juggers. He's plodding along, his head bent into the wind. He's an unknown quantity. Oh dear, I truly hope he doesn't try anything heroic.

Geraldo's plush clinker-built cabin cruiser is nestled against the pier. It looks out of place; a vessel like this would look much more at home somewhere on the French Riviera or, more likely in his case, the Bay of Naples. I've seen them both, you know. If nothing else, war lets one take in the world.

At least the process of boarding is an altogether easier business than getting onto the *Empty Heart*. I think again of Ogden Barclay, and something rather unpleasant comes to mind. It's little things, you know. The wedding ring I'd noticed the day we first met him at the pier, that had disappeared from his finger when he took us out on his boat. At the time, it was part of the horror and tragedy of it all. But you can be sure that such minutiae stick in one's mind for a reason. The trouble he had firing up the engine of the *Empty Heart*, his awkward passage onto the boat. My goodness, the very name of the fishing boat itself.

Unbeknownst to me, these tiny snatches of time have been gnawing away at my subconscious mind. Now, as is often the case, I experience a flash of absolute clarity. Sadly, it appears to have arrived too late.

'I wonder what your husband would say to all this, Mrs Barclay,' say I. If I'm right, it'll hit a nerve.

'You killed him, so we'll never know,' she replies rather too glibly for my liking.

'I remember him poking about at the back of the Skipper, when we were waiting for the doctor and the mortuary van to attend his brother.'

'And what about it?' she replies.

'I thought it rather odd at the time. But things are clearer now. Perhaps he was wondering if his sibling had dropped something on one of his night-time walks? A wedding ring, perhaps.'

'Who knows? Just get on the boat!'

I can hear that she is flustered by this. If I am to go down, I might as well do so fighting.

'Or maybe your husband *was* the man lying dead in the back of the Skipper?'

'What are you babbling on about, Grasby?' says Juggers.

'We met Ogden Barclay, sir. The day we first arrived. The man who took us out to sea and died for his trouble wasn't Ogden, it was Perkin.' I turn to Elizabeth Barclay, her face still hidden by the balaclava. It's strange, but I feel as though I can almost see her expression through the dashed thing. 'You were his lost love, Mrs Barclay. Why you ended up marrying his brother, I don't know. But his midnight perambulations were all about meeting you, weren't they? Meeting you, and plotting. Ogden didn't agree with your plans – didn't want anything to do with them, did he? And you'd realized a long time ago that you'd married the wrong brother. So, you killed him.'

'Shut up!' she cries, her voice wavering, as though on the verge of tears. 'If you're that clever, get yourself out of this!'

I'm halfway down the sea steps when I feel two hands on my back. From there, I'm pushed onto the deck of Geraldo's vessel. But I'm lucky, the accumulated snow cushions my fall, and I feel a sense of pride now because, whatever happens, I worked it out. Aye, and brought Elizabeth Barclay the rightful shame she deserves. Though her armed companions say nothing, if they are local men it must be as big a shock for them as it is for me.

'Hey, this kid's smarter than he looks,' says Geraldo. 'You should let him do some real police work.'

We're all aboard now. One of Mrs Barclay's henchmen helps me to my feet and forces me into a chair in the big cabin. Juggers is seated beside me. Uthley Bay is picked out in little pools of street lamps, like a join-the-dots puzzle, through the big windows at the front of the vessel. It's designed for sight-seeing, though not tonight's sight, I venture.

'How did you know that, lad? I hope it's not just a shot in the dark,' says Juggers.

'Intuition, sir. Nothing more.'

Juggers grunts some kind of approval, as I'm in silent prayer. Where on earth are Deedee and O'Leary?

'You don't expect me to sail this thing, do you?' says Geraldo.

'No, I don't,' says Mrs Barclay. 'It's the good thing about having so many mariners aboard.' She walks over to a tall man in a balaclava. 'Right, let's go. We'll get there just in time.'

Geraldo shakes his head. He's sitting opposite us. 'You believe this?'

'I don't think it's safe to believe anything in Uthley Bay,' says Juggers.

And he's right. This is a nest of vipers, and no mistake. Good and bad, all in one tiny village.

Powerful engines burst into life. They're so different – a deep, guttural roar, not the gentle putter of fishing vessels I've observed since being here.

As we begin to move, I squint out of a large window through the snow and onto the quayside. Deedee, why have you abandoned me? This isn't what we discussed. Then it strikes me hard. What if this cut-throat bunch caught up with her and O'Leary? My heart sinks. Deep down, I know how brave Daisy Dean is. She would never let us be carried off to our deaths.

'Waiting for someone, Inspector?'

There's something in Elizabeth Barclay's tone that sends a chill down my spine. Damn, my expression has given my thoughts away.

'I wouldn't wait too long. Don't worry, your American friends will be far away by now.' She laughs.

'No!' I shout at the top of my voice. 'You harm a hair on her head, and I promise you, you'll be sorry.'

'My goodness, Inspector. You don't mind dishing it out, but I see you're not so happy to be on the receiving end.'

I felt a terrible emptiness when my mother died. I feel it again now. I lower my head to hide my tears.

'That's right, kid. You let it all out,' says Geraldo waspishly.

But I'm not listening.

'I hope you're not blubbing,' says Juggers.

You know, it nicely illustrates the mind of your average Englishman. I saw it right throughout the war. No matter how desperate the situation, tears are not to be countenanced. Take a bullet and die in a ditch with a stiff upper lip, like a gentleman. Well, that's not how it really is.

'Do be quiet, sir,' say I, as a fat tear slides down my cheek.

As we leave Uthley Bay behind in the snow, my heart is broken.

# 38

We can't have sailed for more than fifteen minutes when the drone of the engines drops, and we slow to a halt. I stretch my neck to look out of the windows again, and through onrushing flakes of snow I can see a light. It's moving like a pendulum, to and fro. This is the signal Elizabeth has been waiting for, no doubt a pre-agreed navigation point.

Geraldo shakes his big head.

'Not what you planned, sir?' says Juggers sarcastically.

'It's not the money, it's the betrayal. C'mon, how'd you feel if your young cop friend here sold you down the river?'

'I know that wouldn't happen,' says Juggers with such certainty it makes me feel rather guilty.

I doubt we'll ever live long enough to discuss my *shoelace-tying* absence back in the village.

I can hear voices, Dutch accents on the air. I remember the distinct language from the war. For it is from Holland that the stockings come. I remember Juggers telling me. It's the centre of this smuggling network. I hear snatches of conversation, so there's no doubt that these people know each other.

The talking stops, and I hear the sound of an engine.

Not ours, though, it must be the Dutch heading off back across the North Sea from whence they came.

A pair of seaboots appear down the steps into the cabin. Two great sacks are placed in the middle of the floor.

'And what was once yours is mine, Mr Monza.' Elizabeth Barclay smiles broadly. 'I know you thought we'd do the money handover and you'd cheat us. But, as it turns out, you're the cheated one. Been a pleasure doing business with you.'

'The feeling ain't mutual, lady,' says he.

'Where now?' says Juggers.

'Good question, cop. I wanna see my wife,' Geraldo adds.

I want to see Deedee. Though this isn't the time to say so.

'I think we should so some sight-seeing while you're here,' says Mrs Barclay. 'Don't worry, it won't take long. I've a treat in store. I just hope all this snow doesn't spoil the view.' She wanders off and I hear her muttering to one of her men.

'What does she mean?' I ask Geraldo.

'We was originally meant to meet the Dutch up at the lighthouse. A quiet place to count the dough. But I arranged to pick the money up there without our friendly locals in attendance.' He gives another of those Latin shrugs. 'It was cutting out the middleman.'

'Greed, sheer greed,' observes Juggers, distaste spread across his face.

'Whaddya want? I'm a fat crook from New York. You expect me to stick to the rules?'

'And what about your wife?'

For once, Geraldo doesn't have a smart answer. 'I first met her in a club in Jersey.' His gaze is far away, back in America.

'A golf club?' asks Juggers.

'No, a strip club. You really think I golf? Do I look like a golfer to you?'

'How charming. She must be a special woman,' say I.

Geraldo shakes his head at me with a forced grin. 'You bet she's charming. The lip on this guy.' He bursts out laughing.

The sea is choppier now. I reckon we're going further out from the coast. But Geraldo assures me otherwise.

'It's always a little lumpy round the headlands. Meeting of sea and shore, and all that jazz.'

He's right, for soon after, the cabin cruiser slows again, and two of the men in balaclavas approach us. Our hands are untied. It's such a relief.

'No funny business – any of you!' The man's accent is rough Yorkshire. Two shotguns are pointed at us.

'Hey, you got it,' says Geraldo, his hands raised in faux surrender.

For a moment, I wonder why we've been freed from our bonds. But I dare not follow that thought to its natural conclusion.

'Be ready for a climb, gentlemen,' says Geraldo.

And he isn't kidding. We're hauled to the deck of the cabin cruiser. I look up at a cliff above us. It's not particularly tall, and I can see the top of a lighthouse soaring even higher into the dark sky. Mercifully, a little curl in the headland has produced a tiny bay. They've added a small stone pier, an access point for the lighthouse keepers. It's onto this pier we step, each of us helped off the boat by two men in balaclavas. Though this would normally be a bit hairy, the tide seems to be just at the right height for us to get ashore safely.

'What now?' say I. Our captors have produced sea

lanterns to light our way. The snow has eased to a gentle fall but it's perishingly cold. I can see a gibbous moon jostling with felted clouds beyond the cliff and the lighthouse, adding to the unreality of it all.

'We go up,' says Geraldo. He points to what looks like a scar on the side of the cliff. In fact, it's a long staircase.

I'm no great shakes at climbing things. My gaze follows the zig-zagging steps. It looks ghastly.

'I don't know what the point of all this is,' say I.

'You're not as quick as I thought, kid,' opines Geraldo. 'We go up there, there's a scuffle, a couple of shots, or maybe we fall to our deaths. Hey, what's the betting Old Ma Barclay over there tells the tale of how you brave boys tried to save her and her crew from the vicious mobsters? Yeah, and she'll get away with it too. Because none of us will be there to contradict her. I just wanted to make a little money providing a service. Everyone got a piece. It became real vicious when Mrs B appeared. The other villagers are pussy cats. Not Barclay – or the other one.' He shrugs.

What *other one*, I ponder.

'I doubt she'll go that far,' says Juggers. 'I think you'll find that people in this country have too much respect for the police to kill us.'

'Don't underestimate these guys – certainly not her.' He nods towards Mrs Barclay, still in her mask. 'You might believe me when I say I know a lot of bad people. From what I've seen, she sure is like them.'

I note that Geraldo doesn't see himself as a bad person. Odd, really. I recall my meeting with Mrs Barclay, when I told her that her husband had died at sea. She was so sweet, so distraught. I can hardly believe it. But then another horrible thought crosses my mind.

'You killed these people. You killed Wardle. You strangled

him with a stocking because he wouldn't let you use his vessel. Maybe he was going to blow the whistle. I think Mrs Barclay has some way to go to be as bad as you.'

The shake of Geraldo's head has a weary resignation about it. 'Listen, kid. Whatever you think of me, whatever movies you've seen, I'm a businessman. Hey, do people get killed in my line of work? Sure they do. But that's a last resort. You wanna know why?'

'Go on.'

'Because it's bad for business. It attracts attention, unsettles the guys. Would you be here if that old fisherman hadn't been found dead beside that boat? Don't finger me as your murderer, because I ain't.' He looks at Elizabeth. 'She's clever. I don't know how, but she knew enough to kill using a pair of stockings. Guys I know always try to send a message when they kill someone. If you're an informer, hey, there's a rat next to you when you're found. Everything has meaning. It's an Italian thing. She knew what she was doing, knew I'd get the blame. I ain't killed nobody.'

Before I can probe any further, I'm nudged in the back with the barrel of a gun. It's time to climb the steps.

Juggers takes the lead, I'm next, followed by Geraldo. There are armed men above and below us as we make the ascent. The steps are treacherous, slimy with weed, and slippery with ice and snow. I look on as Juggers stumbles. One of our captors reaches out and grabs his arm, saving him from the sheer drop below. A rope affixed to the cliff acts as an improvised handrail. There is nothing to arrest a fall on the other side of the steps. It all seems rather pointless to me – a bit like rugby. If they're going to kill us, why not get on with it?

I don't know about everyone else, but my knees complain with each step, as we get higher and higher. Mercifully, just as I think Juggers is going to collapse with the effort and fall backwards onto me, we make the top of the cliff. There's snow in my eyes, and my face is numb with cold. So numb, it's beginning to feel warm. It's quite a pleasant sensation, though I know it's a very bad sign. I feel so tired of it all.

And so, we are gathered on the cliff, a strange little band, our faces gaunt in the light of the flickering sea lanterns and the shifting moon.

'What about my wife? I keep asking and get no reply,' says Geraldo.

'And my constables?' says Juggers.

'I promise you both, they're safe. Once we're away from here, they'll be released unharmed,' says gun-wielding Elizabeth Barclay.

I look on with my hot face. It all seems so inevitable now. Even my fear and dread has abated. I'm resigned to my fate. I can even imagine the headlines.

## DETECTIVES KILLED ON CHRISTMAS DAY
## THE CHRISTMAS KILLINGS
## BRAVE FRANK GRASBY DEAD – A NATION MOURNS

Well, maybe not the last bit. But you know what I mean. I am a most reluctant hero.

'If you two could step to the edge of the cliff, please?' Mrs Barclay points our way with a rifle. The lighthouse is towering above is. It's only now I note it's casting no warning beam across the sea for vulnerable mariners. I wonder why, as I begin the walk to my ultimate demise. I'm determined not to be found battered to death by the fall and the relentless tide on the rocks below. So, despite general cowardice, I'm ready to fling myself at one of the armed balaclava-wearers, and damn the consequences.

I take a look round on top of the cliff. These are the last things I'm ever going to see. It makes me really sad – so sad it's painful. But something inside me just wants to rest. Perhaps it's because of the cold, maybe just pure fear. But I begin to feel tired, disconnected from this horror.

In this state of disconnection, I casually observe Juggers fiddling with the zip of his trousers. Surely not! Even he's not mad enough to try this – is he?

Before I can say anything to him, there's a loud pop, and my brave superintendent is engulfed in a fiery orange cloud. Everyone backs away – unlike me, astonished at this turn of events. Knowing exactly what is happening, I can see his rotund figure at the centre of a huge plume of orange smoke. And I remember my father's description of the burning of Protestants under Bloody Mary, Elizabeth I's sister. This must be what it looked like. Poor Juggers! But he may just have saved my life.

There's only one thing to do. In the confusion, I turn on my heels and I'm off, belting away. Juggers has made the ultimate sacrifice, and by doing so, he's given me a chance. Shame to waste it, really.

I hear voices raised in confusion. When I look over my shoulder to find out if anyone's following me, all I see are silhouetted figures dashing about under the orange plume. There's a shout, the crack of a gunshot, a scream.

It's right now something very strange happens. I hear Deedee's voice in my head.

*'Frank, Frank! Stop, stay where you are. You're going to be safe!'*

Honestly, it's as clear as day, as though she were standing right next to me. I've taken a hit, I know it. This is my desperate brain trying to soothe my passage onwards to the great beyond. So close, and yet so far. I'm so confused, taken aback, that I stop in my tracks. If she is calling me from another realm, I'm fine with that. I'm happy if Deedee's there.

Then my heart sinks. I feel strong fingers grasp my arm. I've missed my chance to escape!

'Frank, stop, it's me!'

I look down as a shaft of silver moonlight lights up Deedee's face. Her blue eyes sparkle like diamonds in a coal mine.

It's true. I must be dead, for this is most certainly heaven.

'Here, take this and come with me.'

Deedee thrusts something into my hands. A pistol. I'm not sure they're permitted past the Pearly Gates.

'This way, Frank.'

Blindly, without thought, I follow her back into the fray.

All is madness, lanterns are flashing here and there. I catch a glimpse of Payne the grocer. He's pulling off his balaclava, and has his shotgun levelled at Elizabeth Barclay. She's backing away. He's one of us!

Suddenly, out of the orange slather of moonlight, comes an enormous figure. He lifts one of Barclay's henchmen and fairly flings him to the ground, as though he were a rag doll. The man screams in agony as he writhes on the snow.

I see O'Leary throw a punch at a dark figure, felling him like a pine. Note to self: if he has any romantic intentions towards Deedee, best let him get on with it unhindered.

All around, the balaclavas are standing with their hands in the air. They're beaten, defeated. I'm going to live!

But just as this joyous thought passes through my mind, a hideously malformed shape is crawling towards me from out of the orange cloud. Where there should be a face, there's just a blackened mass of flesh. To my horror, this monster reaches out to me with a dark, clawing hand. It's death, and I know it.

'Leave me alone!' I screech, ready to flee.

'Grasby, give me a hand up, will you, lad?'

It's then I realize this beast of my most tortured imaginings is, in reality, Juggers. I pull him to his feet. Moonlight is banishing the orange cloud now. Under it, Juggers appears to be covered in soot. He blinks at me, the whites of his eyes bloodshot from the smoke. He begins to cough heartily.

'Bloody hell!' he manages to splutter. 'Damn thing blew out the gusset of me slacks!'

'Just as well the barrel was pointing in the direction it was, sir,' say I, altogether astounded that he's still in one piece.

'Aye, like as not,' says he. 'It were a grand show.'

Gosh, you have to admit, he's a stoic old sod.

While Juggers clears his lungs, I look to my right. Geraldo is walking towards Tommaso the chef, his arms outstretched in filial greeting.

'You're some guy, Tommaso. How did you know we was up here? Come here, I wanna kiss that beautiful big face of yours.'

Instead of embracing his gangland boss, though, Tommaso raises a rifle. 'You stay where you are, Gerry.'

Geraldo looks puzzled at first, then he frowns. 'You're the rat? Aw, come on. You're kidding me, right?'

The big man shakes his head. 'No kidding here,' he shouts.

'But our fathers grew up together on the boot. Don't that mean nothing to you?'

But Tommaso isn't in the mood for nostalgia. He grabs Geraldo, spins him about, and soon the singing mobster's hands are cuffed behind his back.

As if by magic, Deedee is at my side.

'Right, Frank. Let's get you back to the hotel, make sure you're still in one piece.'

'What about Juggers and the constables?' say I.

'You leave that to us, Frank.' She squeezes my hand. 'Everything is fine. I'll explain later.'

'I have something to tell you, Deedee,' say I, giddy with all that's gone on, fear and the bitter cold.

'It can wait until tomorrow. You need rest, you understand?'

'I love you, Deedee.' But as I say these words, she's dashing off across the snow, no doubt bent on bringing another criminal to justice.

And so, I've been rescued by the woman I adore. Gosh, that's handy. Promptly, my world starts to spin, and everything goes black.

# 39

They must have taken Juggers for treatment, for when I awake at the Trout, not knowing how on earth I got here, I'm lying across the double bed in our room, blissfully alone.

For a few moments, I'm not sure that I haven't woken up from a nightmare, lingering on into my wakefulness. But it's no dream. I was about to be flung off a cliff by a mad stocking smuggler last night. As a precaution, I pass my hands across my legs to make sure they're still there. I remember a chap in the war waking minus legs, and not realizing this horrible fact until the blanket was lifted from his stumps.

Of course, I want to find out what on earth happened. I can't remember getting back to the hotel from the lighthouse. It's all a blur. Though Deedee's eyes were real enough, even now. I've never seen such a gorgeous pair of peepers.

To my horror, I notice that it's nearly midday. I almost never sleep in, so get myself to the bathroom to spruce up.

My ablutions complete, I feel hunger pangs. I recall that Dot's fish was the last meal I had, yesterday evening. So much seems to have happened since then. I grab a suit, the one that's most presentable, and head downstairs to find a bite to eat.

When the lift doors open, the lobby is deserted, though I hear a hubbub coming from the dining room. It's only spotting the great decorated tree that reminds me it's Christmas Day.

I head for the noise. Gosh, I'm looking forward to some goose and Christmas pudding for the first time this festive season. But the sight that greets me isn't what I expect.

When I open the dining-room door, you can hear a pin drop. It's like the Westerns; you know, when the gunslinger opens the door and the whole saloon descends into a deathly hush.

Quickly, though, I realize that nobody is looking at me. Despite the room being packed with elderly, festive guests, all eyes are on the improvised little stage, constructed from beer crates and some plyboard, where Geraldo sang last night. But they're not looking at the Italian-American singer-*cum*-gangster. Oh no.

On this impromptu stage, a tall, elderly man is doing his best to get down on one knee, with the aid of an odd-looking old woman in a bowler hat with a red feather in its band.

'Henrietta Gaunt, will you take my hand in marriage?' says the buffoon, staring hopefully up into her face, desperately trying to keep his balance on one knee.

'Oh aye, I do, Cyril. I do!'

All of a sudden, the room is in uproar. People are clapping, cheering and hallooing as though they've just watched Norman Yardley hit a century at Headingley. One old codger pops the cork on a bottle of that new Babycham. My father tasted it recently and thought it 'disgusting perry'. I'm not so refined when it comes to palate. If it's wet and gets one drunk, heigh-ho! There pipes up a chorus of 'For He's A Jolly Good Fellow', followed by the inevitable *Hip-hip!*

I feel sick to my stomach. He may well be a *jolly good fellow*, but he's also a jolly bad father. Dash it all!

But it's amidst all this cheering and general celebration that I have another flash of inspiration. And to be honest, I don't know why it never occurred to me before.

I make my way from my father and Hetty's ghastly engagement celebrations and head to the small reception office. Sure enough, Dot's head barely appears across the desk. She stares at me rather sheepishly.

'I'm so sorry,' says she. 'We had no idea what was going on towards the end. We just wanted it to go away. I knew some loved the money beyond all. I've seen the other side of so many people I thought I knew.'

'Dot, I need a favour.'

'Yes, anything,' says she, looking quite relieved that I'm being pleasant.

'Those we met with last night – in the house when you kidnapped us. I'd like to meet them all there again, please.'

'Oh. Can I ask what for, Inspector Grasby?'

'Don't worry. Just to clear up a few things, you know. I'll have a long report to write, as I'm sure you'll appreciate.'

'Yes, of course.' She's relieved when she looks at her watch. 'Now's not a good time. How about around five o'clock? We have our second sitting for Christmas dinner at seven-thirty. We'll be finished before then, I hope?'

'Most certainly,' say I with a smile. 'Can I borrow your phone, please? I hope they're back on?'

'Yes, they were working first thing this morning, though the road's still blocked. Be my guest. I'll get everyone together.' She hesitates. 'We're all so pleased that you're none the worse for it all. Oh, and I'm supposed to tell you, Superintendent Juggers is well, too. Just minor burns to his legs.'

'Just his legs?'

'Yes, I think so. He's not in danger, I know that. The doctor kept him in the surgery overnight. Something about bandages and balm?'

Gosh, Juggers has been lucky. Things could have been worse – much worse!

Dot shows me through to the phone and bustles off.

I have a friend in the Metropolitan Police's Special Branch, you know. Memory, as I've said, is a funny thing. Thankfully, mine is pretty good. But I must talk to him now. Just to be sure – to be absolutely sure.

I head for the phone. Luckily, Detective Inspector Jonathan 'Chubby' Mainwaring's home telephone number is engraved on my mind. You see, I'm to be his best man next June. He too survived Hymers, our mutual alma mater. It's funny we both joined the police. Though, it has to be said, his career has been rather more stellar than mine. Two things I'll say for Chubby: he's a bloody good left-handed batsman; and there's nothing he doesn't know about England's criminal underworld.

I listen to the phone ringing, and shortly I hear his rather plummy tones.

'Hello, Chubby,' say I. 'Sorry to disturb your festivities and all that, but I need to pick your brains, old boy . . .'

As I ascend to our room in the lift, I'm chuffed that Chubby has confirmed my suspicions. I ponder on the vagaries of fate, how some things happen as they do. Many police officers will tell you that to do this job all that's required is a strong arm and an even thicker head. Not true! The old grey matter is paramount when it comes to catching crooks. But there's something intangible about it all too; maybe even preordained. It's hard to put into words.

341

Funnily enough, as I stretch out on the bed, my hunger has vanished. It's the excitement of being right, I suppose. Even my father's engagement can't shift my good mood. I decide to lie down for a while and work out how I'm to go about it all.

Just as I settle to this task, there's a knock at the door. Damn hotels, one never gets a minute's peace. If it's not housekeeping, it's something else. I've never found them to be restful places.

'Who is it?' I shout testily.

'It's Jeremiah Payne – you know, the grocer. I'd like a word, if I can.'

The previous evening comes flooding back. I see Payne as he hauls off his balaclava and detains Elizabeth Barclay. Wheels within wheels. I open the door, and he's standing there like a shorter version of Nelson's Column, straight as a die, and in a smart suit.

'Gosh, you scrub up well, old chap,' say I, showing him in.

'Yes, sorry about that. One has to do one's duty, you know.'

Gosh, he's posher than me.

'I just wanted to thank you and Superintendent Juggers for last night. Is he here?' Payne looks around as though the old boy might be under the bed.

I explain that Juggers is being tended to at the surgery and ask what I can do for him.

'I feel rather bad about you both, to be honest. You see, we just couldn't flush them out – the important ones, that is. I've been undercover here for a while. I thought I'd gained the trust of the locals. But no, they're as tight as a drum.'

'So, you needed two old-fashioned coppers and the State Department to help you out, eh?'

Payne lights a cigarette. 'It was always a joint operation.

The Yanks wanted Monza, and we wanted to stop the smuggling. Communities like this are delicate – soft touch, and suchlike. We knew you chaps would cut through.'

'You mean risk our lives while you all worked behind the scenes?'

He looks rather embarrassed. 'Well, I wouldn't say that, Grasby.'

He's Special Branch. It stands out a mile. Gosh, I should have asked Chubby to find out more about this operation.

'You see, we couldn't work out who was behind it all. How clever of you to identify Elizabeth Barclay. It's a jolly good show.'

'And you think you have your mastermind, do you?'

'I should say. She'll be coming with me to London as soon as this damnable snow clears. Her and the rest of her accomplices.'

'Then you'll be short one,' say I. 'Come to the prof's house at five, and I'll be sure to keep you right.'

'I don't quite know what you mean, Inspector. If you know something else, why can't you just tell me now?'

'It has to be done this way.'

And I mean it, too. I'm pretty sure of one more bad egg. But I'll only know by the reactions of the others.

'See you at five, then,' say I, ushering Payne back through the door.

Even though I've had a good sleep, I feel dog-tired. I find that when I've been thinking a lot, don't you? Now it's time to get to the nub of the Uthley Bay smuggling operation. But first, a short nap.

# 40

I oversleep, and it's dark when I awake – almost a quarter
to five. Not to worry, though. Best to keep them in sus-
pense. I drain Juggers's whisky bottle and enjoy the heat as
the spirit slides down my gullet. To be fair, there was only
a decent dram left.

By the time I reach Professor Blunt's big house at the
end of the village, it's nearly ten past five. Though the snow
is still heavy on the ground, the air is clean and fresh, the
sky a carpet of stars. Out to sea, a ship is all lit up, no doubt
for Christmas. I think of all the families on this little island
of ours. The bottles of beer, singsongs round the family
piano, Christmas puddings, the new Queen's speech on
the wireless, children playing with their toys – if they've
been lucky enough to get any. It's still so hard for far too
many. I sometimes wonder how it would have been if the
war had never happened. It was a beastly time, no doubt
about it. But there was poverty before and there is still. I
can't help thinking we're doing something wrong. But now,
I must concentrate on the job in hand.

I knock the big oak door, thankful not to be blindfolded for
this visit. The professor himself lets me in, all smiles and
thanks for bringing the real crooks to justice last night, etc.

Of course, I take this with all due modesty. In fact, had it not been for Juggers blowing up his trousers and the arrival of Deedee et al, I'd likely have been feeding the cod by now.

I'm slightly taken aback when I'm shown into the drawing room, mind you. There are the five who sent us on our mission, plus Deedee, Juggers, O'Leary and Payne. Though I was only expecting the latter, I suppose the more the merrier. It'll save me having to explain myself over and over again.

Juggers sidles over to me with a distinct limp.

'What's all this about, Grasby?'

'Don't worry, sir. I have everything in order.'

'I hope so. These folk are already traumatized, thou knows.'

'Hi, Frank!' calls Deedee from the corner of the room. She beams at me, and for a moment a memory flashes through my mind from last night. Did I really tell her I loved her? Gosh, I do hope not.

O'Leary nods to me like the all-American hero he is. He has a black eye, a remnant of his bravery on the cliff. But I'm grateful to him, nonetheless.

'Don't worry, Frank,' he says. 'We have your constables looking after last night's miscreants. Hey, and you'll be pleased to know that Geraldo has been reunited with his wife. Through bars, but better than nothing, right?'

'Geraldo and his men are up in the station under lock and key. The Uthley Bay lot are in the cellar of the Trout,' says Juggers. 'Everyone under the watchful eye of Special Branch and the State Department. Hardly ideal, but the best we could do at short notice. I hear the road will be cleared in a matter of hours.' He smiles, something I'm not accustomed to.

Payne is taciturn. Though he has every right to be, having been undercover in Uthley Bay for so long. It can't have been easy or good for the digestion.

The five Uthley Bay locals are seated before a blazing fire. The room smells of roast goose, cinnamon, red wine, brandy, pine needles from the decorated tree, and pipe smoke. Professor Blunt is sitting on the Chesterfield couch, in between Dot and Mrs Smith-Wantley. Meanwhile, Wilf is on the left side of the fireplace in a winged chair, mirrored by Dr McKay, sitting on an identical piece of furniture across from him.

I decide to make my way onto the hearth rug. It's the colour of a good Merlot, with a thick pile. Rather fancy, actually.

Every eye is on me. I glance at Deedee, who gives me a smile of encouragement.

I clear my throat. 'As you know, a number of people were apprehended last night, in connection with the smuggling of hosiery.'

'How awful,' says Mrs Smith-Wantley. 'Could you pass me the sherry bottle, young man? I do find these circumstances most vexing.'

I do as I'm bid, happy to look on as she pours herself what could best be termed a *gentlewoman*'s measure.

'Now, given you all know about the smuggling, we have to take a look at culpability.'

There's a collective gasp at this.

'Hang on, old chap,' says the prof. 'What chance did we have? When some of the villagers fell in with Geraldo, what could we do?'

'We did tell Constable Armley, Inspector. Look how that turned out.' Dot folds her arms in defiance. 'He buggered off to France!'

'Yes, it's too harsh, young man,' pipes up Dr McKay. 'None of us have committed any crime, apart from that of saving our skins. You saw what they did to poor old Wardle and Ogden Barclay. None of us wanted that. And neither would you if the roles had been reversed!'

I notice she's nursing a large whisky. My late mother would have called it a *bumper*.

'What if I were to tell you that one of you – sitting in this room – was the mastermind behind this whole thing?' I stroke my chin for effect.

'I do hope you've got this right, Grasby,' whispers Juggers, looking suddenly agitated.

But I'm just getting started.

'I knew this would happen,' says Wilf, shaking his head. 'Give a dog a bad name, and it sticks forever.'

'Are you referring to the three years you spent in Wormwood Scrubs for theft, Wilf?'

He nods. 'Yes, what if I am?'

'I know you have all the right qualifications to be involved with this crime. Borstal at the age of twelve, some punch-ups with the wrong sort when you were young. In and out of trouble, until gaol beckoned, eh? You alluded to it when we first met you. It all checks out.'

'I see, so you blame it on me. Coppers, you can never trust them,' he snarls, his Cockney accent to the fore.

'Just you watch your mouth, young man,' says Juggers.

'Well, I'm pleased to say, it isn't you, Wilf,' say I.

A smile spreads across his face. 'Y'see, free as a bird, me. What have you lot been up to, then? Naughty, naughty,' he cautions, wagging a finger at his fellow villagers.

'Dot, you have one or two secrets, don't you?'

'Sorry?' she says, looking quite surprised.

'You and the professor have much more in common than a mere employer–employee relationship, don't you?'

Dot bursts into tears and is comforted by the older man.

'I must protest!' says the prof. 'This is going too far. What are you suggesting?'

'Aye, lad,' says Juggers. 'What exactly are you suggesting?'

'I don't know why you're being so defensive, Professor,' say I. 'Most men would be proud to have a daughter like Dot. After all, she runs your hotel. You see, I've a good memory – the note you left for me at reception and the Christmas card for Dot from her father both bore your handwriting.'

'I said you should have been straight with people, Daddy,' says Dot, tears in her eyes. 'This isn't the Dark Ages.'

The professor raises his chin. 'She's right, I'm ashamed of it. Things were different before the war, at least in academic circles. I could have lost my job – all respect – had news of a child born out of wedlock come to the fore. I still might. I'm sorry, Dorothy. You know how much I love you. Please forgive me.'

'Where are you getting all this, Frank?' says Juggers, now utterly bamboozled.

'And you, good doctor . . .' I turn to McKay.

'You'll be hard pushed to find out anything untoward about me, young man. I have nothing to hide.'

'Apart from the little retainer you negotiated with Monza, maybe?'

'I beg your pardon?'

'The deal that meant you would treat any of his men, whatever their need, no questions asked.'

If looks could kill, she has me.

'I had no choice, and you must realize that. And in any event, I took the Hippocratic Oath!'

'The same way you had no choice buying that nice house in Scarborough with the proceeds? The mortuary men are chatty souls – they told me about your little purchase. The rest was pretty easy to work out.'

'It's none of your business, Inspector!'

'I beg to differ, Doc.'

I turn next to Mrs Smith-Wantley.

'I think we all know that you sold smuggled stockings in your shop, didn't you? Your attempt to appear confused on the matter didn't work, I'm afraid.'

She takes rather more than a sip of sherry. 'I had nothing to sell. The price was good, and so I bought them. Surely, it's just part of the entrepreneurial spirit, young man? We all had to survive, you know. Like my fellow villagers have said. The whole thing was insufferable.'

'You all see the point I'm trying to make, don't you?' I look round the room, my eye catching Deedee's. Gosh, she looks quite fascinated. There are murmurs to the contrary amongst *the five*. 'What this illustrates is that you were all open to being coerced in order to keep a secret. Professor, you and Dot kept it quiet that you were father and daughter, just in case your colleagues found out. Therefore, you could be influenced. Your cheap stockings, Mrs Smith-Wantley. Your prison term, Wilf. And your turning of a blind eye in return for cash, Doctor. It's called blackmail, and it makes you vulnerable. I saw Perkin Barclay at the hotel the night we arrived. Just his back, mind you. But it all makes sense now. He was keeping you right. Making sure you didn't give anything away to us. I'm pretty certain that money coming into the village was welcomed by you all. But when people started to die – well, things were different. At least for some of you.'

'Doesn't make any of us master criminals,' says McKay. 'Any jury would be hard pressed to find us guilty, under the circumstances. But feel free to try, Inspector.'

And she's right, of course. Such were the oppressive conditions the people of Uthley Bay were forced to endure at the hands of gangsters, convictions, even prosecutions, are unlikely. After all, the likes of the prof only obfuscated the truth to save his job and reputation. That isn't a crime, but it left him open to blackmail.

Gosh, I'm enjoying this. Bit like that Parrot chap from the novels. Dutch, isn't he? Well, he hasn't got a patch on F. Grasby, you know.

I look at each face in turn. 'I have to ask myself, why Uthley Bay? I mean to say, there are many little villages along the coast that Geraldo Monza could have picked. But he was particularly drawn to this one.'

There follows a collective shrug.

'When I first met Elizabeth Barclay, she reminded me of someone, but I couldn't put my finger on who. Now, of course, we know she was about to rob poor Geraldo of his ill-gotten gains, not to mention take his and our lives, and anybody else's that stood in her way. She'd already killed her husband, Ogden, and passed him off for his twin brother, with whom she was not only in league, but in love.'

It's already old news. The good folk of Uthley Bay found this out earlier today via the gossips. But I press on. Though there's still shock on some faces. Not all, mind you.

Now, for fate. I remember the old cases I'd been reading back at York Central when I was feeling under the weather, before Juggers and I came to Uthley Bay. Life is indeed odd.

'It takes a lot for a fisherman's wife to have the brass neck to do such a thing. So out of character, wouldn't you say?'

'What are you driving at?' says the prof.

'You don't just become a killer or a robber overnight, do you? But then I remembered a case I was involved in just after the war. I was reading up on it recently. Larry Hood, a well-known criminal from the East End in London. You see, he'd married well, the granddaughter of a minor aristocrat, no less. When he escaped prosecution, many said it was this connection that ensured his freedom, and helped him disappear. That may or may not be the truth. In any case, he did disappear without a trace, both he and his wife. About three years ago, the word came from the underworld that poor old Larry had died, but that he was onto something big when he did. You simply can't trust criminals, you know.

'To run and hide successfully, one needs a support net-work of some kind. Money, Larry had. But where could he go? Where better than to the little village your sister-in-law disappeared to when she was seventeen? Again, never found. Simply vanished off the face of the earth – or so it seemed.'

'What on earth?' says Juggers.

'It was one of my first jobs as a detective. Going round with some pictures of Larry, his wife, and his sister-in-law. The case stuck with me all those years. I don't know how often it crossed my mind between then and now. Good old Larry had contacts with mobsters in New York. What better than to go into business together? But then Larry passes away, and those left behind are being short-changed by Geraldo.'

Again, I catch every eye, just for effect, you understand.

'But his wife and her sister had learned a lot from dear old Larry over the years. They knew how to use greed and shame to manipulate people for their own ends. They knew what they wanted, and how to rope in others.'

I pause, place my finger to my lips, and stare at the ceiling, pretending to think.

'This little notion only occurred to me when I recognized a similarity between Elizabeth Barclay and another person I'd met in the village. Then it all came together. You see, I think Elizabeth Barclay was the late Larry Hood's sister-in-law. But she didn't take over when Larry died. That needed someone with guile and calculating ruthlessness. Someone who could play both sides of the game, when necessary, just to make sure they'd always land on the right side. Someone like you, Mrs Smith-Wantley.' I point at the elderly haberdasher.

I have to admit, I admire her sang-froid. Smiling, she knocks back her sherry and holds the glass out for more, while the other four stare open-mouthed.

'My goodness, that's going to be hard to prove, Inspector.' The manner is different now. She's calm and reasoned. There's a dark intelligence behind her eyes, with none of the befuddled old lady I first met. 'The Americans won't say anything – it's against their code or something like that. And as for those who threatened you up at the lighthouse, they are responsible for their own actions.'

I swear, she absolutely winks at me.

'You forget something, Mrs Smith-Wantley.'

'Which is?'

'There are plenty of people who will remember you from your old life. And a good few who'll be happy to confirm your identity. And let's face it, evidence came to light before and after you and your husband disappeared that implicates you in a number of crimes. In effect, you were a team.' I smile. 'You may escape your part in the stocking smuggling and the other heinous crimes committed in Uthley Bay, but your past will catch up with you.'

Her expression morphs from an arrogant sneer of confidence to the scowl of a villain caught bang to rights, despite her best efforts.

'Now, then,' says Juggers. 'You're absolutely certain, Frank, one hundred per cent?'

I nod emphatically.

'Then I was right all along! I thought it were Mrs

Smith-Wantley, if you remember. Copper's intuition, is that,' says Juggers.

How typical. He takes a guess based on nothing at all but, being the senior officer, intends to take all the credit. Damn!

'In the light of what Inspector Grasby has had to say, you'll be taken for questioning at Scarborough, Mrs Smith-Wantley. Just as soon as the road is clear. I place you under arrest in this house until then. If that's fine with you, Professor?'

And do you know, Juggers gets a ragged cheer from all those in the room apart from Smith-Wantley – or, more correctly, Mrs Larry Hood.

Juggers's face displays mixed emotions: surprise, confusion, caution and maybe just a little bit of pride. Though his fists are bunched, and I know he'd happily punch me on the nose if I'm wrong. But he has nothing to fear. I'm absolutely right.

Like any performer, my act over, I long to leave the stage. Deedee grabs my arm.

'Walk with me,' she says. 'O'Leary, Juggers and Payne can tie all this up.'

Soon, we're out of the prof's mansion into the cold evening, under a magnificently starry sky. I look up and see Pleiades and feel as though the world is back on its axis again – especially with Deedee at my side.

We cross the road, tramping through the snow. Distantly, I can hear a choir. At first I think I'm imagining it, but Deedee hears it too. There are children singing 'In The Deep Midwinter'.

We stop on the promenade and gaze out to sea. The great moon, almost at its zenith, has picked out a silvery path across the waves. It's as though it's begging us onwards, onwards to a new life, just Deedee and me.

'I wasn't supposed to be on this case,' says she.

'Oh, why are you here, then?' say I, my heart thudding.

'I saw they were sending you. And Monza and his men are tough – dangerous.'

'You wanted to protect me, then?'

She grins. 'Well, not that I think you need protection, Frank.'

Suddenly, everything is still. There's not a whisper of wind, the choir has stopped singing and even the waves appear silent, as they lap at the sea wall. Deedee stares into my face with her hypnotic blue eyes. The real magic of Christmas is in the air, as our faces move closer, our lips part. I feel quite giddy, actually.

As our mouths touch, in a moment I've dreamed of for a whole year, I hear a crumping through the snow from behind. I turn to face it.

'Francis, at last! Where on earth have you been? I've looked all over.' My father is standing wrapped in an overcoat that's at least two sizes too big for him. Though it's bitterly cold, his face is flushed, no doubt by the over-consumption of strong drink.

'I have something to tell you. Hetty and I are engaged, like it or not. We'll be wed next Christmas. Just to let you know. I've a prelate friend I've known for years; done rather well for himself, in fact. Better than me, at least. He lives in an old country house on the North York Moors. It'll make the perfect wedding venue. Has a little chapel, too. You're invited, of course. No choice, really. You too, Deirdre.'

And hey presto, the magic has gone. My father's wedding plans have ruined my romantic moment with Deedee. Dash it all!

# AUTHOR'S EPILOGUE

*And so ended my adventure in Uthley Bay. I must admit, though, the whole thing left me uneasy. It showed up human nature for what it is, and then some. People are people, no matter what. And when in danger, they'll do almost anything to stay safe. Aye, and some will do the wrong thing through greed, jealousy and the like.*

*The Christmas Stocking Murders, as the case has become known, shocked the nation back then. Nobody could have imagined that the smuggling of such a humble garment could lead to awful murder and mayhem in a tiny Yorkshire village. But it did. And though Juggers and I were little more than lures to flush out the real crooks, we became rather celebrated for our part in the whole thing.*

*I was mostly right in my summing up that night so long ago. I was wrong to think that justice would be visited upon Mrs Smith-Wantley, mind you. No jury would convict this sweet old lady, despite her past. My, she played it up in court and just about everywhere else. And she would never confess to being the wife of the late Larry Hood, even though a few old lags identified her. Perhaps this had more to do with the perceived unreliability of their testimony, than her bravura performance in court. I never found out what happened to her in her later years. I suppose I'd done what I could, and the rest was up to others.*

*While some young fishermen received short prison sentences, Elizabeth Barclay was sent down for five years for her part in the smuggling operation. She blamed the murders on Geraldo Monza and his men back in America. Our judiciary appear to have given up the ghost, happy to leave things in the hands of their counterparts across the Atlantic.*

*The case of Geraldo Monza was a strange one, though. He was taken home to the United States and charged with various crimes, including murder, robbery and extortion. But, somehow, he was found not guilty. I discovered later that he had turned against his former friends and colleagues, giving the police and the FBI so much information that it nearly stopped the organization to which he belonged in its tracks. We all know it better now as the Mafia.*

*I heard nothing of him until about two years ago, when I picked up a copy of the* Daily Express *and there he was: a grey old man lying dead on the floor in a Florida hotel, having been shot through the head. I must confess, I rather liked him. And by golly, he could sing. It's odd the chaps one takes to in the course of a lifetime. I often wondered if anyone would have died had it not been for the intervention of Smith-Wantley, her sister, and Perkin Barclay. We shall never know.*

*In the end, the snows cleared, winter gave way to spring, and eventually our government decided to stop banishing foreign goods from our country. All it took was the usual nonsense in Parliament, and the Queen's signature on a piece of paper.*

*I've never been back to Uthley Bay. Though every time I see it on a postcard in a newsagent, it makes me shiver. Good men died for stockings in that place. Gosh, I nearly did, too.*

*Life's a funny old business, and no mistake.*

*As for me – well, there's much more to come. And not what you might expect. I had my father's wedding to look forward to. Though I'm not sure those were my feelings at the time.*

*Frank Grasby*
*York, May 1976*

# ACKNOWLEDGEMENTS

As always, I must thank my wife Fiona for her constant support. She has to put up with my moaning on a daily basis, as well as my horse obsession. It's a thing!

To my editor, Finn Cotton; what a chap he is! Remember the name, for if you're involved in publishing circles and don't know him already, you soon will. And not forgetting other members of the team: Emma Fairey, Melissa Kelly, copy-editor Fraser Crichton, and all at Transworld Books who work so hard behind the scenes.

At this juncture, I'd like to thank my friend Douglas Skelton, though I'm not sure for what. So, instead of gratitude, I'll just commend his fine books to you. Please seek them out.

Thanks are due to my audiobook narrator Tom Turner, who has truly made Grasby et al his own. Marvellous stuff!

To all those who buy my books, I thank you. Without your support I'd be nowhere.

And to the good folk of Yorkshire, who have taken Frank Grasby to their hearts and bookshelves. Bless you.

And finally, my profound gratitude is due to all those who go to work every day in order to sell books. I'd like to mention Kurde at Waterstones Horsham for her extraordinary help and encouragement. Without you all, there would be nothing to read.

DAM
Loch Lomondside, May '24

Denzil Meyrick is from Campbeltown on the Kintyre Peninsula in Argyll. After studying politics, he enjoyed a varied career as a police officer, distillery manager, and director of several companies. He is the No.1 bestselling author of the DCI Daley series, and is now an executive producer of a major TV adaptation of his books.

Denzil lives on Loch Lomondside in Scotland with his wife Fiona and cats. You can find him on Twitter @Lochlomonden, Facebook @DenzilMeyrickAuthor, or on his website: www.denzilmeyrick.com.